Kate Johnson was born in the 1980s in Yorkshire and now lives in Essex, where she belongs to a small pride of cats. She has a second cousin who made the Guinness Book of Records for brewing the world's strongest beer and she also once ran over herself with a Segway scooter. These two things are not related.

Kate has worked in an airport, a lab, and various shops, but much prefers writing because mornings are definitely not her best friend. In 2017 she won Paranormal Romantic Novel of the Year from the Romantic Novelists' Association with her novel *Max Seventeen*.

katejohnson.co.uk

 x.com/K8JohnsonAuthor
 tiktok.com/k8johnsonauthor
 facebook.com/catmarsters

ALSO BY KATE JOHNSON

Best Hex Ever

Hex Appeal

Hex and the City

Hex and Hexability

THE PROMISED QUEEN

KATE JOHNSON

One More Chapter
a division of HarperCollins*Publishers* Ltd
1 London Bridge Street
London SE1 9GF
www.harpercollins.co.uk
HarperCollins*Publishers*
Macken House, 39/40 Mayor Street Upper,
Dublin 1, D01 C9W8
This paperback edition 2025

1

First published in Great Britain in ebook format
by HarperCollins*Publishers* 2025

Copyright © Kate Johnson 2025
Kate Johnson asserts the moral right to be identified
as the author of this work

A catalogue record of this book is available from the British Library
ISBN: 978-0-00-868483-9

This novel is entirely a work of fiction. The names, characters and incidents portrayed in it are the work of the author's imagination. Any resemblance to actual persons, living or dead, events or localities is entirely coincidental.

Printed and bound in the UK using 100% Renewable Electricity
by CPI Group (UK) Ltd

All rights reserved. No part of this publication may be reproduced, stored in a retrieval system, or transmitted, in any form or by any means, electronic, mechanical, photocopying, recording or otherwise, without the prior permission of the publishers.

Without limiting the author's and publisher's exclusive rights, any unauthorised use of this publication to train generative artificial intelligence (AI) technologies is expressly prohibited. HarperCollins also exercise their rights under Article 4(3) of the Digital Single Market Directive 2019/790 and expressly reserve this publication from the text and data mining exception.

To Spike.

PROLOGUE

The voice of Ember's mother echoed in her head, as it did every time she broke into someone else's house. *You can do it, little ferret.*

Ember hadn't been little for a good long while now, and the days when her mother stood waiting below to catch her if she fell were long gone. But the instinctive knowledge of where the handholds were, which shadows to hide in, and when someone might be coming – those hadn't faded with adulthood.

Somewhere inside Baron Varne's mansion was the High Lord's Stone. Ember didn't know what this was, but she'd heard Varne excitedly telling the mayor about it a few days ago as she did a little light pilfering in the town hall. It had cost him a great deal of money and was very rare indeed, and Ember needed to buy Pa more of his medicine, so it had been a bit of a no-brainer.

She eased the tiny basement window open and slid inside, silent as a snake, waiting until she was sure there was no one else in the tiny room. Carefully, she tucked a little bit of paper into the casement to keep it from closing entirely. *No sense getting in if you can't get out.* She crept forward, her boots soft on the stone floor, and eased open the door.

The room beyond was lit by candles, which was weird. Mansions like this usually had sarel-oil lights everywhere. Why light hundreds of expensive, messy, dangerous candles like you were in a High Lord's temple?

Then she heard a whimper, and her spine prickled with unease. She peered slowly, carefully, further around the door.

In the centre of the room, which was really a large, vaulted cellar, was a large stone slab. And on that slab lay a woman in a long white dress.

She was chained down and gagged.

Ember hesitated. On the one hand, this looked bad. On the other hand, it also looked a bit like that weird sex thing she and Cracksman Jack had stumbled upon in the back of an opium den once.

'Um, are you here willingly?' she said, and the girl shook her head frantically.

Ember pulled her gag away, and the girl gibbered, 'They kidnapped me! I was coming home and they grabbed me and I woke up here and—'

'Shh,' said Ember. She thought she recognised the girl from the bakery her brothers liked. Not because their bread was better than anyone else's, but because the flaxen-haired girl behind the counter was as lovely as a statue of Lady Feara herself. 'Dandelia, right? I'll get you out of here.'

Dandelia sobbed prettily. 'It was that horrid Baron Varne! He said – he said it wouldn't hurt for long!'

'What wouldn't?' Ember asked darkly.

'He didn't say! But that was ages ago and I'm so frightened!'

Ember slid her lockpick from her pocket. The catch on the basement window hadn't been complicated, not for the daughter of the best clockmaker in the Clockwork City, and neither were the locks holding Dandelia down.

Dandelia bit her lip and looked up at Ember with pleading eyes. She really was lovely, in a way Ember knew she'd never be.

But that was fine, because people noticed lovely girls, and Ember preferred to go as unnoticed as possible. Dandelia squirmed in a manner that Ember was quite sure was unnecessary, her bosom heaving and the purple stone on its chain around her neck catching the light.

Wait. 'That yours?' Ember asked, working on one of the wrist manacles.

'What? The necklace? No! I'd never wear something so ... gaudy.'

Ember ran a practised eye over it. Purple sarelstone, weird cut, decent clarity, cheap setting. Nah, not what she was looking for. Wouldn't put food on the table for more than a week.

She got Dandelia unfastened and helped her to her feet. The purple stone winked in the light, and Ember figured a week's food was better than none. She reached out, ignoring Dandelia's flinch, and unfastened the necklace. The stone felt warm in her hand.

'There's a window open through there,' she said, pointing.

'Aren't you coming?' Dandelia peered at her with those lovely eyes. 'Do I know you? Why are you here?'

'You didn't see me,' said Ember. 'I've got something to look for. Go on, go.'

She gave the girl a little shove, and turned to the only other exit from the creepy cellar. She'd have to be quick, because no one lit this many candles and then just left them without coming back.

She hesitated as Dandelia disappeared into the little side room. Maybe she should go, too. Someone would be coming back soon. She'd got the purple stone, not that it was worth a lot, but maybe she could dress it up a little. She slipped it over her head, and the heat of it pulsed through her.

For a moment, Ember couldn't move as the stone beat in time with her own heart and its warmth spread through her. *Yes*, it seemed to say. *I belong with you.* It felt ... right. Like she was home, somehow. Like the stone had been looking for her all along, and was so happy to have found her.

Ember stood, overwhelmed, until the door opened and several men in robes entered, bearing knives, ceremonial bowls, and swinging censers.

At the head of them stood Baron Varne, and Ember saw the pistol in his hand a second before she heard the bark of it firing.

CHAPTER 1

Rhaell had never seen the Great Chamber so bedecked, not even for one of the king's weddings. Great banners bearing the green and silver Sacred Tree of Yskara had been raised to flutter high above the crowd, and every inch of air fluttered with bunting. The great and good – or at least, the wealthy and powerful – of Yskara milled about, everyone wanting to say they'd been present when the Promised One arrived. The sound was deafening.

Speculation had been mounting for years, but the last few months had been almost unbearable. Where would she come from? Would the Tree open a portal between worlds for the first time in generations? What would she look like? How would she save them?

Rhaell lit up a sootweed and leaned against the wall. The poor woman would be little more than a sacrificial lamb, whoever she was.

'You'd better stub that out before the king sees you,' said Phoebe, at his elbow. She eased her weight onto one foot, scrunching her toes in the shiny heeled shoes she never usually wore.

Rhaell squinted at the sky, barely visible through the dome past the layers of banners and bunting. 'We've got time.'

'Barely. He's charging around like a maddened aurochs today.' Phoebe took the sootweed from him and inhaled deeply, closing her eyes on a moment of bliss. 'I just saw him yelling at Lady Sarea that her dragon didn't match the colour scheme.'

Rhaell whistled. 'Do you think our Promised One will care about colour schemes?'

'Leaves and branches, I hope not,' groaned Phoebe. 'I've worked my fingers to the bone making adjustable outfits for her every requirement. Do you know how hard it is to make court-resplendent gowns for someone you've never met?'

'I salute you.' And Rhaell did so, badly, then took back his sootweed. Above them, the sun moved closer to its highest point.

'And have you seen who he's picked as her ladies-in-waiting? Cowbags, the lot of them.'

Rhaell side-eyed his oldest friend, who had been chosen to be the Promised One's personal servant, the only reason she was in attendance today. 'Your tact knows no beginning. Remind me how you got your job?'

'Blackmail and nepotism,' she replied with a tart grin. She poked at the hair escaping her neat lace cap, and peered up at the dome. 'Come on, best get a move on before the crowd's too thick to let us near the Sacred Pool.'

Rhaell clamped his sootweed between his teeth and laid his hand on the hilt of his sword. He rolled his shoulders, straightened up, and looked down from his full height at the assembled crowd. 'They'll let me in.'

The sun was sliding towards its highest point as he pushed through the crowd to stand at the edge of the pool. Opposite him stood the king, magnificent in his green and silver robes. The green stone at the centre of the Crown of Ysarriel on his head seemed to glow in the light. He glared pointedly at Rhaell's sootweed.

Rhaell stubbed it out beneath his boot, then looked up as something splashed his face.

'Rain?' murmured someone. 'Indoors?'

'The Promised One works miracles!' cried someone else, as Rhaell brushed the wetness on his face, unease running through him.

His fingers came away red.

Then more of it splattered his face, and Phoebe's and the king's, and then everyone around them was gasping and screaming.

Rhaell saw something red and white fall from the sky and stepped into the Sacred Pool, arms braced to catch it. It was a woman, and she crashed into him, knocking him to his knees, the sacred water turning red with her blood.

The Promised One had arrived exactly when the prophecy said she would, only no one had said she'd have a knife in her chest when she did.

~

'Well, that wasn't quite what we expected.'

King Onas, third of his name, King of the Sacred Realm and Yskar Sea, Protector of the Tree and Beloved of the Ancestors, gazed at the woman on the bed and didn't bother to conceal his disappointment.

Thanks to her landing in the Sacred Waters, the maid Phoebe had been able to heal her wounds, which were numerous and baffling. He hadn't even been able to work out what caused some of them, but the creature had been a mess, bleeding everywhere, limp and pale as a corpse.

The maid had cleaned her up and put her in a fresh nightgown, but it hadn't done much to improve her. Short of stature, busty like a tavern whore, and sort of ... nothing-coloured, as if she'd been designed to be forgettable. Was this ... *person* really the Promised One?

He'd been expecting a paragon of beauty and perfection. 'They insult us by sending us this – this...' He waved his hand in disgust.

She lay very still in the bed, vulgar chest rising and falling evenly. Her hair was the shade of something you'd find in the privy, and ridiculously short.

From behind Onas came the grunt of a wild animal. *The two of them are well matched.* 'She came when the prophecy said she would. Who else was going to arrive like that?'

'It could be a trick,' said Onas mulishly, even though he knew it wasn't true. Nobody had the magic to pull off a trick like that anymore.

'By who? To what end? We've no enemies capable of it.'

Onas glared at the plain woman asleep in the bed. The queen's bed, awaiting her future status. 'Her ugliness insults the Tree.'

'Perhaps this is the standard of beauty in the Iron World.'

Onas turned, and beheld his grandson, hulking there in the shadows. He truly was monstrous, massive and misshapen. How had his lovely daughter given birth to this? Were the Ancestors punishing him for something?

'What? What would you know about beauty?' He beheld the heavy brow, the thick lips, the mane of beastly hair, then turned back to the girl. Compared to Prince Bronadyr, she was a fucking beauty. 'Well, I suppose she has childbearing hips, at least.'

'That's not the only thing she is here for, Your Grace,' rumbled the prince.

'No, but it's her primary use to us,' said the king. *The seeds she shall nurture will thrive.* That was what the prophecy said. And Onas was sorely in need of some thriving seeds. 'If she doesn't fulfil that single, basic need then why did they send her?'

'Perhaps an heir is not the only thing we need to cure the Tree,' rasped Bronadyr. 'The prophecy said she would save the realm and restore the magic.'

'She can save the realm later, after she's given you an heir,' said Onas. He regarded the dull-coloured woman, so short and dumpy compared to the graceful willows of the court. Willows who had failed to bear a new generation of late. 'Since no other woman in the kingdom will bed you willingly, this must be who the Tree has sent to answer our prayers. Bed her, Bronadyr, and breed her.'

'And if her fate is the same as my mother's?' growled Bronadyr.

The king gave a mirthless laugh. 'You survived, didn't you?'

Bronadyr exhaled hard, like the beasts that snorted and stamped in the stables. The court called him the Beast, Onas knew, when they thought he wasn't listening.

'Should I take her now?' the Beast said. 'While she sleeps? She can't scream and run away from my repulsiveness then, can she?'

Ugh, he would, too. Onas had tried his best, with tutors and instructors, but there was no civilising a mindless beast. Best to get an heir out of him, and then Onas was sure some tragic accident could be orchestrated to befall the creature.

'She is to be your wife, you lecherous oaf. At least wait until she is awake.'

'Your Grace,' said Bronadyr, and made a mocking bow. 'I await further instruction.'

He clomped away, the floors shaking under his monstrous weight, and Onas heard the door to the Queen's Chambers shut behind him.

He moved forward to the bed that had once belonged to his wife, and then to their daughter. The bed that would see this woman, this Promised One, crowned in the blood of childbirth. He pushed back the curtain and leaned closer, inspecting her freckled face, her thick brows, her untidy hair. Her figure was curved, which might be a good sign. Vulgar hips were more likely to bear fruit.

Bronadyr was his only heir. Following that, it was that grasping cow Lady Sarea. He needed heirs to push her further down the line of succession, where she wasn't a threat. Onas couldn't afford to get rid of the Beast until he'd got a few replacements lined up.

'If my daughter can be sacrificed for an heir, then so can you,' murmured His Grace. 'After all, if you birth a monster that tears you apart, at least we'll know it's his.'

He let the curtain fall and walked away.

∼

Ember's head was fucking killing her.

But she remained frozen until she heard a door close, and even after that only breathed in tiny, rabbit breaths, terrified either His Grace or his monstrous heir were still standing around, waiting for her to wake.

She waited for what felt like hours before she even opened her eyes.

She was in a massive bed, hung with rich, heavy curtains. They were partially pulled back, revealing a bedchamber so large and luxurious she wondered if she really had died and was in the realm of the High Lords and Ladies.

No. She must still be in the mansion. Unless Varne had passed her on to someone else? Neither of those voices had sounded like his. The older one had been even colder and more autocratic and the younger... She shuddered. It had been like the bastard offspring of a wolf and an ox.

Slowly, very carefully, she sat up and peered under the neckline of the nightdress she appeared to be wearing. It was very fine fabric – might it even be silk? – and exquisitely embroidered. It was also clean of blood, which was fascinating because the last time she was awake she'd been drenched with the stuff.

Bandages covered her chest, her arms, her legs. She'd been shot and sliced and stabbed, her blood collected in bowls and consumed by chanting, hooded figures. And then the knife – jewelled, curved, ceremonial – had stabbed her in the chest—

Ember thought she must have dreamt the whole thing. But the

healing wounds were there. Proof she hadn't imagined the whole nightmare. Although ... the wounds appeared to be mostly healed. She'd been stabbed in the chest and now she felt almost fine. How long had she been here?

Lying against the bandage bound over her breasts was the cheap purple sarelstone she'd taken from Dandelia. Well, at least she'd got something out of this whole stupid ordeal, even if it was definitely not worth the trouble.

Her stomach grumbled. She had eaten a light supper before she set out to rob the mansion, and she had no idea how long ago that had been now, but it felt like hours. Maybe days. One small lamp burned by the bed, not doing much to keep away the darkness from the tall windows.

There was a pitcher of water and a glass by the bed, but Ember wasn't sure she trusted it. It was entirely possible Varne, or some vile friend of his, had some even worse plans for her.

Bed her and breed her, Bronadyr.

Ember didn't know what a Bronadyr was, but she wasn't going to find out and she sure as hell wasn't going to fuck it. She was going to damn well escape.

Right, what did she have? A silk nightgown. A cheap jewel. Her own mind and body. A body that was not going to be given to that Bronadyr monster, or anyone. It was like Ma used to say, *Once you start letting people tell you what to do with your own body, they'll never stop. You're the only one as can make choices for yourself.*

Whoever had captured her this time had put her in a room with a balcony. A balcony! It was laughable. Ember had been climbing walls and trees and rooftops for longer than she could remember.

Come on, little ferret. Slip into that casement up there, then come down and let Ma in.

She tied a blanket around her shoulders, wrapped her hands and feet with strips torn off the bedsheet, and shinned down the side of the building like it was a nice day out at the park. Granite, somehow sharp and slippery at the same time, not her favourite to climb.

She was halfway down before she remembered that Varne's mansion didn't have balconies. And it didn't have granite walls.

Below her was a sound that might have been waves, only Ember wasn't sure because she'd only heard waves as a sound effect at the theatre. Baron Varne's mansion definitely did not have a moat.

So, this wasn't his mansion. This was a huge edifice, and she was climbing pale slippery granite, not the smoke-stained grey sandstone of Bleakburn. What the fuck was going on?

This was a castle. It was huge, and round, and sat on a rocky shore. Ember had no idea where she was, but that didn't matter right now. What mattered was getting away. Her feet hit the rocks and nearly slipped, but she held on to the helpfully ancient wall. The pale stone was simply full of foot and handholds. It was like they wanted her to escape.

Wait, *did* they want her to escape?

Ember's head swum as she looked back up at the balcony she'd climbed down from. It looked hellishly far up now, just a dark shape against the bulk of the wall. The moon must be on the other side of the castle, which was good, because it gave her more cover to get off these slippery rocks. *More granite, wet but not tidal.*

She made out the edge of the castle in the darkness, the waves lapping against a rocky bay, and was only a few dozen yards from it when a hissing, sibilant voice came from behind her.

'Thiss one looks tassty.'

Ember froze. That voice had not sounded ... human.

'But we ate one yessterday.'

The first one whined, 'But thiss one looks *taasssty*.'

Oh Lords, were there two of them? Ember didn't waste time looking. She scrambled faster over the rocks, not trying to find handholds in the wall anymore.

Something wet squelched behind her.

'We can take it to the larder for later,' said one voice.

'But I like them fressh,' said the other.

Ember's skin prickled with freezing sweat, her pulse flickering.

'It'ss on the rocks! That's ourss!'

'It iss our right,' agreed the other.

Oh Lords, I don't want to die! Ember ran faster, and then something touched her ankle and she yelped, kicking back.

It's on the rocks. It's ours.

So get off the fucking rocks, moron!

She grabbed for a handhold, her fingers digging in straight away, but something cold and clammy grabbed her ankle.

'No you fucking don't!' she snapped, fear making her angry. She kicked back, and then swung forward, smashing what felt almost like a hand into the wall.

The creature made an inhuman wailing sound, and Ember climbed higher. And higher.

And only when she was a whole storey up did she look back. She very much wished she hadn't.

The ... *things* that squatted on the rocks weren't even nearly human. Ember had seen children's books with pretty mermaids, but these weren't the rosy-cheeked, cheerful creatures of illustration.

Their skin was a gleaming, sickly white, their arms far too long for their bodies. There were gills on their bony chests, and their long thin tails were backed with sharp, spiked fins. And their faces...

Nothing should have that many teeth. Nothing.

Ember whipped her head back towards the wall, trying not to gibber with fear. Her fingers trembled and she almost slipped. Dizziness swamped her. What the fuck were they?

'It'ss off the rockss,' said one.

'It'ss got to come down though,' said the other.

'Like fun I do,' muttered Ember, and climbed a bit higher. Then sideways, which was a much harder manoeuvre, but suddenly became terribly easy when the alternative was monstrous mermaids with teeth the length of her fingers.

'Shall we ssing to it?' said one.

'Ssoftly,' said the other, 'so the Kingbeast won't waken.'

Sing? Why would they sing? Ember scrambled away, but the song that followed her was pure and high, the sweetest melody she'd ever heard.

Oh, nothing that sang so sweetly could ever harm her! What was she thinking? She should go back down and listen to them. Her feet were already making the descent. Yes, she'd sit on the rocks and listen to their sweet, sweet harmonies.

Her foot touched the rocks and a moment later, a cold hand touched her ankle. But that was all right, because the singing was so sweet. Nothing could harm her anymore.

She turned to face the mermaids, whose singing revealed their mouths full of rows of needle teeth, and she smiled. Everything would be fine.

Until something reared from the water, so suddenly it shocked the breath from her, and snapped its massive jaws over the tails of the singing mermaids.

Their sweet song abruptly turned into a hideous screech, and claw-tipped hands scrabbled for Ember.

'Lords and Ladies and all their little babies,' she gasped, as the huge creature snapped its jaws again, mere inches from her legs. The mermaids vanished, screaming, into its maw, and Ember ran.

She damn near flew over the rocks, skirting the round wall of the castle, and her feet suddenly hit dry ground.

A garden. A fancy, formal garden, which appeared to have either just hosted a very fine party or some kind of localised, confetti hurricane. At the other end of it was a copse of trees. She ran for it like the hounds of hell were at her heels and had just made the cover of the trees when a man stepped out from behind one of them and she cannoned right into him.

He was large, and he was hard, and he was in her way. Ember tried to move around him, but he simply put out his arm, which was like running into an iron bar.

She stepped back and raised her fists.

'Well,' he said, his face invisible in the darkness. 'You're interesting.'

CHAPTER 2

He was a big man, large with muscle; it showed in the biceps that bulged as he folded his arms across his chest. He wore a sort of old-fashioned leather tunic with a sword belt, and a hood that concealed his features from the moonlight. She could see no insignia that might mark him out as a guard or member of any of the Clockwork City guilds.

He wore a hood. It was nothing like the ones Varne's accomplices had worn, but it was a hood nonetheless, and it had her rabbit-hearted with fear.

Be brave, Ember. Be ... lion-hearted. Or at least ox-hearted or something. A fucking badger would be an improvement at this point.

She looked around wildly. To one side was a cliff edge – and the rocks, and those *creatures* – and to the other was ... more cliffs, because apparently, they were on a narrow spit of land. Behind her were formal gardens that led right back to the castle, and ahead the copse of trees that this large man had emerged from.

And hanging high above the trees was a pair of moons. A pair.

Two moons. Two moons, there were two moons, *there were—*

Ember gaped.

'Is this the bit where I look over my shoulder to see where you're staring, and you escape?' said the large man.

Ember shook herself. It had to be some kind of optical illusion, or maybe the fact that she hadn't eaten in a day or so and had just lost a large amount of blood was playing tricks with her vision.

'Let me pass,' she said, because nothing could be worse than what awaited her in the castle.

Bed her and breed her.

He tilted his head. 'How did you escape the hafmey?'

He had a pleasant voice, deep and cultured. She tried to peer up at his face, but he angled it away from her, so the shadows hid him even more. Shadows made by *two moons*. 'What?'

'The hafmey? Tails, teeth, arms? I heard them singing. It's really hard to escape the song.'

'But you did?'

'Yes, well, I'm supposed to,' he said vaguely. 'They can have anything that's on the rocks. It's a pretty powerful deterrent. Not many people get past them.'

'I got off the rocks,' Ember said, because that was a better explanation than 'a really big creature came and ate them'. 'The wall – it's full of handholds. You must've got people breaking in there all the time.'

He shrugged. 'There are some pretty powerful wards against people breaking in. But I don't suppose anyone thought about them stopping someone breaking *out*.'

She cocked her head. 'Then how did you know I had?'

'The gargoyles told me,' he said, as if that was a completely normal sentence.

Ember wondered if she had gone mad. She folded her arms. 'So, what, you've come to take me back?'

He didn't answer straight away. 'Why did you run?'

Bed her and breed her.

Ember shuddered, and the stranger stiffened. ''Cos I heard

what they wanted to do with me,' she snapped, her voice shaking with what she told herself was anger, but was mostly fear.

His voice was even as he said, 'Which is?'

'Do you know what a Bronadyr is?'

He gave a slow nod.

'I heard he's a fucking beast!'

'Did you?'

Why was he so calm? 'They want me to – to – I'm supposed to — They said he ripped his mother apart! That he's an *abomination*. A *monster*. And they want him to—' *Bed her. Breed her.* Ember wrapped her arms around herself, suddenly freezing in her nightgown and blanket. 'I ain't doing that. I can't. Please. Just let me go.'

She had to get home. Pa and her brothers would be worried – well, at least they would be concerned there was no food on the table. And Pa only had a few days of his medicine left...

'Go where?' He gestured to the cliffs on either side. 'You've already met the hafmey? There are worse things in the Sacred Sea.'

'The huge thing with the jaws?' She shuddered again.

'The Kingbeast. He woke for your coming. It was an omen,' the man said gnomically. He fished in a pocket and Ember tensed, but all he was doing was fetching a cigarette of sorts, which he propped between his lips and – well, she wasn't sure how he lit it, exactly, but he did something with his hands and then the tip of it glowed. 'You could try the river, I suppose, but that's only passable until you get to the Sacred Forest.'

'And if I do?' said Ember, who couldn't swim and had no idea how to row or sail a boat. *But I'm a fast learner.*

'Then you'll wish the hafmey had got you. Then there's the Skipta river,' he indicated somewhere to his right, 'but even if you make it past the fort, you'll be in the Myrlent, and it's an unwise traveller who tangles with the Myr—'

'All right, I get it, escape is impossible,' she said, throwing up her hands. 'You're going to take me back there and sacrifice me, again, this time as a bride to a monster that wants to fucking *breed* me.' Bile rose in her throat.

'Again?' he murmured. He blew out some smoke, the scent deep and earthy.

'Is this a punishment of some kind? Am I in hell? Have the High Lords and Ladies decided to punish me? What's next? I'll be eaten alive?'

'No one's going to eat you alive,' he said.

'Sure?' Ember was aware her voice was rising into hysteria, but there didn't appear to be anything she could do to stop it.

'I promise, now just—'

'Well, it'd be a damn sight easier to believe you if you weren't wearing that hood!' she shouted.

He paused, mid-drag on his cigarette. 'What?'

'Oh, like you don't know. Did Varne send you?' She looked around wildly, as if the baron was hiding behind the topiary. 'Is this all part of one of his sick little games?'

'I don't know who that is,' he said slowly.

'Sure, sure,' she babbled, her rabbit-heart pounding again. 'Hafmey and Myr and giant things with jaws, everything here wants to kill me – are you the next one? Are you going to drink my blood and stab me in the chest?'

'No,' he said firmly. 'I'm not.'

'And I'm supposed to believe you? At least show me your face!'

Her voice came out as a shriek, and it seemed to hang in the air for a terribly long time before the stranger reached up and slowly pushed back his hood.

And all the words vanished from Ember's throat, because she'd never seen anyone so beautiful in her life.

He had dark hair and his eyes were blue, but the details almost didn't matter. He had the face of a god; and with that height and those shoulders it seemed he had the physique of one, too. And not one of those gods who sat around drinking wine and seducing maidens; oh no, he had the face and body of the sort of god who led his legions into battle. Broad-shouldered. Square-jawed. Full-lipped. She bet he'd never had to seduce a maiden. They probably threw themselves at his feet. Begging.

His jaw – his perfect, chiselled jaw – tightened, and he looked away, which only served to make him look more broodingly beautiful. His long thick hair fell in shining waves to his shoulders, throwing the planes and contours of his face into exquisite light and shade.

He took a long drag of his weird cigarette. 'Happy now?' he grated.

'Uh-huh,' Ember managed. She was feeling a bit dizzy. Was that from being stabbed and shot and climbing down a castle wall, or was it the smoke, or was it simply from looking at him?

'I won't hurt you,' he said, still looking away. 'I promise I won't harm you.'

'Yeah, sure,' she said, still slightly dazzled.

'But – look, what is your name?' he asked, glancing at her.

'Ember,' she murmured.

Ember had found plenty of men attractive before. Some of the actors who trod the boards at the city's many theatres, for instance, had legions of female fans, and Ember counted herself among them. A couple of the lads who worked at the sarelstone mill had taken her fancy for a while. And there had been a young, broad-shouldered guard with a handsome smile who she'd once or twice considered allowing to catch her.

But even all of them combined didn't have a hundredth of the devastating appeal of this man.

'Ember? Like a spark? Like a new beginning,' he murmured, and then louder, 'Where are you from, Ember?' he asked, as if speaking to a frightened child.

'Clockwork City,' she said, and when he looked blank, gave the city its real name. 'Bleakburn. You know? Where the three rivers meet? In Coldonia?'

'Coldonia! Yes!' He seemed delighted, and Lords, was he even better looking when he smiled. 'I know this place! Well, I know of it.'

'You do?' Relief flooded her. 'Thank the Lords. Can you take me there? Or show me the way? I have to get back to my family.'

'Ah.' The smile faded. 'I cannot.'

'Please.' Ember took a step towards him.

She wasn't proud of this kind of tactic, but it had worked more times than she could count. She took a deep breath, letting her blanket fall away a little, and looked up at him with big eyes. 'I'll do anything.'

His square jaw firmed. 'There isn't anything you can do.'

'Are you sure?' She let the blanket fall to the floor. It wouldn't even be a hardship with this one. He was *gorgeous*. 'I would be very, very grateful.'

Those blue, blue eyes – so bright, even in the moonlight – were drawn inexorably downwards. Ember made her chest heave a bit more. It was a good chest for heaving.

His nostrils flared.

'What shall I call you?' she asked softly.

His eyes narrowed. 'Rhaell,' he said.

Ember put her hand on his chest. Lords, it was firm. So firm. 'Rhaell? That's a nice name. Why don't we go and find somewhere more private, Rhaell?' she said. 'And make ourselves...' she trailed her fingers down the leather of his doublet, 'more comfortable?'

He stepped back, and Ember cursed herself. Too forward? Or maybe she was just looking an absolute horror. A man like this could have his pick of beauties.

'Well, much as I'd like to,' he drawled, 'I've never been a fan of an audience.'

Her head whipped around at the sound of a cracking twig, and her heart sank so quickly she was amazed she didn't drown.

There were soldiers advancing from the castle, men in smart green and silver outfits with fancy swords at their hips – but soldiers, nonetheless. While she'd been attempting to seduce this man, she hadn't been paying attention to her surroundings. Stupid Ember!

'I won't go back,' she said, stepping away from Rhaell, and from the men – but there were more advancing from the trees. 'I won't!'

'It's all right,' said Rhaell, holding out his hands to her placatingly. He made a very quick gesture to the soldiers, and they halted. 'I won't let anyone hurt you.'

Rage was making her dizzy. 'What? Did you hear what I said? They want to marry me to this – this – this *beast*, and let him fucking *ravage* me!'

'Thirty seconds ago, you were up for being ravaged,' Rhaell murmured, low enough that the soldiers probably couldn't hear.

'Um, no, that's different, because firstly, I was the one initiating it and secondly – did you hear the part about him being a monster? They said he ripped his mother apart at his birth!' Great, she was back to shrieking again.

Rhaell flinched. 'They do say that,' he said evenly.

'And! It's on the orders of the ... of His Grace! Who even is that?' she demanded, because they didn't have graces in Coldonia, not anymore. A duke? A bishop?

'That would be the king.'

Ember's hand went to her chest. The king. This place had a king! And he was the one who'd ordered the Beast to bed her.

She was really starting to feel light-headed now.

She glanced around at the men in their smart green and silver uniforms. They didn't look much like the tired, underpaid city guards in ill-fitting kit that she was familiar with. These men looked more like finely honed warriors in exquisitely tailored couture. King's guards. Of course. And they were deferring to Rhaell, which meant he was probably their captain or something.

'But why?' she whispered, futile tears gathering behind her eyes as the world started to dull at the edges. 'Why've *I* got to marry him?'

Rhaell's beautiful head tilted, fading in a cloud of smoke.

'Because you are the Promised One,' he said. 'You have been sent to save us all.'

'But I can't even save myself,' Ember whispered, and then to her great annoyance, she fainted.

~

'Feisty little thing,' remarked Phoebe, as Rhaell laid the Promised One down in her bed.

'You have no idea,' he murmured. She looked soft and small like this, her hands and feet bound with scraps of filthy fabric, her nightgown torn and muddy. Her hair was oddly short, barely reaching her shoulders, and she had a bosom the likes of which he'd only seen on tavern wenches. She was also at least a head shorter than him; maybe more. She had strong brows, full lips, and a chin he could only describe as stubborn.

She was as unlike any of the ladies of the court as he'd ever seen.

'She said her name was Ember,' he said.

'You mean, looks like nothing but capable of burning everything down?' Phoebe considered her. 'Appropriate.'

Rhaell wouldn't agree that she looked like nothing, but she was sure as hell capable of more than she looked. Ember. *The thing that starts a fire.* He watched Phoebe check her head, her chest, feel for her pulse and concentrate.

'There's nothing much wrong with her,' she said. 'She probably just fainted at the sight of you.'

'Ha,' he said humourlessly. She had stared at him, apparently unable to speak, but then he had that effect on a lot of people.

And then she'd tried to seduce him.

This was not something Rhaell was used to from the ladies of the court – who usually looked at him as if he were an aurochs that had rolled in its own dung – and it had been ... well, it had been really nice, actually.

'She did lose a lot of blood quite recently,' Phoebe said, somewhat deflating his ego. She added pointedly, 'I prescribed bed rest.'

Rhaell raised his hands. 'It's not my fault she climbed out of the window.' He narrowed his eyes and regarded the Promised One more critically. It was a long way down from her window; she had a serious amount of strength in her upper body to manage that. Her arms were strong, her core toned. He'd tried really hard not to notice the firmness of her thighs as he'd picked her up.

'Stop looking at her like that.'

He looked away, cheeks heating. 'Like what? I'm not looking.'

'Like you want to lick her all over.'

'I don't. I'm not.' *Liar.* 'I was just wondering why she wanted to run away,' he improvised. 'Because, you know, she's in the Queen's Chambers and they're almost as luxurious as the king's. Most people wouldn't run away from that.'

Phoebe scrunched her nose. 'I don't think she was as asleep as she seemed earlier.'

Rhaell groaned and rubbed his hands over his face. Ember had seemed to have some idea of the king's plans for her. 'Right. Yeah. Wonderful.' He'd have to do some damage control there when she woke up.

He rolled his shoulders, trying to dispel the imprint she'd left on his body. Strong and soft at the same time. That was a dangerous combination.

Phoebe glanced at him, and her shrewd gaze narrowed. 'Are you all right? She can't have been that heavy.'

'I'm fine. She wasn't.'

Phoebe hesitated. 'Rhaell – your back, does it—'

'It's fine,' he said curtly.

'Because I could take a look if you—'

'I said it's fine,' Rhaell said, and even Phoebe, the one person in the world who had no respect for his authority, backed down.

'Does anyone else know she got out?'

'A few of the guards heard us and came to investigate. They won't say anything.'

'Are you sure?'

Rhaell rested his hand on his sword hilt. 'I know my own guards, Phoebe. They're more loyal to me than they are to the king.'

'Don't let him hear you say that.'

He rolled his eyes at her, but he knew it to be true. He trained with those guards – hell, he was in charge of their training. If he told them to keep something quiet, they'd damn well keep it quiet.

He frowned. Ember was still wrapped with bandages over her chest, but through the fabric of her nightgown he could see something purple. The necklace she'd been wearing when she fell from the sky.

It appeared to be very faintly ... glowing?

Rhaell suddenly felt like someone had doused his brain in iced water.

'Yes, well,' Phoebe prattled on, while Rhaell stared and marvelled, his mind racing through very old memories. 'The walls have ears in this place. There's nothing the court likes more than gossip. If word got around the prince's bride tried to run away—'

'Can you blame her?' Rhaell said distractedly.

'What, for running away from luxury?'

Rhaell filed away this revelation for later examination. 'No – the poor girl thought she was going to be handed over to be the...' what had she said? '... the broodmare of a monster.'

Phoebe made a face. 'Are we still saying monster?'

'The king is,' said Rhaell evenly. He looked down at Ember: small, fragile, fierce, and apparently possessed of the climbing skills of a damned lizard – and felt his jaw tighten. 'And you know what the worst part is?'

'That I've got to launder this nightdress?' said Phoebe, poking at the mud and slime.

He couldn't even raise a smile at her attempt at humour. 'That she's right.'

Ember woke in the same huge, deliciously comfortable bed, but this time there was someone bustling around the room. Bustling in a rather obvious manner, as if she wanted Ember to wake up.

'Oh, there you are,' she said, coming closer. The silk-lined bedcurtains were all tied back, Ember noticed, probably so she'd have nowhere to hide. 'Back with us again. Apologies for the lack of nightgown, I didn't think you'd like to sleep in a dirty one.'

There was something pointed in that comment, Ember thought, and realised as she moved that she was completely naked beneath the sheets. Even the bandage on her chest was gone.

'Who——?' she began, and then caught sight of the woman approaching with an armful of linen. She felt her eyes go wide.

This woman was also very beautiful. Perhaps not in the god-tier of Rhaell, but still in possession of the sort of face that made men walk into lampposts and spill tea all over themselves. She wore a long dress and an apron, and her dark hair was tied back from her lovely face and kept neatly under a lace cap. There was a faint scar on her cheek, but it seemed to only enhance her beauty.

Rhaell. Had he brought her back here? He'd told her something ridiculous about being the Promised One, and then – well, she was going to blame her faint on lack of food and loss of blood.

'Who undressed you? Me, I'm afraid. That's my job. I'm Phoebe, and I'm your body servant. Do you need me to curtsey?'

'What? Oh. Er, no.' Ember sat up, holding the sheet to her chest. Her chest, which hardly hurt at all now. All the little cuts had vanished. Even the wound on her arm where Varne's men had shot her was little more than a dull ache. 'Look, I think there's been some kind of mistake.'

'Has there?' Phoebe was unfolding what seemed to be a silk robe.

'Yes. Rhaell – the guard from last night – he said I was this …

Promised One, or something.' It sounded really stupid when she said it out loud. 'I mean – obviously I ain't.'

'No, of course you are,' said Phoebe unconcernedly. She held up the robe as if expecting Ember to step into it.

'I'm not! I can't be. I'm just ... just an ordinary person,' she said, and then since she was naked and Phoebe was politely holding up the robe, Ember felt herself move to get into it. 'I'm not supposed to be here. I think you were supposed to be getting this girl called Dandelia...'

'Dandelia? Sounds like a weed,' said Phoebe, tying the sash around Ember's waist from behind.

'She's really pretty,' said Ember, although truthfully, she wouldn't hold a candle to Phoebe.

'How nice for her. The problem is, though,' said Phoebe, holding out her hand to help Ember rise from the bed, 'she's not here. And you are. And since we were promised the Promised One, on the twin moon before the eclipse in the forty-seventh year of the reign of the third King Onas, at the sun's highest point – the exact time that you fell out of the sky – I rather think you're her. Small step down here, my lady, mind how you go.'

'Fell out of the sky?' Ember said, following Phoebe across the room, which was massive, the sort of room you needed to hike across. Ember wasn't sure she'd ever been in a room this big before, not even when she was robbing mansions. The ceilings were vaulted and painted, the walls draped in what might be more silk. There were mirrors everywhere, and a long line of tall, arched windows opening onto the balcony she'd climbed off last night. Or had it been last night? How long had she been out?

Mermaids. Sea monsters. Twin moons.

Out of the windows was a gorgeous view of a lake, or maybe the sea, a bay fringed with forests and waterfalls and distant mountains. The sun sparkled on the water where last night, there had been monsters.

'Yes. Well – out of somewhere below the ceiling of the Great

Chamber, but it's basically high enough to be the sky anyway in there. Thunderclap, lightning flash, and there you were, falling straight into the Sacred Pool.' She made a whistling noise, demonstrating the fall with her hand. 'Good job, too, or you might have needed a bit more mending than just your chest, and that arm.'

Ember rubbed said chest. 'Yeah, about that—'

'I can't say I'm not intrigued. We weren't expecting you to turn up ready for Mnorir.' Phoebe opened a door that was twice the height it needed to be, and a gentle, sweetly-scented steam wafted out. 'Was it a ritual thing, or did you have to fight someone for the honour?'

The chains. The knives. The hot ooze of her own blood over her skin. The murmured chants, the incantations to the High Lords and Ladies, the flash of jewels on the knife as it plunged toward her chest—

'Er, ritual,' she said, somewhat distantly.

'Ah. Well, it's been a while since we've been to the Iron World, so we weren't expecting that. Would you like a hand with your bath?'

Ember gazed at a bathing chamber approximately the size of her father's house. It contained what seemed to be a sort of indoor waterfall, water cascading gently over small pools and marble basins before collecting in a large pool, big enough to swim in. Steam rose from it, and a scent that might have come from the lush green vines growing all around. They bore glossy leaves, lush pink and white flowers, and fat pink berries.

'Bath?' said Ember. A bath was a tin thing that hung on the back of the door, and you filled it up with water heated on the stove. She'd heard rich people had fixed bathtubs, with hot water straight from taps, but she couldn't see one of those, either.

Phoebe gestured at the largest pool. 'It's not as deep as it looks, and there are benches all around the edges. If you'd rather have privacy I can turn my back.'

But not leave. Clearly Ember was not to be trusted alone.

'Er, no, it's all right,' she mumbled, and fumbled with the sash of the robe. As she looked around for somewhere to hang it, Phoebe took it from her, and the silk seemed to fly from her hand to hang neatly on the plain marble wall.

No. She must have imagined that.

The water was warm. Except that warm didn't quite do it justice. It was the perfect temperature, the sort of temperature Ember had dreamed a bath should be. She sank in with a whimper, right down to her shoulders. And then she tilted her head back and let her hair float in the water.

She'd done that when she was a small child. Her mother had laughed and said she looked like a mermaid, only Ember knew that to be categorically untrue now.

She looked down between her breasts, where the bandage had been removed, and a healing pink scar remained. Which was almost more confusing than no scar at all. How could she have been stabbed in the chest and then just ... recovered?

Resting gently against her sternum was the sarelstone necklace, the purple stone garish in its cheap setting. It really didn't look worth anything at all. Let alone being stabbed for.

'The berries are quite good on your hair,' said Phoebe. 'And the petals crush nicely into the skin. Or I've oil, if you'd prefer a strigil.'

'Strigil?'

'To scrape the oil off. Very cleansing.' At Ember's puzzled look, she explained, 'It was all the rage last time we were in the Iron World.'

Ember reached for a petal and crumbled it with her fingers. The texture was slightly oily, and the scent was almost creamy.

'What's the Iron World?'

Phoebe sounded surprised. 'Where you're from. Is it not? Rhaell said—'

Her head whipped round. 'You know Rhaell?'

'We grew up together. Hard to believe, isn't it?' she added, with a self-deprecation Ember didn't quite understand. 'He said you're from a country called ... Coldonia?' She pronounced it with an uncertain intonation, as if the word was terribly exotic.

'Yes. Bleakburn. And I want to go back there,' said Ember firmly.

Back to the Clockwork City, with its smoke and smog and dirt and noise. Back to overflowing sewers and skeletal factory workers and coughing miners. Back to Pa, who often forgot she existed, and her brothers, who only remembered her if the dinner table was empty.

'Yes, and I want a winged pony. We call your realm the Iron World. The Ancestors knew of Coldonia, although it was rather a small, undeveloped country at the time. The real power in the world seemed to be the Iusmian Empire. Has that changed?'

Ember laughed incredulously. 'Has that changed? Er, yeah, hundreds of years ago! Iusmia hasn't had an empire in ... I don't know how long.' She hadn't exactly studied much history in her brief schooling. She sniffed at the deliciously scented petals again. 'Can I eat these?'

'Only if you like being sick. That goes for the berries, too.'

It was weird to wash yourself with leaves, no matter how good they smelled. Ember experimentally rubbed some of the crushed petal into her arm, where the bullet wound was likewise healed. 'Don't you have any proper soap? You know, made with sarel.'

Phoebe looked blank. 'I don't know what that is.'

How did she not know? Wasn't all soap made from sarel? 'Sarel? Well, this is sarelstone?' She gestured to her necklace.

Phoebe's brow drew down. 'Why would you wash yourself with a stone?'

For a moment the two of them frowned at each other, as Ember tried to work out what Phoebe was saying. Of course, the necklace wasn't the type of sarel you could wash with; that was a product refined in factories. But it came from sarel, didn't it? Everything did, in Bleakburn.

But it had been a long time since Ember's teachers had tried, ineffectively, to explain how sarel could be a stone and a liquid and made into soap and burnt on a fire, so instead of trying to explain this, she tried another tack. Phoebe seemed a fairly frank person, and much more inclined to answer questions than the secretive Rhaell. 'Where exactly am I?'

'Exactly? In the Queen's Chambers, Castle Yskar,' Phoebe answered promptly.

Ember returned her blank look.

'In Yskara.' Phoebe waited expectantly, and then her face fell. 'You don't know where that is, do you?'

'I'm not very good at geography,' Ember mumbled, rubbing the crushed petals into her other arm.

'It isn't exactly geography,' Phoebe said slowly. She came forward, and sat down on a small bench, gracefully switching her ankle-length skirts out of the way. 'It's more like ... well, perhaps theology. Did they truly not tell you?'

Theology? 'Did who not tell me what?'

'The people who sent you here. My lady—'

But right then her head whipped around, and a second later Ember heard the sounds of knocking coming from the outer room. Phoebe huffed and rolled her eyes.

'I'll go and see who that is,' she said, and hurried away before Ember could demand to know more.

Theology? The study of ... the gods? Coldonia had a variety of religions, but most people believed, however vaguely, in the High Lords and Ladies, a sort of set of ethereal beings who had been known to visit the mortal realm on occasion. There were ancient texts describing their aid to humankind, and a few accounts of supposed encounters that trailed off markedly with the rise of science. They were said to be inhumanly beautiful, tall and graceful, full of gentle wisdom and kindness, and far faster, stronger, and braver than any mortal being.

Ember looked around the high, beautiful bathing chamber, with its warm waterfalls and lush vines, and thought about the gigantic castle, the unearthly hafmey, and most of all the unrealistic good looks of Rhaell and Phoebe, and a very unpleasant suspicion began to creep into her mind.

Voices sounded outside the room, coming closer. She recognised the imperiousness of one of them – the same voice that had ordered Bronadyr the monster to bed her last night. The king.

The king who thought she was ugly, unworthy, and only fit for breeding.

Ember had never really considered her looks to be anything other than average. She wasn't beautiful, but she wasn't ugly, either. She was just ... forgettable. Why did this man hate her so much? Why was she so unworthy of his grandson?

A grandson, she reminded herself, she really didn't want to marry. So that part didn't matter. Except that it did, somehow.

'... really must stress the importance to Your Grace of my lady's dishabille,' Phoebe was saying as her voice rapidly neared the door.

'I have seen her near naked before,' the king said, as Ember wondered if she could reach her robe in time. She stretched out a hand, trying to get it to fly across the room to her, but nothing happened. *Must've imagined that.*

'Yes, Your Grace, but that was out of medical necessity, and also—'

'And also?' said the king, his voice very clipped, and even Phoebe's confidence seemed to dim at his tone.

'I will advise her of your presence,' she said.

'You are stalling,' the king said. 'Is there some reason I should not see her?'

'She is very modest,' Phoebe tried, and Ember nodded vigorously, despite this being colossally untrue.

'Well, that won't last. Is she whole?' the king boomed. 'Deformed? Mentally deficient? What?'

'Well, she's not deaf,' said Phoebe resignedly, and the next moment someone was pushing the tall door open. Ember shrank under the water, wrapping her arms over her breasts and sinking down to her chin.

He was a tall man, probably about the same age as Ember's father but with absolutely nothing else in common. He was no stooped, crippled clockmaker, squinting through cracked glasses and dressed in thrice-darned clothes. The king looked as a king should, in sumptuous fur-trimmed robes and a doublet made from some fabric that glittered like a sarel-oil slick. He wore no crown on his thick brown hair, but he didn't have to. Authority exuded from him in waves.

For a long moment they regarded each other, the thief and the king.

The king who wanted to wed her to a monster. Ember lifted her chin, ready for a fight.

He swept into a bow that knocked it out of her.

'My lady,' he murmured. 'King Onas of Yskara, at your service. We are honoured and privileged by your presence.'

Ember couldn't think of anything to say to that. What came out was, 'I'm in the bath.'

'Yes. For your health, I am sure. The waters of the Sacred Sea are known for their healing abilities. You came to us with unfortunate injuries,' he probed, straightening.

Behind him, Phoebe spread her hands helplessly.

'I got stabbed,' Ember said. 'And shot.'

'I see. A warrior queen, then, like Ysarriel herself. Truly, the Ancestors have blessed us.'

'Um,' said Ember.

'May we know your name, Promised One?'

Ember considered making one up, but her mind had gone blank. And besides, maybe if she explained they'd made a mistake... 'Ember,' she said. 'Ember Hart. But the thing is—'

Behind the king, Phoebe was making frantic throat slitting motions and shaking her head rapidly. Ember trailed off.

'Ember Hart!' proclaimed the king, as if this was the news he'd been waiting for. 'A strong name. Kindling the fires of the heart. An apt name, because...' He trailed off, hesitating just a little too theatrically. 'Are you aware of the expectations of Yskara regarding your arrival?'

Ember cleared her throat and tried to act like she wasn't floating naked in a rock pool. 'What expectations would those be?'

He gave her a sincere look. 'It has long been our hope – indeed, our most fervent prayer – that you will be our next queen.'

Her surprise must have shown in her eyes, because he smiled slightly and said, 'No, my lady, not my queen. My grandson's. He is my only heir, and the future of the throne is anything but assured. He must have an heir, and yet the women of our court remain unblessed.'

Ember waited for him to mention the monster part. Maybe it was an exaggeration. This man looked anything but misshapen.

Wait – what did he mean by unblessed? Bronadyr had not managed to get any of them pregnant? Was he just tearing through them all like a beast? Ugh!

'For our birthrate is falling, and has been for some time. Yskaran women have been forsaken. But the women of the Iron World ... you remain fertile, yes?'

Her mother, life drained away with every child she bore and every child she lost, until she died in her own blood—

'Have you borne a child?' he asked, with some hope.

'No,' Ember rasped.

'Are you a maid?'

'No,' she said, grasping onto that with relief. Maybe, since she wasn't a virgin, they'd send her back—

'Ah, good, then you will know what to expect. Bronadyr is a man of ... voluptuous tastes,' the king said. He was almost rocking on his heels. 'No shrinking violet would suit him. Of course, you will be properly wed, but nobody at all would mind the wedding being ... anticipated.'

Ember thought she might be sick.

'Of course, you will wish to settle in, get to know our ways, meet your people. We shall prepare a court presentation for the eclipse, and we shall take a progress around the country so that you may meet the great and noble houses of Yskara. Then the wedding ... perhaps a month after that? The astrologers tell me this is an auspicious date.'

A month? A fucking *month*?

The panic must have shown on her face, because Phoebe said, 'Your Grace. My lady is still recovering from her injuries. Her physiology is not the same as ours, and it seems the sacred water is not performing for her as it should. I am sure,' she pressed on, when a tiny frown appeared between the king's brows, 'that given time, she will acclimatise, and soon it will be just as if she was born Yskaran.'

'Not just as if,' the king glowered. He shot a look below the surface of the water, and Ember tried not to shudder as she recalled him ordering the monster to bed her and breed her. Clearly, the idea of her being considered anything like his exalted people was an insult.

'No, no, of course, Your Grace, I only meant that she has to heal from her injuries,' said Phoebe quickly. 'And, of course, I am sure Your Grace would wish the wedding celebration to be as spectacular as possible? To show the Promised One off to as many heads of state and vassal lords as possible? I am sure that is what Prince Bronadyr also suggested,' she added meekly.

The king stroked his chin, which bore a small beard. It was only slightly peppered with grey, as was his hair. On his wrist jangled an incongruous bracelet, hung with small charms. A snake, a rainbow, a fruit of some kind.

'Are you now my adviser?' he asked Phoebe, who shrank back against the door.

'No, Your Grace. My most ardent apologies, Your—'

'Oh, stop snivelling, girl, it doesn't suit you,' the king snapped.

He looked Ember over as if she was a horse he didn't really want to buy. 'When will she be healed?'

'It's hard to say, Your Grace,' Phoebe murmured.

He narrowed his eyes. 'I will consult my advisers on the matter,' he said. 'No more than a month, for sure. In the meantime, get her healed, get her dressed appropriately, show her how things work here.' To Ember, apparently having remembered he was supposed to be being gracious, he performed another bow. 'My lady,' he said, and swept out.

Phoebe pressed her finger to her lips, and waited at the door until they had both heard the outer door shut. Then she closed the bathroom door and hurried over.

'I am so sorry,' she whispered, 'I couldn't stop him.'

'It's okay,' said Ember, although it wasn't really. But she didn't want to get Phoebe in trouble.

'I mean, he is the king. And this is his castle. And you are the Promised One.'

'Will everyone please stop saying that?' said Ember. 'I'm not! I'm not supposed to be here. I—'

'But you are here,' said Phoebe, looking her in the eye. 'And there's nothing either of us can do about that, so come on, let's get your hair washed and we'll see what we can do about clothes.'

The library of Castle Yskar was huge, many storeys high and shapelessly sprawling. Learned scholars wafted about, thinking important thoughts, their brows furrowed under the weight of all their knowledge. Rhaell nodded to a few and stepped out of the way of others, too lost in their lofty thoughts to notice him.

He opened a door and walked through a room of books chained to the shelves, some of them faintly rattling. Went through the door at the end into a large hall of popular books on Yskara's celebrated history. Opened the next door using the sign of the Tree, and walked through the room with the chained books again. This time he emerged onto a wide balcony, where two scholars sat smoking pipes and debating the death of Ysarriel. He smiled politely as he passed them, opened the next door and walked past the rattling books for a third time.

He hadn't understood this the first time he'd encountered it, and he wasn't sure he understood it now. But that was how things sometimes worked around here: the third time was definitely the charm.

This time, when he opened the door, he entered a circular room with a high ceiling and shelves that were liberally coated with dust. He waved a werelight into existence, crossed the dusty floor to one shelf in particular, carefully removed a book, and turned it to a page where it fell open easily.

'The heart of Yskar will be healed by her hand and the seeds she shall nurture will thrive.'

The heart of Yskar. He'd heard it so many times, especially in recent years as the arrival of the Promised One drew closer. Everyone knew the heart of Yskara was the Sacred Tree, right at the centre not just of the land of Yskara, but of the whole continent. The precious Tree, source of all their power, to whom the monarchy was inextricably tied.

If one failed, the other failed.

And yet...

The memory was years old, scratched and faded by time. A book on a high shelf – no, a scroll! He had pored over the bright colours and the incomprehensible words, a puzzle he thought he'd never solve until one day he saw a scholar reading the same sorts of words and asked for help.

He'd never told anyone about the scroll. But bit by bit he'd learned to decode it. And the story it told...

If the king knew he was here, there'd be hell to pay. But what more could the king do to him that he hadn't done already?

His back throbbed in memory. *Don't even ask that question.*

He peered up at the high, dusty shelves. He hadn't even looked at the scroll for years and years, his life filling up with duties and obligations he couldn't shirk. He'd forgotten about it, a childish fantasy that had faded from his memory. Until now.

It took several wrong tries and a lot of sneezing before he found it, a fragile roll of vellum tied with string that fell apart when he touched it. Carefully, he unrolled it on the dusty table and conjured more lights.

Its colours glowed up at him, as they had so long ago. The words carefully inked in an ornate style that was hard to read, the language centuries old and the spelling somewhat optional. The images depicted the Ancestors, the seven founders of Yskara, each lovingly rendered in their signature colour.

He scanned the text until he found the bit he was looking for.

'*They removed the heart, and cut it into seven pieces.*'

He stood back and stared at nothing. He'd heard the story so many times: how Yskara was founded by Ysarriel, the First Queen, and her husband Ruvaen the Rogue, who betrayed her with her best friend Ephyrea. And as punishment, Ephyrea was bound into the Tree forever, a living death.

But nobody talked about her heart. Nobody said that it had been cut out and split into pieces and the pieces had been hidden, so she couldn't die. Nobody mentioned how one piece had been hidden so thoroughly by Ruvaen that it would never be found.

Until the Promised One came to *heal the heart of Yskara*.

He looked back down at the scroll. There was Ysarriel, in Yskaran green. Ephyrea, in lover's pink. And Ruvaen, in roguish purple. Purple as the stone around Ember's neck.

The green stone in the king's crown had seemed to glow at the moment Ember appeared. He hadn't noticed if her purple one had glowed too, what with it being saturated in her blood, but...

Rhaell reached out a hand without looking, and a chair scraped across the floor to him. He sat down heavily and began rereading.

The clothes on offer to Ember were, quite frankly, ludicrous. Silks and brocades and satins, embroidery and gemstones and endless, endless acres of skirt. Quite apart from which, they all appeared to have been modelled after someone who had twice Ember's height and half her cleavage.

Ember didn't even wear skirts most of the time. Trousers weren't yet completely acceptable for women in the Clockwork City, but she wore them when she went out thieving, and a divided skirt the rest of the time. Dresses were for Solsdays and fancy occasions, and she attended mercifully few of those.

'This isn't working, is it?' she said, after Phoebe tried and failed to get her modesty concealed inside the scanty little bodice of a blue silk number. 'One deep breath and it's hello, boob.'

'I admit we weren't expecting someone so, er, generously blessed,' Phoebe said, tweaking a bit of fabric that crumpled under the weight of Ember's breast again.

'You don't have short stays, I take it?' she asked, and got a blank look in return.

Ember had never considered herself particularly busty. Or particularly short. She was completely average in every single way, which was a huge advantage when your chosen profession required you to be extremely unmemorable. But she was beginning to wonder if everyone at court was as willowy as Phoebe, in which case she was going to look simply absurd.

Eventually, Phoebe found her a dress that wasn't slit to the navel, under which she could wear a sort of girdle that seemed designed to flatten her figure, rather than enhance it. Ember let Phoebe dress her up like a dolly and fuss around with her hair because it gave her time to think.

She clearly had to get out of here. Firstly, to get back to her father and her brothers, and secondly, to get away from marrying

Prince Bronadyr. Being a queen held no appeal for Ember. Who even had royalty anymore?

A plate of bread, cheese and fruit was delivered by a curtseying maid. The bread and cheese looked normal enough, but she didn't trust the berries, which were a suspiciously bright purple. Should she trust any of it?

Her stomach growled, and Ember realised she probably hadn't eaten in a couple of days. Well – she could try the cheese, at least...

Damn, it was delicious.

But she couldn't just climb out of the window and hope for the best again. This was a royal palace, and even a Coldonian knew such places were fortified and guarded. By evil mermaids, in this case, and possibly sentient gargoyles and definitely guards with pikes.

Ember absently ate some bread. It was the fluffiest, crustiest bread she'd ever eaten.

So she'd have to get to know the lie of the land. Root out weak spots and escape routes. Discover where, exactly, she even was. Ember's education had been pretty basic, but there had been a world map on the wall of the schoolroom, and she didn't remember any Yskara.

Oh, fuck it. She ate a berry, and the sour sweet taste exploded on her tongue.

Phoebe was just doing her level best to avoid complaining that Ember's hair was too short, when another knock sounded on the outer door.

'If it's more food, I really liked the cheese,' Ember said, licking her fingers. The plate was empty. Phoebe gave her a smile through the mirror and bustled off to deal with it.

The bedchamber and bathing chamber appeared to be only part of Ember's suite. Phoebe had to cross a sitting room and what appeared to be a private dining area before reaching the outer door. The rooms all had tall, intricately arched windows that looked out over a vast lake – what Rhaell had called the Sacred Sea – with a distant waterfall thundering over high cliffs. She couldn't see much else, apart from the unrealistically blue waves and cloudless sky.

After trying and failing to hear Phoebe's low conversation with the visitor, Ember was treated to a louder, 'I shall enquire,' and then she was back, fixing a smile upon her lovely face, and hesitating.

'Rhaell would like to see you,' she said.

'The Captain of the Guard?' Ember said. 'The guy who brought me back here even when I begged him not to?'

'Well—' began Phoebe.

'Forgive me, Sparks,' said Rhaell's deep voice from the outer chamber. Ember glowered at the doorway as he appeared in it, even more beautiful in the daylight. She didn't want to like this man, with his ruffled dark hair and his shining blue eyes. He wore grey, which might have looked plain on another man, but gleamed like silver on him.

She'd thought he looked like a wolf last night. Now he reminded her more of a guard dog, large and implacable, but absolutely capable of tearing you to pieces if he needed to.

She tried to dispel the image. At the sarel mine where her brothers worked, there was a huge dog chained to the payroll office. He spent most of his time lying in the meagre sun, eyeing people as if to decide if they were worth eating, but rumour had it he'd torn the leg off the last man who'd tried to rob the place. The lads called him Buttercup.

'You had fainted—'

'I don't faint,' she said, trying to ignore the hot blush that warmed her cheeks.

His eyebrows rose. 'Perhaps we are divided by a common language,' he said. 'You were conscious, and then you were unconscious...?'

'No, that's passing out, from lack of food and blood and stuff,' Ember corrected. 'It's not fainting. I ain't a fainter.'

Amusement crossed his face, twitching at those fine lips. 'A thousand pardons,' he said with no sincerity whatsoever. 'But I had to bring you back here after you … passed out. I could hardly leave you for the hafmey, could I?'

'Maybe you should've. Maybe I'd have preferred taking my chances with them to being locked up back in here.'

'You're not locked up.'

'Really? So, I can leave whenever I want?'

His smile faltered. 'You can leave this room.'

'Wow.' Ember injected as much sarcasm into the syllable as she could. 'Thanks. So generous. And when I do, will I be able to keep on leaving, until I'm back in Coldonia?'

Rhaell sighed. 'I'm sorry. I truly am. But you can't go back there.'

'Watch me,' snarled Ember, getting to her feet and shaking out those stupid skirts.

'You don't understand,' Rhaell said. He pushed his hand through his hair and winced. 'It's not that we won't let you. It's that you can't.'

CHAPTER 3

At the other end of a long corridor leading from the Queen's Chambers, a large solar had been laid out overlooking the Sacred Sea. One long, curved wall was made of windows, the delicate arch of their frames draped with trailing vines and sweet-scented flowers. In the summer, they provided shelter from the heat of the sun, and in the winter their bare limbs allowed magnificent views over the Sacred Sea.

Now it was autumn, and the banks of the Dagrai Falls were rippling with shades of red and gold. The wind blew leaves against the windows and the sun was pale and cool, laying deep shadows across the carpets and chaises of the solar.

Rhaell took Ember to a section not far from the fireplace, where the view across the sea was particularly fine. Herbs had been strewn by the fire, scenting the room with cosiness. He sat her down on a deep sofa and asked if she was warm enough.

She didn't respond, still staring out at the sea.

'What are they?'

Rhaell looked at where she nodded and saw a pair of perytons tumbling over and over in the sky. It was rutting season, and they'd be clashing antlers until one admitted defeat. Ember seemed fascinated.

'Perytons. You don't have those?'

'No. Deer don't fly,' Ember said, as if he was an idiot.

I used to know a deer who did. 'They're not deer. They're perytons.'

Ember squinted. 'They're flying deer.'

'Which are called perytons. May I pour you some wine?'

Her gaze flicked back to the table, where servants had laid out spiced wine and little cakes. 'How do I know it's not poisoned?'

His brows went up. 'What would be the sense in that? You're our Promised One. You've been sent to save us.'

Her eyes narrowed. 'First, says who, and second, I don't care 'cos you could've just made that up to lull me into a false sense of security. I've read penny dreadfuls. I know what dastardly villains do. I'll probably wake up chained to another stone slab about to be stabbed to death. Again,' she added irritably.

'Can you be stabbed to death more than once?'

She spread her hands. 'Well, I'm still here. And I haven't heard an apology yet.'

Rhaell paused in the pouring of the wine. 'For...?'

'Getting stabbed to death! Come on, where is he? They? There was a whole bunch of them.'

He put the carafe down. 'Of who?'

Ember Hart looked at him as if he was trying to kid her. 'Of the men who chained me to a stone slab and stabbed me to death! To be fair, some of them might have been women, but that's not the point,' she said, grabbing the wine and drinking it anyway.

Well, that explained the knife to her chest at any rate. Rhaell wanted badly to light up a sootweed, but that was considered uncouth, and she was the Promised One after all, even if she was ... not exactly what he'd expected.

For one thing, he really didn't think the Promised One was supposed to try to escape the minute she got here.

'Could you just ... walk me through exactly how you got here?' he said, and Ember set down her wine cup and fixed him with a look.

'Buckle up, Buttercup,' she said.

'What?'

'So there was this girl, right? Really pretty, you'd have liked her. She was supposed to be your Promised One. Only I didn't know that, did I? I only knew I'd found this girl chained up in a cellar and there were all these candles and shit, and like I said I've read penny dreadfuls, I know what *that* means, so I helped her escape. I'm good with locks,' she explained. 'My pa's the best clockmaker in the Clockwork City. Like, officially. Or he would be if he hadn't quit the Guild 'cos of what they said about our ma, but that's not the point,' she said again.

Rhaell nodded helplessly. She was using words, and they were mostly real words, but the order she put them in made no sense.

'Anyway. I helped her escape, but then these fellas with guns came in and they were kind of mad, and...' She rubbed her arm, where there had been a puzzling circular wound made by something that had shattered bone and shredded muscle. 'Well, anyway, next thing I knew, I was chained to the stone slab I rescued Dandelia from, and they were chanting and there were—' She broke off, inhaled sharply, and continued, 'They had knives. Like, not normal ones, sort of ritual ones. With fancy handles and curved blades and shit.'

Rhaell grimaced. One such knife had been embedded in her chest when he'd caught her in his arms. Phoebe said it had just missed her heart.

'And they cut me all over, and collected the blood and drank it,' she said, as if she was describing a dull court event, 'and then Varne said something like, "High Lords and Ladies, accept our sacrifice, please return and share with us your power."'

'Varne?'

Ember fixed him with a look that pinned him in place. 'Baron

Varne. He's got the big mansion outside the city. On the hill. In the woods.'

Rhaell returned her look and said, 'There are no mansions outside this city. We are on the hill. The woods contain the Sacred Tree. And I have never heard of any Baron Varne.'

She glared at him for a long moment, then slumped. 'No. Course not.' She gazed out of the window at the perytons. 'I don't think I'm anywhere near the Clockwork City anymore, am I?'

Rhaell, who had never even heard of it until last night, said, 'I don't think so. No. I'm sorry.'

'And the High Lords and Ladies?'

He shrugged. 'We have many lords and ladies, but I'm not sure about the "High" part. Lord Addor, Lord Keenor, Lady Feynrith...' They were some of the more powerful courtiers. But Ember just shook her head.

'Lady Sarel, Lady Feara, Lord Nori?'

Rhaell shook his head in turn. 'I'm sorry.'

Ember sighed and poured herself more wine, which was a novelty. Rhaell had never seen any member of the court pour their own drinks.

'What about your necklace?' he asked casually. 'Family heirloom, is it?'

Her hand went to her chest, which had the unfortunate side effect of drawing Rhaell's gaze there. 'It was a gift,' she said.

'From?'

'A friend. You don't know her,' she added, almost automatically.

'I don't think I know anyone you know,' Rhaell said slowly. She was clearly lying. 'May I see it?'

Ember eyed him suspiciously, but she fished the stone from her bodice and held it out.

There was a faint – very faint – purple glow from it. Rhaell leaned closer, trying not to gaze at her breasts as he did.

The stone was an uneven cut, the setting cheap. It was not a jewel he imagined anyone wearing by choice, and it didn't go with Ember's outfit.

Men had chained her down and stabbed her, and in return for this 'sacrifice' they expected power. Was it possible this was the ritual set down by the Ancestors to bring their Promised One?

'It's just a cheap sarelstone,' Ember said, tucking the stone away. 'It ain't worth nothing.'

The green stone in the king's crown had glowed when Ember appeared. Rhaell had seen that crown on countless occasions, and never once had the damn thing glowed. Green for Ysarriel, the First Queen. Purple for Ruvaen the Rogue. It absolutely couldn't be a coincidence.

'Your friend,' he said. 'What was their name?'

Ember eyed him suspiciously. 'Dandelia,' she said.

'The girl you rescued?'

'Yeah. She gave me the necklace. For safekeeping. I didn't steal it,' she said.

Rhaell fought a smile, because Ruvaen wasn't named the Rogue for nothing. 'Of course,' he said smoothly, but before he could ask any more, she went on.

'Is that why I'm here? 'Cos I had the necklace? It was meant to be her. She's really pretty. You'd like her,' she repeated.

'I'm sure,' said Rhaell, 'but you're who we've got.'

'That's what Phoebe kept saying,' muttered Ember. 'But I'm the wrong one. I've got to go home,' she said, striking her hand on the chair arm for emphasis. It wasn't a neatly-kept hand, he noticed. It was covered in small scars and calluses, the nails brutally short. 'I've got a crippled father and two little brothers. They need me.'

Rhaell ran his hand through his hair and winced. 'I'm sorry,' he said. 'But I meant what I said. It's not that we don't want to send you home. It's that we can't.'

The Promised One folded her arms and muttered something that sounded like 'fuck's sake'.

Rhaell gazed out at the solar, empty but for the two of them.

They'd encountered only a few people on the walk here, all of them curtseying and bowing and clearly desperately curious about Ember. Which they would be, her coming having been foretold for generations.

He sighed. 'Listen, here's what I know. The Tree links all worlds – yours and mine and hundreds of others. The Yskar used to travel to the Iron World frequently. It's why I'd heard of your country. It's why we can understand each other.'

'You're speaking Coldonian.'

'Technically, you're speaking Yskaran,' Rhaell began, saw her mutinous face, and decided not to fight that fight today. 'The Ancestors used the power of the Tree to open portals to different worlds, but we don't have the power to do that anymore. All we can manage now are portals around the castle.' He didn't add that if the magic faded any more, they'd barely be able to do that.

'Magic?' she said doubtfully.

'Yes. The magic...' He shoved a hand through his hair again. 'It has been fading. Incrementally, but steadily, for generations. Where once it powered portals to other worlds and allowed Yskarans to fly and to raise mighty castles in a day,' he indicated their surroundings, 'now we use it to make lights and travel around the castle. The days of great and powerful sorcery are long behind us. Even the Great Dragons are gone.'

'Dragons?' said Ember, her eyebrows going up. Maybe it was because they were thicker and darker than the other ladies' at court, but they seemed to make her face more expressive. Or maybe the other ladies were just excessively languid. 'You have dragons here?'

'Only lesser ones,' Rhaell said. 'The Great Dragons haven't been seen in generations. We assume they're all dead. The magic couldn't sustain them.'

'What's a – you know what, never mind. If you can't open a portal to my world because you don't have the magic, then how did I get here?'

Rhaell sighed. 'Do you want the long answer or the short answer?'

'I want the honest answer.'

He spread his hands. 'I don't know.'

Ember slumped in her seat and glared out at the sea.

'There's a prophecy,' he said. 'It's existed for generations. No one knows how old it is or even who wrote it. But it declares that when Yskara is in great peril, a saviour will arrive and save the realm. She is to bring an end to the blight and restore power to the rightful. She will heal the heart of Yskar and the seeds she plants shall thrive.'

He watched Ember carefully for her reaction. She looked frankly disbelieving. 'And you think I'm that saviour?'

'The prophecy,' Rhaell went on, 'gave the exact date and time of your arrival. In case we might miss it, the Kingbeast awoke, stars fell from the sky, and at Jaonos Yllanala's memorial last week the Tree put out a single pure flower.'

She gave him the sort of look he used to get as a small child telling fibs. 'Shooting stars? Trees? This is all nonsense.'

Rhaell winced, and hoped his face didn't betray that he actually agreed with her. 'I'd advise you not to go around saying that.' He thought about the fervent hope on the faces of the court as they'd waited for the Promised One's arrival. How the city had been decorated with bunting and banners, how the Sacred Forest was overrun with pilgrims. He'd needed to double the guards and add extra patrols all through the night.

'But it is. It's all bollocks. I ain't a saviour. The king called me a warrior queen! I've never even been in a fight!' She thought about that for a moment. 'Well, maybe with my brothers when they were being little shits, and maybe that time with the Bonerun Gang, but not a *proper* fight. I don't know how to use a sword or a gun or anything.'

'A ... gun?'

She blinked at him. 'Yes, a gun. You don't have those here?' She made a strange gesture with her hand, pointing two fingers and sticking her thumb up, and made a noise he could only describe as 'pew'. 'No?'

Was it some sort of spell? Was it meant to hurt him? It had no effect. He'd never been more baffled. 'Er, no.'

'The thing that shot me?' She gestured to her left arm, where the mysterious wound had been healed. 'What do your guards carry, then?'

He shrugged. 'Pikes, swords, bows.' Some had lesser magic that increased the effectiveness of their weapons. 'But you needn't worry, they are here for your protection.'

'The sort of protection that means I can't leave? We've a word for that where I come from,' she groused.

Rhaell sighed. How could he explain it to her?

But before he could even try, movement at the door caught his attention. A flurry of coloured silks and a girlish giggle. He groaned.

'For what's about to transpire, Sparks, I'm truly sorry,' he said, and hauled himself to his feet. 'Ladies, you might as well come in.'

They came like a flock of exotic birds, shimmering and fluttering, dropping curtseys that had them vanishing in billows of silken skirts.

Ember stared up at them in some horror.

'Lady Ember,' said Rhaell, 'may I present your ladies-in-waiting.'

The five young ladies all rising from their deep curtseys would have made the lovely Dandelia look as plain as a piece of paper. They were probably not much younger than Ember, but all of them seemed so fresh, pretty and lovely, in a way that said they'd never known a moment's hardship. Their hair was styled in a variety of ways, but each boasted luscious, flowing locks they could probably use to climb out of a tower window. Each of was them dressed in a gown that had clearly been tailored and styled to suit their tall, willowy forms, showcasing slender arms and neat, perky little breasts.

Ember shoved her short hair behind her ears and folded her arms across her own overflowing cleavage, wondering why she had to have fallen into a world where everybody was physically perfect.

Rhaell gestured to them each in turn and began a series of introductions that seemed to go on for hours. It was just word soup to Ember. Lady this and Honoured Daughter of that. They each dropped elegant curtseys as Ember tried hopelessly to remember their names and titles.

Ember said, 'Um, hi?'

They all giggled.

'These are to be your ladies,' said Rhaell, with what sounded like thin patience. 'They have all been chosen as daughters of important families, all allies of Yskara. Their character and education is of the very highest quality.'

Daughters of allies... Something in the way he said it gave Ember pause, but he was already continuing.

'They are to be your eyes and ears at court. They are to assist your day-to-day activities, your dress, your correspondence, your schedule. If there is a tradition of the court you are unfamiliar with, they will instruct you.'

Oh, I bet they will. 'It's nice to meet you,' Ember said, and they giggled and curtseyed again. She was at a loss as to what to say next. Or do. Ladies-in-waiting? Whoever heard of such a thing? 'Do you want to sit down?' she asked, and they all fluttered over, arranging themselves elegantly on the sofas and chairs nearest Ember's.

Rhaell, she noticed, gave up his seat, but none of them sat in it. In fact, the looks they darted him were downright hostile. Perhaps a mere captain of the guard was beneath them.

Before she could think of anything else to say to them, a guard in a green and silver uniform appeared in the doorway. He bowed his head sharply, saluted, and said, 'Sir, if I might have a word?'

Rhaell, his relief barely disguised, nodded and bowed to Ember, which was absurd. And then he was gone, and she was alone with these five exotic and beautiful creatures.

'So,' she said, and they looked at her expectantly. 'Um. Nice weather we're having?'

'It's autumn,' said the one in the blue dress, as if nobody could ever possibly be expected to like autumn.

Ember refilled her wine. The ladies all gasped. *Great, looks like I wasn't supposed to do that.*

'How refreshing your manners are,' said the one in pink, and Ember knew she was the one she'd have to look out for.

This wine was smooth and rich, rather like an expensive-looking bottle she'd helped herself to from the manor house last Wintertide. It went very well with the little cakes, so she ate a couple, which meant her mouth was full when the girl in the pink dress said, 'What a lovely shade of blue that is on you, my lady.'

Ember chewed and swallowed so fast she nearly choked. 'Mmm,' she agreed, covering her mouth with the wineglass. 'Er, thanks.'

'Your girl has an eye for colour. It is a pity about the cut, however.'

'My ... girl?'

'Your maid. You should really have her flogged for putting you in something cut so poorly.'

Flogged? 'It isn't her fault,' she said. 'She didn't know what I'd look like. I don't expect she could just magically run up a new dress for me while I was asleep.'

The girl in the pink dress – Lyndis, perhaps? – frowned as if in surprise. 'Well, of course she could. That is the skill set of a maid. Although...' She tapped her lips thoughtfully. 'I did hear she is misplaced as a maid. Not well trained. Wanted to be a healer.'

'What?' said the one in the green dress. 'But her mother was a servant. To the princess. It was a personal favour from the king to make her the Promised One's body servant.'

Ember really wished they wouldn't call it that. It made her sound like a corpse. Although twenty-four hours ago she supposed she nearly had been.

'Yes, but apparently that's given her ideas above her station. I mean – look. She clearly has no interest in dressmaking.'

Ember felt compelled to defend Phoebe. 'She's a good healer, though,' she said, not really even sure what she was talking about. 'I mean – I was stabbed and shot and now I'm fine.'

They all gazed at her, wide-eyed. Shit, was she not supposed to say that?

'I mean – what princess?' she deflected, grateful the unfashionable dress covered her healing wounds. Did the monstrous prince have a sister? Was she just as monstrous as he?

The five ladies exchanged looks. 'The king's daughter,' said the one with the bangles. 'Princess Nephinae.' All five of them cast their eyes down and made a complicated gesture with one hand. 'May the Tree shelter her.'

'May the Tree shelter her,' the others murmured.

'The king's daughter?' Given Prince Bronadyr was the king's grandson... 'Was she the...' *don't say monster don't say monster*, 'the prince's mother?'

All five of them shuddered.

'They say he ripped her apart,' whispered the one in pink.

'The *horns*,' said the one in blue, with a shudder that had Ember feeling sick.

'Born a monster,' said the one in green.

'Always will be a monster,' said the one with the diadem.

The one with the bangles glanced at Ember, and said quickly, 'He is not as bad as we are saying. It is merely gossip—'

'Gossip?' interjected the one in pink. Her dress was slashed nearly to the waist. 'No, Thalissa, I've seen him leaving one of the brothels just before dawn.'

'What were you doing outside a brothel just before dawn, Lyndis?' scoffed the one in blue.

Lyndis's cheeks coloured. 'Well, my maid saw her,' she said.

'And what was your maid—'

'Are you calling her a liar?' said Lyndis, and they all backed down. 'He is debauched,' she pronounced, with satisfaction.

'Debauched,' said Ember, her voice coming out a little high.

'Oh, yes. No lady in the palace will go near him. I heard it from Lady Eyvinby's girl that he's completely deformed under his clothes.'

'The men he trains with call him the Beast,' said Lyndis.

'And you know what he did to Lady Alais,' said the brunette with the diadem. They all shuddered.

'I heard—' began the redhead.

'I think that's enough,' said Thalissa, who Ember vaguely recalled being introduced as the daughter of a foreign queen. 'We are here to aid her ladyship, not to terrify her.'

Ember tried to smile at her.

'After all, the union has been foretold for generations, so there is no point in fretting about it,' Thalissa added, in a manner that was presumably supposed to be reassuring. 'Now, let us have some wine and discuss what sort of gowns might be more appropriate for our Promised One. We have a progress to plan for, after all.'

Ember gratefully let the chatter wash over her. *The union has been foretold for generations.* Well, that didn't mean it was inevitable.

The king wanted her married in a month. Ember intended to be long gone by then.

CHAPTER 4

In the attics, Deer and Rainbow ran.

They were huge, as attics went, and there were dusty windows to the sky every now and then. Some of them opened, although Mama forbade them to go near them if they were any more than a hands-breadth ajar.

'But Mama,' said Deer, folding his arms. 'I can fly.'

'And what happens when you get tired?' said Mama. 'I know you, Deer. You'll fly and fly and then you'll be sooo tired and sooo sleepy, and then you'll go to lie down for a nap, and oh!' Her mouth and eyes snapped into shocked ovals. 'There won't be any floor! And dooown,' she made a whistling sound, 'and down you'll go and then splat!'

She blew a raspberry at them, and both children giggled madly.

'Splat!'

'I'll go splat!'

'Exactly. Splat. And Mama can fix a lot of things, but she can't fix splat. So, stay away from the windows, all right?'

Then Mama went back to doing boring things like folding clothes, or whatever she did all day, and Deer and Rainbow raced off into the next attic room.

'It's so unfair,' Deer complained, flexing his wings.

'What's unfair?'

'I can't go anywhere!'

'Mama's taking us outside tonight,' said Rainbow. 'That's somewhere.'

Deer scowled. 'She still won't let me fly. Not properly.' Mama worried if he went too high, or too far, and she constantly begged him not to go anywhere near the castle walls.

'Well, what if someone saw you? We couldn't be spies if someone saw us.'

Deer considered this. They watched the people in the court all the time, diligently recorded their activities and wrote them down. He wasn't sure why. Mama carefully filed them and sometimes quizzed them on stupid things, like who Lord Addor had been talking to about the mantises, and how far the Myr had progressed into Valoris. Boring things like that.

He fluttered into the air as he thought. Below him, Rainbow put her hands on her hips and sighed. 'Show off.'

He smirked. He couldn't help it. Having wings was awesome! They weren't very big right now, but they were getting stronger all the time, and Mama said that when he was grown, they might reach from one side of the room to the other. And then he could fly anywhere he wanted!

'Well, I can stand on my head,' boasted Rainbow, but then they both froze because they heard a knock at the door.

'Quickly, quickly,' Mama gasped, but they were already rushing into the big dusty armoire and shutting the door.

They could see through the cracks in the door, but only a sliver. Enough to see Mama standing there, blocking the entrance to the room.

'I am perfectly capable of cooking meals,' said Mama, as the smell of food came in. Deer could just see a person pushing a trolley.

Rainbow sniffed appreciatively. 'Ptarmigan,' she whispered happily.

'No, it's peryton.'

'Don't be stupid! It's roast ptarmigan!'

'...we're stupid? We'll just bring you up knives and pans for you to use as weapons?'

'You think I want weapons when I've got two children around the place?' said Mama. They heard the rattle of serving dishes. 'Ptarmigan. Would it be a crime to send up some vegetables?'

Rainbow nudged Deer, looking smug. He rolled his eyes at her.

'You're to be reminded we have an important event today, with a reception afterwards in the gardens, so no taking ... *it* anywhere near the keep or gardens. Not tonight.'

'No one will know we're even here,' Mama promised, and they waited until the door had shut before they tumbled out.

'I said it was ptarmigan,' said Rainbow cheerfully. 'Deer said it was peryton but peryton smells nothing *like* that.'

'Indeed.' Mama looked thoughtful.

'It smells sooo good,' said Rainbow.

'I'm *starving*,' said Deer, gazing longingly at the covered dishes. He could eat a whole ptarmigan by himself, probably.

Mama nodded. 'Well, come on, set the table. We have our manners. What are we not?'

'We're not animals,' chorused both children, Rainbow fetching plates and Deer flying over with fistfuls of blunt knives and forks.

'Quite. Now, we can't go to the gardens tonight—' she waited for them to make appropriate groans of disappointment, which they dutifully did, 'but how about the library? We can look at the old books.'

'Will you tell us the story of the Ancestors again?' said Deer. He liked that one, although some of the words were too complicated for him to read.

'Of course. It's important you learn as much as you can. Now, eat up. You want to grow big and strong, don't you?'

CHAPTER 5

Rhaell lay on his back on a bunk in the guardhouse, blowing sootweed smoke rings towards the stained ceiling. The bunk was both lumpy and hard, and the room was only warm on one side, where a somewhat pathetic fire sputtered. The floor shook slightly with the trample of soldiers' boots outside and the air was heavy with woodsmoke, sootweed smoke, and the scent of healthy young men who didn't wash often enough.

He liked it here. Liked it far better than the court above, where all the lords and ladies wafted around in their silks and high heels, sneering at him while they plotted their boring little personal intrigues.

They were fascinated with Ember, just as they'd been fascinated with each of the king's new wives; only more so, not just because she'd been foretold but because there was an actual chance she could end their blight.

No babies had been born in the court for several years. Rhaell had to think quite a long way back to last time he remembered even seeing a newborn.

For a while it had been assumed the king would take the Promised One as his own wife. But the old man had married five more times after his daughter had died, and none of those poor girls had blessed him. And the old goat would never admit that his days of siring children were over, so he'd passed on the responsibility to his monstrous grandson.

They want to marry me to this – this – this beast, and let him fucking ravage me.

The king believed that if Ember could provide him with an heir, the Tree would heal and the magic would be restored. Rhaell was pretty sure he'd got it backwards, but voicing that would probably have his head on the block before he got to the end of the sentence.

The Heart of Yskar will be healed by her hand...

A shadow darkened the doorway. 'Hiding from something?'

Rhaell didn't look round. 'What makes you say that?'

''Cos that's the only time you take a bunk in the guardhouse, lad.'

Rhaell scowled at the ceiling. 'I stay here all the time.'

'I said what I said.'

Brock wasn't an especially large man, but he didn't need to be. Rhaell had never seen anyone move so quickly, or with such precision. Brock could down a man twice his size, and frequently did. Rhaell always savoured the first day of a new season, when the cockiest new recruits decided they could definitely beat the wiry, laconic man who handed them their practice swords.

Brock glanced at him and sniffed. 'I smell the Spreading Branches on you, lad. Had a good drink?'

Rhaell took another deep draught of his sootweed. He had indeed had a good drink at the tavern. Among other things. 'I introduced the Promised One to her new ladies.'

Brock grimaced. 'In that case I'm surprised you're not drunker. How's she getting on, our great saviour?'

'She wants to go home,' said Rhaell, rubbing his hands over his face.

'Back to Coldonia?' Brock looked mystified. 'I looked it up in the old texts. They said it was a bleak place, always damp, always cold, always muddy. People lived in miserable dark little hovels and died of plague.'

'That was many generations ago,' said Rhaell, which was true, even if he didn't know whether it was relevant.

'Be that as it may, didn't she volunteer to come here?'

Rhaell winced, but before he could enlighten Brock, a shadow appeared in the doorway. One of the king's pages, looking at the barracks as if it might be diseased.

'Yes, lad?' said Brock.

'I come with news of justice,' the page said portentously. 'In the trial of the heinous murderers and their conspirators.'

'The accused,' corrected Rhaell, a little sharply. The young man's gaze strayed to him and the pompous light faded slightly from his eyes as Rhaell stood and loomed over him.

Maybe a little on purpose.

'The accused?' he repeated.

The page swallowed and looked up at him. 'Sentenced this very afternoon, uh, sir.'

Rhaell pinched his nose. He knew what the sentence was going to be before he even asked, but he still had to. 'Death?'

'Yes, sir. Two more for the block, but one, er ... he's pled the sword, sir.'

'Leaves and branches,' swore Brock.

Criminals sentenced to death technically had a choice. Death by beheading, or death by combat, which came with the tantalising prospect of a pardon, if you won the fight.

But no one ever won the fight.

'Did they say anything?' Rhaell asked. 'In their defence?'

The page scowled. 'What they all say, sir.' He spat on the ground.

Rhaell didn't ask for the exact words. He'd heard every variation. He'd heard every argument, for and against. And he knew there was no point trying to change the law whilst King Onas sat on the throne.

'When's the execution?' Rhaell asked.

'Tomorrow,' said the page.

'Terrific.' What a wonderful introduction to Yskara for the Promised One. He rolled his shoulders, and asked the page, 'Have you ever seen a trial by combat?'

'Er, only once, sir, I haven't been here long.'

'Enjoy it?'

The boy went even paler.

Rhaell said to Brock, 'Order extra sawdust for the royal box. And have the hinges on the sky door oiled. The hafmey will feast tomorrow.'

Deciding she needed to find her way around before she could escape, Ember asked for a tour of the castle, but the ladies just stared and then giggled as if what she'd said was hilarious.

'Do you have a spare week?' said one of them, and they all laughed.

'More like a spare month,' said another.

'A spare year!' They all howled.

Ember smiled politely. 'You're saying the castle's big?'

'Come and see,' said one, rising elegantly to her feet and leading Ember over to the wall of windows. She opened one, and the others all shivered theatrically. 'Here, look.'

There was a veranda outside, large enough to hold a party on. The wind buffeted them both as they crossed to the marble balustrade, the air as crisp and clean as a knife.

Spread out far below them – below a high, rocky cliff she now knew to be infested with hafmey – was the Sacred Sea, glittering bright and blue like a child's painting. Ember could just make out the far banks, pale cliffs rising to woodland and hills. The faint smudges in the distance might even have been mountains.

But that wasn't what Eletha – the brunette with the diadem

and a jewelled necklace depicting a flying dragon – wanted to show her. She gestured back at the castle. 'Do you see?'

Ember turned. And she stared.

In the daylight she could see what the night had hidden. And now she knew she'd have never attempted the climb if she'd known.

Ember tried to count the rows of windows – the double- and sometimes triple-height windows – and gave up. Both below and above they soared, a cliff face of hewn, polished white stone and glittering glass curving off out of sight. The veranda sat on the edge of a huge, circular building, which itself was dwarfed by the even huger wing stretching off to her right.

There was no possibility of counting the windows in that direction. She couldn't even see them at the far end. And it didn't even end there. It was twinned with another huge white edifice, both of them crowned with spikes of turrets, joined by a high, narrow bridge above a gorge. A tower rose in the middle of the bridge, itself already queasily high above the gorge.

Ember quite literally couldn't take it all in. The far end of it was impossible to make out.

'But—' she began.

'It's actually even larger than you can see,' said Eletha. 'I tried to walk from one end to the other of the castle when I first came here. Gave up after six hours. I didn't even get to the bridge.'

'The bridge is six hours' walk from here?' That was surely a couple of miles.

'No, from about halfway down the East Wing. That's this bit,' she gestured to the wing closest to them. 'The other side of the bridge is the West Wing, and we're in the Keep. From here to the far side of the West Wing?' She shrugged. 'I don't even know how long that would take. There are races to the tower in the middle, sometimes. I think the winner does it in about half an hour. But you can't go the whole way across, of course, and some horses just refuse the bridge altogether.'

It was hundreds of feet above a narrow, rocky gorge. Ember couldn't blame the horses in the slightest.

'So,' she said, 'how the hell do you get around?'

Eletha's pretty face lit up. 'I'll show you.'

She hustled Ember back inside, where the others were clustered around the window. Nobody noticed Ember slipping a folded cake wrapper into the door as it was closed.

'We're going to show Her Highness around,' Eletha announced.

The ladies led her out of the solar, and into the wide corridor. Ember took in the plush carpets, the huge artworks on the walls, the decorated pillars and carved wall panels and vaulted ceilings – and the two guards in their smart uniforms with their large pikes who flanked their group as they set off back towards Ember's rooms.

But before they got there, they reached an alcove in the wall that contained a bellpull. After some jostling, as if ringing the bell was a privilege, Thalissa stepped forward and pulled it smoothly.

There was no sound, but after a slightly awkward short wait, a panel in the opposite wall opened, and a young man stepped out. He wore silver and green, but unlike the guards' longer tunics, he wore a short doublet and what Ember could only describe as tights, shielded at the crotch with a nattily contrasting codpiece. His boots had buckles and high heels, and his shining chestnut hair fell halfway down his back.

He bowed. 'Where would you like to go?'

The ladies giggled again. Lyndis said, 'We're showing Her Highness around.'

'I'm not a Highness,' Ember said, but they ignored her.

'Where should we go first?'

'The Great Chamber!'

'The orchard!'

'The library!'

'The training yard!' That was Eletha, and her cheeks went a bit pink.

The young man bowed again. 'Might I suggest the gardens?' he said. 'The light there is pleasant this time of day.'

'Yes,' said Ember, partly to see if there was an escape route visible in daylight, but mostly to shut the others up.

The young man turned back to the panel he'd emerged from, laid the fingers of his left hand on it and made a sign with his right. The same sign the ladies had made at the mention of Princess Nephinae. Then he lifted the panel upwards, and a delicious scent – like baking pastries – wafted from it. Over his shoulder, Ember could see shelves of the most delicious-looking cakes. She made to move that way, but Thalissa's arm stopped her, and the door was abruptly shut.

Puzzled, Ember watched him close then open the door again, this time hinged to the right, and now she saw a flawless white beach, lapped by an azure shore. The scent of hot sand and sea salt drifted across the corridor.

'Impossible,' she said, even as Eletha sighed.

The beach vanished, and then the door was pulled down, and on the other side of it was a garden, filled with bright flowers and lush greenery, intoxicating scents filling the corridor.

'The gardens,' said the young man, standing back and gesturing them forward. One of the guards went first, and then Lyndis, and as she stood in the garden and beckoned to Ember, she supposed she'd better go next.

She left the corridor, walked across the pulled-down panel of wood, and stepped onto a gravel path, flanked by beds of flowers that grew taller than she was beneath the bright blue sky.

Ember breathed in the fresh, floral-fragranced air, heard the buzz of an insect nearby, and *marvelled*.

She turned back just in time to see the young man pull up the panel and vanish behind it, and as she looked, it became part of a hedge. Which was impossible, because it had been panelled wood, she'd seen it, she'd walked over it—

'Pretty good, right?' said the girl she thought might be Caeda, as Ember groped at the hedge. 'You just ring the bell to summon a porter, and tell them where you want to go. They can send you anywhere in the castle.'

'Well, almost anywhere,' said Eletha.

'Oh, and the most important part,' said Thalissa. 'Never, ever go through on the first or second opening.'

They all nodded. 'No matter how tempting it might look,' said Caeda.

'But – it was just a bakery,' said Ember, and they all shook their heads.

'It's not real,' said the one who might have been Zentha.

'Or if it is, you really don't want to go there,' said Eletha.

Ember wanted to ask how any of it was possible, because how could one panel open into a garden, a bakery, and a beach? But the girls seemed entirely unconcerned, their attention already elsewhere. 'Look, Your Highness, the flowering inkberry is in bloom!'

Rhaell said their magic was fading. But all of this was miraculous to Ember. Last night, she hadn't noticed the complex hedge mazes, the avenues of trees, the complex topiaries. There were plants and flowers she'd never seen before, not even in books about exotic lands.

Ember was so taken with them she almost forgot to scope out the hiding places and exits.

'What's this?' she asked, finding a fountain carved of pure white marble – slick and slippery, but the shape gave plenty of handholds to climb – in the shape of a shrouded young woman with her arms raised. At her feet were five more young women, all shrouded and languishing.

'It's the Heirs Memorial,' said Zentha. 'Here, in the centre, is Princess Nephinae, the king's daughter. And around her are the king's lesser wives. May the Tree shelter them.' She made the sign with her hand again.

'Lesser?'

'Yes. They gave him no children. The Sacred Water weeps over them,' Zentha said.

Ember scanned Zentha's face. 'Not having children makes them lesser?'

'Oh – well, no, of course, most women these days – and it is a blessing and a gift from the Ancestors to bear a child, of course, I pray to the Tree that I shall one day be so blessed, but...' Zentha didn't seem to know how to finish that sentence. She rallied, 'Queen Amatheis's memorial is in the Great Chamber. She was Princess Nephinae's mother, may the Tree shelter her.'

Bearing a child got you a special memorial. Not doing so made you lesser. That couldn't be fucking clearer.

Ember sighed, and looked at the shrouded, faceless women. 'Five of them?'

'Yes.' Zentha's eyes were suitably downcast. 'None survived.'

'Survived what?'

Zentha hesitated.

'Childbirth?'

'Well, yes.' Zentha reached for Ember's hands, and said earnestly, 'It's why you're so important. You must save the Tree, because without it nobody is having children. The king is tied most closely to it, and he only has one heir, who is hideously misshapen. The royal line cannot thrive if the Tree does not thrive, do you see?'

'Not really,' said Ember.

'The king must have an heir,' Zentha said, as if it was simple.

The king must have an heir. His daughter had died, his grandson was a monster, and his other wives had... What? Died in childbirth? Ember peered closer at them all with mounting dread. Two held tiny bundles in their shrouded arms. Three looked as if they had simply died, artistically and tragically.

What had happened to the king's wives?

'Your Highness, would you like to see the Great Chamber?' said Zentha. 'It is where you arrived in Yskara, after all.'

Yeah, with a fucking knife in my chest. 'Sure,' said Ember.

All around the garden were little arbours and benches, and some of them contained bellpulls. Another porter was summoned, and the six of them watched him pull a section of hedge to the left, to reveal a sunlit chamber; then to the right, to show a room lined with hourglasses, and then back to the left again, to a huge room, larger than any she'd been in so far.

Ember watched his movements very carefully.

The Great Chamber was well-named, seeming approximately the size of the Clockwork City itself. It contained dozens, maybe hundreds, of well-dressed people, all milling around and talking in groups. Every one of them was tall and slender as a reed, long-haired and elegant, as perfectly composed as a lovely picture. A slight hush fell over all of them as Ember and her party entered.

Fucking Promised One. Ember resisted the urge to melt into the shadows and ignored them.

The far walls were a mere blur, and the ceiling so far above that she half expected to see clouds there. Instead, there was a great dome of tiny pieces of coloured glass, which even from this distance she could see depicted a beautiful woman with flowing hair, conjuring forth a shining building of immaculate white.

'That's Ysarriel,' said Caeda, craning her neck back to look up with Ember. 'The founder of Yskara. They say she raised the Keep in a single day, and then a year after that, both the East and West Wings on the same day, with the help of her husband Ruvaen. There's a tapestry of them over here.' Ember obediently followed.

'Look, here's Ruvaen with Ysarriel. That's before the betrayal, of course.'

Ember let their boring history lesson wash over her. There had to be a way out of this castle without being caught. The damn place was basically a city in its own right – how many staff went in and out all the time? Did they all live here? What about supplies – there had to be piles and piles of food being delivered every day.

The ladies took Ember all over the castle, and at one point she realised they were on the other side of the bridge in the West Wing.

Each time they went through a portal, Ember paid close attention to the gestures of the porter. Was there a reason these specific people opened the portals, and the ladies couldn't do it themselves? Or was it one of those things nobby people didn't do, like drive their own carriages?

They took her to a long gallery filled with statues and paintings, and led her to one of a handsome youth in heroic pose. 'That's Jaonos Yllanala,' said Zentha. 'The king so loved him that when he died, he had this statue erected to his memory, and we observe the anniversary of his passing every year.'

Ember gazed up at the serene face of a boy who'd never become a man. 'The king loved him, huh?'

'Indeed,' came a cool voice from behind her. 'His Grace says that Jaonos is the man who taught him that sacrifice is necessary to do one's duty.'

She turned and found the speaker to be a richly dressed and extremely beautiful woman on the arm of an equally resplendent man.

Ember had noticed that nobody in this castle had hair that was merely blondish or brownish – they had shining locks the shade of ripe wheat, or burnished copper, or raven's wings. Their eyes were emeralds or sapphires or deep mahogany. Nobody here was ordinary. But this woman put them all to shame.

The hair rippling down her back was the red of freshly spilled blood, and her skin gleamed like the white marble of the castle itself. She wore an amethyst gown that matched her extraordinary eyes, which tilted like those of a cat, and around her neck was an elaborate necklace fashioned into the shape of a dragon, studded with diamonds.

But even with all this, it was the tiny dragon on her shoulder that had Ember staring.

It was about the size of a ferret and feathered down the length of its sinewy body. Its little head was scaled and horned, and its mad little orange eyes blinked sideways. Its scales were a ruby red, and its feathers raged through all the colours of a living flame. The end of its tail ended with a barb that flicked back and forth.

It cocked its head and regarded Ember beadily.

A dragon. I'm looking at a dragon. Lords, that's a dragon!

The ladies all dropped into smooth curtseys. Eletha smiled – with some apprehension, Ember noted distractedly – as she said, 'Uncle Addor, Aunt, how lovely to see you.'

'Perhaps you could introduce us, niece,' said the man, looking somewhat unimpressed by her greeting.

Eletha puffed herself up a little bit. 'Lord Addor, Lady Sarea, may I present'—the girl was practically rocking forward on her feet —'the Promised One, Ember Hearth.'

'Hart,' corrected Ember, and Eletha went bright red. 'Ember Hart. Nice to meet you.'

She held out her hand to shake, and both of them stared at it, as if she'd just handed them a fresh turd. The dragon skittered about on Lady Sarea's shoulder.

'We don't shake hands here? Okay,' said Ember, resisting the urge to wipe her hand on her skirts.

'Ember Hart,' purred Lady Sarea. 'What an interesting name.'

'It's the one I've always had,' Ember said.

'Indeed. Well, here you shall surely be known as Lady Ember – or will it be Princess Ember, already? Just so you get used to it.'

Those amethyst eyes were cold. Ember realised this woman hated her – had never met her before but already despised her.

Well, two can play at that game, sweetheart.

'I suppose I had better get used to it,' she said cheerfully. 'As a sort of stepping stone, before I become queen. That's what the king told me, anyway.' She met the amethyst gaze. 'I'll be queen one day. Apparently it's written somewhere.'

'In the sacred text,' murmured Lady Sarea. Her hand idly stroked the dragon curled around her shoulder.

'Sacred text now, is it? Is that printed on paper from the Sacred

Tree?' Ember said, and immediately realised she'd said the wrong thing.

Everyone around her — not just in the immediate vicinity, but everyone else browsing the gallery — froze in horror. Lord Addor's cheeks puffed up. Zentha covered her mouth. Caeda looked like she might cry.

Lady Sarea barely moved a muscle, but her expression turned somehow calculating, and the dragon on her shoulder gave Ember a look that said it could probably turn her to cinders if it wanted.

'We don't print on the Sacred Tree?' Ember said, her voice coming out a little high. 'Good to know, good to know. I'm new here. Don't know how things work. No offence meant. Very sorry to cause upset. Ladies, maybe we could move on?' she said desperately. 'Nice to meet you.'

'And to have met you. We leave overmorrow,' said Lady Sarea.

'Oh no,' Ember said with as much sincerity as she could manage, which wasn't much.

'But it shall not be for long. It is our honour to host the king's progress,' Lord Addor said.

'The king's what now?'

Lady Sarea's smile slid just a fraction towards condescension. 'The king's progress. His tour of allies and vassals. He, of course, wishes you to meet as many of your future subjects as possible.'

Show off his new pet more like, Ember thought darkly. 'Well, that sounds lovely. I look forward to it. Must dash.'

'A message, before you do?' said Lord Addor, regarding her haughtily. 'From His Grace?'

Ember ran cold. Had he heard about her escape attempt? 'Yes?'

Lord Addor drew himself up. 'The king is pleased that you are getting to know the castle but realises you must be tired from your exertions and bids you rest this evening with a quiet supper in your rooms.'

That's me fucking told, Ember thought.

'Tomorrow,' he went on, eyes glinting, 'an important event is to take place, and all are required to attend.'

Ember's stomach hollowed. *He's moved the wedding up.* 'What event?' she managed.

'The execution of a prisoner,' said Lord Addor, and Ember shouldn't have felt relieved, but she damn well did.

'He is a murderer,' said Lady Sarea, her eyes still on Ember.

'Well, I'm sure he's getting what he deserves,' she lied.

'He deserves to have his skin stripped from his bones in tiny pieces,' snapped Lady Sarea. 'But the king is merciful.'

'Is he, now? What,' Ember asked, already dreading the answer, 'is the punishment?'

'He will face a trial by combat,' said Lord Addor.

'Combat? So, if he wins, what then?'

Lady Sarea laughed, the sound like the chiming of bells that got right on Ember's nerves. 'Oh, Your Highness,' she said. 'He will not win.'

'How do you know?'

'Because he faces your future husband,' the lady purred. 'And Prince Bronadyr was born for slaughter.'

CHAPTER 6

The next day came fine and cold, and Phoebe dressed Ember in a high-necked gown that did her few favours. Her maid had, however, been industriously working on a support garment that was somewhat more comfortable than the girdle Ember had worn the day before. It wasn't quite the same as the short stays she used to wear, but it was a start.

Last night, Ember had intended to go exploring around the castle as soon as Phoebe left. But Phoebe hadn't left, simply retired to a small chamber hidden behind Ember's vast bedroom. Ember had tried to stay awake to sneak out later, but all the exploring and planning she'd done meant she was dead to the world as soon as her head hit the pillow. She'd dreamed of a tree, vast and forbidding, its branches like skeletal hands trying to catch her.

Phoebe had taken one look at her sweat-soaked sheets and ordered her into the bathing chamber. When she emerged, a huge and ridiculous outfit was waiting for her.

Ember had already been dressed in layers of petticoats and silks, and now it was the turn of the headdress, heavy and awkward, with an array of silver spikes wreathing her like a halo.

'It's going to fall off,' Ember said, trying to stay still whilst also cramming her face with delicious pastries. Say one thing about this place, the food was incredible.

'It's not going to fall off. I will add more pins.'

'I don't have enough hair for more pins.'

'No, there's a bit here that's still free.' A sharp jab to her scalp. 'Sorry.'

'I'm more pins than hair already.'

'Perhaps if I added a hairpiece...'

'So you can pin some fake hair to my real hair in order to add more pins?'

'That's the basic idea, yes.'

Ember regarded herself in the mirror. She looked ridiculous and she felt even stupider.

'This is absurd,' she said.

'You are the Promised One. You have to look...'

'Insane?'

'Regal,' said Phoebe, but her mouth twitched. 'This is the first time the Court will see you.'

'You mean, apart from the people I saw yesterday?'

'Oh, that won't have been the Court. I mean the king's inner circle, and all the important lords and ambassadors. There is Lord Keenor of Valoris, our ally against the Myr. His daughter Lyndis is also one of your ladies...'

Ember let the names wash over her. There was no way she'd ever remember them all. And then one caught her attention.

'Lord Addor – the uncle of Eletha, whom I'm told you met yesterday,' Phoebe said, in an entirely neutral tone of voice. 'Addor is our neighbour to the north and west, across the Sacred Sea. His wife, Lady Sarea, is a cousin to the king.'

Well, that explained something about her attitude, at least.

'I met them yesterday,' Ember said, in the same neutral tone.

'Indeed? What a treat,' said Phoebe briskly. 'They are our allies against the Rakaa, although of course that threat has faded somewhat in recent years. Indeed, it was seen by some as an insult that they did not send a more prestigious hostage.'

Ember jolted, the headdress nearly coming unmoored. 'Hostage? Lyndis is a hostage?' That would explain her attitude.

'Yes.' Phoebe seemed entirely unbothered by this. 'All of your ladies are.' She paused at Ember's obvious discomfort. 'This does not happen where you come from?'

'Er, no!'

'Really? It's very common here. Most of the king's younger cousins are hostages in other states. He himself was fostered as a child, out in Vaesturness. He often speaks fondly of his time there. He made friends he still has today. The court still marks the death of one of them, Jaonos Yllanala, commended to the Tree on the anniversary each year. It was last week, actually.'

Ember blinked. 'When you say "hostage"...?'

'Perhaps foster is a better word. Usually it's children, but sometimes older relatives.' Phoebe's fingers pulled a strand of hair a little too tight, and Ember winced. 'Sorry. They are honoured guests of esteemed allies, growing and forging lifelong bonds with the children of other nobles. Whose parents will, incidentally, be much more reluctant to invade or declare war, when their precious child is in residence.'

'Ah. I see now,' Ember said, and chewed her thumbnail. 'We don't have this where I come from. Most people have more children than they know what to do with. I reckon they'd be glad to give some of them away.'

'More children than—?' Phoebe shook her head in disbelief. 'Truly, your people are blessed.'

'Yeah? You wouldn't say that if you had to figure out how to feed four mouths on the income of one crippled clockmaker.' She wondered if Pa and the boys had figured out how to feed themselves yet. The boys would probably have spent all their weekly wages on hot pies and beer and Pa would have forgotten to eat entirely.

Phoebe went to a stand where a long, heavy cloak rested. It was green velvet, heavily trimmed with silver embroidery. The fastening across the chest sparkled with what looked like real gems. It was clear from the way Phoebe lifted it that it weighed a ton.

'Am I going to be able to walk in that?' Ember was already wearing her own body weight in clothes.

'You are the Promised One,' Phoebe told her, as if that was enough.

The cloak was indeed heavy, but well-constructed and easier to move in than Ember had expected. 'Just take things slowly, let the ladies help arrange it when you sit and stand, and you'll be fine,' Phoebe said, moving her to stand in front of a huge mirror.

The woman reflected back at her was almost unrecognisable. Phoebe had applied cosmetics that ranged from subtle smoky eyeliner to a line of bright silver running the length of her nose, branching out across her forehead and her tightly slicked-back hair to meet the massive headdress. Which, now that she could see it as a part of the whole, resembled a tree.

'I'm ... the Sacred Tree?' she said doubtfully.

'You are here to save the Sacred Tree,' Phoebe said gently, brushing invisible specks from the velvet cloak.

'But I don't even know what it is.'

'It's a tree. It's sacred. Now, this outfit was intended for tomorrow, but more people will see you today, and of course you won't need the cloak tomorrow.'

'What's tomorrow?' asked Ember, with some dread, as Phoebe helped her into her mercifully flat shoes.

'A double moon eclipse. You will be formally presented to the Court.' Phoebe hesitated, then added, 'And formally betrothed to Prince Bronadyr.'

King Onas, third of his name, King of the Sacred Realm and Yskar Sea, Protector of the Tree and Beloved of the Ancestors, looked upon his heir and didn't even bother to conceal his disgust.

The boy was useful, he supposed. Stories of his monstrous bulk and hideous deformities had spread far and wide, largely because Onas had spread them. Now Yskara's enemies knew that should any of them challenge the sacred realm, they would have the monstrous Prince Bronadyr to answer to.

It was good, having his own pet Rakaa. Even if Bronadyr was half the size of the barbarian creatures, he was still twice the size of any good Tree-fearing Yskaran.

'Full armour,' he instructed, as the Beast gazed down over the balcony at the courtyard being turned into an arena. 'Keep your helmet on. Don't want to scare her off.' He picked at some fruit, and gestured at the wine cup in front of him.

It failed to refill. Time was, the wine would have just leapt out of the bottle into the king's cup, and warmed itself along the way.

'You think the helmet isn't scary?' Bronadyr rasped. 'Perhaps it needs a redesign.'

'Not as scary as your hideous mug, boy,' said Onas.

Bronadyr just grunted.

He wasn't stupid; Onas knew that. He'd arranged for proper tutors for the creature, when it became apparent no other heir was going to be forthcoming. Bronadyr knew how to run the kingdom, and quite probably would make a decent job of it, if only because everyone else was terrified of him.

Onas studied his grandson and heir. Taller than any other man at court, and two or three times the width at the shoulders. Bronadyr had the build of an ox, massive in the chest, his arms like branches of the Tree itself. Vulgar, to say the least. And that was before you got to what topped it, a face whose features more properly belonged on a gargoyle. And those horns—

'The official presentation is tomorrow,' he went on. 'Double eclipse and all that.'

'Auspicious,' muttered the Beast.

'Aye! A good omen for your future offspring.'

Bronadyr snorted. 'And how am I to get these offspring?' he said. 'When any woman of breeding runs screaming from the sight of me?'

'Aha!' cried Onas triumphantly. 'She is not a woman of breeding. One can tell,' he added, as his grandson looked at him in surprise. 'Broad-backed, dull-coloured, and those vulgar tits. I haven't seen tits like that since I used to go whoring.'

Bronadyr didn't respond to that. He raised his voice and bellowed, 'Leave a gap for the corpse cart!' to the men constructing the scaffold.

'They still have tits like that?' Onas pushed.

'Who?'

'The whores. Don't play coy with me, boy, we all know where you spend most of your time.'

'Tree forbid I should violate any of the ladies of court,' Bronadyr replied.

'Violate whoever the fuck you want, so long as you get them with child,' said Onas. Up until now, he hadn't really cared if Bronadyr knocked up another man's wife, or even a whore. The baby was the most important thing. Its mother was little more than a vessel.

He had to continue the line. The heir had to be his direct descendant. Or that bitch Sarea would take the kingdom.

But now he had the Promised One. The prophecy had foretold she would bear his heir. It was inevitable.

Bronadyr sneered at him. 'Don't you recall, Your Grace? It is surely my repulsiveness that soured their wombs. Isn't that what Lady Alais said?'

Onas snorted. He remembered Lady Alais, all right. She'd had dreams of grandeur, of marrying the prince, no matter his hideousness. But one glimpse of the deformity he hid inside his breeches had her screaming and hiding behind the furniture. The story didn't take long to spread throughout the castle: the prince's cock was an abomination, capable of ripping apart any decent woman.

Alais had been married off to some other lord, but their union had never borne fruit. She claimed it was Bronadyr's fault, that the sight of his unclothed body had soured her womb, and who was to say she was wrong? The Beast had pursued other women of the court, and the birthrate had continued to drop.

Onas had even made discreet enquiries among the taverns and brothels as to whether the prince had sown his seed among any of their girls, but even with the prospect of a juicy reward, none would lay claim to it. It seemed that even whores didn't want to admit to bedding such a monster.

'But now the Tree has blessed us,' Onas said. 'The Promised One has childbearing hips, and she tells me she is not a maid.'

Bronadyr sliced him a look from beneath heavy brows. By the Tree, he was ugly.

'And will she let me fuck her?' he said. 'Once she catches sight of me?'

Onas signalled for more wine. 'I don't care if you have to blindfold her and shackle her to the bed,' he said. 'You'll swell her belly, boy. That's your duty. Besides, the prophecy promised that the seeds she plants will bear fruit and Yskara will thrive.' He spread his hands. 'Your seed will take.'

And if it failed, Onas would see to it that someone else's did.

The roar of the crowd hit Ember before she stepped out into the courtyard.

She concentrated on holding her skirts so she didn't trip; keeping her head up so the headdress didn't tilt and fall off and take most of her hair with it. She kept her eyes down as the steward ushered her to a canopied seat right at the front of the stand. Most of the other seats were full, Ember's skirts brushing silks and velvets and gorgeous embroidery. Everything was bedecked in green and silver bunting and ribbons and swathes of fabric, as if this was a festival, and not an execution.

The ladies had been vivid in their chatter at supper last night. Prince Bronadyr never lost a fight. He was faster and stronger than everyone else. It was like trying to fight a Great Dragon. A thunderstorm. A Great Dragon in a thunderstorm. Once, he'd cleaved a man entirely in two, top to bottom, with a single stroke. His sword was so heavy no one else could lift it. He was a demon in barely human form.

He was a beast. He was The Beast.

Ember didn't dare look up. She concentrated on breathing as she took her seat. She felt vaguely sick.

Public executions had not been legal in Coldonia for several decades, and even before that, they had been largely discreet affairs. Schoolteachers loved to tell stories of huge crowds gathering to watch a historical hanging, of bodies left to rot in gibbets.

Ember had lapped them up with the other children. Gore did not frighten her. She had witnessed her mother's childbed labours. She had laid out her corpse. But she had never heard of a prisoner being condemned to death by fighting. It was barbaric.

And the man who would – apparently, almost certainly – be the executioner, was to be her husband.

She became aware of a roaring. Was it in her ears? No, it was the crowd.

'Your Highness, listen,' whispered Thalissa, beside her.

The roar had a rhythm. Ember didn't want to hear it. She couldn't look.

'They're shouting for you,' said a voice on her other side. The chair there was larger than hers, and more carved and gilded. A throne. Of course, she should have realised who'd be taking it.

'Your Grace,' she said as he approached, wondering if she was supposed to stand up and curtsey.

'Wave at them, girl,' said the king, smiling at her through his teeth. 'Stand up.'

Her palms sweating, Ember made it to her feet and lifted a hand. The stands beyond were a blur, and only partially because they were so far away.

'Smile,' hissed the king. 'The people have come to see two things: the execution, and you. And we will give them what they want.'

Ember forced a smile. The courtyard was more like an arena, lined with stands that groaned under the weight of the people filling them. She couldn't even begin to imagine how many there were. Thousands. Many thousands.

They all screamed, 'Promised One! Promised One!'

Ember waved for what felt like hours, until the king finally stopped and sat down. Gratefully, she collapsed onto her own seat, barely aware of Thalissa fussing over her cape and skirts.

'Wine,' said the king, and a servant hurried up with a tray. Ember took the glass that was offered to her, but turned down a cake from the next tray.

'I'd advise you to eat,' said the king. 'These things can drag on.'

'But,' said Ember, 'I thought it was one fight? How long do they last?'

'Oh, not long, usually. Sometimes half an hour, but not usually. No, we have other executions first. I do hope you're not squeamish, Promised One.'

Ember wanted to protest again that she wasn't the damn Promised One, but what would the king do to her in front of everyone if she did? So she took a deep breath and said, 'I'm not afraid of blood, Your Grace.'

'No?'

Time to see if he was squeamish. 'Most women over the age of thirteen or so aren't.'

The king went still. So, it seemed, did her ladies, and all the staff. Then he let out a bark of laughter.

'That's good to know,' he said, which was a strange comment.

A fanfare sounded, and Ember let her attention move down into the arena for the first time. There were trumpeters with sort of flag things hanging off their instruments, and as they stepped back, a man with a scroll stepped forward.

But Ember wasn't looking at them. She was looking at the scaffold that had been set up with a block at its centre.

The king waved a hand, and the herald's voice carried to them clearly over a few hundred feet.

'In the name of His Most Gracious Majesty King Onas, third of his name! May the Tree protect and shelter him!'

'May the Tree protect and shelter him,' murmured the ladies, and everyone else in the arena.

'Presented to you this day are the following condemned! Amra Byllyng, for the crime of murder! The condemned did plead as follows...'

'Murderer!' shouted the king, spraying crumbs. 'Let her blood water the ground!'

The herald appeared to read out a summary of the woman's trial, but the sound was lost under the booing from the crowd as the prisoner herself was led by a couple of guards from a tunnel on one side of the arena, and up to the scaffold. Her hands were tied behind her back and she had a sack over her face. She was pushed down to her knees, her head forced down onto the block.

People screamed and threw things. The hatred and disgust was so thick Ember could almost taste it.

She wore only a ragged shift, stained with blood. Her arms and legs were swollen and split with wounds, and she stumbled on bare, dirty feet. The awful realisation dawned on Ember that this woman had been tortured.

'Who did she murder?' she asked Thalissa.

Thalissa's face was tight as she murmured, 'Her unborn child.'

Ember's head whipped around to the trembling figure kneeling at the block. Beheading for abortion? Dear Lords, she had to leave this barbaric place!

The jeers grew into a buzz and then a roar, as a figure emerged from a tunnel on the other side of the arena. The boos took on a different tone, as if the people feared this newcomer more than they hated him.

The figure was simply enormous.

He wore armour, massive over the shoulders and chest, the plates of it gleaming with intricate inlays that flashed in the sun. The breastplate was enamelled in green and silver with the Yskaran's beloved Tree. The shoulder plates were built up into spikes that resembled branches. Along the arms were scales patterned like leaves, which also covered the skirt of the armour. His heavy thighs were encased in mail, and his metal-plated boots thudded against the stone floor.

But it was the helmet that really drew the eye. It was huge, crowned with massive horns and sculpted with a mane of spiky leaves and branches. The nose and cheek pieces covered most of his face, the metal fashioned into more leaves and vines. The whole of it resembled a wild animal, a beast made from leaves and thorns.

His heavy footsteps thudded slowly up the steps of the wooden scaffold, echoing over the noise of the crowd. He carried a double-headed axe that was probably the same height as Ember. It glinted wickedly, light dancing over the razor-sharp edges of the twin blades, each the length of his forearm.

The prisoner on the block shook so violently that Ember could see it from this distance. She also saw the puddle of urine the condemned woman now knelt in.

Prince Bronadyr – because who else could it be? – murmured something to the prisoner that was too low to hear. Then he raised his axe, and in one quick moment, cleaved the woman's head from her body.

Blood sprayed, spurting and pumping from the neck, even as

the body slumped. It sprayed over the guards, who reared back in disgust, and the prince, who did not. The crowd roared.

'May the Tree have mercy upon her!' cried the herald, and promptly moved onto the next.

Ember watched the headless corpse being dragged to the edge of the scaffold and shoved off into a cart that rested to one side. The head was kicked along after it, like an unwanted football.

Ember's fingers clenched into fists.

Bronadyr stood like a statue, awaiting his next kill. Blood dripped off the silver and green of his breastplate.

By the time he had made seven more kills, the muzzle of that beastly helmet was dripping in blood, as if he'd killed each prisoner with his bare teeth.

Beside Ember, the king went on eating and drinking, occasionally laughing or cheering if one of the prisoners stumbled or tried to make a final speech. Ember grew cold as she sat back in her seat, almost unable to move as her future husband killed, and killed, and killed.

Finally, there was some sort of pause, and the herald was handed a new scroll.

'Presented to you this day one final spectacle!' cried the herald.

Spectacle. Ember's nails dug into her cold hands.

'One Piers Rykeworth, who did commit grievous crimes against the sanctity of life! In collaboration with one Amra Byllyng, he did conspire to destroy the precious blessings of the Tree...'

Ember leaned forward, straining to hear, but the crowd booed loud enough to drown out the herald's voice. Ember gave up on trying to listen as she watched Bronadyr walk slowly down the steps of the scaffold. At the bottom of it, a minion waited to take his axe and hand him a sword.

The sword was just as big as the axe, its blade gleaming even sharper in the sunlight. It was a huge weapon, double-handed and as wide at the base as his fist.

The prince swung it a few times, as if testing it, then he nodded and started across the arena towards the royal stand.

Her heart quickened. Was he approaching to speak to her?

But he stopped, about halfway between the scaffold and the stand, and bowed his head to the king.

'You're in for a treat,' said Onas, nodding in acknowledgement. 'It's much more exciting when they fight for it.'

'Fight for what, Your Grace?'

'To die, of course.'

'What if he wins?' asked Ember, not taking her eyes off the giant standing motionless in the middle of the arena. Behind him, the scaffold was quickly being dismantled, a process that had clearly been undertaken many times before, the pieces being stacked on top of the corpses. Horses were hitched to the cart, their tails flicking away the flies that already gathered, and the headless bodies were led away.

'They never win,' said the king.

'But theoretically—'

'They never win,' he repeated firmly, almost glancing at her as he spoke.

The herald neared the end of his speech. Ember knew this, because two guards marched out of the tunnel, flanking a man dressed in armour that even Ember could see was shoddy. A mail shirt, an ill-fitting breastplate, and a helmet that was too big for him.

The king settled down with a happy sigh, as if he was about to watch a production of his favourite play. He made a gesture at the herald, whose voice was suddenly magnified against the noise of the crowd.

'...fight in honourable combat against the king's Champion, Prince Bronadyr,' he shouted.

Bronadyr raised his sword. The crowed screamed his name.

'Should the condemned man win, he will be granted his freedom!'

The crowd actually laughed at that. The king muttered something that sounded like, 'Not for long.'

Ember gazed at the man, who looked lanky and hopelessly unfit, shoving his helmet back up out of his red-rimmed eyes. He carried a sword and a small round shield; he didn't look like he knew how to use either of them.

'Only one may leave this arena.' The herald glanced at the king, who nodded. 'You may begin!'

Bronadyr faced the king, and clanged his sword hand against his breastplate, the ring of metal echoing around the arena. The prisoner did the same, his sound tinny and thin.

'This isn't fair,' Ember murmured. Beside her, Thalissa rapidly shook her head in alarm. 'But it isn't.'

'Fair?' grunted the king. 'For the crimes he has committed there is no "fair".'

For a long moment, Ember entertained a fantasy of telling him exactly what she'd paid a woman to do to her in a back alley all those years ago. How the blood that had started at thirteen had been stopped a few years later and never come again. That no matter how hard Prince Bronadyr bedded her, he would never breed her.

And then she thought about the noise the prince's sword had made as he hacked off that woman's head, and kept her silence.

The prisoner threw himself sword-first at the Beast. His sword clattered uselessly off the great breastplate. Well, of course it did. It was like attacking a tank with a toothpick.

The Beast swiped the smaller man easily aside and swung an almost casual blow at him with that great, two-handed sword.

It really wasn't a fair fight. The Beast's sword was twice the length of his opponent's. The smaller man danced back, out of its reach, and Ember found herself leaning forward to see what he did next.

Rykeworth lunged and was parried. He went low and was parried. High, and was parried. His tiny sword went nowhere near the big man, who swiped the blows aside as if he was being attacked by a small, fluffy animal.

The prisoner feinted, and the Beast moved to parry, but Rykeworth threw himself into a roll and came up by the Beast's feet, jabbing up with his sword. The crowd sucked in a collective breath as the smaller sword darted up into the gap under the skirt of the Beast's armour—

But Rykeworth wasn't the only one with an impressive turn of speed. The Beast leapt backwards, somersaulting over to land on his feet.

Ember's mouth dropped open. That should not be possible! He'd gone from basically a standing start to three feet in the air, as if his feet had springs on them. Was he some sort of ... of frog?

Rykeworth rolled to his feet, trying to right the helmet that had shifted to one side, only to hurriedly duck again as the Beast lunged for him. The massive double-handed sword missed him, but the Beast used the momentum to swing it back, slamming the smaller man in the ribs.

The crowd made a sound of dismay as Rykeworth staggered back, shoving at his helmet. His chest visibly heaved. The Beast seemed barely exerted, standing with his great sword aimed low at the ground as if letting the prisoner recover.

Then, without warning, he attacked in a flurry of blows that Rykeworth could hardly manage to defend against. Several hit him on the arms and chest, another on his thigh, and he staggered, clearly tiring.

Ember realised he was being driven back, darting to the left and right to avoid the blows, whereas the Beast simply moved forward, one implacable step at a time. He paused, then with something like delicacy, used the tip of his sword to flip Rykeworth's ill-fitting helmet off his head.

The king laughed. The Beast could have slit his opponent's throat then, but he was playing with him. Playing!

Rykeworth panted, his face red, hair plastered to his head with sweat. He was a young man and might have been quite handsome if his features hadn't been twisted into desperation. His gaze darted around at the arena, at the people screaming for his blood.

He glanced at the cart that held the headless corpses. He shouted something, but the sound was lost.

The Beast reached out his hand, palm up, and made a 'come at me' gesture.

Hopelessly, Rykeworth did.

The Beast battered him some more, and then the flat of his sword hit Rykeworth's wrist. The blade clattered from it, and the prisoner leapt back, shaking out his wrist.

For a second, both of them stared at the fallen sword. Then Rykeworth lunged for it, but he was too slow. The Beast made a gesture, and the sword flew into his hand.

Flew there. Just as Ember's robe had flown to the bathroom wall yesterday.

Who *were* these people?

The crowd screamed as the Beast stood there with two swords in his hands. Rykeworth knelt, panting, clearly expecting his death. He shouted something again, the words lost but the hoarse desperation clear. The crowd booed him down.

And then the Beast did something completely unexpected. He threw his great sword down on the ground, in front of the prisoner, and waited, ready in a crouch with the smaller sword in his hand.

The crowd roared with laughter. The tiny sword looked absurd in his massive paws, like a bear with a butter knife. But he stood waiting, apparently not even out of breath, as Rykeworth reached for the huge sword and attempted to get to his feet with it.

'He must know he's being toyed with,' Ember murmured. Her hands twisted in her skirts.

But even if he did, he still went for it. He found the sword's momentum and swung it at the Beast, managing to catch him on one armoured shin.

Ember kept her cheer to herself.

The Beast simply changed feet and lunged, his longer reach making a mockery of the shorter sword. It jabbed into Rykeworth's shoulder, hard enough to make him howl.

The prisoner managed to raise his sword a few more times, parrying the Beast's blows, but it was clear the bigger man didn't mean anything by them. He was watching Rykeworth tire, the cheap mail shirt rising and falling erratically, the sword slipping in his sweaty hands.

And when the prisoner couldn't raise the great sword anymore, the Beast swung in a graceful arc and chopped into Rykeworth's wrist.

Rykeworth sobbed, as if he no longer had the energy to scream, and the huge sword clattered to the ground. The crowd bayed, howling and hooting for his blood.

Rykeworth fell to his knees, clutching at his wrist as it gushed blood.

Ember didn't want to watch the end of the fight, but she didn't really have much choice. Beside her, the king was leaning forward, shouting encouragement.

'Go on, boy! End it!'

The Beast did not pick up his great sword. He simply swung the smaller one at the prisoner, chopping into his neck.

Up on the scaffold, he had decapitated his victims with a single blow. Perhaps he needed his mighty axe for that, or perhaps he simply chose to prolong Rykeworth's death.

It took nearly a dozen blows to sever Rykeworth's head, the latter half of them performed on his toppled corpse. Even then, the Beast had to lean down, one foot on the dead man's back as he grasped his hair in one gauntleted hand and ripped the remaining tendons and skin away. The grisly sound it made echoed around the arena.

Ember choked down her vomit.

As the Beast straightened, his gory trophy held aloft, the crowd screamed and stamped. 'Bronadyr! Bronadyr!' they yelled, in exactly the same cadence they had shouted 'Promised One!' earlier.

Ember made herself concentrate on breathing, watching her future husband turn in a slow circle with the prisoner's head held high. Rykeworth's face was frozen in fear and shock, his eyes and mouth wide, flaps of skin and muscle trailing loose from his neck.

The king stood, his voice as magnified as the herald's had been. 'Your champion, Prince Bronadyr!' he cried, and the crowd somehow howled even louder. 'Justice has been done this day!'

The prince completed his circle, and threw the severed head in front of him. It bounced and rolled and came to a stop not far from the royal stand.

Blood dripped from his massive horned helmet. 'By its leaves and branches,' he bellowed, 'your will be done!'

'For the Tree!' shouted the king, leaping up, and the crowd took up the cry.

'For the Tree! For the Tree!'

Ember's ladies joined in, rising to their feet and pounding the air. Ember followed suit, disgust roiling in her gut, terrified that if she didn't she'd be the next one in the arena.

The Beast stood for a moment, arms upraised, and then he tossed the small sword aside, and simply walked away.

The king sat back down, as the herald moved forward and began announcing that refreshment stands were open. In the arena, the cart was being brought forward to remove Rykeworth's remains.

Lord Ruven and all his little thieves, if I ever told him the truth it'd be me on the block.

Ember looked at the howling, baying crowd. Hawkers were beginning to move among them, selling food and drinks, and there were booths opening up around the edges of the arena, people already queueing up at them. This was a day's entertainment for them.

'For the Tree!' cried the king one last time, taking to his seat and gesturing for more wine. He glanced sideways at Ember, who knew she probably looked like shit run over twice. 'You are pale. Drink up, my lady.'

'It's just,' Ember covered, 'I don't really understand. About the Tree. What does ... this,' she gestured at the arena without looking at it, 'do for the Tree?'

The king looked her over. The tree headdress was so heavy on Ember's head.

'We will show you,' he said.

CHAPTER 7

Ember had little affinity for boats. In the Clockwork City, the rivers were crossed by bridges, and the docks had their own network of thieves she'd never wanted to tangle with. But the barge waiting at the quay beneath the castle was large and luxurious, its prow fashioned into the inevitable tree, its deck scattered with cushions and low tables, covered by a silk canopy.

Ember fought to keep the contents of her stomach as the deck swayed beneath her feet, and she had just collapsed into a low seat when one of the ladies screamed and pointed, and everyone looked up.

What appeared to be a human body was flying rapidly towards them.

Behind it, Ember realised as she looked back, was the impossibly high bridge that linked the wings of the castle, and under that the river ended abruptly in what she realised was a waterfall, cascading down to the Sacred Sea.

'Ugh,' muttered the king, apparently unconcerned. He waved his hand, and the body was flung back, towards the waterfall. Ember saw as it hit the water that it appeared to be headless.

Her hand flew to her mouth, the vomit threatening again. 'Was that'—she managed, as the barge began to move away—'one of the—?'

The king was busy stuffing his face, so it was Zentha who answered. 'The executed prisoners are given to the hafmey,' she said. 'Sometimes one of them falls the wrong way.'

'Falls?' Ember said, looking up. Even as she peered at the high bridge, she knew the answer. From far above, more shapes tumbled, mostly falling on the other side of the waterfall where presumably, the hafmey caught them as they tumbled over the water. 'Do the hafmey come up to the river?' she asked apprehensively. The barge was quite low in the water.

Lyndis laughed. 'No. The waterfall is warded. They can't get into the Sacred River.'

The barge began to move forward, although Ember had no idea what the means of propulsion was. Back home in the Clockwork City, the smaller and cheaper boats were rowed or sailed, and the larger ones ran on sarel engines. But none of the boats she could see on this river had sails or paddles. Was it the same magic that had allowed the king to just push that body away?

The barge moved serenely down the river, other vessels moving out of its way. Ember saw people cheering and saluting from the banks as they passed. The roads that lined the gorge, low and high, appeared to be festooned with bunting and banners, all in silver and green, and flags that displayed the Yskaran's beloved tree. Some of the larger buildings had massive banners running down their sides, four and five storeys high, and as they passed under a high bridge there were flags hanging from it, too.

All the buildings she could see, even the ones at the docks, seemed tall and elegant, carved out of a rosy stone that blushed in the afternoon light. There were endless spires, high and narrow, tapering off into carved points that seemed almost translucent. Arched windows sparkled with coloured glass. Even where the steep sides of the gorge threw the streets into shadow, bright lights twinkled.

It was as pretty as a storybook.

Ember looked up at the soaring towers, the shining lights, the bridges arching hundreds of feet overhead, and her heart ached for the smoky, filthy, badly lit mess of the Clockwork City, with its streets full of horse dung and its teetering, unsanitary tenements. What she wouldn't give to see a mechanical carriage puffing along these shining streets, billowing out scalding, lung-choking sarel steam!

She glanced back over her shoulder at the impossibly high bridge linking the two wings of the castle. Tonight, she'd get out of her rooms and go looking for a way out. Even if she had to seduce a porter and half the guards. She was going home to Bleakburn.

The barge continued serenely down the river, eventually leaving the built-up areas of the city for lower cliffs, lined with smaller buildings. Ember still didn't see anything that looked like a slum, or even a suburb. Everything in Yskara seemed to be beautiful, and only beautiful.

It was kind of boring.

'Over there,' whispered Caeda, 'is where I saw a Myr!'

'In Yskara?' scored Lyndis. 'They wouldn't dare.'

'I know what I saw! It had that weird nose they have, all flat and slitted. Ugh. It was hiding under a cloak, but the breeze blew it back, and then I saw it had webbed fingers.'

'Caeda,' said Lyndis patronisingly, 'don't be absurd. If there were Myr in the city the guards would drive them out.'

'I know what I saw!'

'I'm from Valoris!' Lyndis said. 'My uncle has a dead Myr stuffed in his study. Believe me, if one of them was in the city, we'd all know about it.'

'Well, now you do,' said Caeda, and Ember tuned out of their squabbling.

Eventually the buildings were replaced with trees, growing

thicker and thicker. They approached a series of boats blocking the river, but the royal pennant on the barge had them moving aside. The king barely stirred in his drinking, only rousing when the barge moved towards a dock.

'Now you'll see,' he said, lumbering to his feet and nearly falling over the side. 'Damn boat,' he muttered, as guards steadied him.

Ember followed him onto the dock, where more guards waited, in their shiny silver and green livery. These ones held large pikes, crossbows slung across their backs and swords at their hips. This was no ceremonial force.

So many men surrounded them that Ember didn't see the queue at first, and then she wondered how she'd ever not noticed it. More people than she could entirely believe were lined up, a dozen thick, standing and sitting and in some cases lying on the sloping ground that led away from the river.

Some were in chairs, some on stretchers. Many leaned on crutches. There was a pregnant lady surrounded by what appeared to be well-wishers touching her belly. And there was a family clustered around a sickly-looking child.

And Ember suddenly realised what had been missing since she'd arrived in Yskara. At home in the Clockwork City, children ran everywhere, underfoot in the streets and the factories and the mines. Nobody took time off because they were pregnant or had just given birth, and the newspapers were full of scandalised stories about women having babies on factory floors and going straight back to work.

But here ... no pregnant ladies. No children. Not in the castle, in the arena, or out on the streets.

You must save the Tree, because without it nobody is having children.

These people were here for a miracle.

As they strolled up the hill, people cried out, 'For the Tree!'

'Tree save His Grace!' 'By its leaves and branches!' People bowed and curtseyed to Ember.

Over the tops of the other trees in the forest, Ember could see silver leaves. Not just silver-coloured, but real silver, gleaming in the afternoon light.

Her heart began to beat faster. Was the Sacred Tree made of silver? How much would that even be worth? Her thief's brain was already trying to calculate the value of single leaves and entire branches.

As they neared the Tree, the presence of the guards intensified until they were very nearly forming a human fence around the clearing at the top of the hill. At the sight of the king's guards, they smartly formed an opening, and the royal party sailed right through.

I'm with the royal party. This cannot be real.

And then the Sacred Tree was there in front of them, and it was...

Ember had been prepared for disappointment, for the Tree to be just a tree. But what stood in front of her was a perfect, idealised tree, gleaming as if not just its leaves but its trunk and branches were made of precious metals and gems.

The leaves were silver, yes, but also gold and copper, and there were some that gleamed translucently, as if they were made of diamond and emerald. The trunk could have been burnished bronze, but it was less metallic than that, somehow organic and living even as it shone in the sunlight—

Wait. There was no sunlight on the trunk; the branches of the tree blocked it out. The bark simply shone with its own light. It reflected off the faces of the supplicants kneeling before it, gibbering their desperate prayers.

Even the moss gathering on the trunk, the beads of sap, looked like precious jewels. Ember reckoned if she ran her hand over the trunk she could probably feed her family for a week.

She would come here, and steal some leaves, before she made

her escape. Given the ease with which the king had passed by the guards, she figured that an imperious attitude could probably get the Promised One in.

'Is it not magnificent?' said the king, and then, to Ember's astonishment, he bowed. She glanced hurriedly at her ladies, who all curtsied deeply, their eyes on the ground. Not wishing to be sent to the scaffold, Ember gave a curtsey that lasted long enough for the king to see her.

'Very magnificent,' Ember said, and meant it. The Tree was not just beautiful, it was unearthly, and it was huge. She'd never seen a tree that size before. It towered over the rest of the forest, which even her city-dweller's eye could see was clearly very mature. 'How old is it?'

'We do not know,' said the king.

'We cannot know,' said Lyndis.

You could cut it down and count the rings, Ember thought idly, and then hoped no one here counted mind reading among their accomplishments.

She had grown up in a city, but it did contain green parks. Ember knew what oaks and sycamores and firs looked like. She knew the ornamental copper beeches and cherry trees that the wealthy grew in their gardens, mostly because she'd climbed quite a few of them. But the Sacred Tree was nothing like any tree she'd ever seen. The twisting shape of its trunk was massive – easily larger than the house Ember had grown up in – and the heavy, thick branches seemed to defy gravity. The leaves were all different shapes, as if the Tree was somehow *all* trees.

The purple stone at her breast seemed to throb.

She gazed at the Tree for a while, and then became aware that people were watching her. The king, of course, sipping from a flask, and her ladies, but also the supplicants kneeling by the Tree. Some of them whispered among themselves, some pointed, and some stared, their mouths wide open.

Ember tried not to sigh too visibly, and moved forward so they were out of her eyeline. 'Can I approach it?' she asked. *Don't steal anything while they can see you.*

The king looked wary, but he said, 'You are the Promised One.'

'So you keep telling me,' she muttered.

The air beneath the spreading branches of the Tree was cool, cooler than it should have been in the shade. The ground itself seemed to be emanating cold, despite the day being relatively mild. But even with that, the Tree still drew her closer, as if it was some kind of giant magnet. Perhaps it was; although the closer she came to it, the less metallic it seemed. It was almost as if the Tree was made of real bark, but the bark itself shone like precious metal. Which didn't make any sense.

Ember's hands came up of their own volition. She had to touch the Tree. The compulsion grew stronger and stronger with each inexorable step she took, until it was no more possible to resist it than it would be to stop breathing. The purple stone pulsed in time with her heart.

And when her fingers finally touched the bark, it was not cold, but soft and warm. A living thing.

It shivered as she laid her palm against it, tensed, and then seemed to press gently back against her. Like a nervous horse, or a wary cat.

And then *something* flowed into her.

Ember could never say what it was. Power would probably be the closest word, but that didn't ever feel quite right. It was almost as if the Tree was welcoming her, recognising her. As if it knew her, and had been waiting for her, and was so glad to meet her.

'I'm glad to meet you, too,' Ember murmured, and laid her face against its soft bark. The Tree somehow nudged her back fondly. The purple stone beneath her dress warmed like a living thing.

She stayed for a moment, soaking up the Tree's warmth. Ember had never enjoyed many warm hugs from either of her parents; her father too absent-minded and her mother too frail with exhaustion and ill-health – but this felt like she'd always rather hoped a hug would.

Eventually she straightened, but even when she lost direct contact, she could still feel the warmth of the Tree, as if it had left its imprint on her. She turned back to the king and the rest of the party, and then she realised they had all gone very, very silent.

Everyone stared at her with wide eyes. The supplicants, the guards, the ladies and even the king.

Shit, shit, shit. She wasn't supposed to hug it? Why hadn't anyone said? How was she supposed to know?

Her eyes darted around, trying to find an escape route. Could she make it back to the river? 'I'm sorry—' she began, but the king spoke over her.

'Touch it again,' he said, his voice hoarse.

'Again?'

He nodded. All the ladies nodded.

Ember tentatively reached out, and the Tree damn well *nuzzled* her, like a favourite pet. She found herself smiling, and stroking her hand over its soft, spongy bark. The stone glowed beneath her clothes.

This time, she heard the reactions. Heard the gasps, the muttered prayers, the audible shock. When she glanced back, she saw plenty of people making that complicated motion with their hands.

'Look at yourself,' Thalissa whispered, and Ember looked down at her free hand.

She was *glowing*.

Hurriedly, she snatched her hand back from the Tree, and the glow faded. Tentatively replaced it, and the glow returned.

'By its leaves and branches,' breathed the king. 'She truly is the Promised One!'

∽

There was still a banquet laid out in the Great Chamber, but somewhere between the slaughter and the disposal of the bodies, Rhaell had somewhat lost his appetite. He lit a sootweed, but that didn't help.

Rhaell had been walking alongside Mnorir for as long as he could remember – death was not new to him. He'd forget Rykeworth's grisly visage by tomorrow. But the appalled, sickened expression on Ember Hart's face as she watched the slaughter: that made him realise how numb he'd become to it.

He took a portal to the servants' quarters and found Phoebe in the upper servants hall, labouring over a complicated undergarment he didn't want to ask too much about. A few other superior servants bustled around, all of them giving Rhaell a wide berth. *And I bathed and everything.*

'She's gone to see the Tree,' Phoebe said, without looking up from her stitching.

'With who?'

'The king and her ladies.'

'You didn't want to go?' Visits to the Tree were usually treated as a special occasion.

'I assumed she could be spared my attentions for the afternoon. And I needed to work on this.'

Rhaell squinted at the garment, which had some complex structure to it that involved stiffening and boning. 'Dare I ask?'

One of the other lady's maids gave a sniff. Rhaell thought she might work for Lady Sarea.

Phoebe made a face behind her back. 'Apparently the ladies of Coldonia wear significantly different undergarments from the ladies of Yskara. Or perhaps it's just the ones with a lot of … um…' Phoebe glanced down at her own modest chest, 'support needs.'

Rhaell closed his eyes and tried not to think about the soft mounds of Ember's breasts rising over the neckline of her gown. It was a better image than Rykeworth's corpse, he supposed.

'Well, er, good. Was she all right? After the...?' He waved his hand in a not particularly illustrative manner.

'You mean, after watching her intended fiancé slaughtering criminals?' Phoebe appeared to consider this. 'She could have been worse, I suppose.'

Rhaell sighed. 'Always a comfort, Phoebe.'

She shrugged, still not looking up from her stitching. 'It's not my job to comfort anyone.'

'Fair enough. Right. I'm going to get some food.'

'There's probably still banquet stuff going on.'

'For some reason,' said Rhaell, 'I wasn't hungry.'

'Gouts of blood don't do it for you?'

He pointed at her. 'Less of that. Or I shall faint from hunger and then it'll all be your fault.'

'I am always happy to contribute to your reputation,' Phoebe said, as he left.

He was just heading down to the barracks when the ball rang for the king's personal body servants. Two men stood, groaning, and headed to the porter who always stood ready outside the servants' hall. Phoebe heaved a sigh of annoyance and carefully gathered her sewing into her basket.

'I'll take it with me and work on it when she's asleep,' she said, and nodded to Rhaell.

'Here, I'll portal you,' Rhaell offered. 'I'm going that way.' He wasn't, but he wanted to see what Ember had made of the Tree.

The porter politely stepped aside for Rhaell, who made the sign of the Tree, opened the door once, twice, and thrice – and let the king's servants into his corridor. Then he worked the door again for Ember's chambers.

'You'll do the porter out of a job,' said Phoebe.

'I'm sure the castle's economy can survive me opening my own doors every now and then,' Rhaell said, opening the door up onto a quiet library. He closed it again.

'Ooh, that looked nice,' sighed Phoebe.

Rhaell glanced at her as he opened the door left. 'After some peace and quiet, are you?'

She shrugged. 'I could stay in my room in the Queen's Chambers, but then everyone calls me unsociable.'

'So be unsociable.' The next door opened onto a rowdy tavern. Rhaell sighed.

'That's fine for you, but some of us would rather not be outcasts. Is that where you're heading later?'

He closed the door on the tavern. 'Maybe.' Definitely. But not for the reasons Phoebe expected.

The third door opened upwards, onto the corridor outside Ember's rooms. He gestured Phoebe through and followed her, and she'd barely put down her sewing bag when Ember entered her chambers.

'...you don't want to join us for supper?' one of her twittering ladies was asking.

'No,' said Ember. 'An early night for me.'

The guard behind her nodded to Rhaell as he closed the door. There would be someone stationed outside her rooms at all times.

'My lady,' said Phoebe, bustling over. 'You must want to get out of that headdress. Can't go around looking like a tree all day.'

Ember shrugged and leaned against a chair back. She looked ... wan, Rhaell decided was the best word. As if something had exhausted her and shocked her at the same time.

Such as her fiancé hacking a man to pieces. 'Are you all right?' he asked, as Phoebe began untangling the stupid thing from her head.

Ember glanced at him as if surprised he was there. 'Oh. Yeah. Fine. Just ... tired.'

'How was the Tree?' he asked.

'Oh, it was, you know. A tree,' said Ember, and before Rhaell could even question that, she started laughing. 'A tree made of silver and gold and fucking diamonds, oh my Lords, are you kidding me?'

'It's very impressive,' agreed Phoebe.

'Impressive? The thing practically purred at me. I think it tried to hug me,' said Ember, and Rhaell felt himself straighten.

Phoebe's hands stilled. Her eyes met Rhaell's, wide and bright.

'Hug you?' Rhaell said. He tried not to look at the shape under her dress that Ruvaen's Stone made.

Ember clutched the back of the seat so hard he thought she might fall. He moved quickly to slip another chair behind her, and she collapsed onto it.

'Have you seen the Tree?' she asked, still seeming dazed.

'Yes.' Many times.

'Have you touched it?'

'Yes.'

'Did it...'

Rhaell shook his head. He'd felt the warmth of the Tree, of course; everyone did. But never any other reaction.

'Phoebe?'

She cleared her throat, hands still working on the absurd headdress. 'It felt warm to my touch, no more.'

'You didn't, like ... glow?'

Glow? They both shook their heads, Rhaell trying very hard to keep his face politely interested, and not completely delighted. The Tree recognised her, because Ephyrea's Stone recognised her! Or at least, it recognised the stone she wore.

The green stone in the king's crown had glowed just before she arrived in Yskara. It could not be a coincidence.

'Maybe it's the necklace,' Ember said, and moved to try to take it off. But the clasp didn't move.

'Maybe it's you,' said Rhaell, to distract her.

Her eyelids sank closed. 'Don't you start with all that bollocks again,' she said. 'It can't be me. I'm not...' She wiped her hand across her face. 'I'm tired. I don't understand any of this.'

'Of course.' Rhaell stepped back. 'Get some rest.'

'Tomorrow's a big day,' said Phoebe, and Rhaell glared at her.

'Why's it... Oh. Yeah.' Ember's brown eyes turned pleading. 'Have I really got to meet this prince? They say...'

'Don't pay attention to gossip,' said Phoebe. 'Now, Rhaell, I'm sure you had somewhere to be?' she said pointedly. 'A tavern or somewhere, wasn't it? Sorrows to drown?'

He narrowed his eyes at her. Yes, drowning sorrows did sound like a good idea, although he had another agenda in mind.

'A tavern sounds so good right now,' groaned Ember.

'Promised Ones don't go to taverns,' he said apologetically, and moved towards the door. 'Get some rest. Don't try to escape.'

'Wouldn't dream of it,' said Ember, and Rhaell made a note to double the guards outside her door.

CHAPTER 8

'News from the Great Chamber,' said Mama. 'Report!'

Rainbow stood up straight, hands behind her back, the way the guards did. She would quite like to be a guard one day. She was good at fighting with sticks, although Deer usually beat her anyway because he could fly.

'The court is gossiping,' she announced. 'About the new lady.'

Mama was sorting socks as if Rainbow's report wasn't very important, but she knew it was. 'Do we know the lady's name?'

Rainbow shook her head sorrowfully. 'They just kept calling her the lady. They say she's going to be queen one day.'

'What do you know about her?'

'That she came from somewhere far, far away. So far no one even knows where it is. But the king is very pleased because she has,' Rainbow frowned, 'child-bearing hips? What does that mean? Does it mean her hips are like bears? Baby bears?'

Mama's lips twitched like they did when she was trying not to smile. 'Not exactly, no. It means the king is hopeful of a new heir.'

'But doesn't he have one?' said Deer. 'They talk about him a lot. They say he's a deformed—'

'Deer. This is your sister's turn. Rainbow, continue.'

Rainbow stuck her tongue out at Deer and continued trying to remember what she'd overheard, whilst storing the word 'deformed' away to ask about later.

'Um... Oh! Lady Sarea doesn't like her.'

'Lady Sarea doesn't like anybody,' Deer said.

'But like, she really doesn't like her. She said, she's just like all the others, and it's stupid trying new girls when it's him that's the problem.'

'Who him?' said Mama.

'She didn't say who him, but everyone seemed to know. Then she said something about a blight.'

'A blight?'

'Yes. That it's him who's blighted, and he'll just keep spreading it until something is done. That he shouldn't even be trying to pro-cree-ate.' She carefully pronounced the word, having no idea what it meant.

'Ah,' said Mama. 'Anything else?'

Rainbow scrunched up her nose. She and Deer had spent half the afternoon behind the panels of the Great Chamber, but they'd had to keep moving whenever they heard someone coming.

'We sort of saw the lady,' said Rainbow, glancing at Deer doubtfully.

'Sort of?'

'Well, there were a lot of ladies together. And they all had very pretty dresses. And everyone was whispering and talking about them, like this.' Rainbow put her hand to her mouth and went 'pspsps' behind it.

'I see,' said Mama gravely.

'Lady Sarea said she'll be with Mnorir soon enough,' piped up Deer. 'Who's Mnorir?'

'Someone I hope you won't meet for a very long time. Now. Go and put these socks away, and we'll play a game of Grandmother's Footsteps.'

CHAPTER 9

The portals inside the castle couldn't take you absolutely anywhere – everything had its limits. Maybe in the old days, Rhaell might have been able to portal himself to Jalaros or Sehari, but the Tree's magic was so diminished now he could barely make it into the city.

The tavern at the sign of the Spreading Branches was a familiar route, however, and familiarity made portalling easier. He stepped into the sudden warmth and noise of the back corridor, closing the portal carefully behind him, and deliberately adjusted his posture into the slump of a tired man looking for a no-strings thrill.

'Oh, look who it is!'

The young lady greeting him wore a smile and not a lot else. Wine sloshed from the jugs that vaguely concealed her modesty.

'Genna,' he said. 'You're looking...' *naked naked don't say naked*, 'well.'

'Oh, you know how it is, Mister Knight! Can't hardly stop to get my chemmy back on. Be a lamb, will you, open the door for me?'

He obliged, and the sounds of the Spreading Branches' main room hit him like a wall. Music and bawdy singing and laughter, and the occasional whoop or yelp as a hand found its way under a skirt or inside a trouser.

And the smell of the place. Cheap wine, cheaper perfume, sootweed smoke. Bowls of stew and plates of snacks. And sex. The place reeked of sex.

Because while Rhaell told Phoebe he was going to the tavern, the inn at the sign of the Spreading Branches rented rooms by the half hour, and the tariff framed by the door listed an awful lot more than food and drink. Girls and boys lounged around in states of undress, fondling and being fondled by the punters. Rhaell held the door open for one young man leading a well-dressed fellow towards the corridor and its collection of private rooms.

The young man winked at him. The punter looked faintly terrified. Rhaell vaguely recognised him from court.

'What happens at the brothel stays at the brothel,' he said, as reassuringly as he could.

'Doesn't it just?'

Rhaell turned to the speaker, a generously endowed woman somewhat older than him. She had hair so red it was nearly purple, and very good skin.

'Merelle.' He leaned in, and she accepted his kiss on her lightly perfumed cheek. 'Always a pleasure.'

'Will you have some wine with me, Mr Knight?'

'With you, anything,' he agreed.

She led him to a table, and Genna poured them wine. It was not good wine, but that didn't matter. Rhaell wasn't here for wine.

'I hear it's all very exciting up at the palace, Mister Knight!' the younger woman said brightly, her breasts in his face as she leaned forward. 'Have you seen the Promised One?'

'Seen her, touched her, held her in my arms,' he said. Merelle lit two sootweeds and raised an eyebrow.

'Held her – oh, Mister Knight, you are a card!' Genna laughed and sashayed away.

'Yes, Mr Knight,' said Merelle, handing him one of the sootweeds, her eyes slightly narrowed. 'You *are* a card.'

He grinned at her around the cigarillo. 'Would I tell lies in an honest house?'

She snorted. 'Are you even a knight?'

He shrugged. 'I've got a very big sword.'

'Oh yes, we all know about your big sword.' She gestured to someone, and a languorous young lady wandered over. 'Private room for Mr Knight,' she said. Her eyes scanned his body. 'Drinks for three and go tell his special request he's here.'

'Three?' murmured Rhaell. 'Lucky me.'

'Oh, I've just the pair for you,' said Merelle. 'They're busy preparing for you right now.'

A plate was set down in front of him, bearing various snacks designed to be popped into the mouth by a lover. 'To keep your stamina up,' she added.

He smiled. Oh, she was good at this. Rhaell ate, and flirted with some of the girls, and smiled broadly at any punters he happened to recognise. It never did any harm to remind the courtiers he knew where they'd been, and it did no damage to his own reputation at all.

'I was sorry to hear Kissu was sick,' he said casually, after a while.

'Yes, a shame. She's much better now,' said Merelle, with equal nonchalance. She lit a new sootweed. 'Your contribution towards her care was gratefully received.'

'But anonymous?' Rhaell pressed. 'It wouldn't do for this sort of thing to get back to the castle.'

'Oh, of course. We are very discreet,' Merelle assured him.

He smiled and waved for more wine, relieved. Kissu's affliction was not an uncommon one among the ladies of the Spreading Branches, but if anyone at the castle heard that Rhaell was contributing towards its cure, his headless body would be joining those being fed to the hafmey.

Eventually, the languorous girl wandered back. 'Everything's ready for you, Mr Knight,' she rasped, dangling a key fob from painted fingers. Her eyes travelled his body as he stood. 'Be gentle with them.'

'Oh, I wouldn't dream of hurting anyone here,' he said. A beat, then he added, 'Unless that's been added to the tariff?'

'We cater for all tastes,' said Merelle, tapping the ash off her sootweed.

Just as Rhaell turned away, he heard the girl say, 'I've never met anyone with tastes like *him*.'

He grimaced as he pushed open the door. He was not a man for looking in mirrors, but he knew what people saw when they looked at him. Even Merelle's girls wouldn't lie to him about his looks.

The room he favoured was right at the end of the corridor, by the back door. This was not by accident. He tapped briefly on the door, and went in.

One of the women there was twice his age. The other had pale blue skin.

Rhaell beamed at them. 'Well, this makes my night much more exciting,' he said.

Ember knew how to be whisper-silent when she needed to be. She had crept unheard through countless drawing rooms and servants' halls and even bedrooms, her pockets full of pilfered jewels. Breaking into her maid's room presented no challenge at all.

She crept in, silent as the grave, and stood barely breathing until it became clear Phoebe wouldn't stir. Then, her eyes adjusting to the gloom, she quickly scooped up Phoebe's plain dark dress and cap, grabbed her boots and the shawl hanging from the back of the door, and let herself out to get dressed in her own room.

The boots were too big, so she added another pair of stockings, and regarded herself in the mirror. The dress was a sensible ankle-length on Phoebe, which meant Ember had to hitch it up into its own belt, and it was too tight in the bust, but the shawl covered that.

It also covered the purple sarelstone necklace she still wore. The thing creeped Ember out, but at least it had stopped glowing, and she figured she could fence it in order to finance her trip home. If she could get the damn thing off.

She nodded at her reflection, and then set out to retrace the route she'd planned. Over the balcony, climb to the solar, quietly let herself out without drawing the attention of the guards stationed outside her room, and head towards the nearest portal—

That part went as easy as the plan. At least, until she cracked open the solar door.

There were guards outside her room. Two on either side of the door, and two facing them across the corridor. Rhaell really didn't want her getting out.

Dammit, she should have climbed up or down a storey, but she didn't know what would be there...

Would they recognise her? Would they wonder who she was and demand proof of identification? Or would no one know who she was, without her make-up and her finery?

Ember thought for a moment, then unfastened the straining ties at her bodice. She pinched her cheeks, pulled some hair out from under her cap, bit her lips and let her shawl slip from her shoulders.

Then she exited the solar, eyes down, doing her best to blush as she headed for the portal. Coming the other way, their arms laden with heavy baskets of laundry, were two sturdy young women in white caps and aprons. Ember didn't have time to avoid them.

'Oh, Lor – lawks,' she gasped, stooping to help pick up the bits of linen she'd knocked from one basket.

'No harm done,' said the maid, setting the basket down and helping her. 'Hey, do I know you?'

'Um, no,' said Ember, flashing an embarrassed smile. 'I don't usually work up here, I'm, er...' She glanced back at the solar door and tugged at her overflowing bodice. 'Well, he likes the view of the sea, so...'

Both girls cackled. Ember tried to blush.

'Mine wanted to go up to the bridge the other week,' said the taller of the two maids. 'I said, no way. It's freezing up there!'

'Wow, that's quite a rock you've got there,' said the other, and Ember froze. She'd unfastened her bodice too far!

But she was good at lying her way out of tight spots.

'Yeah, you know how it is. They're selling them cheap in town, you know, like the one the Promised One has?'

'Already?' said the taller one.

'Oh, you know the artificers,' said the other. 'Their lesser magic can make a bit of glass look like whatever you want.'

'Yeah. He got me one, because he wanted to...' Ember pressed her hands to her face as if trying to cool her cheeks. 'The real reason he wanted to come up here wasn't the view. It's because it's where *she* is. You know. He wanted me to wear the necklace and...'

They gasped, suitably scandalised. 'Pretend he was fucking the Promised One?'

Ember nodded, gulping.

'Well, I hope that doesn't mean your fella looks like the Beast,' said the tall one.

'Oh, no, he's quite, um ... unbeastly,' said Ember, trying not to think of Rhaell.

'Especially in the trouser department.' They both shuddered, and Ember joined in. 'Can you even imagine?'

'He's a monster. He's not even human.'

'My cousin used to work for Lady Alais, and she said,' the taller maid leaned in closer, conspiratorially, 'that his – *you know* – is the size of a forearm.'

The shorter maid held out her own and they all looked at it

speculatively. Being that she thumped laundry around all day, it was quite a sturdy limb. Ember tried to rein in her horror.

'Imagine trying to fuck that?' said the taller one, and Ember did not have to hide her revulsion.

'I heard even the whores in town turn him down.'

'Doesn't surprise me. Imagine being faced with that!'

'By the Tree! I wouldn't want to be the Promised One!'

'Me neither,' said Ember firmly.

Thankfully, their speculation ended before Ember accidentally did something like scream, as a voice called out, 'All right, enough of this, what are you all gossiping about?'

It was one of the guards, and he was sauntering over.

'Nothing,' said the taller maid. 'Just making sure we have everything.'

'Well, be off with you. The Promised One had a long day and she doesn't need to be disturbed by the likes of you.'

They all bobbed hurried curtseys, and scurried – thank the Lords! – to the portal's bellpull.

'Are you headed to the servants' hall?' asked one of the laundry maids.

'Uh, no. Back to my mistress. You go first,' Ember said, and when the porter appeared, she smiled and waved them through into a steamy laundry, much like the one she'd worked in for all of five minutes in the Clockwork City. It seemed some things were universal.

She waited for the porter to come back. What was she going to say to him? Could he portal her out of the castle entirely? Her ladies had asked for specific locations, but now she thought of it, one had mentioned portalling to her dressmaker, so they clearly could go out of the castle, which was a relief. She'd ask for a tavern or something. That was probably the sort of request people forgot about.

'Miss?' said the guard.

Ember flashed him a smile. 'I'm just waiting for the portaller to come back,' she said, and winced at her own mistake. 'Porter. Sorry. Been a long day.'

He looked her over and frowned. Ember clutched her shawl around herself a bit tighter, but his gaze had already gone to her chest.

'What's that you have there?' he asked.

'What? Oh, nothing. A cheap gift. From my boyfriend. He's a blacksmith,' she improvised wildly. 'Arms like steel bars. Could punch out a rhino. This porter is taking his time, isn't he?'

'You didn't pull the bell,' said the guard. He was still wandering closer. Had Rhaell told the guards what she looked like? 'What's a rhino?'

In Bleakburn, Ember was wallpaper. Average height, average build, average hair and eye and skin colour. But here, she was short and round and her hair wasn't long enough and he'd recognise her, oh Lords—

'I'm going to need to see that necklace, miss—'

She had no time to grab the bell pull. She copied the gesture she'd memorised yesterday from watching the porters, laid her hand on the panel, and whispered, 'Take me where I need to be.'

To her astonishment, she felt a pulse of power, just like the one she had when she'd touched the Tree.

The power that had flowed into her...

'Miss?' The voice was coming closer, footsteps echoing on the stone floor. Her heart pounded, despite knowing that she could just tell him she was the Promised One and have him wake up Phoebe to prove it.

But then she'd have to go back, and she was so close...

The door opened with a soft click. Ember so nearly went straight through it, but the smell of baking bread had her abruptly remembering the ladies' advice. She shut the door, hurriedly pulled it open again, ignored the sweet voices singing to her, closed it—

'Miss, I'm going to have to—'

113

He was right behind her, but Ember didn't even look back to see how close. She threw herself through the door, and kicked it shut the second she'd cleared it.

The air where it had been simply became a wall, the lath and plaster crumbling. Ember lay on dusty boards that had been strewn haphazardly with dried stalks.

From somewhere very near came the sound of music, although she didn't recognise the instrument, and raucous singing. Ember knew a bawdy song when she heard one. And she knew bawdiness did *not* belong in Castle Yskar.

Exhilaration stole over her as she realised she'd finally left the castle. She was halfway to being free!

She sat up carefully, and got to her feet, shaking out her borrowed skirts. She was in some kind of back corridor, lined with crates and boxes and racks of clothing that, even to someone unfamiliar with the fashions, were clearly quite tawdry. A few niches on the wall held mundane candles, not even the warm clean lights she'd already become used to in the castle.

The scents that came to her were queasily familiar, however, even if they were technically new: cheap perfume that had gone stale, spilled wine and sour beer breath, bodies that were sweating alcohol. Some kind of food, and— Oh yes.

Ember knew the smell of sex perfectly well.

The portal had sent her into a brothel. Why? Was this where it thought she needed to be? Were the damn things sentient?

She looked about her and made her way towards the end of the corridor, away from the music and laughter. *No sense getting in if you can't get out, little ferret.* Here were a few more doors, but the one she was really interested in was the one at the end, which looked like an outside door. And she was nearly there when a door at the other end opened.

A woman stood there, a decanter in her hand, and blinked at Ember. Her eyes narrowed. 'Can I help you, love?'

Her clothing proclaimed her profession. The expression on her face said she was in charge. And her enquiry was not being made out of kindness.

'I think I'm lost,' Ember said, trying to look ditzy.

'I should say so.' The woman looked her over. 'Maid at the castle, are we?'

'That's right.'

'Hmm. Come to bring someone a message, have you? Long walk from the castle. Used a portal, I expect?'

'Er, yes,' said Ember. She tried to calculate if it would help to say she was there for Rhaell, but it was too late. A door opened a few feet away, and his massive presence loomed over her.

'Merelle? Is there a problem?'

CHAPTER 10

Whilst the city wound down to sleep and the court carried out its boring little intrigues, the whorehouses of the Upper Bazaar were just getting started for the night. Outside the private room Rhaell had bespoken, catcalls and laughter and rough grunts occasionally penetrated the door.

He winced at his own choice of words. Best not think about penetration, given the location.

'I mislike this place,' said the Myr woman. She flicked back her hair, which had an oily sort of sheen to it, and glared at him.

'Nothing wrong with a good honest fuck,' said the artificer Merelle had found for him, placidly setting out her velvet cloth. 'There any handsome young men available here?'

'Quite a few,' Rhaell assured her.

'Oh good. Prices reasonable?'

'I believe so.'

'Should be a decent evening for me, then.'

The Myr wrinkled her nose. It was flat, and slitted. Rhaell had heard they breathed through their skin, but he wasn't about to start asking how.

He knew there were a few Myr in the city, mostly well-disguised, some of them working on the river and some, inevitably, in establishments like the Spreading Branches. He'd met Neris, briefly, when he'd gone to sort out a problem with disappearing cargo at the docks and had tried to interview the hafmey. They were recalcitrant with him, and had even become threatening, but to his surprise the slit-nosed woman had emerged from the shadows, and they had immediately behaved themselves. Myr, it seemed had dominion over other creatures of the water. He had thanked her and promised to keep her presence secret in exchange for her silence.

'Sex should be free,' she muttered.

'A fine sentiment, but not all of us can get it,' said the artificer, as she finished setting out her stones, each roughly the size of a gold leaf coin. 'Now. This is as close as I could get to the colours and shapes you asked for. I can make more if you can tell me more.'

Rhaell regarded the stones set before him in their seven shades. He had made brief, crude sketches from the old manuscripts, but he had plenty of comparisons to make with the various statues, paintings and tapestries he'd seen every day of his life.

He sorted through them for shape and size. He had the king's crown and Ember's necklace to go by as regarded depth of colour and size, but that wasn't much. The artificer had not been impressed with his single-word descriptions of the shade. Apparently even black could come in different colours.

'That one,' he selected the green, 'and that one. A few more like this, if you could?' The artificer made notes. He looked up at the Myr. 'Well?'

She cocked her head and peered at the stones. When she blinked, a second vertical eyelid snapped across her pale eyes.

'I could tell you false,' she said. 'Our people are not friends.'

'They could be,' said Rhaell.

'Are you in a position to make demands of the king, *erlish*?' Neris asked mockingly. 'No. I will take the payment in gold leaf, as discussed.'

'And the stone? Gaeleath's Stone?'

She was pushing some of the blues aside, pausing over others, picking one or two out. Deep, dark blues, as he'd suspected from the tapestries. She hesitated over one with a slightly greener light to it.

'Choose several,' said Rhaell. 'It's better to have options.'

The Myr snorted. 'Says he who will not be making the substitution.'

Rhaell said nothing. He still hadn't actually found anyone to do that. Thieves, it turned out, were untrustworthy bastards.

A tap on the door made them all freeze. The artificer hurriedly flipped the velvet cloth over the stones.

'It's Merelle. Can I bring you anything?'

They all relaxed – at least, as far as the Myr was capable of relaxing.

'I could kill for a whisky,' said the artificer, and Rhaell nodded. He gave Neris an enquiring look.

'Do you have gin flavoured with roe?' she asked, somewhat patronisingly.

He sighed. 'I can ask.'

Merelle did not, so the Myr declined a drink. Rhaell asked Merelle to bring the whisky. The artificer certainly deserved a drink for her work.

'These are excellent,' he said.

'I know. I'm good at what I do.'

She didn't ask what he wanted them for. Rhaell appreciated that.

He heard footsteps in the back corridor, and expected Merelle to open the door, but instead he heard voices. Female voices, but not staff and not clients. Merelle wasn't happy with whoever she was talking to.

Rhaell sighed and stood up. He didn't mind acting the heavy for Merelle, but he'd actually really rather wanted that whisky.

He slipped through the door so no one could see inside. 'Is there a problem?'

And there she was, the Tree-damned Promised One. In some kind of maid's uniform, a stupid cap on her head, glaring at him.

'You?' she said.

'Me,' he said stupidly. Her bodice was very tight, and only half fastened.

'So this is your *tavern*, is it?'

For a second, Rhaell didn't know what to say. Where to even start. Why was she here? *How* was she here?

So he settled for, 'What are you doing here?'

She folded her arms. It didn't help the bodice situation. 'I could ask you the same question.'

'It's a brothel, honey. What do you think he's here for?' drawled Merelle.

Rhaell raised an eyebrow at Ember, but she didn't even blush.

'Why the hell are *you* paying for it?' She looked him over. 'Don't get enough for free?' She held up a hand before he could answer. 'No, don't tell me. It's the power, isn't it? Always the bloody power.' She sounded weary.

Rhaell glanced at Merelle, who said, 'She's got a point, darling. Now, would you mind taking this little lovers' tiff outside? Voices carry, and it's bad for business when the girlfriends come to collect.'

'I am not his girlfriend,' said Ember, at the same time as Rhaell protested, 'We're not lovers.'

'Either way,' said Merelle. She sashayed languidly away, the decanter still in her hand. 'I'll see you tomorrow, darling,' she called over her shoulder, and then she was back in the main room and he was standing there with Ember glaring at him.

'It's not what you think,' he said.

'No? Book club, is it? Quiz night? Philosophy club?'

He opened his mouth to say he didn't know what a book club was, but stopped. 'Did you follow me?' he said.

'No, I just picked a brothel at random,' she spat. 'This one looked like your taste.'

'You know what my tastes are, do you?'

'Well, you seem to like tits, and those aren't hard to find.' She put her hands on her hips, which somehow managed to emphasise her own.

He ran his hand through his hair and winced. She'd definitely followed him, although he was damned if he could figure out how. The porters would never give away where they'd taken someone. 'How did you even get out of your apartments?'

She shrugged. 'That's for me to know and you to find out,' she said.

'Oh, I will,' he said grimly. 'And in the meantime, I'll have guards stationed on your balcony.'

'You can't keep me locked up like that,' she said. 'I'll find a way out.'

'It isn't safe—'

'It isn't safe in there!' Ember gestured in what he supposed was meant to be the direction of the castle. 'Did you see what the Beast did to those people in the arena today?'

'They were convicted criminals,' Rhaell said, because even here, the walls had ears.

'He hacked them to death! For *entertainment*!'

He glared at her, forced to defend something he didn't even agree with. 'That's the law.'

He saw her fists clench. She shuddered. 'You still think it's right to taunt them with the prospect of freedom then have them hacked to death in public?' she said.

Rhaell sighed. It was brutal; she was right. 'There isn't really anything I can do about it,' he said. 'It's the will of the king.' The king who had wanted to make a very definite example of people who interfered with what he called the Will of the Tree.

Deep down in the most secret parts of his mind where he didn't even like to think out loud in case someone heard, Rhaell suspected that this was because the king suspected one of his wives of such an interference, and it had robbed him of a replacement heir.

'I didn't see the Beast complaining,' Ember snapped.

'The king is the king,' he said, not sure how else to explain it. 'His will is our command.'

'Even his own grandson?'

'Especially his own grandson.'

Ember's face was pale with anger, her finger trembling as she jabbed it at him. 'And that's who he wants me to marry,' she said, her voice cracking. 'That ... creature, who toys with men he's about to kill.'

I would stop that if I could. I would send you home if I could. 'There's not much I can do about that, either,' he said.

'Do you know what the maids told me this evening?' she demanded. 'He's got a cock the size of my forearm. Look at it!' she said, brandishing said limb at him. 'Do you think I can take that?'

Rhaell covered his face with his hands and groaned. 'I really don't want to think about that,' he said.

'Well, I've got to!'

'Look, it's just stupid rumours,' said Rhaell. 'Who told you this?'

Ember folded her arms again and shrugged. 'Is it true?'

Two could play at that game. 'What's true,' said Rhaell, reaching for her, 'is that you're coming back to the castle with me right now.'

'No,' said Ember, stepping back. 'And if you force me, I'll run again.'

'Then I'll find you again.' *And that purple rock around your neck.*

'You can't keep me locked up forever! I'm supposed to become the queen!'

'Then act like it,' he snapped. 'Queens do their Tree-damned duty.'

'I didn't ask for this! I'm not supposed to be here! I need to go home,' she said, and her voice broke a little on the word. 'Please. I have to care for my father. Do you have a father?' she asked, eyes big and pleading.

Interesting. She'd done the same thing that first night. 'No,' he said.

'Or siblings? I have two little brothers and no one to care for them.'

'Two brothers?' Rhaell whistled.

'Yes?'

He couldn't remember the last time he'd met anyone with a single sibling, let alone two. 'Very impressive,' he said. 'But still no. I *can't* send you back.'

She narrowed her eyes at him. 'You'd need a portal, right? I opened a portal tonight. One of the castle ones.'

Rhaell couldn't hide his surprise. 'You did?' But ... that wasn't common magic. Only a few people had the skill, and most of them worked as porters. A handful of higher-ups in the castle could open their own, but Ember wasn't even Yskaran. And from the castle to the city was about the furthest that could be portalled.

She went to see the Tree today.

Leaves and branches, maybe she really was the Promised One.

'It's still not the same,' he said. 'I'm sorry, Sparks. But you're stuck here.'

She was shaking her head. 'No.' She backed away from him. 'No. I don't accept that.'

'I'm afraid—'

'You can't make me.'

He sighed. Ember was not large – by Yskaran standards she was positively petite. Rhaell could deal with her with one hand tied behind his back.

'I probably could,' he said. 'I don't want to, but—'

'Gotta catch me first,' she said, and then suddenly the door was open and she was flying through it.

Rhaell swore, and raced after her.

The city of Yskara was built into the gorge. Ember knew this, had seen it from the river, but that was very much not the same thing as skidding out of a door and finding herself several hundred feet up in the air.

'Loooooord Ruven and all his little thieves!' she gasped, limbs pinwheeling at the edge of the pavement. Below her, the river rushed, lights twinkling along its length on the bows of small boats and on bridges that crossed it high and low, like strands of spider-web. There was a railing, but below that were rooftops and more pathways, and below that more roofs and more paths and ... well, it was a very flimsy railing.

But Rhaell would be right behind her, so she didn't waste time hanging about to enjoy the view. She could hear him crashing through the door behind her.

Ember had run from bigger meaner bastards in her time. Well, maybe not bigger, because the man was enormous, but that was to his disadvantage. She cut down a narrow alley, turned left then right, switched back on herself. Surely she'd have lost him now—

Rhaell's broad shoulders blocked the far end alley in front of her.

'You have got to be kidding,' she muttered, and ricocheted off the nearest wall to turn herself around and shoot back the way she'd come.

'Ember,' he shouted, as if she was a dog and she'd just come back when he called her name. She didn't answer, racing back towards the lights glittering up from the river.

She swung over the railing and onto the roof below, rolled to her feet and leapt to the next roof six feet away.

Which wasn't something she knew she could do.

'Holy fuck,' Ember whispered to herself as she raced across the roof and dropped down into an alley, dodging a trysting couple there. Jumped and grabbed a gutter, swung onto a steep roof and ran up it as if it was downhill.

How am I doing this? This isn't possible!

The river gaped up at her again. Ember shook off her confusion and decided to switch back, towards the cliff face, into the darker streets. Yes. She knew this. Tiny, twisting alleys, the shadows of tall buildings, the shadier parts of the city where respectable men didn't go—

'Guards!'

Oh hell, just what she needed. Reinforcements.

Everything here was built on top of everything else. She skipped another roof, getting a little out of breath now, swerved around a woman in scanty clothing and bounced off the corner of a building to come out over the river again.

There was a bridge, high and narrow over the gorge. Too obvious. He'd see her running all the way across it. Ember dodged away from it to head downhill, but there were men racing up it, torchlight glinting off their armour. Fuck. *Fuck*.

She reversed again, but there were people up ahead. Lords dammit, the bridge was her only option.

It was so high that even Ember thought about becoming vertiginous, and the strong wind didn't help. The sides of the bridge were balustraded, but that did little to keep the wind from trying to knock her down. It was probably a graceful arch over the river, but Ember wasn't really in a mood to appreciate the architecture. Pale granite, like everything else around here, her brain catalogued automatically. If she climbed over the edge was there anything below she could drop onto?

Maybe, with these mad new skills I seem to magically have.

A quick glance told her that would only be a good idea if she was tired of having quite so many bones and fancied pulverising a few. She raced ahead, grimly aware of how exposed she was. But they wouldn't shoot her or anything, would they? They needed her. She was their Promised One.

She was halfway across when a shadow dropped towards her from above and the bridge shuddered.

'Ember.' It was Rhaell, straightening from the crouch he'd dropped into. What the fuck? Had he come from another bridge? Ember turned to run back, but the entrance of the bridge was blocked by men in helmets.

She swung back, panting. The wind filled her ears and chilled her skin, blowing her cloak around her legs. Below her the river glittered blackly.

Her heart pounded. *Little ferrets don't get scared.*

'I'll jump,' she blurted.

Rhaell cocked his head. The bastard wasn't even out of breath. 'No, you won't.'

Fury boiled over in her. 'Oh yeah, and how do you know? You know me that well, do you?'

'You want to get home to take care of your family. Can't do that if you're dead.'

Lords damn him for being so logical. 'I'd rather be dead than held captive.'

'You're not a—'

'If you say I'm not a captive, I swear I'll fucking jump,' Ember snarled.

Rhaell held up his hands, as if trying to calm a wild animal. 'All right. All right. Ember. Please. Don't do anything rash. Come back to the castle and talk to me.'

'We've talked! All you've said is you can't get me home! And I won't stay here.'

'But you are the Promised One...'

She threw up her hands. 'Not this old shit again.'

'The prophecy said—'

'I don't care about your stupid prophecy!' Ember screamed. 'I am not your fucking Promised One! I'm the wrong person! Why can't you get that into your stupid head?'

'Because you're the one who's here,' Rhaell said implacably.

The one who's here. Ember heard a desperate laugh wheeze out of her own throat, and for a moment she couldn't breathe, bracing herself on her knees as she laughed and laughed.

'What's so funny?'

'What's so funny?' She sucked in a breath, hacked it back out again. 'What's funny, Buttercup, is *why* I'm the one who's here.' She fished inside her cloak and held up the gaudy purple stone. 'I was in that manor house, getting stabbed in a ritual and sent here, because *I broke in to nick this*.'

He stared at the stone, then at her for a moment. 'You what?'

'Yeah.' Ember managed to straighten up, still dangling the stone on its pendant. 'I told you I helped the real girl escape, but I didn't tell you why I was there in the first place. I went in to steal stuff. I'm not your Promised One. I'm a thief.'

For a long moment Rhaell was silent, his eyes wide. Then he started laughing.

'Yeah, all right,' Ember muttered, her own mirth gone. What was he going to do now? Arrest her? 'It ain't that funny.'

'Funny?' Rhaell wheezed. He straightened, gasping and grinning. 'No, Ember, it isn't funny, it's perfect. By the Tree! You're perfect.'

Ember had no idea what to say to that. The wind blew Rhaell's shining dark hair across his face, the lights of the torches gilded his sculpted face, his eyes glittered blue as sapphires, and he called her perfect.

As a much younger girl, she'd had fantasies about this kind of moment.

Rhaell was still laughing. 'You were there to ... the climbing down the wall! The way you— Wait, are your pockets full of jewels now?'

Slowly, she nodded.

Rhaell laughed delightedly. *Damn, he's pretty when he laughs.*

'You're a thief,' he said.

'I'm also your Promised One and you can't hurt me, remember?' she said quickly, and then winced, because she'd just told him she wasn't and he was *laughing*, why was he laughing?

'Oh, you are definitely the Promised One,' he said. He rubbed his face, still grinning. 'Leaves and branches. Sparks – the prophecy said we would be sent exactly what we need and by the Tree, we were.'

She stared in incomprehension. 'Come again?'

'You're a thief. And that's exactly – *exactly* – what I need.'

What *he* needs? 'For what possible purpose?'

'To steal the scattered pieces of the Heart of Yskar and restore magic to the realm.' His blue eyes glittered in the moonlight. 'And when magic is restored, Ember Hart, we can send you home.'

CHAPTER 11

It was late, and not many people were around in the Scholar's Quarter. Rhaell flicked his hand at the library werelights, and they came on, illuminating the vast space lined with shelf after shelf of books.

'Whoa,' breathed Ember.

He began leading her through the complex set of stacks and anterooms to the archive.

'We've already been through here,' Ember said as he opened a room where the books were chained to the shelves. She was looking at everything as if calculating its value, and he could see her scanning for exits everywhere they went.

'Yes, but some rooms you have to go through more than once,' he said.

'What? Why? That doesn't make any sense,' she said, and then he opened the door onto a room filled with hourglasses, and she made a small, frustrated noise. 'Are you trying to trap me? Is this like a maze or something?'

'It's a maze for sure,' said Rhaell, 'but I'm not trying to trap you.' He led her through the hourglasses, their sands whispering secrets, and through the door back to the chained books. 'When I've explained everything to you, you can leave if you want.'

'And go where?'

'Where were you going before?'

'Anywhere but here.'

Rhaell led her into the final room, which was still very dusty, apart from the tracks he'd made yesterday.

He saw her gaze flick distrustfully towards the door they'd come through. There was no other exit.

'You said you opened a portal,' he said.

'Yeah?'

'That's not something most people can do.'

She shrugged, as if to wonder why that mattered. *She is the Promised One.*

'What're you going to show me that'll miraculously make me trust you?' she said, folding her arms. It did rather impressive things to her chest that Rhaell tried very hard not to notice.

Rhaell motioned her to a seat, which she ignored, and floated the books and scrolls he wanted down to the table.

'That's a trick I'd like to learn,' she said.

'You'll probably have to stick around in that case,' he said, and moved in next to her to open the first scroll. 'All right. Has anyone told you any of our history since you've been here?'

She shrugged. 'It was founded by this warrior queen and then her husband betrayed her. It's on those tapestries in the Great Chamber.'

'It's on half the tapestries I've ever seen,' Rhaell said, carefully unrolling the scroll. 'It's a very popular subject. Okay, here's the standard depiction of the founding of Yskara. Here's Ysarriel, the foundress, raising the keep.'

He gestured to the image in the style of the Ancestors: richly coloured and decorated, with every bit of space filled in with allegorical images, but the figures themselves crude and lacking detail.

Ysarriel was shown as shining with a halo, her long golden hair cascading to her waist, her gown deep green.

Flanking her was the figure of Ruvaen, her husband, dark-haired and mantled in rich purple, and the maiden Ephyrea, gowned in blushing pink.

'What was here before?' Ember asked.

'In some versions, nothing. They found the Tree and decided to raise a keep beside it. Here, this is the Seven discovering it.'

The Tree, Yskar itself, blazed off the page in real gold and silver leaf. The Ancestors ringed it, gazing on in awe.

'And in other versions?' said Ember, a little too perspicaciously.

Rhaell reached for the scroll he had carefully read the other night. 'This,' he said, 'is not something we're really supposed to see.'

'Hence the whole'—she waved her hands at the door—'secrecy thing?'

He shrugged. 'These books in here, they don't want to be found. They've protected themselves.'

'Then how come you could find them?'

'Because I didn't mean them any harm.' Rhaell carefully pointed to a section of the hard-to-read text. 'It says there were people here before. They lived in harmony with the Tree, and at first so did the Ancestors. They learned to harness the Tree's power, but they grew greedy on it, and tried to keep it for themselves. They built a stone castle and vast walls surrounding the Sacred Forest and drove out anyone who would not pledge fealty to them.'

'Oh yeah, we have those,' Ember said. 'We call them colonists.'

'Do they thrive?'

She shrugged. 'Pretty much, yeah. Only in my world it's sarel they're after, not trees.'

'Sarel?'

'Yeah. You don't have that here? It's like ... you find it underground, as a liquid, and you can use that as fuel. Or sometimes it's solidified, and that's also fuel. But sometimes – they told us how at school but I can't remember it – it gets turned into precious stones. Like this one.'

She fished out Ruvaen's Stone from beneath her cloak.

'That's ... sarel?' Rhaell said doubtfully.

She nodded. 'Not very good sarel. See, there's all kinds of fractures in it, and the colour's kind of gaudy. And the shape is weird, too. Who cuts a stone like this?'

The Ancestors, Rhaell wanted to tell her, but he knew he was getting ahead of himself.

'Let me explain who the Ancestors were,' he said, and went back to the first scroll, with its bright illustrations. 'Ysarriel, the founder of Yskara, was the one who discovered the Tree. Her husband Ruvaen helped her raise the castle we're standing in right now.'

'In a day, if the ladies-in-waiting are to be believed,' Ember said.

Rhaell made a so-so motion with his hand. 'It's possible that's poetic licence, but the point is they could raise the castle by themselves. That's what their magic could do.'

Ember was silent for a moment. Then she said, 'That's horrifying.'

'Horrifying? Why?'

'If you can raise a castle in a day, what else can you do? Crumble it? Is it just buildings or can you destroy the earth, too? Bury people under it? You could be a mass murderer with that power. You could be a tyrant.'

He blinked down at her. Generally, people were in awe of the Ancestors and their astonishing feats. Not many people even considered that they could have been terrible.

'Were they?' she asked, as if it was a matter of academic interest. 'Tyrants?'

Rhaell sighed. 'Ysarriel was said to be a wise and just queen,' he said.

'Said?'

'Said.' Rhaell tapped the scroll.

'And it was her historians who wrote all this down, was it?' Ember gave him a knowing look, and Rhaell felt a smile curve his lips.

'Don't ever say that out loud around here,' he said.

She shrugged. 'I don't trust people with too much power,' she said.

'Nor should you. You'd have liked Wynric,' he said, pointing to the figure clothed in yellow with a quill in his hand. 'He was Ysarriel's scribe, said to be the wisest man who ever lived. Many of the sayings and mottos of Yskara come from him.'

'As well as the official histories,' Ember murmured.

'Maybe you wouldn't have liked him. How about Gaeleath, the founder of the healing order?' They traditionally wore blue, and a serene expression.

'That trained Phoebe?'

Rhaell winced. 'Um, no. Phoebe is ... not formally trained. She has the aptitude, but...'

'But what?' The pale lights shone on Ember's short, waving hair, her upturned face, her enquiring eyes.

But she is being punished for her mother's loyalty. 'But she is a maid instead. It is a position of great esteem,' Rhaell said, and quickly moved on. 'Here, in the black, is Mnorir.'

'I've heard of that one. Death?'

'That's how he's usually invoked these days. But back then he was a sorcerer of great power.'

'Greater than raising a castle in a single day?'

'Greater even than that. It was he who bound Ephyrea into the Tree.'

Ember blinked. She frowned down at the seventh figure,

graceful in pink. She alone did not have a halo of light emanating from her.

'Why? Who was Ephyrea?'

Rhaell sighed. 'She was Ysarriel's companion and greatest friend. Reports differ about their exact relationship but suffice it to say, they were close. They shared everything. Even, unknown to Ysarriel, her husband.'

Ember's brows twitched. 'Ah.'

'Yes. When she learned of the betrayal,' Rhaell gestured to the next section of the scroll, 'Ysarriel's fury knew no bounds. She banished her husband, but an even greater punishment was reserved for the treacherous Ephyrea. Mnorir bound her into the Tree, where she would live a half-life forever, alive but not, never dying, aware but unable to move or speak.'

'That's hideous. I said she was a tyrant.'

Ember gazed at the illustration of Ephyrea being imprisoned in the Tree, her arms outstretched as if in plea. Ysarriel stood unmoved, pointing to the Tree, where black swirls surrounded Mnorir.

'So, she's still in there? Just ... trapped? That's fucking gruesome.'

'It's just a story.'

'Is it?'

Rhaell could only shrug. He was never sure if he believed it or not.

'All right,' Ember said, looking up at him. 'So that's the history lesson. But you said you needed a thief. Why?'

He nodded at the stone around her neck. 'Because that stone is strangely cut for a reason. It's one of seven. They're the pieces of the Tree's heart.'

Ember rubbed her face and exhaled as if she was very tired. 'Trees don't have hearts,' she said. 'I didn't do that much schooling but I'm pretty sure on that one.'

'Ah, but the Tree is not an ordinary Tree. It powers the magic of the whole land.'

'The magic that's dying?'

'Yes. Because the Tree's heart has been cut out. Look – it's not in the official record, it's in this scroll, which was'—he gestured to the secret room around them—'reluctant to be found. When the Ancestors found the Tree, they knew its worth, but also its vulnerability. While it stood, it could be cut down. But if they removed its heart, it could not die.'

'That doesn't make any—'

'It's a magic tree, Sparks,' Rhaell said impatiently. 'Don't look for logic. The Ancestors have stories of babies being born from flowers and visiting the dead under the sea. They removed the heart and cut it into seven pieces. One to remain in the tree, and the others scattered for safekeeping. Because so long as the pieces of the heart existed, the Tree could not be destroyed.'

To say Ember looked sceptical would be a huge understatement. 'Which bit did they leave in the Tree?'

'Ephyrea's. She classically represents love. Mnorir is death, Wynric wisdom, et cetera, but Ephyrea was love, and so who better to represent the heart of the Tree?'

Ember groaned. 'This is some metaphorical bollocks.'

Rhaell laughed. No one had ever called the stories of the Ancestors 'metaphorical bollocks' before. 'That doesn't mean it's not true. Look,' he said. 'There's a stone in the king's crown that's always been called Ysarriel's Stone. It's green, of course.'

'Of course?'

He gestured to the Tree on the scroll, to the emblems in the ancient stone of the library walls, to the stamped and painted crests on the official histories. 'You haven't noticed everything around here is green?'

'Oh. But the Tree isn't?'

Rhaell shrugged. 'I didn't say it had to be logical. Ysarriel is usually depicted in green, and so is her stone. The others were said to have been hidden by their owners. Where exactly isn't easy to decipher. The scroll is ... cryptic,' he said, with feeling. 'But there was one that even this scroll never knew the whereabouts of, because it was taken by Ruvaen.'

'The cheating husband?'

'Yes.' Rhaell looked down at her and couldn't help smiling. 'Classically, Ruvaen represents traitors, but also gamblers, chancers ... and thieves.'

'Ha,' said Ember idly, her fingers twirling the necklace, and then she stopped and looked up at him. 'Wait, what? Are you saying ... I found the necklace because I'm a thief?'

'Maybe. Yes. But it's been lost for generations. And you have it.'

Rhaell pulled a book towards them. It wasn't old; it didn't need to be. The prophecy had been repeated in scrolls and books for years. Rhaell had gone back to some pretty old scrolls and found it unchanged. 'Here. This is what it says about you.'

He watched her lean over and read it, frowning. Her finger traced the words, as if literacy was not a skill she was comfortable with. Or perhaps reading classical Yskaran was the problem.

'"And when ye sacred land of Yskara faces Critical Peril, a great Saviour will arrive to restore and protect the Realm. The One who is Promised will be delivered on the day the twin Moons do rise before they block the Sun in its path in the seven and fortieth year of the reign of the king of Peace, the third of his name, when the sun does reach its zenith. Though the land be Blighted she shall end it, and by her will shall Power be restored to the Rightful. The Heart of Yskar shall be healed by her Hand and the seeds she shall nurture will thrive." Well, that's clear as mud.'

Rhaell leaned over the manuscript, trying not to notice how nice she smelled. 'Which parts are unclear?'

'Um, all of it? This is like those flowery plays they made us read at school. Who's the king of Peace?'

'King Onas. It's an old meaning of his name.'

'Oh. What's yours mean?'

Rhaell blinked at the manuscript. 'Uh, it means my mother liked the name, I think. The stuff about the sun and moons just gives the date. The blight must mean the magic dying.'

'Must it?'

'Well, what else could it mean?'

Ember shrugged. 'I dunno, maybe the whole "nobody having babies" thing?'

'Well, the two are linked.'

'Are they? Are you sure you haven't tried fucking?'

The word hung in the air between them for just a fragment of a second too long. Ember stood very close to him, her hip brushing his, the scent of her skin rising to him. The light caressed the curve of her cheek. He wondered what it would feel like to let his fingers do the same.

'We've tried,' said Rhaell shortly, willing his body to control itself.

'Sure.' She tapped the book. 'What's this about seeds being planted? 'Cos I ain't much of a gardener, and if we're talking a more, um, human kind of seed I ain't nurturing any of those either.'

Rhaell felt his cheeks burn. 'That one's open to interpretation,' he said.

'Ri-ight,' she said, drawing the word out doubtfully. 'And the Heart of Yskar? Is that a metaphor, too?'

Rhaell chose his words carefully. 'The king believes so.'

Her brows went up. 'And you?'

Rhaell sighed. He gestured to the ancient scroll. 'There are many versions of the story of the Ancestors, but most of the details that vary are small. This one differs in its account of the Heart, and also ... the exact details of the prophecy.'

'Such as?'

'Well...' He rested his finger over the lines. '"And when our native land be—" This word here, *skoli*, it's sometimes translated as wrong or sick, but sometimes also stolen. "When our native land be stolen she shall restore it. And *vallr*" – that could mean power as in authority, or power as in strength – "power shall be restored to the *reatlottr*" – that could be rightful or righteous.'

'You're losing me,' said Ember.

He tapped his fingers together, trying to work out how to explain it. 'The official translations are clearer. And they cast things in a more favourable light – there's a big difference between a land being stolen and being sick.'

Ember cocked her head. 'Do you think the land has been stolen?'

Rhaell shrugged. 'I don't know. But if you were the king, would you want that theory being bandied about?'

'I suppose not. So this scroll is like ... contraband?'

'Essentially, yes.' He gestured to the entrance it had taken three tries to find. 'If the scholars know about it, they've kept it quiet. It isn't supposed to exist.'

Ember was quiet for a moment, gazing at nothing. Her fingers tapped her lips.

'So, this scroll that isn't supposed to exist says Ysarriel might have stolen the land, and also had the Tree's heart cut into pieces? And you think it's true?'

Rhaell nodded.

'All of it?'

He took in a deep breath and blew it out. That was the real question, wasn't it? 'To question the legitimacy of the king is treason,' he said. 'By even looking at this, we could be considered traitors.'

Ember threw up her hands. 'Now you're telling me?'

She pushed away from the table and paced, arms wrapped around herself. Rhaell waited.

It had been a gamble, bringing her here and telling her this. She might listen to him and walk away. She might declare it wasn't her problem and leave him to it. But this way...

This way, she was already complicit. She couldn't go telling tales on him without also getting herself into trouble. Would she be immune from punishment, as the king's cherished Promised One? He wasn't sure. But the king wanted those heirs. He probably wouldn't have Ember executed.

The thought occurred that the king could have her chained up in a room somewhere, being repeatedly bred. But that wasn't a thought he was going to share with her. Best not give her imagination nightmare fuel.

She turned around and glared at him. 'I know what this is,' she said. 'This is like when Newcomb Salty hired me to go lift the mayor's gold chain from his mistress's apartment, only it wasn't 'cos he wanted to sell it, it was 'cos he wanted to blackmail the mayor.'

Rhaell blinked. 'Was he successful?'

That startled a laugh out of Ember. 'Uh, yeah.' She cocked her head. 'You don't mind that I was liberating stuff from people's private apartments?'

He shrugged. 'It's what I want you to do. And, by the way – those words in the old scroll? The word *afrelte*, it could mean restore, or rescue. Or liberate.'

'You want me to steal the land back?' Ember fiddled with her cap, which wasn't doing much to contain her hair anymore. 'Mate, I nick jewels and paperwork and shit. I can't nick a whole country.'

'Are you sure? Wars do it all the time,' Rhaell murmured. 'Listen, here's the bargain I have for you.'

He faced her, and she rolled her shoulders and folded her arms and raised an eyebrow.

That should not have been a massive turn-on, and yet it was. *Control yourself, you pathetic creature.*

'You help me retrieve these stones and restore them to the Tree. And when magic fills the land and I can open a portal between the worlds, I will use one to send you home.'

Her eyes narrowed with scepticism. 'How long's this going to take, then?'

He shrugged. 'I don't know. But the king is scheduling a

progress to tour you around the country, and I think some of the stones might be retrievable from there, if we plan things carefully.'

'You can tell the king where to go?'

'I don't have to, he's very predictable. Addor, Valoris, Varalhen, some hunting in the grasslands, get bored, sail back up the Sacred River in time to thank the Tree for the harvest.'

'The wedding is supposed to be in a month.'

He winced. 'We'll be back by then,' he said, very much hoping this was true.

'The engagement is tomorrow.'

Rhaell ran a hand through his hair. 'I can't do anything about that. But an engagement is not a marriage. And I will get you home before you have to marry him.'

'What if he follows me?'

'What if I stop him?'

Her chin came up. 'You'd stop him marrying me?'

Rhaell looked at Ember and saw a woman who would gladly stab a man in the dick if he touched her where she didn't want. There was no way she would allow herself to be forced into marriage. She was not the sort of woman who needed his protection at all. And yet...

She is not yours to protect.

Rhaell looked her in the eye and said, 'Yes. I would stop him marrying you.'

Ember eyed him for a long moment, and then she gave a nod, as if she had made a decision.

'Rhaell, in the gardens I saw a fountain. The Heir's Memorial.'

He exhaled, slightly confused by her non sequitur. 'Yes. It's very beautiful. The carving on the shrouds is a work of art.'

'It is,' Ember said, distracted, 'but – like, it was the king's daughter, who died, and his wives, who had babies who ... also died?'

He nodded. 'Yes. The monarchy is inextricably linked to the

Tree. That's why we must restore the Tree and bring life back to the land.'

'But all of them...?'

He knew what she was asking, and sighed. 'Ynasell and Lyrai died in childbirth, and their babes with them. The Lady Syllia had a series of miscarriages in a very short period and it ... disordered her mind. She was last seen wandering the grounds, tearing at her nightclothes. Nothing was found of her but some blood-soaked scraps of silk on the rocks.'

Ember's eyes were wide. 'The hafmey ate her?'

'It would appear so. Aravae carried her first child nearly to term, but it was not to be. After that, the king told his courtiers more than once that she had conceived, but her health was fragile. She was found at the bottom of the tower stairs, her neck broken.'

'An accident?' said Ember sharply.

Rhaell spread his hands. 'What else could it be? Then there was Umily. She was young and healthy, but never conceived. It upset her greatly, and nothing would bring her comfort. She became withdrawn, and frequently harmed herself. One day she was found hanging in her chamber.'

Ember's eyes were narrowed. The king had told the court these stories with great sorrow, everything draped in black, all silent with mourning. Each time he had redoubled his prayers to the Tree, sacrificing his own blood in penance.

'No one questioned any of this?' said Ember.

'He is the king,' said Rhaell simply.

Ember was silent for a long moment. Rhaell could see her thoughts. The king's wives died when they did not present him with a child. His own daughter had died giving birth. What was going to happen to Ember?

Nothing, because she will be long gone.

She cleared her throat and squared her shoulders, looking down at the colourful scroll. 'You said this is one stone, and the king has another. So that's five we've got to get?'

'Four. Ephyrea's is in the Tree.'

She blew out a breath. 'Four. From where? In the castle?'

Rhaell shook his head. 'Further afield. I believe one of them may be in Addor, and one in Valoris. Both are important allies.' Best not to tell her where he thought the others were just yet. Or that his plan to get them was ... in need of some finessing.

'Eletha is from Addor,' she said. 'And Lyndis is from Valoris, I think.' She made a face.

'You don't like Lyndis?' Rhaell said, trying not to smile.

'Oh, no, she's very...' He enjoyed watching her try to come up with something diplomatic. 'Pretty,' she tried.

Rhaell laughed. 'And doesn't she know it?' He carefully began rolling up the scrolls. 'You should get some rest. Is there anything you'll need to go, um, stealing? Equipment, I mean?'

Ember gave him a sly look. 'Offering to find me a set of lockpicks, are you?'

'I'm a very resourceful man,' he told her.

'I'm sure you are.' She pinched the bridge of her nose. 'Pa's tools were excellent for cracking doors. But you don't have clockwork, do you?'

He shook his head. He still didn't know what that was.

'Get me something practical to wear. Dark. Trousers, not another bloody dress. Nothing loose and trailing, but nothing too tight if I've got to go climbing. Gloves. The fingerless kind. Soft boots. A good tool belt. With pockets. Something with a hood.'

Rhaell blinked, and nodded. Most of that could be found at the barracks, if he looked hard enough. He tucked the ancient scroll away behind some dusty tomes on the history of agriculture.

'Oh, and knives,' she said.

'Knives?'

'Sharp things. You use them for stabbing. Black blades,' she added, 'so they don't shine.'

'Anything else, Sparks?'

She narrowed her eyes at the colourful scroll. 'A plan,' she said.

'I have that,' he said, with more confidence than he felt.

Ember regarded him steadily, her eyes reading his face in a way he wasn't sure he liked. 'Not just a plan for getting in, Buttercup,' she said. 'There's no sense getting in if you can't get out.'

Rhaell had a feeling it was already too late for that.

CHAPTER 12

King Onas surveyed his grandson and heir with contempt. 'That's what you're wearing?'

The Beast shrugged. It made a clanking sound. 'I have to ride out to Aurvik later to see some dead mantises.'

'Why? If they're dead?'

'Because there might be more nearby that aren't?'

Onas tipped his wine cup to his lips but it was empty. He gestured for more. 'Sure you're not being a coward?'

Prince Bronadyr went very still. He was good at being still anyway, for such a big creature, but this was a different kind of stillness. This was a dangerous kind of stillness.

'Coward?' he said, a growl so soft it was almost lost inside his helmet.

He stood at parade rest, gauntleted hands behind his armoured back. His great horned helm rested on his head, the beastly visor flipped up to reveal his hideous visage.

'Scared to show her that?' Onas said, gesturing to the Beast's face as his wine was refilled.

His eyes narrowed under his hulking brow. 'No sense in frightening her off,' he rumbled.

'Ha! Like I said, coward.' Onas drank some more wine. 'Hallas, where are we on the progress?'

He hated going on progress, most of the time. All that endless travelling and pretending to be polite about whatever tree-damned accommodation the local lords could cobble together for you. But he'd got a reason for going this time. Something to show off.

His Promised One.

'We are to sail to Addor first, Your Grace, for two days,' said Lord Hallas. 'Then, down the Shadowmelt to Rivelor—'

'Not going to Kearsby, are we?' said Onas. 'It's a shit-hole.'

'Not anymore, your Grace,' said Hallas smoothly. 'At Rivelor we will stay two days—'

'Make it overnight. Rivelor's a shit-hole, too,' said Onas. 'All Paren's a shit-hole.'

'Yes, Your Grace, although Paren will take offence if we do not progress there.'

Onas curled his lip. He'd caught something embarrassing in Paren as a young man, and while the lady in question was doubtless long gone, the memory lingered. As did the itch, sometimes.

'From Rivelor we shall cross the estuary to Valoris and stay at Castle Keenor three days. After this, a three-day tour of the grasslands, bringing us back to the Sacred River...'

Onas stopped listening. The grasslands were boring as death, just one small town after another. They'd no doubt have to camp in tents, and while the king's tent was more luxurious than most palaces, it was still a fucking tent.

On the table lay a copy of *The Story of the Ancestors*, brightly illustrated, with real gold in some places. It lay open, as it had most of the last few weeks, at the prophecy.

By her will shall Power be restored to the Rightful. Onas flicked his fingers at the fireplace, and the flames barely grew at all. *The seeds she shall nurture will thrive.*

'We go to Addor three days hence,' he told Bronadyr. 'Bed her there.'

Bronadyr's gaze flicked to his. 'We are not to wed for a month. The astrologers—'

'Bah! Who cares about the wedding! It's the bedding that's important!' His fingers stabbed the book. 'The seeds she nurtures! She can't nurture any fucking seeds if you don't plant any in her, can she?'

Bronadyr stared straight ahead. 'I suppose not.'

'Exactly. Fuck her. Swell her belly. Once the line is secured, we will thrive again. A tree can't survive if it's got roots but no branches, can it?'

'No, Your Grace.'

'And I want lots of branches. I don't care if you have to lock her up and tie her to the bed to get them.' Onas got to his feet. The room tilted a bit. The page clearly hadn't watered his wine properly. 'Crown,' he commanded, and Lord Hallas put down his stupid itinerary and picked up the Crown of Ysarriel from its green velvet cushion.

Onas didn't wear Ysarriel's Crown very much. It was heavy and it hurt his ears. But it did look very impressive. Styled in gold, for once not the usual Yskaran silver, it formed intertwining branches with leaves of emerald. Diamonds studded the band, and it was trimmed at the base with the glittering silver fur of the flame-eared asena. But the real glory of it was the stone, said to have belonged to Ysarriel herself, glowing at the base of the main branch, right above his forehead.

He grunted as it was settled in place, then straightened. His mantle was brought forth.

'Princess is ready, is she?'

'She's not a princess yet,' rumbled Bronadyr.

'She will be soon enough. Bind her today and bed her within the week. I want her belly swelling by the time you say your vows, you hear me?' A thought occurred to him. 'As a matter of fact, I want that helmet staying on your head until she says her vows, you understand? Don't go scaring her off before she's got the ring on her finger and a babe in her belly.'

'You want me to fuck her wearing this?' said the Beast, flipping down his visor. The green and silver beast leered at him, all tusks and snarl.

'It's an improvement on your face. Now, come on. We've an engagement to formalise.'

~

Ember had been dressed for an hour or so – it was hard to tell, there were no clocks in this place – and sat at a table picking at food while her ladies twittered around her. Eventually, someone tapped on the door and whispered to Phoebe, who tweaked Ember's outfit and sent her after the guards leading her down to the Great Chamber.

She tried to hide her tremors in her giant, trailing sleeves. Today's dress was green and blue, embroidered with silver and trimmed in matching fur. The stupid tree headdress was back on her head, controlling every movement she made, and the necklace Rhaell had called Ruvaen's Stone was tucked into her bodice, the chain hidden by an elaborate neckpiece made of silver and jewels, styled into the inevitable tree.

The king's wives died when they didn't give him children. What's he going to do to me?

'Your Grace, you look beautiful,' said one of the ladies. Caeda, maybe.

'I can't bleedin' move,' Ember replied, wondering when she'd become a Grace.

'All you have to do is walk and stand,' said Lyndis.

They carried her train for her, a feat in itself as their own outfits were hardly less elaborate than her own. Each of them wearing coronets and diadems, long fur-trimmed cloaks and jewel-toned gowns, each of them dripping in jewellery that made Ember's fingers itch.

We could live for a year on one pair of earrings, she thought, then told herself to stop thinking about Pa and the boys. She'd be home soon. When she'd done this job for Rhaell and got his magic back.

But first she had to go through this engagement charade.

It's just pretend, she told herself as she slowly progressed towards the portal. *It's not going to come to anything*. The portal took her to a small antechamber, where more refreshments were set out, and the ladies sat around gossiping as Ember's heart quivered in her chest like a frightened rabbit.

I just have to get through this, then I can get this stupid sarcophagus of an outfit off and go talk to Rhaell about these stones. Yes. I can go and nick some stuff. That'll make me feel better.

That little pep talk lasted her until they heard trumpets from the Great Chamber, and a herald popped in through a small door.

'Your Grace,' he said, bowing. 'Their Graces King Onas and Prince Bronadyr have arrived, so once they have taken their places, we shall announce you.'

'Can't wait,' Ember muttered.

He beamed at her, apparently oblivious to her sarcasm. Lyndis took Ember's hand and said sympathetically, 'I'm sure it won't be that bad. I heard he filed down his horns for you.'

Ember's terrified little heart started tap dancing in her chest. 'Is that supposed to make me feel better?' she hissed.

A tap came on the door, and the herald straightened his silver and green tunic. He opened the door with a flourish, stepped forth, and those damn trumpets sounded again.

'The Promised One, Saviour of Yskara, Blessed by the Tree, Her Grace, the Lady Ember Hart! May the Tree protect and shelter her!'

The cheer that followed this was almost deafening. Ember froze. *Rabbit heart rabbit heart rabbit heart.*

'Your Grace?' whispered one of the ladies.

I'm just a thief. I nick shiny things. I'm not anybody's saviour.

The room before her blurred in front of her eyes. Her heart beat so fast she was surely vibrating.

'Simply walk to the prince and take his hand,' whispered the herald.

Oh yes. That.

She just had to take one step forward. Then another. Yes. That was it. She was walking normally. Well, as normally as anyone wearing a dress that was basically a suit of armour and a headdress the weight of a full-grown stag could do.

The crowd had parted in a wide avenue for her to walk down. Ember concentrated on putting one foot in front of the other, on breathing regularly, and not on what awaited her at the end of the walk.

But eventually even the blurred shapes had to resolve into people. Ember forced her gaze up, over the gleaming mass that stood in front of the throne, up above the throne itself, and fastened onto the king's crown.

There. A gleaming green jewel, as gaudily bright as the purple one tucked into her bodice. Ysarriel's Stone? How much would that be worth, then? If it was the same poor quality of sarelstone she had around her neck, not much. But that was Clockwork City values. Here, in Yskara, where anything to do with the sacred Tree or the blessed Ancestors had people wetting their pants, it was probably priceless.

Heh. Literally priceless. You couldn't shift something worth that much. Who'd buy it? Hmm, maybe the king had some enemy who'd like to humiliate him ... start a war...

The stone tucked under her bodice gave a sort of throb. It felt ... warm, the way she'd felt when she touched the Tree. Dear Lords, were the stones really magical?

A gleaming silver mass filled her vision. Ember realised with a start that she'd made it all the way to the dais at the base of the throne, and the great lump of metal in front of her was Prince Bronadyr.

So he's cleaned the blood off his armour, she thought, the hysteria back again as he extended one gloved paw. She was face to chest with the green tree on his breastplate, only it wasn't painted or enamelled as she'd thought, it was jewelled. Hundreds, thousands of tiny emeralds winking at her in the light. Lords, he probably just had to stand in the sunlight and half his enemies would be blinded.

She daren't look up. Not at that fearsome face, with its gleaming silver tusks and horns. Or worse: what if he wasn't wearing the helmet and she had to look at his actual face. Would that be tusked and horned, too?

Ember felt sick. She was getting engaged to a monster.

Everyone seemed to be waiting for something. Behind her, the ladies settled the train of her dress. Silence fell.

'My lady,' rumbled the giant beside her, and his engraved silver gauntlet filled her vision. Right. Carefully, trying not to look like she was shaking like a leaf, Ember placed her hand in his.

She didn't think she had small hands. She'd never thought anything about her was particularly small, or large come to that, until she'd washed up here. But now it was like taking the hand of a giant. A cold, metal giant who wanted to *bed her and breed her*.

He stepped forward, and in order to keep her arm attached so did Ember, and they stepped up onto the dais, then up another step, until they faced the king.

'Prince Bronadyr,' proclaimed the king. 'My grandson and heir.'

The beast inclined his massive, helmeted head. The horns on top were longer than Ember's forearm. *Like his cock, those girls said it's the size of your forearm, oh Lords—*

'Lady Ember. The Promised One.'

Ember managed some kind of grimace.

'Do you both enter freely into this betrothal?'

No, of course fucking not! Ember wanted to gibber, but what would happen if she said so? If she told them the truth about why she'd never be the queen they wanted? They'd send her to the block, and the Beast beside her would chop off her head with his great war axe; or worse, she'd be forced to defend herself against him in the arena as he hacked her to pieces, bit by bit—

'Yes,' rumbled the giant at her side.

'Yes,' squeaked Ember. *It's not real. I'll be long gone before anyone finds out the truth. Just say what they want to hear and don't make waves.*

'Then let us seal the bargain.'

The Beast let go of her hand, and Ember looked up in confusion. But he was simply unbuckling and pulling off his gauntlet. She braced herself.

It was a hand. He had a normal hand. A large hand, callused and scarred, the nails cracked and torn, but just a hand. Not a paw. No talons.

She reached out to take it, wondering if he'd be cold or hot, when someone cleared their throat.

The king. He held up a knife.

—a much larger knife, its blade curved and gleamingly sharp, the drumming, her heart, her heart was drumming, it was Varne, he was going to plunge it into her heart—

'Breathe,' murmured the Beast, and the rumble of his voice startled her enough that the king took her hand and sliced the palm before she even realised what was happening.

'What the – sonofabitch!' Ember yelped, and there was a startled murmur from the crowd.

The king held onto her wrist with one hand, while his other used the knife to cut open Bronadyr's hand.

Ember's heart tried to beat out of her chest. The stone pulsed gently, soothing her. And the king pressed their hands together, palm to palm, blood dripping down her arm as her wide sleeve fell away. *So that's why the sleeves are like that*, she wondered numbly as the Beast clasped her palm in his.

Her heart beat against her palm. His blood pulsed in time with her own. Ember found her gaze dragged up, over that jewelled breastplate, over the tusks and snarl, to the shadowed aperture above.

Eyes gleamed out at her from the darkness. The great horned head inclined in a brief nod.

Their joined hands gave a throb that shook Ember's whole body.

'It is done,' said the king in satisfaction. 'May the Tree protect and shelter your union.'

Ember stared at those dark eye sockets, dread filling her as she realised she was bound to the Beast by more than words.

CHAPTER 13

'Hands over cocks, fellas, I'm coming in.'

The barracks fell silent at that, as she'd expected it to. It was a large, low-ceilinged room, lit by a few lamps and a large cosy fire, which did nothing to dispel the odour of sweat, farts and feet that suddenly reminded Ember of her little brothers.

The men sitting at trestle tables, eating and drinking and laughing, all turned to stare at her. Ember glared at them, rage throbbing in her. They might not recognise her as the Promised One, not in the practical dark clothing Rhaell had sent up for her, but she clearly didn't belong here.

'Ma'am?' said a man in slightly shinier armour than the rest, rising to his feet.

Ember ignored him and looked around. At the back of the room were various curtained alcoves holding large tubs. Most were empty, but one had the flicker of lamplight around the edges.

'You know who I'm looking for.'

The man who'd stood said nothing, but too many other pairs of eyes flickered towards the curtained alcove at the back.

'He's back there? Oi! Buttercup! I'm coming in.'

'No—' said someone, but Ember was fast and light on her feet, and she got to the curtain before anyone could stop her, fury propelling her forward.

'Don't you dare bloody hide from me! You knew, you evil rat bastard, you— Oh.'

The bathing alcove was lit only by a werelight, but it was enough. Enough for her to see Rhaell standing by the tub, skin gleaming wetly in the dim light, dressed only in a pair of trousers he hadn't fastened. Blood and dirt streaked his torso, grime clumped his hair into dark strands, and his blue eyes glowed angrily at her as he turned away.

Dear Lords and all their little angels. His muscles shone, bunching and flexing as he turned away from her. He looked like some sort of primal god, fresh from battle. Like he only needed to crook his finger at her and she'd go to her knees before him.

'Fuck's sake,' he snarled, turning away from her. 'You don't knock in the Iron World?'

Ember opened her mouth to make some retort about there only being a curtain, but right then the light fell on his back and all her words deserted her.

Somebody – some *thing* – had gouged two deep lines in his back: massive, ragged canyons in the bone and muscle that ran either side of his spine. Around them, the tattered remains of intricate tattoos remained, hacked and defaced in a seemingly deliberate manner. The scars were old, the skin well-healed, but the agony they must have caused stole her breath.

'What happened?' she breathed.

'Mantises,' he grunted, slapping a cloth into the tub and scrubbing at himself with it. 'Look, fuck off, will you, and let me bathe?'

Ember managed a small noise of agreement and stepped to the other side of the curtain. 'Are you all right?' she asked through it, not quite willing to face the rest of the barracks.

'Fine. What do you want?'

What had made those scars? Mantises? She must have misheard. He looked like someone had hacked at him with an axe. Ember's fingers curled in sympathy, and then she grimaced, and remembered why she'd come here.

'When were you going to tell me?'

'Tell you what?'

Ember stuck her bandaged hand through the curtain. 'That this engagement is a fucking *blood oath*?'

Water splashed. 'You don't do that where you're from?'

'No! We wear *rings*, you lunatic.'

'Rings? Forged into place, you mean?'

'What? No!'

'So you can just ... take them off?'

'Yes!'

'What's the point of that? Look—' Rhaell shoved back the curtain and glowered down at her. His hair was wet, and his shirt clung damply and quite lovingly to his muscles. Damn him, even surly and grim he was bloody gorgeous. 'Maybe we could talk about this somewhere less ... full of people.'

Ember glanced back. Everyone in the barracks was pretending, badly, to ignore them.

'Fine.'

He grabbed a cup of ale, didn't offer her one, and led her across the courtyard to a bench where at least there was no one else around to overhear. The night air settled around them, cool and clear, and if Rhaell was cold in his damp clothes he didn't seem to mind.

He looked her over, in the clothes he'd sent up for her. Ember had to admit they were practical for sneaking out of her rooms. 'Enjoy your engagement feast?'

She glowered at him. 'The king was drunk and the prince fucked off immediately after the bargain was sealed.'

Rhaell saluted her with his beer and drank some. Ember waved her bandaged hand at him.

'Why didn't you tell me someone was going to slice me open with a bloody knife?'

He shrugged. 'It never occurred to me. That's just how we do it.' He drank some more beer, sighed, and admitted, 'Usually it's just a fingerprick though.'

The bastard was grinning. 'Usually?' she gritted.

'Well. Yes. But things are always ... bigger at court.'

Ember snorted. 'Oh yes, I hear there are no small pricks in the royal family.' She picked at the bandage. 'What happens if I break the engagement?'

'Oh, the sky will probably fall in or something. Don't worry about it,' he added, when she looked alarmed. 'Nothing will really happen. Especially because you won't be here, will you?'

That was a good point. 'Phoebe's packing for the progress.'

He nodded. 'And our first stop is Addor. Which is important because...'

He glanced around and made a small motion with his hand that seemed to deaden the sound coming in around them. Another of his little tricks.

'Because?'

Rhaell lowered his voice anyway. 'Wynric's Stone. The stone of wisdom. According to the ancient scroll, it was given to the dragons.'

'I thought you said there weren't any dragons? I mean, apart from the tiny ones, like Lady Sarea has.'

'Just like the one Lady Sarea has.' He was so casual, but the idea of dragons still thrilled her. 'You know he was a gift from her husband, on their marriage? Because the symbol of Addor is the dragon.'

'So ... you think Wynric's Stone is in Addor?'

Rhaell nodded. 'Which will be first on the list of destinations on the king's Progress. Quite probably they will be decked out in all their finery for the state visit. We should be able to see if Wynric's Stone is part of their regalia.'

'And if it isn't?'

Rhaell grinned at her. 'Then I guess we go snooping.'

Snooping, Ember thought three days later. *He thinks we can go snooping when there's this many people about.*

It appeared that when the king moved, the whole court moved. Many of the actual courtiers stayed in Yskara, but the sheer number of servants and baggage trains required for a few dozen guests utterly astounded Ember.

I wonder what they did when they had proper magic.

They travelled by ship to begin with, a method of transport Ember had grave misgivings about. Sure, the Clockwork City was at the convergence of three rivers, but those rivers had bridges over them. You walked, or if you could afford it, took a carriage across the water. Boats were something Ember had seen from a distance and had no wish to encounter.

The king's royal barge was, admittedly, very fancy. It had a giant sail and banks of oars, but they appeared to be mostly for show. As Ember stood at the rail with her ladies, trying not to look down at the water, Eletha said, 'Look, Your Grace, the seahorses.'

'I love seahorses,' said Thalissa. 'We don't have them in Sehari.'

'Seahorses?' said Ember, slightly puzzled. She'd seen seahorses in picture books as a child, and once in an aquarium in some rich banker's house. Tiny things, smaller than her finger.

She smiled to herself. That rich banker had bragged about how he'd hidden jewels in the bottom of his aquarium, amongst the rocks. It hadn't taken Ember very long at all to scoop out a handful of them. She wondered if he'd even noticed yet.

Then something swam under the water near the ship, a large

shape that had her recoiling from the rail. A hafmey? That giant creature that had eaten the hafmey?

Her knuckles were white on the ship's polished railing as the creatures broke the surface – and then suddenly she was laughing.

'They're ... actual horses!'

As she looked closer, she could see that beneath the water, the horses had flippers instead of legs, and their sleek bodies were hairless. Each of them swam towards what Ember had taken for an oar, but which seemed to have a sort of halter under the water.

And when a few dozen of them had affixed themselves to the ship, it began to move.

Ember watched them for a while, their heads just barely above the water, and then she gazed at the scenery a while. The cliffs upon which the castle stood receded, until the shore was lined with low hills and green woods. Every now and then a settlement appeared, a cluster of pink and white cottages with small boats bobbing at the tide. People came out and waved at them, and Ember waved back, bemused.

There were no children with the waving villagers.

After a while, as she was getting bored, Phoebe appeared and bobbed a curtsey that bordered on insolent.

'Your Grace,' she said, which wasn't what she called her behind closed doors. 'I wonder if perhaps there might be time for that fitting we talked about?'

They had talked about no fitting, although the previous three days had mostly involved trying on clothes while Ember attempted to learn the names of the people they were going to visit. But Phoebe had a knowing look in her eyes, so she nodded and excused herself to the ladies.

'Is there really a fitting?' she asked, as they went inside. The salon was luxuriously appointed, with low benches and tables, food set out everywhere. Phoebe led her down a steep set of stairs with a rope handrail, and along a narrow corridor lined with polished wood.

'There's always something to be fitted,' sighed her maid, opening a door. 'However...'

Ember had never been in a ship's cabin before and had never really thought about what a luxury one would look like. She supposed the small bed and the rich hangings were probably standard, but that they probably usually didn't contain a large, handsome man poring over a scroll.

Her heart beat a little faster. 'Are you in my room or am I in yours?' she asked.

Rhaell looked up. 'I'm in yours,' he said. 'Don't worry, I'm very discreet.'

The scar on Ember's palm gave a throb.

'Something I can help you with?'

'Yes.' He opened a leather pouch, and out spilled a few dozen yellow gemstones.

'Ooh,' breathed Ember, and Phoebe shook her head.

'Last time I saw that expression on anyone's face, the court was hosting an orgy,' she said.

'Don't get too excited,' said Rhaell, as Ember blinked at her maid. 'They're all fakes.'

Ember found herself gazing at his full, firm lips and wondering how they might be employed in an orgiastic setting. 'I doubt that,' she murmured.

There was a short silence. Ember felt her face burn.

'Phoebe,' sighed Rhaell.

She threw up her hands. 'I'll do some sewing.'

'We don't need a chaperone.'

'Did I say I was going to do it here?' She gathered an armful of clothing. 'I don't want to be party to whatever you're planning. When they come to put your head on the block, I shall disavow all knowledge of your activities.'

'Your compassion knows no beginning,' murmured Rhaell, and she clucked her tongue at him and left.

The cabin really wasn't that large, and Rhaell really, well, was.

He had on a sleeveless leather doublet and a shirt of fine linen that did little to disguise the muscles beneath. His dark hair fell loose to his shoulders, and when he looked up at her there was an adorable wrinkle between his brows.

Suddenly the small cabin bed seemed to loom large in the edge of her vision.

Don't think about orgies. Don't think about his lips. Or his biceps. Or what that hair might feel like if you grabbed at it in ecstasy.

On his back were those two long scars. Deep, jagged, and clearly completely horrific. It was very, very wrong of Ember to wonder what their texture would feel like as she clutched his back and screamed his name—

'The stones,' Rhaell said.

And around the jagged craters had been tattoos, intricate and intriguing, disfigured by the scars. She wanted to learn them with her fingers. 'Mm-hmm?'

He stood up and gestured her to the only chair, which she took reluctantly. It was warm, and in the small cabin there was nowhere else for him to go but to loom over her.

'I had an artificer make these to the best parameters I was able to give her,' he said. 'There aren't many illustrations of the stones, as you might imagine – at least, not the ones whose whereabouts are unknown. So we have a variety of shapes and shades. When we find Wynric's Stone, you'll have to switch it out for the closest match.'

Ember frowned. 'What if there isn't one?'

'That's why I said closest.'

She poked at the stones, all roughly the same trapezoid shape. They ranged in shade from a light buttery yellow to a dark shade she could best describe as 'beer piss'.

'What if it's in a setting? A crown or necklace or something?'

Rhaell looked nonplussed. 'What do you usually do in that case?'

'I nick the whole thing. I'm guessing that ain't an option here?'

He sighed. 'No. Can't you ... prise it out?'

Ember raised her eyebrows. 'What am I, a jeweller?' She picked up the nearest stone. 'You get me any tools?'

Rhaell nodded and handed her a velvet roll. Inside it were various slender picks and pliers; the sort of thing a jeweller might use. She supposed she could try, at any rate.

'What about the other stones?'

Rhaell leaned against the edge of the bed, which was not helpful for Ember's libido. 'Well, one of them I'm pretty sure went to the Myr. I have a contact there, who said their Speaker has it in their regalia.'

'Speaker?'

'My understanding is this is their current leader. The one who speaks for them.'

'They don't have a king?'

'No.' He looked puzzled. 'She said they ... choose the Speaker?'

'Democracy. Nice. Didn't know you lot had heard of the concept.'

She watched him try the word out a few times, then look at her helplessly.

Ember rolled her eyes. 'It's this radical concept where the people get to decide who's gonna be their leader, and what they're allowed to do. O'course, in practice this means it's mostly men who get to do the voting, and men who get to do the leading, but it's better than the alternative.'

'What, having a king?'

She nodded. 'Our last king was so inbred he had six toes and no chin and married his sister. Spent his final days running round the palace talking to cushions.'

'Could his advisors not run the country for you?'

She gave him a sharp look. 'Advisors the mad king had chosen himself? Advisors who had no problem with him making laws that everyone had to wear green on a Tuesday, or that names containing the letter B were illegal?'

Rhaell smiled. His eyes crinkled very attractively when he did that. 'That doesn't sound too bad.'

'It's swell if your name is Ember. He also endorsed child sacrifice, locked his wife in a metal chastity belt, and had his enemies flayed alive and eaten by foxes.'

'Ah.'

'Yeah. So we had a revolution and cut his head off. They say it was a mercy.'

Rhaell looked as if she'd just told him she'd eaten the moon. *One of the moons. Lords.* 'You ... cut off the king's head?'

'Well, not me personally. It happened a couple of hundred years ago. Generally speaking these days we elect our madmen. At least we can vote them out after a few years. Well, I say "we"...' Ember pointed to herself.

'Only the men?'

'Yeah. Apparently women aren't to be trusted.'

Rhaell looked down at her, and right then Ember didn't think she could be trusted, either. His thigh was really very close to her arm. She could reach out and touch it, if she wanted. See if it was as firm as it looked. See what would happen if she slid her hand up, just a little bit, let her fingers explore what was under that dark leather because from here it looked like he'd got quite a lot to be proud of...

Rhaell cleared his throat and straightened up. 'The, ah, the other stones,' he began, and Ember tore her gaze away from his crotch. The scar on her palm throbbed again.

'Yeah. Stones,' she said. 'Uh-huh. Tell me all about them.'

He leaned forward, over the side of the desk, and Ember tried not to whimper. He was right there, the heat rising from his skin through that thin shirt, his hair falling over his face, and oh dear Lords he even smelled good. Like bitter oranges. She wanted to lick him.

'The Healing Stone, Gaeleath's Stone, is the one with the Myr.

We can probably slip away while we're visiting Valoris for that. Neris is expecting us in a week or so.'

'Neris being your Myr friend?'

He made a so-so noise. 'She's not my friend. The Myr aren't anyone's friend. Remember that.'

'Sure. Chock-full of enemies, me. No friends at all.' She was babbling. Rhaell was very distracting.

He glanced sideways at her. 'You have your ladies.' Ember rolled her eyes, and he grinned. 'You have Phoebe.'

She considered this. She liked Phoebe, but then the woman was her servant, and Ember didn't know how to feel about that.

'You have me,' Rhaell said gently, and Ember looked up to see him giving her a soft smile that had her rising out of her seat, reaching for him—

The door opened, and Phoebe said, 'I'm not here, I'm not listening, I just need that bodice to trim. Lalala ... can't hear you.'

Ember thumped back in her seat. This was going to be a long voyage.

~

As it happened, they were at sea for less than a day, and on arrival at the small port at the northern end of the Sacred Sea, there were carriages waiting for them. Night had fallen, and the air had the bite of frost in it.

Exhausted from the early start and long day of not jumping Rhaell's bones, Ember yawned as she followed her ladies from the royal barge. The torchlit docks were already busy with people unloading crates and trunks. Her gaze fell on a nearby vessel, its shape hulking in the darkness.

'Is that a military ship?' she asked, eyeing the metal plating and the massive harpoons glinting along its bow.

'No, it's a supply ship,' said Eletha. 'For Bronavon Point. All the ships heading north from here look like that.'

'Why?'

'Because of the Rakaa,' she said, as if this was obvious, and bundled Ember into a waiting coach. It was comfortable and spacious, and Ember knew she'd be asleep before long, especially when Eletha tucked a warming blanket over her knees.

'What's the Rakaa?'

The ladies exchanged glances.

'A barbarian people, from the mountains,' said Caeda.

'Don't worry, they rarely come down this far,' said Lyndis.

A barbarian people who necessitated the use of armoured ships? 'Rarely?'

'Never,' said Eletha firmly. 'I've never seen one, and I'm from Addor.'

'Yes, but you were fostered in Yskara from the age of five,' pointed out Lyndis.

'The Rakaa aren't dangerous,' said Thalissa, soothingly. 'Yskara beat them very thoroughly in the war. There's hardly any left.'

'What war?' yawned Ember.

'It was years before we were even born,' Zentha said. 'It's not important. Eletha, how far is it to Kasteladdor?'

Ember let their chatter wash over her and dozed. She was woken some time later, as the carriages rattled towards a fortress, and her ladies fussed over her hair and the wrinkles in her dress.

The castle in Yskara was undoubtedly highly defensible, but Kasteladdor really wanted you to know it was a war fortress. They approached over a high mountain pass, which tapered into a somewhat terrifying drawbridge over a gorge, complete with a series of portcullises. The castle bristled with battlements and arrow slits, and once they were inside the courtyard the bleak grey stone of the keep was hardly any more welcoming. *Bluestone dolerite, rugged but not impossible to climb.* The windows were high and narrow, the walls pitted as if they'd withstood a siege. It was vast, and the door was halfway up, accessible only by a wooden staircase. They really weren't kidding about this place.

At the top of the stairs stood Lord Addor and Lady Sarea, her dragon curled around her shoulders. He wore ceremonial armour and she sported a fur cape with armoured shoulders. Ember peered blearily at them, but no yellow jewels shone at her.

Eletha gave Ember a brave smile as the carriage halted. 'Welcome to Addor, Your Grace.'

~

The dead peryton swung, upside down and bloody, from the poles slung between the shoulders of two Addoran soldiers, its antlers occasionally dragging in the mud.

'Careful with that!' shouted the king, riding alongside, as smug as if he'd shot the beast himself. 'Those antlers will go on the wall at the castle.'

The soldiers hoisted the beast higher. Its rain-bedraggled wings had been bound to its body so they didn't get trampled. They'd go on the wall, too. No doubt with a plaque beneath to boast of the king's achievement.

Ah yes, the great achievement of watching as one of his marksmen shot the poor bastard down. Rhaell felt sour today, and not just because he'd been up since the crack of doom, organising the hunting party.

He'd been up all night, thinking about Ember.

He couldn't have her, and that was the end of it. At least, that should've been the end of it, but now he kept thinking about how close she'd been to him in that little cabin, and how her breasts had risen and fallen above the neckline of her dress, and how she smelled of crushed petals from the bathing chamber, and how she'd looked up at him with those big brown eyes and he'd wanted to – to—

He swiped the rain from his face. There was no point in thinking about what he wanted to do with her. He couldn't have her. And even if he could, she was probably leaving forever in a month or so.

And even if she wasn't, the memory of her face when she'd seen his back was imprinted on him forever.

She'd come out after breakfast with the other ladies, to wish the men well on the hunt. He'd watched Eletha and Lyndis and the others all giggle as they handed over favours to the gentlemen mounted on horseback, and eyed Ember as she stood, eyes narrowed, clearly unwilling to participate despite the silken scarf Phoebe handed her.

'A favour for your fiancé!' bellowed the king, and he saw Ember wince, clear across the courtyard. 'Well, boy, don't leave her waiting – take it, and don't forget to return it in person later!'

It had been awkward, the way she handed it over. Bronadyr's steed was the largest in the Kasteladdor stables, and even if Ember had held it high above her own head, she'd have been unable to reach more than the prince's knee. Not that she did. She held it out, flat ahead of herself, not looking at him, until he took it and tied it to his own saddle.

Rhaell found it trampled into the mud some time later, the little embroidered leaves and vines stained forever.

He avoided her for the rest of the day, which wasn't hard as the Addors had definite ideas about activities that were suitable for men and suitable for women. He couldn't imagine her particularly enjoying embroidery, but she might have some fun touring the castle. The Addors had plenty of impressive jewels. Rhaell found he wouldn't begrudge her stealing some.

Especially if she stole the right one.

He ate with the soldiers that evening and was just preparing to go out to the training yard, when a hand grabbed him and dragged him into a side chamber.

Ember stood glaring up at him, foot tapping, arms folded.

'Um?' said Rhaell.

'Ember,' she supplied. 'My name is Ember. I know it's been a while.'

He rubbed a hand over his face and grimaced. 'I've been busy.'

'So I heard. Hunting, was it?' Her tone was as sharp as her face. 'Deer? Grouse? Women?'

She sounded jealous. Rhaell filed that away for later. 'Have you found anything?'

Ember folded her arms. 'You mean jewels? Oh yeah, fucking hundreds. They're rolling in them. I had the full tour today. You know they've got a jewel tower? Imagine having so many jewels you've got a whole tower for them.'

Castle Yskar had vast rooms full of them. Rhaell knew because he'd searched them for the Heart Stones.

'And no yellow ones?'

'No. And I figure I'd know, right? I mean, this,' she slapped her chest, thankfully concealed by her dress, 'reacted to the King's Stone, so—'

'Wait, what?'

She looked surprised. 'Yeah. It sort of ... pulsed. Like a heart, I suppose. It felt like it glowed, but if it had, you'd have seen it. Oh no, wait, you wouldn't've, because you weren't even there.'

Rhaell sighed and leaned against a small table nearby.

'It's fine, I was just sealing a blood oath to a monster,' Ember said.

'I told you, it's just symbolic.'

'Oh yeah? Why's it throb when I ... er, sometimes?'

He shrugged. 'Because it's a cut on your palm? Get Phoebe to heal it. It doesn't have to stay. Listen, is there anywhere you haven't looked yet?'

She scowled. 'I mean, there's a whole castle. But I figure, you've got a jewel tower, you're gonna keep your jewels in it, right? Either that or your personal rooms.'

'You want to break into Lord and Lady Addor's rooms?'

She sighed. 'If I can't find it in the tower, yeah. Look, I'm gonna need your help. I'm used to breaking into places where people rely on nice complicated locks for their security. Maybe one or two nightwatchmen who are usually asleep, or dogs – and I've never yet met a dog who'll say no to a sausage, even one laced with sleeping pills. But this place? It's crawling with people, and those people have pikes. And if I get caught, what excuse am I gonna have?'

'How can I help?' said Rhaell.

She lifted her chin, as if she didn't like what she had to say next. 'Well, there's one old trick that rarely fails, if you're caught somewhere you shouldn't be.'

'What's that?'

Ember looked down for a moment, then met his eyes. 'You fake fucking in a corner, of course. A man, a woman – nobody's going to look too closely at our faces. You dress as a guard, I'll nick Phoebe's cap, people'll just think we're hooking up.'

Rhaell felt the heat rush into his face, and abruptly looked away from Ember in her low-cut evening dress. 'That actually works?' he said.

'Would you stop and ask two people with their pants around their ankles what they're doing?'

'Well, now you've told me, yes!'

She gave him a knowing look. 'Sure you will. Look, come and get me, oh ... in an hour. Phoebe's got a bed in the dressing room, so don't knock too loudly. Okay?'

Rhaell pinched his nose. 'Okay,' he agreed reluctantly.

She nodded and slipped out of the alcove. Rhaell shook his head and felt in his pocket for a sootweed.

His hand touched something soft and slightly damp. Dammit. 'Ember?'

He hissed her name softly, but she heard and turned back.

He held out the embroidered scarf, now black with mud, and she frowned for a moment before she recognised it. Then he saw the hurt cross her face, and his heart broke a little.

She lifted her chin. 'I see it meant as much to him as it did to me,' she said. 'Keep it. I'll see you later.'

~

The tap came on her door not long after Phoebe had retired to her pallet in the dressing room, pleading a stomachache. Ember felt slightly bad about that, but she just hadn't been able to stop herself borrowing a handful of herbs from the stillroom on Lady Sarea's tour earlier. It was all the better that Phoebe didn't know what she was up to.

She'd dressed in the jerkin and trousers Rhaell had found for her, the boots pleasingly quiet on the flagstone floors. Over this she'd put one of Phoebe's caps and a dark cloak. It wasn't bad, as disguises went. Hell, she'd got out of Castle Yskar this way.

People had only seen the Promised One dressed up in silks and hairpieces with her face painted. Plain Ember Hart was very forgettable.

A familiar feeling warmed her as she waited for Rhaell. This was what she knew, what she was good at. *You can do it, little ferret.* She wasn't a princess, wasn't a Promised One, wasn't going to save anything for anyone. But this – sneaking into places she shouldn't be and taking things that weren't hers – this, she'd been born to do.

Rhaell looked her over as she opened the door.

'I thought you'd be wearing a dress,' was all he said.

'This is more practical.'

His gaze lingered on her legs for a moment. Ember wasn't sure why; the ladies of the court often wore gowns slit to the thigh, so it wasn't as if he was expecting her to be solid below the waist.

'Fine,' he said. 'Let's go.'

His stride was long, and she had to hurry to keep up. As they left the wide, well-lit corridor, past Lady Sarea's rooms, Rhaell curved his hand around the air and a ball of light appeared in it.

'That,' she said. 'How do you do that?'

He looked surprised. 'This? It's just a werelight.'

She studied the floating ball. It was similar to the ones that bobbed in lanterns around Kasteladdor and Yskara, too, but they didn't seem to move, and she'd never actually seen them lit. 'Can anyone do it?'

'Pretty much, yeah.'

'I can't.'

He gave her a sideways look. 'Have you tried?'

Ember said, 'We don't have magic where I come from, remember?'

'And are we where you come from, now?'

She opened her mouth to say it didn't work like that, then realised she'd got no idea how it did work.

'So how d'you do it?' She curved her hand in the air, and absolutely nothing happened.

He cocked his head. 'How did you open the portal?'

Ember felt herself flush, and she didn't know why; it wasn't as if she'd been forbidden to do it. 'I, er ... just told it where I wanted to go.'

'Well, then,' said Rhaell.

She gave him an enquiring look.

'It's just a ... minor force of will. Just tell the light to exist.'

Ember thought that was a terrible way of putting it, but she curved her hand and thought about a light being there, and when one actually appeared, she stumbled and had to grab his arm.

'What the fuck?' *That's a very nice firm arm.*

Rhaell seemed pleased. 'You see? It's got nothing to do with where you're from.'

'No. Shit.'

She extinguished the light the same way, then lit it again, and kept doing it over and over until Rhaell told her he was getting a headache.

'Besides, we're nearly there,' he said.

The jewel tower was not particularly remote but could only be accessed via a wooden bridge across the rooftops. 'So if the castle is breached, the bridge can be burned,' Rhaell explained.

'Well, that's dumb. Then you just blow up the tower,' she said.

'And the jewels with it?'

Ember shrugged. 'Nah. Jewels are resistant. S'why they're mined with dynamite.'

'Dyna—?'

'Never mind.'

There was a guard at the entrance to the bridge. He looked bored, half asleep, but he straightened when they approached.

'Are you lost?'

Ember giggled and laid a hand on Rhaell's arm. 'No,' she said. 'We were just looking for somewhere ... quiet.'

The guard grinned knowingly. 'Ah. Nowhere around here like that,' he said. 'But if you go back a bit and to the stairs on the left, there's a bit under there you can use. So long as you're quiet.'

Ember had one hand in her pocket. Phoebe's herbs weren't the only thing she'd lifted from the stillroom this afternoon.

'Is that so?' she said. She left Rhaell and sauntered over to the guard. He was young and lanky, and his eyes went right to her breasts when she thrust them out deliberately. 'You seem to know your way around the, ah, nooks and crannies,' she crooned.

He swallowed. 'Well, I've, er, tried some out,' he said.

'Really? You want to...' Ember let her fingers walk up his arm, 'try some out with us?' She glanced back at Rhaell, whose face was like granite. 'Honey? What do you think? Been ages since we had a third.'

His throat worked for a moment, then he said, 'If it's what you want.'

Ember bit her lip and smiled at the guard, whose eyes had gone very big. She caressed his neck, and then her hand slipped to his mouth and pressed a cloth over it. His eyes closed, and he sank to the ground.

Ember caught him as he slid down the wall, easing him quietly to the stone floor. Behind her, Rhaell blew out a breath.

'For a minute there I thought you were serious.'

She winked at him. 'Who says I wasn't, Buttercup? Come on, let's get him to that stairwell.'

'What if he remembers?' said Rhaell, hefting the younger man as if he weighed nothing. Ember took a moment to admire the bulge of his biceps.

'What, being propositioned for a threesome? I'd be insulted if he didn't,' Ember said, and as they deposited the guard under the curve of the stairs – he was right, it was quite secluded down there – she twitched his tabard aside and unlaced his trousers.

'What are you doing?' Rhaell hissed.

'Authenticity,' she hissed back, shoving the guard's hand into his nether regions. 'He wakes up with his hand on his cock, he'll think he was fantasising about us, right – and drifted off after a crafty wank. Come on.'

Rhaell followed her, shaking his head. 'Have you done this before?'

Ember just smiled at him. Truth was, she'd done a lot more than just knock guards out before it got to the trousers-off stage, but he didn't need to know that.

The door to the bridge was locked, but it was a ridiculously simple old thing that barely necessitated a pick at all. She opened the door and gestured to Rhaell. 'After you.'

The wind bit at them on the bridge, high up above the roofs, and Ember was glad for her cloak. She hurried across to the door on the other side, which was also locked but not guarded.

'Weak security,' she sniffed, as they stepped inside.

'Professional opinion?'

She gave him a cold look. 'Yes.'

Rhaell looked like he wanted to say something else, but didn't. Instead, he gestured to the cases and displays of jewels around them.

'It's not on display, or I'd have seen,' Ember said. 'There's gonna be stuff hidden away – the ugly shit, you know, inherited from mother-in-laws and all that...' She crouched down and began picking the lock of the nearest cabinet whose door was solid wood.

'Is Ruvaen's Stone reacting in the slightest?' Rhaell asked, and she shook her head, probing with the pick until she felt the lock give. It wasn't a sophisticated lock. Ember could have picked it when she was a small child.

She peered into the cabinet, gesturing her magic new light over to help. *This is gonna be so useful.* Jewels gleamed back at her, some of them in broken settings, some poor quality, some just very ugly. None of them were yellow.

'Ruvaen was the husband of Ysarriel, right? Who betrayed her with her bestie?'

'Best—? Yes.'

'Why'd he get a piece of the Heart, then? If he was in disgrace?'

Rhaell shrugged. 'Who says he was given it?'

'You mean he stole it?' said Ember, delighted. 'Ha! A fella after my own heart. You know,' she shuffled on her knees to the next cupboard, instead of getting up. 'At home we've got a High Lord called Ruven, and he's meant to be the patron of thieves. I'm not one for praying much, but I do leave an offering at his temple sometimes.'

When she looked up, Rhaell was frowning. 'What do you mean by High Lord?'

She shrugged. 'Uh, they're sort of like ... not gods exactly. More like ... saints? Or like ... folklore. Something like that. The old stories say they were unworldly beings, uncannily beautiful and magical; and when they came, humans were living in mud huts and shit, and they taught us stuff. How to be civilised.'

She sat back on her heels and looked up at Rhaell, uncannily beautiful, a werelight floating at his side.

'There was Ruven, the thief. He taught us how to lie and steal, but also how to dream and how to tell stories. Actors pray to him, too, not just thieves. And then there was Inric, the wise, who taught us language and mathematics and science and shit. And Gilia, who healed the sick.' She shrugged. 'Most people don't ... believe, exactly, in the High Lords and Ladies, but they don't ... not believe, either. They want to hedge their bets, I guess.'

Rhaell had gone still. 'How many of these ... lords...?'

Ember held his gaze. 'The High Lords and Ladies. Seven. Most cities have temples to all of them. There's loads of lesser ones, too, but seven High Lords and Ladies. D'you wanna know what the main one is called?'

He rubbed his scalp, something she'd noticed him doing when exasperated, and winced. 'Something like Ysarriel?'

'Sarel.' She tapped the stone at her breast. 'She's the lady of beginnings, births, of queens and power. S'why we call this sarel-stone. 'Cos people a long time ago, they only used the coarse stuff to burn on their fires, but it was completely necessary to life, d'you see? So they named it after the Highest Lady. And now we have sarel-oil, and sarelstone, and it powers basically everything. But it's still named after her.' She closed the last cabinet and clicked the lock. 'Think we can cross the Jewel Tower comprehensively off the list.'

She watched his face fall. 'No Stone?'

'No Stone.'

'Wrong place?'

'Wrong place. What did your scroll say?'

Rhaell blinked at her a few times. 'Uh, that ... it said, "The house of the dragon shall be the home of the Stone of Wisdom, those whom wise and honest Wynric does call his friends." But some of those words could be translated differently, I suppose—' Distracted, he broke off. 'Ember, are you saying my Ancestors are your gods?'

He seemed flabbergasted. Ember didn't know why. It was completely obvious to her that even now, with their magic hugely diminished, his people were vastly superior to her own. They could draw portals out of walls and make lights out of air and jump like bloody jackrabbits. They were tall and beautiful and elegant. They seemed like gods to Ember now, and she was a semi-sophisticated woman who knew how to engage a clickspring with a ratchet pawl.

'Yeah. Wacky, ain't it? I guess they visited a long time ago and must've seemed like gods to my muddy little clay people.'

'But – why?'

Ember looked up at the most beautiful man she'd ever seen in her life and blinked a few times. His pretend bafflement at his own gorgeousness was getting a little wearing. 'Cute,' she said. 'Now listen – Inric is sometimes portrayed with a snake. Could your word for dragon be anything like snake?'

He sagged against a display cabinet. 'Yeah. It could be serpent, or snake. That's where the name Addor comes from. And Wynric took a wife from this house. Where else could it be?'

Ember shrugged and got to her feet. 'I dunno. It's your world. Somewhere else with dragons. When he was around, the big dragons were real, right?'

'The Great Dragons? Well – yes, but they were dragons. Not friends.'

'Hey, I know plenty of women whose best friends are cats. Don't judge.' She glanced around the room, but they'd barely moved anything and there was no dust to disturb. 'We should probably get going before our friend wakes up. It ain't here.'

Rhaell met her gaze. 'So you'll have to search Lady Sarea's rooms?'

She nodded. 'Yeah. But I can't do that tonight. For one thing, she'll be in them.' A thought occurred. 'Unless you happen to know she has interests elsewhere?'

Rhaell coughed. 'Not that I know of.'

'Shame. Nah, I'm not going in when she or her dragon might be there. Tomorrow, during dinner maybe.'

'How will you slip away from dinner unnoticed? You're the guest of honour.'

She groaned. 'Don't remind me. I'll think of something. Come on, let's go.'

They made it back across the bridge without incident and had just locked the door behind them when footsteps sounded.

'Shit.'

They both looked around, but there were no exits until the stairwell where they'd left the guard. With any luck, he was still asleep and they could hide there.

Ember grabbed Rhaell's hand and ran, but the footsteps grew louder before they got there, and she had only a moment to mutter, 'Sorry,' before she pressed herself against the wall and whirled him into her arms.

Good *Lords* there was a lot of him. And all of it god-like. She grabbed his shoulders and hitched herself up, one leg over his hip, and dragged his head down to hers.

She wasn't sorry *at all*.

'Mmm,' she moaned, pressing her face against his neck. He smelled like bitter oranges. 'Mmm yeah, just like that.' Into his ear, she hissed, 'Move, for fuck's sake, we're supposed to be fucking!'

His every muscle was rock hard, and at her words only seemed to get tenser. He thrust his hips against hers, somewhat unconvincingly, and put one hand on her shoulder.

The blue eyes looking down at her were somewhat incredulous.

'Oh, yeah,' Ember moaned, as the footsteps got a bit closer, and stopped. 'Uh – uh, yeah—'

There was a sort of squeak behind them, and a woman's voice gasping, 'I'm sorry!'

Rhaell growled over his shoulder, 'Fuck off. We don't need an audience.'

That was a dark and dangerous growl, and it reached right

inside Ember to her basic hindbrain. *This is a predator. In a really good way.*

She didn't have to fake her shiver. 'Sure about that, lover?'

This time when his eyes met hers, they were absolutely molten. The blue of flames, of lava, of sarel that burned so hot it consumed everything around it. Ember gazed at them, helpless, and her body gave such a powerful throb her legs tightened around his waist.

Suddenly this wasn't pretend anymore.

'We already tired out the guard. Want a bit of soft, too?' he rumbled.

Ember whimpered helplessly, her fingers curling in his collar. His skin was hot, the nape of his neck smooth and inviting. She couldn't stop touching him.

The girl squeaked again. 'I'm sorry! I got lost! I'll leave you alone!' and her footsteps hurriedly receded.

Ember barely noticed. Rhaell continued rocking his hips against her, and his gaze was so intense she actually moaned for real. Her fingers dug into his back, felt the indents of those scars that ran down his spine. She wanted him, more desperately than she'd ever wanted anything.

Rhaell was the sort of gorgeous Ember had only ever dreamed of. Men like him didn't look at girls like her. But now she had him in her arms, his large, solid body bracing her against the wall, and her brain entirely stopped working. She hungered for him. She *needed* him.

Rhaell leaned down, face to the crook of her neck, and inhaled. He shuddered. Ember arched her body against his, against all that hardness, and grabbed him by the chin to fit her mouth to his.

He drew back, abruptly straightening.

'I think that worked,' he said.

Ember gazed up at him, her breath coming in little pants, her legs clenched tight around his waist. 'It worked, all right,' she whispered.

Rhaell cleared his throat and moved his head back, taking his hands from her shoulders. Ember tried to chase his warmth, but he was withdrawing from her, stepping way, gently untangling her legs from where she'd twined herself around him like a weed.

She grasped the rough wall behind her and stumbled, legs weak. She throbbed and ached for him, panting and whimpering with frustration.

No, you can't leave me like this, I need your body. I need it hard and fast and deep.

Rhaell turned away, quite as if they'd been having an entirely ordinary conversation. 'Come on. Back to your room before Phoebe notices you're missing.'

And off he strode, while Ember failed to remember how to make words or take steps.

Somehow, pretending to have sex with Rhaell had been better than most of the actual sex she'd had.

Whimpering quietly, she stumbled after him. He didn't look at her as he led her back to her rooms. Didn't speak. Went out of his way not to touch her. Clearly, for him that had just been a performance, and the idea of actually fucking her was abhorrent. That doused her ardour pretty sharpish.

He opened the door for her, quietly, and said, 'Do you have a plan for tomorrow?'

Yes, tracking you down and shoving you into a corner and fucking your brains out. 'Eh?'

'For searching Sarea's rooms.'

'Oh.' Right now, Ember didn't have a plan for the next five minutes. Apart from dying of embarrassment. 'Uh, I'll ... um, think of something.' She looked up, straight into his rock-hard chest. 'Distracting. I mean – we need a distraction.'

He nodded, eyes sliding away from her as if she was covered in some kind of repellent. 'Distraction during dinner. I can do that.'

He stepped back and nodded, then turned away.

'Rhaell!' Ember blurted.

He paused, half turning but still not looking at her.

Please come back and touch me. 'Um. Thanks. And, uh, sorry. For the, um. Grinding.' Fuck, why did she say that? 'I, um – I mean the – you're a very good actor,' she babbled.

'So are you,' he replied. 'Goodnight.' And he walked away, leaving her hanging in the doorway, throbbing and fevered and desperately unsatisfied.

~

Rhaell ignored everyone in the barracks until he could shut the door behind himself and lean against it, eyes closed, chest heaving.

She'd been faking it. He knew she'd been faking it.

That didn't stop him being as hard as a fucking rock.

The scent of her skin lingered in his nose. He fumbled in his pocket for his sootweeds and lit one with shaking fingers. Thank the Tree his borrowed tunic covered his groin, and that it had been dark. Surely, she'd felt it? Grinding against him like that, by the *Tree*, he was only flesh and blood!

You can't have her. You know you can't have her.

His cock didn't give a fuck. It wanted to have Ember grinding against it again, hot and soft and moaning. By the Tree, the *moaning*! The way she'd looked at him, as if he was one of the pretty boys of the court and not a great scarred lump of gristle.

Her breath on his neck. Her fingers against his skin, the pads callused and rough and unspeakably erotic for it. The voluptuous warmth of her breasts, pillowed against his chest. Fuck. Fuck. He unfastened his trousers, desperate for relief.

A knock came against the door, and he froze. *Ember*.

'No,' he said, voice strangled.

'It's Brock, lad.'

Of course it wasn't her. 'Still no.'

'Are you all right?'

Absolutely not. He had a hard-on that was never going to go

down and now he knew what Ember felt like in his arms, pressed against him, warm and pneumatic, gasping in his ear—

You can't have her. She's going to marry the prince. She will never love you.

Rhaell sucked hard on his sootweed. 'Fine,' he rasped. 'Late night. See you tomorrow.'

He slapped his own face, nearly putting his own eye out with the burning cigarillo. He had to come up with a distraction for her to search Sarea's rooms. There were reports of mantises south of Kasteladdor; maybe he could organise a hunt and drag one of those to the castle. That'd be a distraction, all right.

He tried to think about mantises, their huge multi-faceted eyes and their snapping mandibles, their razor-like legs, the way they could slice a cow into meat and lay their eggs in its corpse.

It was no distraction at all.

∽

Ember didn't see Rhaell at all the next day, which was probably just as well. Someone said the prince had gone with the guards hunting mantises, which was a weird thing to do. Who hunted tiny insects?

Anyway, she was grateful to be spared his presence, especially after the torturous dreams that had left her sweaty and unfulfilled, moaning to such an extent that Phoebe had asked if she had nightmares. Oh no, the dreams had been very sweet. Very sweet indeed. And completely, utterly filthy.

She wasn't sure she'd be able to look at Rhaell even if she did see him.

He didn't want her. That should be the end of it. But her libido didn't care, constructing elaborate scenarios where she wasn't engaged to the prince and Rhaell wasn't a moody bastard oblivious to his effect on her.

She'd felt his physical interest. Man alive, had she felt it. He didn't find her completely repulsive. Was he just holding back because of the engagement? Maybe he had other reasons. Maybe whatever had made those scars on his back had scarred him on the inside, too.

Maybe she could kiss him better...

Lady Sarea had various cosy rooms set up for the visiting ladies to play music and do embroidery. Ember, whose sewing skills extended to excessively ugly darns and mismatched buttons, sat half watching them, planning her evening and trying not to think about the way Rhaell smelled like bitter oranges. She wanted to lick his neck. Stripe her tongue over the rough stubble, taste his sweat and moan into his ear, feel his hands tighten on her as she made him as desperate as he made her—

At dinner, she was seated with her ladies, while tumblers performed for their entertainment. There was no sign of the prince, who didn't seem to attend any of the formal meals. She heard the king telling Lady Sarea he had no interest in 'sophisticated entertainments, for which I'm perfectly grateful.'

No sign of Rhaell, either. Hopefully he was off creating a distraction. Ember needed to concentrate. She'd managed to come up with a plan, although she kept wandering off into a fantasy where Rhaell came with her and they got caught again and this time they had to take the ruse much further and ended up so desperate for each other they rutted behind a tapestry, hands over each other's mouths to stifle their moans...

Fuck's sake, Ember! Concentrate!

She'd just forked up something that might have been venison, and a bit of unknown vegetable, when the great doors to the hall were thrown open, letting in the spattering rain. A huge figure stood there, horns gleaming in the firelight, carrying the bloody, mauled remains of some hideous, alien creature Ember really did not want to look at.

Yep, that oughta do it, Ember thought to herself, and slipped away amid the screaming.

Her heart pounded with excitement and not, for the first time that day, inappropriate arousal. This part, the bit where nothing had gone wrong yet and her plans were still eminently executable, was her favourite. She was never afraid at the start of something like this. The possibilities were too exciting.

She lifted her long skirts and ran.

In a pouch at her waist, under her skirt, were the yellow stones Rhaell had shown her on the boat. She'd also slipped the velvet roll of tools and a knife onto her belt, which had made the skirt hang a bit weird, so she'd stood around with her hand on her hip all evening. Phoebe had frowned at how long Ember had taken in the privy when she'd fastened things in place, but she'd muttered something about rich food and travel sickness and planned to have another bout of it before she went to bed.

She knew where Lady Sarea's chambers were. Eletha had proudly pointed out that they were in the same wing, which was a great privilege, although whether it was a privilege for Ember or Lady Sarea wasn't clear. She made her way quickly there, ducking into dark corners whenever she heard someone coming. Slipped briefly into her room to shuck her heavy dress and pull a cloak on over her petticoat. There was no time to change properly. Then it was down the corridor to Sarea's chambers. She listened at the door and ducked inside.

And stood for a moment, blinking.

The banners of Addor were gold and red with a black dragon on them. Much of the décor of the castle – at least in the places where it had been decorated – followed a similar theme, with red drapes and gold sofas featuring prominently.

Lady Sarea's room was ... not in the same style.

The drapes and furnishings were green, with silver trim. The cushions were silver, embroidered with trees. The bedposts were carved into trees. The robe warming by the fire was green, with leaves embroidered all over it.

Lady Sarea was the king's cousin, and clearly in no mood to forget it.

Ember shook her head and started opening doors. There was some jewellery on a stand, but it wasn't what she was looking for.

This did not prevent it going into her pocket.

There were closets full of beautiful clothes. Ember felt at the back for hidden compartments and found nothing. Searched under the bed and the back of every drawer. Tugged at the paintings hanging on the wall – but found nothing on a convenient hinge.

She stood in the middle of the room, hands on hips, trying to think. Maybe there was another secret safe somewhere in the castle. In a study or library, or a hidden tower. Either way, there was nothing in this room.

She gave it a quick once-over to check she hadn't moved anything out of place – Ember was very, very good at this – and smoothed the rug with her foot before letting herself out.

Then she flattened herself against the door, because Eletha was coming down the hallway, and she was – shit, shit! – she was knocking at Ember's door.

'Your Grace? Are you all right? Your woman said you weren't well earlier.'

Ember tried to think quickly.

'I know it was horrible, him bringing the mantis in like that, but don't worry, it didn't kill anyone.'

Ember frowned. Mantis? That thing had been the size of a human.

'The guards have been out all day hunting them and they've burnt the nest. We're perfectly safe here. Your Grace?'

Then Eletha squeaked in alarm, because Ember had just pressed a knife to her neck.

'Now don't you make a sound,' she said, roughening her voice and keeping to a whisper. 'No one needs to get hurt.'

'I'll scream, and the guards—'

'Are out hunting mantises. Just tell me what I want to know, and I'll let you go, sweetheart.'

Eletha appeared to consider this. Ember pressed the knife in a little harder.

'What do you want to know?'

'Good girl. I'm looking for a stone. A jewel.'

'I – have this one,' Eletha began, hand going to the rock at her neck. It was a ruby, and quite a nice one. Ember very nearly took it, but what the fuck was she going to do with it? Eletha would tell everyone it had been stolen.

'No. A particular stone. Yellow. Shaped weird. Like a rectangle but narrower at the top.'

'Like a scholar's cap?'

Ember had no idea what that looked like. 'Sure, whatever. About the size of a tangerine.'

'A what?'

Fucking stupid place and its stupid food and stupid hats. 'Half the size of your fist. Do you know it?'

'No...'

Ember pressed the knife a little harder. 'Are you sure?'

'I'm sure! I've never seen a stone like that! But all the jewels are in the jewel tower—'

Eletha was Lady Sarea's niece, wasn't she? She'd lived in this castle. 'No, I'm sure there's somewhere else they're hidden.'

'They're not! They're all there! Apart from the ones Lady Sarea wants to wear on the day, they're in her room!'

'Where in her room?'

'I don't know, on the dresser?'

'No secret compartment? Is there a safe here?'

'Just the one in the steward's office, for the wages!'

A steward wouldn't have a precious stone in his safe. If it wasn't in the jewel tower and it wasn't in Lady Sarea's room, then it probably wasn't here at all. The purple stone at Ember's breast hadn't reacted to anything.

Rhaell had been wrong. Lords dammit.

'Right,' she said. 'Now, you go down the hall and run back to your friends, you hear me? You bring a single guard up here, I'll cut your pretty little throat. Run!'

Eletha ran.

Ember watched her for a moment. *Fine, just leave the Promised One in her room while there's an armed robber about.*

'Speaking of which,' she said out loud, and let herself into her room. She left the dress crumpled on the floor, stowed her tool belt in the bag of belongings she had forbidden Phoebe to investigate, and pulled out some of her hairpins as she crawled into bed. *Good job I ate supper.*

When Phoebe burst in ten minutes later, she was wielding a crossbow. She stuttered to a halt in the middle of the room.

'Ember? Ember! Are you— By the Tree, please don't be dead!'

Ember rubbed her face, blinking as if she'd just woken up. 'What? No. I'm not dead. Why would you think that? I just had a bit of a bad stomach, that's all. What you had, maybe. Must be catching. Came up for a lie down. Stop aiming that thing at me, would you?'

Phoebe panted, but she aimed the crossbow at the floor. 'On your own?'

'I wasn't aware I needed a chaperone.'

Phoebe blew out a breath. 'No. Of course not. But Eletha said there was a robber...' she said, pausing slightly on that last word.

'A robber? Did they steal anything?'

Phoebe narrowed her eyes at Ember. 'No. They were looking for a yellow stone.'

'Oh. Do I have any yellow stones?'

'With your colouring?' said Phoebe. She frowned at Ember. 'No. You don't.'

For a long moment, her maid stood looking at her, and Ember was absolutely certain Phoebe knew exactly what had been going on.

But then Phoebe flicked a catch on the crossbow, laid it down and went to pick up Ember's dress. 'I don't know anything about what's going on,' she said pointedly. 'It's easier that way. We'll be leaving after lunch tomorrow, down the Shadowmelt to Rivelor. Nothing much of interest there, but I'm sure they'll find some local sights to show you. Perhaps you'd like some more practical clothes?'

She said this with her arms full of cloth, pausing in the doorway to Ember's dressing room. And there was a note in her voice that said she knew exactly, *exactly*, what Ember would be wanting them for.

'Practical clothes are always welcome,' said Ember cautiously.

'Duly noted,' said Phoebe, and swept out.

CHAPTER 14

So, Addor was a bust.

Rhaell sat in his tiny cabin on the riverboat and reread the words he'd copied from the ancient scroll. '*The house of the dragon shall be the home of the Stone of Wisdom, those whom wise and honest Wynric does call his friends.*'

It had to be Addor. Where else could it be? But he'd been with Ember when she'd searched, and she had no reason to lie to him. She needed these stones as much as he did.

Unless Wynric actually had taken his stone to the actual dragons.

He lit a sootweed and inhaled deeply. The last anyone had heard of the great Dragons, they'd been in the Shadowed Mountains, and no right-minded person would go anywhere near those frozen peaks. Quite apart from anything, it was where the Rakaa had retreated to when Yskara had finally defeated them after centuries of warfare. Anyone looking like a human, walking into Rakaa territory, would be committing suicide.

He let his gaze slide to the section of his notes about the War Stone. Aywin, the warrior queen, had taken a red fragment of the Heart, and reputedly wore it until her death in battle.

'*Whereupon,*' the scroll said, '*the enemy stripped the armour from her corpse and forged it into a crown, and the Stone of War was placed at its centre.*'

That didn't sound too hard to find, except for the crucial fact that nobody really seemed to know in which battle Aywin had fallen. Her body had been returned to Yskara, and was interred below the castle, but the accounts of the time merely said she had fallen '*in valiant battle against the old enemy.*'

Yskara had been at war with pretty much everyone on the continent at some point in its long history. But there was one enemy they could never find peace with. One whose legacy was fearsome fortresses in the north, memorials in every town, and a bleak canyon where the bones of his father lay. The vicious barbarians, savage and cruel, who destroyed everything in their path when they made war for the fun of it. Yskara had fought them again and again, but still they came back.

The War Stone was with the Rakaa. Rhaell knew that, deep in his bones. And he knew how to retrieve it. But he'd have to leave that one for last because once he walked into Rakaa territory, the odds were good he wasn't walking back out again. Not without turning the peaks and valleys of the Shadowed Mountains red with blood.

Suicidal, indeed.

He tapped away the ash of his sootweed and tried to concentrate on the next part of their plan. Gaeleath's Stone; and then, if all went well, Mnorir's.

Gaeleath had taken their stone to the Myr, amongst whom they had lived for many years. Much of what Yskara knew about the Myr came from their notes: that the Myr could control other marine animals, including the hafmey; the Myr were amphibious to various degrees, depending on complex factors including heredity and caste; Myrish caste and clan systems were incredibly complex and led to near-constant wars; despite this, they all cast votes for their Speaker, who was meant to be apolitical and who served for life, or until they abdicated. An abdication process which, as far as Rhaell could tell, usually involved feeding themselves to sharks or being lowered into a pool of hungry flesh-eating thrask or walking into a raging bonfire.

Gaeleath's notes also included detailed pictures of the Speaker's regalia, helpfully including their blue stone which was set into a kind of chest harness. The Myr believed it to have healing properties, which kept the Speaker alive for years past their time, but Gaeleath had disputed this, claiming that true healing came only at the behest of the Sacred Waters that flowed from the Tree.

Neris had supplied the information that the Speaker never took the harness off, apart from when it needed repairing, which was fairly often due to the leather being repeatedly soaked. She seemed fairly confident she could manage to damage it enough for this to occur during the king's visit to Valoris, after which it was up to Ember and Rhaell how they stole it.

'Why are you helping us steal it?' Rhaell had asked, that first meeting in Merelle's establishment.

Neris shrugged. 'The whore said there was payment?'

'There is.' Generous payment. 'But isn't the stone important to your people?'

'It's just a stone. Your king has dozens. The Speaker won't even know it's gone.'

'You don't believe it has healing powers?'

Neris had snorted, a surprisingly eloquent gesture for someone with no proper nose. 'It's just a stone,' she repeated.

A stone that could heal the Tree and send Ember home. Not that he particularly wanted to send her home, but it was what *she* wanted. Rhaell would actually quite like it if she stuck around.

He shook his head and bent his head to the copy of the scroll. After they had Gaeleath's Stone there was still the question of the others.

Mnorir's Stone. He had, helpfully, taken it to 'death itself'. This, according to the scroll, was a journey Mnorir had undertaken in order to understand the true nature of death. He had encountered many fantastical animals and people along the way, along with things like mountains that breathed fire and seas that sang. Eventually he had travelled to the Land of the Dead, through a hole in the sea where the sun meets the darkness, where he had become the king.

The scroll was not very forthcoming on where this might be geographically located.

But there were stories, weren't there, of how to approach death itself? Old stories, the kind people called myths because they didn't want them to be true. That if you took a token of the dead – a bone, or a tooth, or something precious to the deceased – and cast it into the Dagrai Falls as they thundered into the Sacred Sea, the waters would part and Mnorir would invite you into his lair.

How to get out again, that was the trick; but if water was involved, Rhaell knew a Myr. He hoped Ember could swim.

He sighed and leaned back in his chair, which creaked. Everything on this boat creaked. It was apparently the finest vessel on the Shadowmelt, which really didn't speak well for the other craft on the river.

He knew he was rushing this. He needed a lot longer to read everything he could find in the library. Months. Years. Certainly more time than he'd had before they'd needed to leave for this damn progress. But he was rushing.

Because if he couldn't get the stones before Ember's marriage, she'd leave anyway. Ember was smart and resourceful, and she'd already escaped twice. She could be hidden anywhere on the continent and he'd never find her. Or the stone she wore.

He rubbed his face, and bent back to his notes.

∽

Rivelor was a small town with a local lord who was pleased as punch to be hosting a royal visit. Ember quite liked him, but the king was clearly unimpressed with his moated manor house and the country fair being held in their honour.

They stayed one night, then crossed the Shadowmelt Estuary to Valoris. Lyndis, who was the daughter of Lord Keenor of Valoris, spent most of the short crossing and subsequent carriage ride fretfully telling the other girls their clothes and hair and demeanour weren't fashionable in Valoris. She made several coded attempts to tell Ember the same, but since Ember thought all the clothes and hairstyles here were ridiculous, none of it landed.

Castle Keenor was a large, grand, sandstone edifice, clearly a lot newer than the ancient granite keep that had given it its name. It sat on a bluff over the Skipta River, and on that side was heavily fortified, which, Ember was informed, was necessary to keep the Myr out. Its lord was exactly the sort of man Ember would have expected Lyndis's father to be: well-groomed, handsome, and pompous. His wife was much the same, with a slightly more terrifying air of outdoorsiness.

Ember caught Phoebe's eye as they were being shown to their rooms. Her maid gave an enormous eye roll.

'Apple doesn't fall far from the tree,' Ember murmured, once the door was shut.

'The Tree doesn't have apples,' said Phoebe, frowning.

'No, it's a— Never mind. What are we supposed to do while we're here?'

Phoebe shrugged. 'There's a hunt.'

'And what will the ladies be doing?'

Phoebe acknowledged this with a wry smile. 'Oh, the Keenors are very progressive. The ladies are positively encouraged to hunt. Lady Keenor herself is responsible for many of the trophies on the wall and your own dear Lyndis is said to have quite the predatory instinct.'

'You surprise me,' said Ember, in the same tone. 'Am I expected to hunt? Please say no.'

'Alas, I should not lie to you,' said Phoebe, carefully unfolding Ember's gowns and shaking them out.

Ember threw herself at the large, canopied bed. 'But I don't know how to hunt! Does it involve riding a horse?'

'Unless you know how to ride a vyanka?'

Ember groaned. 'Unless a vyanka is a lusty man, then no.'

There was a short silence. 'It's a flying horse.'

'Still no.'

'It's fine,' said Phoebe. 'You sit on the horse, hold the reins, follow the others. Mill around for a bit and then say you're tired and want to come back. You're the Promised One. They'll have to let you. I'll tell Rhaell to make sure you have a nice placid horse.'

But Rhaell had different plans for Ember. He told her when he visited her room after supper.

'I've got plans for you tomorrow,' he said.

Ember sat still as Phoebe removed her fake hair and headdress all in one. 'Should you be here?'

'I was very discreet.' He looked excited, which was kind of adorable on him. 'Phoebe, could you give us a minute?'

She eyed them both, then shrugged. 'You two kids be careful,' she said, adjusting her hold on the massive, heavy headdress.

'Have you ever known me not to be careful?' Rhaell said.

'My darling, I have personally healed many of your wounds. Get the door for me?'

Rhaell did, and carefully shut it behind her. And then they were alone.

The last time Ember was alone with Rhaell, she'd been grinding her crotch against his rock-hard abs and panting after him like an animal in heat. The sense memory of his large, hard body pressing hers against the wall rushed back to her, stealing her breath.

She looked down at her dressing table to hide her flush. 'I heard Phoebe's mother was one of the princess's ladies-in-waiting,' she said, fidgeting in her uncomfortably stiff dress.

'She was,' said Rhaell.

'How did she end up a lady's maid?'

'It's a long story. And also, she is lady's maid to the future queen, so...'

Ember pulled a face and risked a glance at him through the mirror. Dammit. Still chiselled, blue-eyed and incredibly fuckable. 'Not if I help you get these stones. I assume that's what you're here about? Please tell me you have a plan to get me out of hunting tomorrow.'

He grinned. 'Well, yes, and also no.'

Ember groaned. She rolled her shoulders, then reached behind her back to the fastenings of her dress. But it wasn't designed to be removed by the wearer, and she could barely manage the first couple of buttons.

'There are reports,' said Rhaell, 'of a golden hind to the south.'

Ember met his gaze through the mirror and gave him a 'so what?' look.

'It's a great prize,' said Rhaell. 'They're very rare. Said to grant wishes. That is, if you don't slaughter them and mount their head on your wall.'

'Ugh,' said Ember, trying to twist to reach the buttons and being thwarted by a dress with all the give of a suit of armour.

'You don't hunt in the Clockwork City?'

'No, we buy our meat at markets like civilised people.'

'And where do the markets get their meat from?'

Ember gave up on the dress. 'Look, don't confuse me. What's the golden hind got to do with anything?'

Rhaell came towards her, and to her surprise, started undoing the buttons at the back of her dress.

Heat flashed through Ember with all the speed and devastation of an explosion in a sarel mine. His fingers brushed the nape of her neck, and for a moment there seemed to be no air at all in the room.

'Well, what better prize for the prince to present to his

betrothed? Perhaps she could even hunt with him. The sort of hunt,' Rhaell added casually, as if Ember wasn't fibrillating in front of him, 'that could take several days. In remote country. All alone.'

Well, that doused her ardour. 'You want me to spend several days alone with the Beast?'

'No, I want you to *say* you're going to spend several days alone with the Beast, and then bugger off to meet me.'

Whereupon we will fuck like bunnies. No. Ember frowned at his reflection. 'Won't he notice?'

'Probably not. You can always say you got separated. Pretend you hit your head or something. It really shouldn't take us more than a day or two to get Gaeleath's Stone, and then we can be back here, and everyone will think you've just been out hunting.'

His fingers grazed her upper back. The heat roared back, and this time it sucked all the warmth from her skin, prickling it with goose bumps and puckering her nipples. 'What if he comes back early?'

'He won't. A golden hind is too enticing a prize.'

'But what if he catches it really quickly?'

Rhaell laughed, a low sound that had Ember squirming in her seat as her thighs pressed helplessly together. 'That'll be hard, since I just invented it.'

For fuck's sake man, don't say 'hard' when you're touching me like that. She twisted to look at him. 'Seriously?'

He grinned at her. 'The whole court will be out looking for it. At least, enough of them that they won't notice who's missing. You just make your intention clear to spend some time with your fiancé, and no one will even come looking for you.'

Ember couldn't help her grimace. 'They won't? Even when it's known he's a... Well, he's a...'

'Yes?'

She could still remember the way he'd moved in the arena. How he'd leapt into the air like gravity didn't apply to him, how the ground had shaken when he landed. How he'd taunted that condemned man. The sounds of his sword hacking into flesh, into bone, into muscle and blood. The wet meatiness of it. The bellow of triumph that had roared and echoed from his great horned helmet.

They say he ripped his mother apart at his birth. They say his cock is the length of my forearm.

Ember knew she'd move heaven and earth to avoid spending any time alone with him at all.

'I'm not going to marry him,' she said fiercely.

'You've made that quite clear. There,' Rhaell said, stepping back, and she felt her dress sag. Her hands moved to hold it up, all arousal obliterated by memories of the Beast. 'Now get some rest. Tomorrow, ride with the prince for a little while, then make an excuse and turn back. Make your way to the river and turn north.'

'What?' Ember had grown up in a city. She knew which direction the mines were in, and which direction the slaughterhouses, by the smell and the dirt. She knew if she was crossing the River Bulworth by its colour and the River Rook by its smell, and if she was anywhere near the River Bonerun then she was in trouble. But here, in the – she swallowed – the countryside? 'How am I supposed to know which way is north? Or where the river is?'

Rhaell blinked at her for a few moments. 'Moss grows on the north side of trees,' he said. 'In the morning, the sun will be in the east. Put your back to the sun until you reach the river. Then turn right. Upstream. That's against the flow of the river.'

'I know that,' she said, turning. *He's just taken my dress off and now he's leaving. Such a waste.* 'Moss on the north?'

'Yes.' He stood in front of her. 'If you're facing west, and I'm a tree, which side is the moss?'

She hesitated. Then tentatively put her hand on his right arm.

Well, that was a mistake. His bicep was rock-hard and she could feel the heat of him, even through his leather jerkin. Her arousal zinged to life again.

Rhaell stood very still, tall and rigid as a tree, until she moved her hand.

'That's correct,' he said stiffly. 'Right then. I'll see you tomorrow. Wear something practical.'

He strode away, and Ember stood flexing her fingers. A day or two with him.

Her heart hammered in her chest.

～

The following day dawned fine and clear, damn it. Although given the heartiness of the crowd gathered in the courtyard and the snippets of conversations Ember overheard, it seemed likely that nothing less than a full-scale siege by enemy forces would put them off the hunt today.

Phoebe dressed her in a riding habit with a split skirt and said, somewhat pointedly, 'I've packed a change of clothes in your saddlebag.'

'What, in case the golden hind invites us for afternoon tea?'

'In case you stay out overnight.' Phoebe hesitated. 'There's a bedroll and canteen and things. And a knife. For ... practicality.'

Ember narrowed her eyes. 'What kind of practicality?'

'Just in case you ... you know, get separated from everyone else. Don't...' she began, and looked like she was at war with herself, 'don't do anything silly.'

'Not a silly bone in my body,' Ember promised her.

All she had to do was ride with the prince for a while, fake a headache or something, then go off to meet Rhaell. Simple. Totally simple. How hard could riding a horse be?

'You are fucking kidding me,' she said, when her mount was brought out.

The groom looked nervous. 'He's an excellent hunter, Your Grace,' he said.

Ember stared up at the creature. 'Hunter? He could storm a city all by himself!'

Ember knew horses. Whilst the wealthy of the Clockwork City rode around in their steam-powered vehicles, most people still relied on horses. She knew there were different horses for riding, and for pulling carriages, and for towing barges. Some, like the drayhorses that delivered beer, were truly massive.

This creature was bigger than them all, and it was armoured.

Not armoured like in pictures of Ye Olde Knights in Shining Armour. This horse was armoured like a rhino. It had plates of thick keratin over its head and chest, extending into a shell over its back and flanks. On its nose was a sort of short horn, and instead of a mane it had a series of short spikes. It was almost a shock to see normal horse eyes, brown and gently lashed, looking at her. She half expected them to glow bright red.

'I don't know how to ride that,' she said, backing away. She'd have to stay here, and think of some other way to get away from the castle—

'Then ride with me.'

The voice was rough and slightly metallic, like listening to a lion roaring into a tin can. Ember already knew what she'd see when she turned, her stomach so heavy with dread it sank into her boots.

Prince Bronadyr's armoured horse was twice the size of hers, glaring down at her from deeply hooded eyes and pawing the ground with hooves that could crush her entire body without breaking stride.

Okay, this one's eyes definitely glowed.

The prince himself was only lightly armoured, but still wore that horned helmet. Hanging from his saddle was a collection of blades and bows that could probably take down a whole herd of golden hinds.

And here she was, diligently telling everyone at breakfast she intended to ride with her fiancé today. He hadn't been there – he never was – but he'd clearly heard about it. Ember cursed Rhaell and his stupid ideas.

'You know what, I'm good,' she said, but the prince was already gesturing to the groom. The man unfastened Ember's saddle bag and began the complicated process of finding somewhere to put it on Bronadyr's armoured beast.

The Beast riding a beast. Oh Lords.

'Your Grace,' rumbled the one in the helmet, extending a hand. His horse was so tall he could barely reach her. The groom had to bring a mounting step, and even then, it was an inelegant scramble that caused more than one giggle to be hurriedly shushed.

'Hold the pommel,' the Beast instructed, and Ember gripped it for dear life as the horse pranced a little. She was going to fall off as soon as it started moving, and she'd fall a hundred feet to the ground and be trampled by its massive iron hooves, and—

'Relax,' growled the Beast behind her.

'Relax! It's a thousand feet high up here and I don't know how to – argh!'

The animal began moving, and she jolted wildly. Bronadyr wrapped one arm around her waist, muttering under his breath, and she clung to that, too, because it was basically an iron girder. And then it wasn't so bad, until he did something with his legs and the horse's rhythm changed as it started moving faster.

Ember bounced around, yelping, until he clamped her to his body and growled in her ear, 'Find his rhythm and move with it.'

'Saucy,' gasped Ember, and he snorted. Or maybe that was the horse. But as she forced her stupid racing heart to calm down and felt his body moving behind her, she realised he was right and the horse did have a rhythm. And once she started moving with it, everything became markedly less terrible.

By the time she'd calmed down enough to start taking in her surroundings, she realised they'd already left any sort of path and were travelling through woodland. Or maybe it was a forest. Ember knew how to navigate an urban jungle but not the countryside kind.

What she could tell, once she'd become accustomed to the sounds of the horse and the prince, was that there was no one else around them.

'Where is everyone?'

'Don't know. Don't care.'

Oh Lords, he's taking me away to rape and murder me.

No, stupid, he wouldn't murder you, he needs you to pop out dozens of babies.

Great, so just rape, then.

She could tell him the truth. Tell him about the woman down the back street with her ether and her ghastly implements. Tell him that one choice could take away every future choice. Tell him about her mother and the babies and the blood, and her refusal to live or die the same way.

And then he'd definitely murder me. In the arena, in front of the whole city, as she trembled with a sword in her hand. He would hack her to death for a decision she'd made as a frightened girl.

Her rabbit heart made her whole body tremble. *Don't show fear, Ember.* Surely, she could be braver than a rabbit. A hare, maybe. A ferret. *You can do it, little ferret.*

She blew out a shaky breath. 'Where are we going?' she said.

'Hunting the golden hind.'

'Do you know where it is?'

'I know where it isn't.'

'Where's that?'

'In the middle of a pack of clattering morons who've been drinking since breakfast.'

She supposed he had a point. Maybe he did just want to hunt.

'Do you think we'll find it today?'

He grunted.

'Will we have to ... camp?'

He snorted. 'What, princess? Don't fancy roughing it?'

Of course she didn't. What person in their right mind would want to sleep out in the open when nice soft beds in nice warm rooms were available?

'I've never camped before. I grew up in a city,' she said.

If Bronadyr recognised this as the invitation to conversation it was, he ignored it.

'Where did you grow up?' she asked.

'In a castle.'

Oh. Yeah. Obviously. 'Did you ... go camping?'

'Only on campaign,' he said, armour clinking.

'Right.' Probably best not to start him down that route. She didn't really want any more reminders that the man with his arm around her waist was an experienced killer.

Right then, she felt him go still, his arm tensing. The spikes and tusks of his helmet stirred her hair as he looked around.

Hoofbeats sounded. Bronadyr's hand strayed to a bow strapped to his saddle.

'Oh!'

The horse being reined to a stop a few dozen feet away was smaller and lighter than the prince's, but still armoured, its saddle hung with a couple of bows. Its rider wore a fetching pink habit with a jaunty hat.

Ember squinted. It was one of her ladies. 'Caeda?'

'Your Grace! And... Your Grace.' Caeda somehow managed to convey a curtsey whilst riding sidesaddle.

'Are you lost?' growled the prince.

'Oh! No, I was just ... ah, hunting, obviously,' said Caeda. She nervously twisted a ring on her finger. 'Perhaps I could ride with you?'

It was on the tip of Ember's tongue to say yes, and then she wouldn't be alone with the Beast, but then she remembered she had to slip away and leave him, and Caeda's presence would make that a hundred times harder. The blasted woman would probably insist on giving her a ride back to the castle.

'Actually, we would prefer some privacy,' she found herself saying. 'The prince and I have important things to discuss.'

Caeda blinked, and her mouth worked for a second before she said, 'Of course!' Her gaze flickered over Ember with the prince's arm around her waist. 'Of course. Well, I will see you back at the castle. Good hunting!'

She gave Ember a meaningful look, and then wheeled her horse away.

Bronadyr grunted and slipped the bow back into its holster.

'Were you going to shoot her?' demanded Ember.

'Probably not.'

'Probably?'

He didn't say anything, just kicked the horse into movement again. Ember gripped the saddle, proud of herself for not squeaking this time.

They rode for a while in silence. It was a pleasant enough day, although a little warm to be wearing her thieving clothes under a riding habit. The prince didn't grab her, or ride too fast or say anything unpleasant. He didn't say anything at all.

For an idle moment, she let herself consider just staying with him. Going for a ride in this pleasant forest, camping out with him, bonding a little, maybe. He might take his helmet off and let her see what demonic visage lay beneath. She might not be that shocked. Ember had known some fairly characterful faces in her time. You didn't get an awful lot of pretty boys in the criminal underworld, and you definitely got a fair few who'd survived mine and factory disasters.

She sighed. You also got people like Pa, who'd been hit by an omnibus and needed expensive medication for the pain ever since; and people like her brothers, who'd spend all their money on drink and gambling and girls if she wasn't there to stop them.

Ember mostly did crime so her family wouldn't have to.

They needed her. She couldn't stay here. And just because the

Beast wasn't being beastly right now, didn't mean he wouldn't be in future.

'The other night,' she said. 'At Kasteladdor. When you brought that ... thing in?'

He grunted.

'What was it?'

'A mantis.'

'No, seriously.'

He sounded surprised behind that metal mask. 'You don't have mantises?'

'We do, but they're like'—she held her finger and thumb a few inches apart—'*this* big. They eat their mates, I've heard. But ... I heard they're killing humans here?'

There was a short silence, then Bronadyr said, 'A fully-grown female mantis is about the size of a small horse. Larger if she is a queen. Her head is around the size of yours, with mandibles the length of your hand. They are serrated, flexible, and strong enough to break bones. Her legs are as long as a lance, and spiked all along the length, ending in flexible claws that can grasp an arm or pierce a sternum. They feed on small animals, mostly wild, but sometimes in breeding season, they seek new territory and attack farm animals, and sometimes humans, especially if their nest is threatened. The villages around Kasteladdor saw several attacks in the weeks preceding our visit. We found the nest and destroyed it.'

Ember, whose eyes had grown wider with horror at every word, stared dumbly ahead.

'Oh,' she managed.

He grunted.

'Are there ... um, any ... around here?'

'No. They're usually found in warmer climates.'

'Good.' Then, 'But Addor was much colder than here!'

He made a growling sound. 'Yes. Something is driving them north. It is not the first time they have been seen in Addor. Lord

Addor had ample opportunity to erect fences and traps, to supply his people with effective arms and deterrents. He did not.'

Ember hadn't liked him, anyway. 'Is that why you brought it to the castle? To shame him?'

'To shock him,' corrected the prince. 'Would have been better if it had been one of his courtiers, but...'

A shocked laugh escaped Ember. 'Seriously?'

'Lord Addor does not care for the little people.'

'And you do?'

A movement behind her that might have been a shrug. 'I will be king one day.'

'That's not an answer, is it?'

To her surprise, he gave a rumble of laughter. 'No, it is not.'

She waited, but nothing else was forthcoming.

'What kind of king are you going to be?' she pushed.

'I don't know.'

'Haven't you made plans?'

'Only a fool makes plans for something he cannot foresee.'

Ember rolled her eyes. 'Well, that's bollocks for a start. You can plan to be a good king, or a bad one – but if you don't plan anything you'll almost certainly be the latter.'

'And you know so much of kings? Tell me – who rules Coldonia?'

Ember gritted her teeth. 'A government elected by the people. Because we cut the king's head off.'

'Recently?'

'A couple of hundred years ago. Look,' said Ember, before he started quizzing her on her personal knowledge of monarchy, 'he was a bad king. Loads of them had been bad kings. They got to rule because of an accident of birth, and none of them planned anything, apart from how to amuse themselves and get richer. You can't run a country like that.'

Bronadyr snorted.

'Well, you can, but it'll be pitchforks at the gate before you know it.' She picked at a leaf that had landed on her skirt, realising she had an opening here. 'Are you planning on showing them your face?'

She felt him stiffen behind her. Well, as much as a person could stiffen further when they were already wearing armour.

'My face?'

'Yeah. Might engender more trust if they could actually see you.'

'Trust me, princess, it would not.'

'Well, how do you know? You can't keep secrets from people because of what you've already decided they're going to believe.'

'We cannot tell the people everything. That would be madness.'

'Yeah, but not even showing them your face? They're gonna decide you're a monster and lop your head off.'

'That's harder than you think.'

'Really? I've seen *you* do it.'

'I am much stronger than most men. And I have armour.'

'Oh? Gonna wear it every day, are you? All night? Gonna sleep in it? Bathe in it? Fuck me in it?'

Around them, the wind rustled the trees, birds called, small creatures did whatever they did in the undergrowth. But around Ember and the prince, there was a deep, thick silence.

''Cos you're not gonna get many heirs if you don't take your armour off,' Ember said, recklessly.

'Depends which bit,' rumbled the Beast.

'Oh, sure! What was I thinking! Just the codpiece, right? After all, it's no different to taking a piss, is it?'

'Lady,' said the Beast, 'who the hell have you been fucking?'

'People who let me see their faces,' Ember said furiously. 'And if you can't even do me the courtesy of letting me see yours, then you can weld that codpiece in place, my friend, 'cos you're not putting any bit of you inside me. Stop the horse.'

'What?'

She grabbed for the reins, but he didn't let her have them; and even if he had, what would she have done with them?

'Stop the horse!'

'Why?'

'Because I want to get off. And if you don't, then I'll just throw myself off – and good luck getting any heirs out of my mangled corpse.'

He appeared to mutter something under his breath, but he reined the horse in. Ember pried his arm loose and he let her, but he didn't help her scramble down the ten or twenty feet to the ground.

I'm going to break my neck anyway, she thought, trying to swing her leg over the horse's neck without getting stuck on its neck spikes.

'You're going to hurt yourself,' he rumbled.

'Better I do it than you,' she said.

'You think I'm going to hurt you?'

Ember got her leg over the horse's neck with only a slight rip in her riding habit, and twisted round to give him an incredulous look.

'You think being fucked by a suit of armour is going to be a pleasant experience?'

'I wasn't going to do it right now.'

'No? I've got the next month to anticipate that, have I? Or were you just going to wait until we get the bedrolls out?'

He made a growling sound and Ember pushed herself off the saddle, going into an instinctive roll when she hit the ground. One thing she'd learned very, very early on in her housebreaking career was how to take a fall.

Her shoulder gave a twinge anyway.

She got up, dusted herself off, and gave as dignified a nod as she could manage, before she began walking away, as fast as she could manage.

'Where are you going?'

'Back to the castle.'

'You're going the wrong way.'

She turned to glare back at him. 'At the minute I'm just getting away from you.'

He sat impassively on his massive rhino horse, and watched her. *Oh Lords, please don't follow me.*

'You know,' he said. 'You could give me heirs with all your arms and legs broken.'

All Ember's bravado deserted her, like someone scooping out her insides.

She stopped, and made herself breathe for a moment, and pushed the fear right down to allow rage to rise up.

She turned.

'And I could stab you to death as soon as you got your dick out,' she said, and walked away, her ferret heart pounding.

CHAPTER 15

The king's tent was as luxuriously appointed as any palace quarters and set up an hour's ride from the castle. For while King Onas greatly enjoyed hunting, what he enjoyed even more was waiting in luxury for someone to tell him they'd found the golden hind, captured it, and were waiting for him to make the kill shot.

Currently, he was being aided in this by half a roast ptarmigan and a bottle of excellent Valoran wine.

'Rode out on his actual horse?' he said, testing the crackle of the ptarmigan skin with his fork.

'Yes, Your Grace. Up in front of him on the saddle.'

'You followed them?'

'Yes, Your Grace. They were talking pleasantly.'

Pleasantly. Well, well. Maybe she actually liked him.

Their children would be ugly, of course. The boy was a gargoyle, and she was the sort of wench it was best to bed from behind. But so long as they gave him heirs, Onas didn't care if they each had three heads.

A king with no heirs could be toppled before he even had the bad fortune to die. It was easy to kill one man and take his place; a lot harder if that man had heirs to spare. Onas had made very sure that his people believed in the sanctity of life: even a hideous monster of a child would be protected and cherished.

If Onas died, the vultures would be circling Bronadyr before his corpse was cold. That bitch Sarea would have her knife in his back and her arse on the throne in the blink of an eye, and then Addor would be ruling the land. And Feynrith hated Addor. So they'd find an excuse to declare war on them, and Valoris would be dragged into it, which meant nobody would be protecting them against the Myr... Onas had spent too long carefully cultivating peace to be known as the king who sparked another bloody war.

He forked up some meat and a sliver of vegetable. 'She didn't spend much time with him in Addor. What of her token from the hunt?'

'He did not give it back, Your Grace.'

'No? Perhaps the boy has sentiment, after all.' He regarded his plate. 'She is a coarse little thing, isn't she? Vulgar. Perhaps women like her actually like men like him.'

'Perhaps, Your Grace.'

'Well? You spend enough time with her. What does she say of him?'

His informant paused thoughtfully. 'Truthfully, Your Grace, she seems ... interested by him. Intrigued. She still bears the scar of their betrothal on her palm.'

'Hah! He had his healed immediately.' So much for sentiment.

'She does not seem particularly frightened of him. Nobody in the court has made a secret of his ... differences,' said the informant delicately, 'but she has not seemed as repulsed as a lady of the court might be.'

'You see? Vulgar.' He chewed his ptarmigan. 'Has she taken any other lovers to her bed?'

'Not that I know of, Your Grace. Her sheets are clean. And she is seldom alone.'

'Hmm.' Perhaps he shouldn't have allowed her to be

surrounded by so many twittering girls. If Bronadyr could come upon the Promised One while she was alone and unguarded, he could overpower her easily. And he could get his heir.

He could almost smell those ugly babies.

'Hmm,' he said again. 'Where do we go next? Varalhen? Perhaps some opportunities,' he added meaningfully, 'could be engineered for them to be alone together. You will see to this.'

'Yes, Your Grace.'

'She will have a babe in her belly before the year is out. If the prince has not taken her before the wedding,' said King Onas, 'I will take his place myself.'

It had got to the point where Rhaell was genuinely considering asking the flower sprites to go looking for Ember when she appeared.

Or rather, he heard her. Thrashing at the undergrowth, swearing and occasionally shouting. He could have probably heard her back in Yskara.

'... cut it off and feed it to him,' she seethed as she broke the cover of the trees. 'In pieces. One slice at a time.'

'Sounds delicious,' he said, and her head snapped round to him.

He sat in the boat, sharpening his sword for want of anything better to do.

'Trust me, it won't be,' she said grimly. She marched towards him over the grassy riverbank, her riding habit torn and her hat mangled in her hands. Her hair clung sweatily to her neck, her face was red, and her scowl was fearsome.

He smiled helplessly.

'What's so funny?' she snapped.

He wanted to brush away that sweaty hair from her nape and kiss her there. His fingers remembered the heat and silk of her skin when he'd unfastened her dress. The scent of her, warm and rich, still lived in his mind. He wanted to lick the salt from her skin.

Remember you can't have her. 'Nothing,' said Rhaell. 'At all.' He stood and extended his hand. 'Your vessel awaits.'

It was a rowing boat, old and shabby, with no other means of propulsion than the oars bobbing with the current. There were no water horses here, and he didn't really think the grindylows upriver would be interested in propelling the boat.

Ember looked it over, then stepped back and began unfastening her skirt.

'Um,' said Rhaell, looking rapidly away. Had he spoken his fantasies *out loud*?

'I've had about enough of this stupid thing,' she muttered. He heard the rustle of cloth, and then she swore a bit more and more cloth hit the ground. 'All right, help me in.'

'Um,' said Rhaell again. He didn't look up. He wasn't sure he could cope with the sight of Ember in her underwear.

You've seen her in less, said his treacherous memory, and he told it to shut the hell up. He made himself think about dismembered limbs and pustulant wounds, because otherwise the evidence of his interest would be obvious the minute she glanced in his direction.

'Hello? Fuck's sake, I have had it with bloody men today,' Ember stormed, and even though he was trying not to look he saw her coming closer, her lovely legs so black and matte in the sunlight—

Wait, what? He blinked. She was wearing trousers. The dark, practical trousers he had got her, with the leather at the knees and the pockets front and back, and above them was her belt with its pouches and hooks, and above that her leather jerkin, unfastened over a dark shirt.

'You changed,' he said stupidly, unsure if he was relieved or not.

'I shedded.' Ember gave the pile of riding habit a dark look, and then a kick. 'Fucking boiling under all that.'

'Er, you should bring it with you,' he said. 'For when we get back.'

She made a growling sound in her throat, but bundled up the fabric under one arm and took his hand. The boat rocked as she stepped into it, and Rhaell steeled himself for the feel of her body against his. Lush. Warm. Strong. *Don't sniff her don't sniff her don't—*

She pushed away from him without even looking up and sprawled gracelessly in the bow of the small boat.

'How's this thing move?'

'What?' *Stop staring at her.*

'Is it like, seahorses? River horses?' She peered over the side of the boat. 'Or is there a magic portal, or what?'

'Er.' He took a seat and grasped the oars. Ember sighed. 'Sorry.'

'When we've got the stones and magic is restored, will the boat row itself?'

Rhaell considered this. 'That would be nice,' he said.

'You don't know?'

'Why would I know that?'

She conceded the point with a shrug. 'Okay, tell me what you do know.'

I know you are braver and smarter than anyone else in this wretched land. I know your breasts make my mouth physically water and my hands ache from wanting to touch you. I know the scent of your skin haunts me. I know your fiancé is an idiot.

'About the Myr?' Ember prompted, and Rhaell sighed as he started to row, and told her.

∽

Neris met them in a small inlet upriver. Ember, who had been enjoying the movement of Rhaell's arms as he rowed the small boat, wasn't really looking around at the scenery, so it was something of a surprise when a face appeared over the side of the boat.

'Fuck the Lords!' she yelped, leaping backwards and nearly capsizing them.

'It's all right,' Rhaell said, grabbing her arm. 'This is Neris. Our contact.'

Neris had unsettlingly pale, bluish skin and a flat, slitted nose. Her dark hair lay slick against her skull, and when she blinked, a second membrane covered her large eyes.

'Seriously?' gulped Ember.

'Relax, *erlish*,' said the alien face. The fingers that grasped the side of the boat were webbed. 'I'm not here to harm you.'

'What did you call me?'

'It's just a Myr word for people who dwell on land,' said Rhaell quickly. A little too quickly.

'Yes,' said Neris, with amusement. 'That's what it is.' The pale eyes regarded Ember. 'This is your thief?'

'I'm not his anything,' Ember said. 'But yeah. You're gonna show me where to nick this stone from?'

Neris nodded slowly.

'What's in it for you?'

The Myr gave a smile that was too wide, showing teeth that were pointed. 'Gold leaf. Half of which you still owe me, *erlish*.'

Rhaell nodded and retrieved a pouch from his pack. He checked the contents, then handed it over. The Myr poked at the contents and pulled a few out. Ember peered at them. She hadn't actually seen any Yskaran money, but it figured they'd call them leaves. The coins were circular and very thin, but each was imprinted with a leaf on one side, and a depiction of the king on the other.

'This is acceptable,' said the Myr, sliding into the boat. Ember was half surprised to see an almost human body, with arms and legs instead of flippers and fins, that appeared to be female. Neris was taller and thinner than even the willowy ladies of the court, with skin that gleamed like an oil slick. Her feet were large and webbed, and she wore nothing but a wide belt, to which she affixed the pouch of coins and some strings of shells and small bones around her neck.

Ember was no prude, but she found herself somewhat uncomfortable looking at this naked woman. Rhaell, she noticed, kept his gaze firmly above the Myr's collarbone.

'The Speaker is sick,' she said. 'He lies in his nest, sleeping. It will not be difficult to retrieve the stone from him.'

'I thought you said the harness would be removed for repair?' said Rhaell.

She waved a hand. 'He will not. He says it heals him.'

'Does it?'

She spat over the side of the boat. 'It is nothing but a trinket. You have your decoy?'

Rhaell nodded and retrieved a dark blue stone from his pack. Neris inspected it. 'This is acceptable.'

'But he's still wearing it?' pressed Ember. She'd never stolen anything from someone in their sickbed. Hell, it had been years since she'd stole anything from an actual person. She liked robbing houses, not bodies.

'He is sick,' Neris repeated. 'He will not wake.'

'How do you know?' Ember said, and then realised. 'You've drugged him?'

Neris shrugged.

'And you're sure you won't be disturbed?' Rhaell said.

'The others will be gathering to'—she waved her hand again, as if searching for a word—'pray for his health. It is stupid,' she added. 'He will die.'

Ember opened her mouth to ask how Neris knew this, too, and decided she didn't want the answer.

'When do we go?'

'Now.'

Ember looked around. It was barely mid-afternoon, the sun still bright and high. The creek itself was shaded, but not nearly enough for Ember's liking.

'Shouldn't we wait until dark?'

The Myr cocked her head. 'Why?'

'Er, for better cover?'

Neris stared at her. Ember stared back.

Rhaell cleared his throat. 'The Myr have excellent night vision,' he explained. To Neris, he added, 'We don't.'

'Ah yes. You are blind at night. Here, it makes little difference. There is no sunshine deep underwater.'

Ember's stomach turned over. 'We're not going deep underwater?' she said. 'Because I can't swim.'

'You can't?' said Rhaell.

'No! When would I've learned? You go near the rivers at home, you're gonna need a coffin.' The water that wasn't full of traffic or being diverted into mill races, dams and factory cooling was mostly full of sewage.

'Coffin?' asked the Myr.

'For burial,' explained Rhaell. 'When you're dead.'

'Ah. You go near the rivers here, you will need one, too,' said the Myr. 'You will not be going under the water, *erlish*.'

'She'll be safe?' said Rhaell.

'Yes.'

'You swear it?' said Rhaell.

The Myr rolled her eyes. '*Erlish* oaths,' she muttered. 'Yes, I swear it. Let us go, now, while he sleeps.'

'Wait,' said Rhaell, as Neris turned to the side of the boat. 'What we also spoke of in the city. About the hafmey?'

She cocked her head again. 'You wish to go under the waters of your Sacred Sea?'

'We do?' Ember said. *Great, more water.*

'Yes. Sort of. The hafmey are bound by a spell put in place by the Ancestors, but we don't know how to modify it. If we go into the deep water, they'll probably kill us. Can you keep us safe?'

Neris blinked her inner eyelids. 'For a fee.'

'More gold leaf?'

That too-wide smile again. 'You understand me now, *erlish*. We will speak more of this on my return. Come.'

She slipped over the side of the boat and simply walked up the riverbed to the bank. Rhaell rowed them to the shore, looped a rope around an overhanging tree, then leaned forward and took Ember's hand.

His hand was large and strong, and there were calluses on the palm and fingers. It was a good hand. A distracting hand. The sort of hand that would feel really good stroking and grasping her—

'You're sure you can do this?'

'Sure thing, Buttercup,' she said. It was just a job, and she'd done hundreds of those. She didn't get nervous about them anymore.

He glanced at Neris, waiting for them on the shore. 'Do you want me to come with you?'

'No,' she said. 'You're a big bastard, you'll just get in my way.'

He cracked a faint smile. 'Fair enough. I'll be right here. Okay?'

'Okay.' Ember retrieved her hand and patted his arm. 'This is my manor. I know what to do. I'll get your stone, Rhaell.'

He took in a deep breath and let it out, which did interesting things to his chest. 'All right. I'll see you soon.'

'See you soon.'

Ember accepted the Myr's hand out of the boat, and wished she hadn't. Neris's skin was cold and clammy, and the texture of her skin was unpleasantly rubbery.

She probably thinks you feel gross too, she told herself, and found a smile. 'Let's go.'

The Myr took her across the muddy shore and began walking into a sulphurous marshy area interspersed with soggy, moss-draped trees, moving as if the water offered her no resistance. Ember stalled.

'I don't think I can go through that.'

'There is nothing in it to harm you. It is not deep. See?'

The water was barely past her knees. Ember looked down at her boots, which probably weren't waterproof, and sighed. 'Fine.'

The water was cold and the mud at the bottom sucked at her boots. Neris watched her wading, and shook her head.

'It is better barefoot,' she said.

'Not on your life,' said Ember, as the cold water seeped around her toes.

Around her, the air felt thick and damp, and the sounds that filled it made her skin crawl. Things that chittered, crooned or cackled from the trees. The route was slow and unpleasant, mostly through stinking marshes where strange creatures watched from on or under the water. Ember nearly screamed the first time she saw a pale face with huge dark eyes staring up at her. It had a mouth that opened into a circle filled all the way around with rows and rows of teeth.

'The grindylows will not harm you while you are with me,' said Neris.

'And if I'm not?'

Neris shrugged and walked on.

Finally, the sounds of the swamp were joined by the sounds of ... well, not humans, because Ember had never heard humans make noises quite like this, but she had to presume it was the Myr, doing whatever their equivalent of praying was.

'Wait here,' said Neris, gesturing to a large tree that was thankfully out of the water. Ember squelched over to it and leaned against the trunk, watching as Neris melted into the dappled shade.

She listened to the Myr for a while. She could make out drumbeats, and something that was almost singing but more like keening. They were almost chanting, but not in unison. It was as if every Myr was making their own sound, and not all of them harmonised.

Right as it started to get on her nerves, she heard the crunch of footsteps, and turned.

'There you – *Caeda*?'

Her lady-in-waiting stared at her with huge eyes. 'Your Grace! What is going on?' She grabbed Ember's hand. 'Come on, let's get out of here!'

'Shh!' Ember stared at her. Caeda had knotted her skirts up on her hips, revealing stout boots she'd managed to keep clean and dry. 'How did you get here?' Ember hissed. 'What are you doing here?'

'I followed you! I thought the prince had kidnapped you!'

'The prince? No, it was—' She stopped before she dumped Rhaell in it. 'No one kidnapped me. I'm here of my own free will.'

'Are you sure?' Caeda looked around in fear. 'I saw him. Outside your room.'

Ember went cold. 'What? When?'

'Last night.' She swallowed. 'I've never seen him up close before. He's ... terrifying.'

Try being on a horse with him. 'You need to get out of here. Where's your horse?'

'Tethered back there.' Caeda's big green eyes were earnest. 'I have charms against the Myr. And smoke, too.'

'Smoke?'

'Yes, they hate it.' Caeda raised a bundle of twigs or herbs or something. 'Let me light it—'

'No! Fuck's sake, Caeda – no.' What was she going to do? She couldn't possibly tell the girl what she was doing here. 'I'm – I'm meeting someone. A ... a lover,' she said.

Caeda's eyes got even wider. 'Here?'

'Yes. No one would ever suspect it,' Ember said.

Caeda looked around at the dripping swamp. 'No one would,' she agreed. 'Who is he?'

Rhaell's gorgeous face swam into her mind. 'I can't tell you. It's too dangerous. But you can't follow me.'

Caeda nervously twisted the silver ring on her finger, but she nodded.

'Go back to your horse,' Ember said. 'Go back to the hunt. Don't tell anyone I was here. Okay? You can't blow my cover.'

Caeda chewed her lip for a moment, her perfect brow creased, but then she nodded. 'All right. But how will you get back?'

'The same way I got here. Don't *worry* about me,' Ember said, giving her a little shove. 'Go, and be safe.'

Caeda went, turning back and giving Ember troubled glances. Ember waved at her as cheerily as her racing heart would allow, and the girl was only just out of sight when Neris reappeared. 'Come with me.'

Ember nodded, really hoping the Myr couldn't hear her heart pounding.

Great, that was another complication. Would Caeda talk? Was Ember going to have to bribe her to be silent? How much money did Rhaell have? Dammit – Rhaell would have to be told. She really hoped Caeda didn't run into him. He'd probably be mad at Ember for being followed.

Her heart pounded like the stupid terrified ferret she was, and she pressed her hand to it. The stone beneath her jerkin pulsed with warmth.

'*Erlish?*' said Neris.

'Yes?' Ember let go of the stone. She didn't want to give anyone ideas about what to steal from her.

Neris peered at her and blinked. 'You move silently for an *erlish*.'

Ember shrugged. 'It's a skill.'

She followed Neris around some strange shapes in the ground that she realised were half-submerged dwellings, made mostly of wood and leaves. Some of them were open to the sky, some partially roofed. Some, she saw as they progressed further, were large and sprawling, built of stone and roofed with timber and tiles. They were entering, she was amazed to realise, a city.

More than once, the Myr froze, and bid her hide. Ember was good at that, too. Eventually they reached a large structure, surrounded by a moat with no bridge. It was closed off at the front with a curtain made of some kind of leather, with a small wooden platform in front of it.

Neris grabbed Ember around the waist and slid into the water.

It was too deep for her to reach the bottom. Ember panicked, silently flailing, and Neris glared at her, finger to her lips. She swam easily through the dark moat, keeping Ember's head above the water as Ember's foolish heart nearly beat out of her chest.

At the front of the structure, Neris deposited Ember on the wooden platform and gestured with one hand to the curtain. Ember knelt for a moment, fingertips grasping at the wood beneath her, trying to calm down. *It's just a job. This doesn't need to scare you. Be a lion. A lion wouldn't be scared of a bit of water. Probably.*

The stone at her breast throbbed. The blue stone was nearby. This was going to work. It would be all right.

Eventually she got to her feet, took the decoy stone from her pocket and gestured to the curtain. Neris nodded.

They moved silently to the curtain, and Ember recoiled as she saw it up close. It was made of leather only in the sense that leather was another word for skin. It was stitched together out of ... skin. One piece had a tattoo on it.

Ember let Neris push it aside, creeping past as if it might infect her.

Inside, the platform stopped in front of more open water, in which floated a half-submerged nest. It was made of branches and leaves, but also bones and skins. Curled in the middle of it, apparently asleep, was a skinny, grey-skinned Myr, mottled with age and scars. The Speaker.

He wore scraps of clothing, bits of skin stitched together into a sort of skirt and cloak. The latter had fallen away to reveal a leather harness that criss-crossed his chest, and many necklaces of shell and bone.

Ember peered at the water, then at the nest. She could probably climb into it, but would it dip? Even as she was pondering it, Neris slipped into the water and held the platform steady.

Ember took a breath, then climbed onto the nest.

Things crackled and crunched beneath her knees. Ugh, bones. She didn't want to think what from. Some of them were quite large. *The curtain had human skin on it—*

She reached the sleeping Speaker and heard his rattling breath. Carefully, very carefully, she pushed on the cloak covering his shoulder, so that he rolled onto his back.

There. A large blue stone in the centre of his harness. Ember exhaled in relief and reached out to it. She felt it pulsing before she even touched it, beating in time with the stone at her neck.

The old Myr drew a rattling breath as her fingers landed on the stone. Ember winced. 'May Gilia bring comfort and an end to your suffering,' she whispered, the same thing she used to pray when her mother lay drowning in the blood of childbed.

His breathing eased. The stone was warm under her fingers. Ember grabbed the knife from her pocket to pry it loose. The stone warmed further, pulsing gently, as if saying hello to the one she wore. The setting wasn't sophisticated, just a few metal claws that could be easily bent, and her knife made short work of it.

She was almost done when the Speaker suddenly jolted, and she nearly lost the stone. She froze, eyes darting up to his face, and then she couldn't help her loud gasp.

Dark blood spilled over his chest from the deep gash in his throat. Neris held a sharp knife, its blade dripping.

The stone tumbled from Ember's fingers, and Neris grabbed her hand and shoved the knife into it, pushing her down onto the Speaker so his blood covered her.

Then Neris screamed, and it was a frequency so piercing it made Ember cower, her hands going to her ears, the Myr's dark blood coating her face and her hair.

More screams joined it, and Ember flinched away from them, only to be grabbed by cold, rubbery hands. The knife fell from her nerveless fingers as Myr hauled her away from the dead Speaker. Neris was pointing at her, eyes wide with shock, shouting something in Myrish.

'I didn't do it!' Ember shouted. 'I didn't kill him! She killed him!'

But if anyone understood her, they didn't listen. Nightmarish faces screamed at her, blades swooped at her, and she squeezed her eyes shut, waiting for the death blow.

Not like this, not so far from home, not so scared. Not without having even seen Rhaell naked.

But the blow didn't come. A hand grabbed her face, and cold, fishy breath gusted over her.

'Open your eyes,' said a voice, and she cracked them open a tiny bit.

The Myr glaring at her had lots of bones strung around its neck and piercing its flesh. Its skin was a greenish grey, its head bald.

'I didn't do it,' Ember gibbered.

'Your word against the Myr,' said the grey Myr.

'I didn't! I've got no reason to!'

'You stole from us,' spat Neris. 'Then killed our beloved Speaker.'

'I never! You did!'

Neris looked so appalled Ember began to doubt her own memory. 'I came to check on the Speaker and found you covered in his blood! Filthy *erlish*!'

The cry of '*Erlish*!' echoed around the room, amplified by the water into a sibilant hiss.

'That's a lie! She got me in here!' Ember shouted.

'For what purpose?'

Shit. *Shit*. 'Um, curiosity?' said Ember, but Neris had snatched up the blue stone she'd dropped.

'To steal from us! Our precious healing stone!'

'I didn't—' Ember began, but right then another commotion sounded, and more Myr appeared, dragging someone.

It was a filthy, sodden, spluttering Caeda.

Icy dread filled Ember. 'Let her go,' she said. 'She's done nothing wrong.'

Caeda's bundle of soggy herbs was thrown on the floor, along with a string of beads and teeth. The Myr screamed at the sight of it, and Ember realised with a sinking feeling that Caeda's anti-Myr charms appeared to be made from the teeth and bones of Myr.

'Put them in the cage!' screamed the grey-skinned Myr. 'Let the thrask decide!'

Caeda moaned. 'No! Not the thrask!'

'What's the thrask?' Ember demanded as they were dragged away. 'What are you doing to us? Let us go!'

As they were hauled past Neris, she smirked.

CHAPTER 16

'Psst!'

Rhaell's head felt like he'd been whacked with a tree branch.

'Psst! *Erlish*!'

Wait, he *had* been whacked with a tree branch. He'd barely turned in time to see it coming, but not in time to duck. He'd gone over the side of the boat into the water, and then he didn't remember anything else.

A clammy hand slapped his face. 'Wake up, *erlish*! Don't be dead!'

He grabbed the hand without opening his eyes. It was clammy. 'Don't slap me.'

'Are you dead?'

He wasn't sure. His head really was killing him. 'Do the dead speak?'

The speaker appeared to consider this. 'Sometimes?'

Rhaell groaned. He was soaking wet, but he wasn't in the water anymore. He appeared to be lying on the bank, and when he risked opening his eyes he saw a Myr face peering down at him. It had dappled grey and brown skin and hair, and if it hadn't blinked at him, he might have thought it was just a shadow.

'Can I help you?' he managed, rubbing at his head. Yes, there on the side. The wound was bleeding sluggishly.

'No,' said the Myr.

'Right. Okay then, I'll be on my way.' He tried to sit up, but the Myr was practically sitting on his chest. 'Um?'

'*Erlish* needs to come with me. *Erlish* is in trouble.'

'I am? What did I do? The main river is free for all travellers.' That had been a peace treaty that had cost many lives.

'No! Not you *erlish*! Other *erlish*!'

Rhaell pushed the creature off him and sat up. His head throbbed. Other—

His mind suddenly sharpened. Ember.

'Female? Short? Brown hair?'

'Yes, yes, probably.' The Myr waved its hands. '*Erlish* is in a cage. Going to be fed to thrask.'

'What?' Rhaell was on his feet in seconds, which proved to be a bad idea because his head felt like someone was stabbing it from the inside. 'Thrask?'

He'd read about thrask in Gaeleath's writings. They were terrifying little fish that ate live flesh, and the Myr used them to not only dispose of abdicating Speakers, but also to determine a person's guilt. If the thrask ate you, you were innocent. If they did not, you were guilty, but then the Myr would kill you anyway. Gaeleath had hypothesised that the thrask were attracted to blood, which usually coated the individual in question after they'd been beaten for a confession.

He grasped the Myr by its slender shoulders. 'What happened?'

~

Ember was sure she must be in a nightmare.

She thought she might have blacked out at one point, probably while the Myr were hitting her with pointy sticks, and she'd come to in a bamboo cage, being winched into the air on a rope. The air around her was filled with screams and howls; and from the trees, Myr were throwing things at them.

'Your Grace! Your Grace,' Caeda sobbed as a rotten fish hit her back. 'What are they doing? How do we get out?'

Ember's stupid frightened heart drummed so fast in her chest she thought it might explode. The cage jolted and swayed, and the slats in the bottom were too far apart to stand on easily. Her boots kept slipping and she jolted down to the bottom of the cage, which trembled as if it wasn't going to hold them.

Why put them in something so flimsy? She could probably pull the sides apart, she was pretty strong from climbing, she could get them out and then—

She glanced below and really wished she hadn't.

They were being raised above a pool of water, surrounded by gleeful Myr chucking in fish and chunks of meat. Leaping from the water were... Well, Ember couldn't even see what they were, but they made the surface of the water boil with movement, and in the dappled sunlight she could see the water turning dark with blood.

There was nowhere to escape from this cage that wasn't a thousand times worse than what was below. Not unless she could fly.

Wait. She couldn't fly, but she could climb. And she could jump. That night in Yskara, when she'd leapt over rooftops as if her legs were made of springs.

'Your Grace!' Caeda clutched her, her pretty pink riding habit dark with mud and blood. Her face was bruised, her hair dripping. 'What do we do?'

No sense getting in if you can't get out.

'We survive,' Ember said, and jumped to grab the top of the cage. She missed, losing her balance and putting her foot through the base. The Myr howled.

'Please be careful,' Caeda gasped, plastering herself on the far side of the cage from the hole.

Careful? Hah. 'Why am I always rescuing maidens?' Ember muttered, grabbing the side of the cage and climbing up it as the whole thing swung alarmingly. 'Hold on!'

She grabbed the top of the cage and yanked hard. The bamboo came away in her hands, and she let it fall to the depths below them. Above, was a sturdy rope fed through a winch that hung from a tree. She could climb that and pull Caeda up to safety.

She grabbed the rope with both hands and had just hauled her torso out of the opening, when the cage suddenly dropped.

Caeda screamed, and the breath was knocked from Ember's lungs as they plummeted towards the water.

'No—' she gasped, trying to reach down for the girl, who was clinging to the side of the cage. 'Caeda—'

Gravity smacked up at them as the cage hit the water, bamboo stabbing into Ember with the force of it, and she was breathless from the agony. *Be brave. Be lion-hearted.* Her arm was wrapped in the rope, gripping hard, as she panted through the pain, because she knew she had to reach down to grab Caeda and pull her out of the water.

But she was too late.

Caeda's mouth was torn open in a scream Ember couldn't even hear over the howl of the Myr. The bottom half of Caeda's body was below the water, which seethed with tiny *things* that turned everything red.

Gibbering with fear and horror, Ember tried to get her arm to let go of the rope so she could grab Caeda, but her lion heart had deserted her and for too long – maybe seconds, maybe hours – she couldn't move, couldn't speak, could only freeze.

Then she could move, and she tried to shift down, but the bamboo shattered and she fell, scrabbling desperately for something to hold onto. Her arm wrapped around a sturdier upright as her boot hit the base of the cage and went through it.

She grabbed Caeda around the chest and hauled her up, but then her boot simply dissolved and a thousand knives stabbed into her foot at the same time. The pain was worse than anything she'd ever felt, worse than the time she'd broken her collarbone, worse than being stabbed in the chest, worse than the back-alley woman with her metal implements—

But the lion in her chest roared, and made her move, and she dragged herself up out of the water. She climbed with one foot and one arm and her knee, wedging herself against the bamboo with dogged determination until she could haul herself above the bars of the cage and hang by one arm, her muscles screaming.

Caeda was limp in her arms. Ember's foot was agony, and she dared not look, but she couldn't stop her gaze being dragged down, against her will, and what she saw made her nearly pass out again.

Her boot was gone, and so was most of her foot.

What flesh was left hung in ribbons. She could see her own bones. Strips of sinew hung there, chunks of muscle falling off like shredded meat. Ember stared, unable to process what she was seeing.

'...Grace?'

The word was barely a murmur. Caeda. Ember was still holding onto her, as if the girl was a doll she didn't want to part with.

'Gimme a minute,' she said, or tried to, but then she made the mistake of looking at Caeda.

The things in the water had eaten more than her feet. They'd taken all the flesh off her legs, and the bones had fallen away, and even as Ember looked Caeda's femur slipped free of the gristle hanging from her pelvis, because below the waist *there was nothing left of her*—

Ember stared, and stared, because it didn't make sense that half of Caeda's body was missing. Blood thundered in her ears. She was clinging with one arm to a woman who was half missing, and how could that make sense?

The cage jolted, and the sound of howling reached Ember's

ears. She tried to haul them up but she only had one arm free, and she couldn't let go of Caeda, who was suddenly so heavy, like she weighed twice as much not half, and the arm she had wrapped around the rope was locked, and the water was boiling red and coming closer—

The howls suddenly became screams, and the cage flew into the air, and she forced her gaze up to see what fresh hell had erupted.

It was a big man, large with muscle, blue eyes glowing like fire as he leapt through the trees like a lemur. *Rhaell.*

Rhaell was here, and he had her, plastered tight against his body. The cage fell away, and so did the ground and the screams and the pain. Rhaell was here, he would save them, and she could let go. Just for a moment.

The next time she opened her eyes she was cradled in his arms, and he was muttering, 'Tree protect and shelter her, please, Tree, protect and shelter her...' over and over.

He was praying. That was how they prayed here. Ember wanted to move, to tell him she didn't need his prayers, but she barely felt anchored in her own body.

Then Rhaell sobbed. His body shuddered with the force of it, his arms convulsing around her. This big, tough man who seemed entirely oblivious to her was actually crying over her; great ugly tears wrenching from him to soak her face. 'Ember, love, please,' he wept, 'I can't lose you. I can't.'

No, that couldn't be right. Rhaell needed her for his scheme, he didn't actually care about her. He'd rejected her advances often enough. He seemed utterly uninterested in her. She must be having some kind of weird nightmare.

'Tree take me,' he whispered, 'I'll do anything.'

Suddenly she was right there, feeling his body against hers; but more importantly feeling the pain, the agony shooting up her leg from her foot, and it tore a cry from her. Rhaell clutched at her, gasping her name.

'Rhaell?' Her voice didn't come out right. It was thready, and weak, and her foot hurt *so much*—

'Sparks?' His hand gripped her arm. 'Ember? Can you hear me?'

She nodded and blinked. Everything was quiet now, and still. Darkness surrounded them. There was just Rhaell, holding her so tight in the dark, his chest heaving as she clung to him. He was real. He was so solid, more real than anything, too vivid to be imagined. The buckles on his jerkin pressed into her face as she burrowed into him, crawled closer as if she could draw on his life and energy and the certainty that being with him was right.

Pain swamped her, robbing her of breath and sense. 'Don't let me go,' she gasped. If he let go, she'd fall, she'd die—

'Never,' he promised, fingers digging into her flesh. 'By the Tree, Ember, I thought I'd lost you.' His voice broke. 'I thought I'd lost you.'

She tried to squirm closer to him, but there was no space left between them and her foot hurt so much, her whole leg was agony. She let out a sob, and he cried with her.

'Don't let me go,' she repeated, darkness dragging her down again. If she could just stay with him, she'd be all right. 'Don't let me go.'

'I'm here. I'll keep you safe. I promise. I've got you, love. I've got you.'

She breathed in the scent of bitter oranges and blood, and let go.

CHAPTER 17

Rain beat down on the windows, a noisy drumbeat that echoed around the attic rooms. Deer liked days like this, when the sky was dark and low, and Mama lit lanterns and they sat by the fire for lessons.

He watched her light it with a wave of her hand. She didn't let Deer do that, not unless she had a bucket of sand nearby to smother it.

'Now,' she said, as they sat on cushions on the rug. 'What news did you hear today?'

Rainbow's hand shot up, the little swot.

'There was a Myr attack.'

'Where?'

Rainbow's face screwed up. Deer knew she'd forget this part.

'Valoris,' he said. 'Where Lord Keenor is from.'

'Lady Krislynn says we should burn them all with fire,' said Rainbow, glaring at him.

'And what do you think about that?'

'That it's horrible!' said Deer. 'You can't burn people!'

'Are the Myr people?' asked Mama.

'Everyone's people,' said Deer uncertainly.

'That's correct. But why else can't we burn them with fire?'

He tried to think. 'Because we don't have dragons?' he said.

'No, silly,' said Rainbow. 'Because they live in a swamp. Swamps don't burn.'

'They could,' said Deer mulishly. He stretched out his wings to feel the warmth of the fire.

'So could those wings, if you're not careful,' said Mama mildly. 'Why did the Myr attack?'

'Because they're—' Deer began, and then caught himself. 'Lady Krislynn says,' he corrected, 'that they're little better than animals. But you said they're people.'

'Right. And am I usually wrong?'

'No, Mama,' they both chorused.

'Right. So why do people attack?'

'Because they're mean,' said Rainbow.

'Because they're afraid,' said Deer.

'Yes,' said Mama. Thunder rumbled outside. 'And because they're trying to protect something.'

'Like when you try to steal my dinner,' said Deer to Rainbow.

'I don't! You eat twice as much!'

'I don't! I'm just bigger than you!'

'Children,' said Mama, giving them the look that said they'd better settle down.

'The Myr can't attack here, can they?' said Deer.

'Are you going to fight them?' said Rainbow. 'With your wooden sword?'

'It gave you a bruise,' he said with satisfaction.

'Ooh, a bruise, that'll scare them off!'

'They won't come here,' said Mama. 'There are a lot of soldiers outside the castle, and the Sacred Forest is full of fenrir who fight very fiercely.'

'For who?' said Deer, and this time Mama's look was approving.

'Good question. For us, for now.'

'For now?'

'The castle is well protected. We have nothing to fear from the Myr,' said Mama firmly. 'Would you like to hear a story? About the Ancestors?'

Deer, who was old enough to know he was being distracted but still young enough to want the story, nodded, and they settled down under blankets with Mama, watching the fire as she spoke.

'This is the story of Ephyrea and Ruvaen, and why she was imprisoned in the Tree.'

'But we know this one,' said Rainbow. 'They betrayed Ysarriel.'

'Yes, but that's not the story of why she ended up in the Tree, specifically. You see, back then, things were very much more brutal when it came to things like marriage.'

Deer thought about the scar on Mama's palm that proclaimed her a married lady, and wondered what was more brutal than cutting into someone's flesh to prove you owned them.

'It would have been very much within Ysarriel's rights to kill Ruvaen right there on the spot, the moment she discovered the lovers together.'

Both children obliged with a scandalised gasp.

'But Ysarriel felt the far greater betrayal had come not from her husband but from Ephyrea, her best friend. Ysarriel and Ephyrea had known each other for many years and shared many things, and indeed it was Ephyrea whom Ysarriel first told of her love for Ruvaen, back when he was a dashing knight of no court. It was Ephyrea who attended Ysarriel as a bride, and who rode by her side in every battle. So while Ysarriel's heart was broken into pieces by Ruvaen's betrayal, it was Ephyrea who hurt her the most, and so Ephyrea became the subject of her revenge.'

'So she imprisoned her in the Tree?' said Rainbow, curled up on Mama's other side.

'Not at first. She had them both imprisoned in the usual sense, in the dungeons below the castle. There are those who say you can still hear them weeping and calling out for each other down there.'

'Ooh, we have to go and see!' cried Rainbow.

'I think I'll be ill that day,' said Deer.

'Ephyrea and Ruvaen knew that Ysarriel would punish them, but they didn't know how. Would it be banishment? Would she send one away but keep the other near at hand, or would she make them both slaves? She might send one slave away and keep the other close, to humiliate them whenever she chose. Ephyrea and Ruvaen whispered to each other of the islands we now know as Dethari, where the worst of all convicts were sent to do hard labour, so punishingly cruel none ever returned.

'Or perhaps she might take a physical revenge upon them. Her rage might be a knife, or a whip, or the breaking stone. She might give them to the fenrir or the hafmey. Or she might simply execute them.'

'I'm not sure I like Ysarriel anymore,' said Deer in a small voice.

'You have never been betrayed, my sweet boy,' said Mama, hugging his shoulders. 'Down there, in the dungeons, the poor lovers drove themselves mad with speculation, whispering from cell to cell all the terrible things Ysarriel might do to them. And Ephyrea said, "Do you recall that day, my love, when you gave a piece of your heart to me?"'

'Ugh, sappy,' said Rainbow.

'It had been many moons before, when their love was new and secret. Lying in a meadow together, Ephyrea had said to him, "I wish I could give you a piece of my heart, so that you might carry it always," and suddenly a voice came from nowhere. "If that is what you wish, I can grant it to you."' Mama spoke in a sepulchral tone, and the children gasped.

'Who was it?'

'A sorcerer, shrouded all in black.'

'Mnorir?'

'You might think that. But he never revealed himself. He told the lovers that he could take a piece of each of their hearts, and give it to the other. And that as long as they held them, they could never truly die.'

'Wait,' said Rainbow. 'You can't actually do that, can you? If you cut a bit of someone's heart out, don't they, well, die anyway?'

'This was magic, darling, not people with knives,' said Mama. 'Besides, in stories, anything is possible. The Ancestors told of babies being born from flowers and visiting the dead under the sea.'

Rainbow scrunched up her nose in irritation.

'The sorcerer took a piece of Ephyrea's heart and embedded it in Ruvaen's. He said he could feel her heart beating beside his. But when the sorcerer moved to take a piece of his heart, suddenly they heard the wings of a flying horse, and saw Ysarriel herself approaching. When they looked around again, the sorcerer had vanished.'

'So, he had a piece of her heart, but she didn't have his?'

'Correct. Now, Ysarriel took Ephyrea from the cells and told her to prepare herself for execution. In those days death could be by stoning, a truly awful way to die. But while the stones broke her bones, they could not kill Ephyrea. They tried again, this time with a rope to hang her. Still she did not die. This time Ysarriel herself used her great war axe, but it stopped before it could cut off her head. Incensed with fury, Ysarriel demanded to know what sorcery was upon Ephyrea.'

'Did Mnorir confess?'

'Did I say it had been Mnorir? He came forth and reached for Ephyrea's heart and told Ysarriel that a part of it was missing, and that without her whole heart, she could not be killed.'

'I still don't think that's true,' muttered Rainbow.

'It is in stories. So Ephyrea told her the truth, that a piece of her heart belonged to Ruvaen the Rogue and always would. Ysarriel ordered Ruvaen to be brought above to verify the story, but when the soldiers returned, they said his cell was empty.'

'He escaped?'

'He escaped. The soldiers searched the whole land for him. Mnorir cast spell after spell. But Ruvaen had vanished. It seemed he had left the world entirely.'

'How?'

'By the Tree, of course. The Tree links all worlds. And in those days, you could use it to travel there.'

'But why? Why didn't he take her with him?'

'Ah,' said Mama. 'That is a question we will never know the answer to. Now, this made Ysarriel even more angry, and in her rage she declared that if Ephyrea could not be killed, then she would be imprisoned evermore in the one place no one would dare to touch her.'

'The Tree?' Nobody would dare harm the Tree, the source of all their power.

'The Tree,' agreed Mama. 'And before she did, Ysarriel had Mnorir cut the remains of Ephyrea's heart into six pieces. She kept one for herself and gave four to the others, to hide where they would, so that Ephyrea's heart would never be whole again.'

Deer was counting on his fingers. 'And the other piece?'

'That one she left with Ephyrea. Because Ysarriel believed Ruvaen would use it to find his way back to her, and she could trap him too.'

'So they'd be trapped forever together? That's sort of romantic,' said Deer.

'Ugh, it's horrible. They'd still be trapped,' said Rainbow.

'Perhaps Ysarriel wanted him for herself. At any rate, the trap didn't work. Ruvaen never came. Ysarriel never saw her love again, and neither did Ephyrea.'

'So there's no happy ending?' said Deer.

'Life doesn't get happy endings,' said Mama. 'But if you are good, it gets endings. And for you two, that means bed.'

They moaned and groaned, but Mama got them to bed anyway. And just as she went to pinch the light out, Deer asked, 'Will Ruvaen ever come back?'

'Maybe,' said Mama. 'Maybe.'

CHAPTER 18

Like many of the great houses that swore allegiance to Yskara, Valoris had long ago been presented with a rare seedling from the great Tree itself. Hundreds of years later, it was still little more than a sapling, but it was enough to power the healing waters of a deep well.

Perhaps the bath house built onto the side of Castle Keenor had once served the people of Valoris, or perhaps it had been used by soldiers after a battle. Today it was little more than a private health spa, used by the Keenors and their court for pick-me-ups.

Except for the last three days, when it had been used to save the life, not to mention the foot, of the Promised One.

Phoebe had refused to leave Ember's side, and Rhaell had had to physically remove her to a cot to sleep whilst the Keenors' personal healer took over. Anyone in Valoris with an ounce of healing skill had been brought forward to assist, lending their strength much in the way they had on the day Ember first appeared.

Why did he only get to hold her when she was bleeding to death?

She stirred against him, and he squeezed her fingers. *I've got you.*

It was his fault she'd been in that Tree-forsaken swamp in the first place. His fault she'd nearly died. His fault Caeda was dead. If he hadn't recruited her to this stupid plan...

And for what? They didn't even have the stone.

There were many dark stains on Rhaell's conscience, and this should not have been the worst. And yet it definitely felt like it. His head ached, and tears burned his eyes. The way she'd shuddered in his arms, gasping for breath, pain robbing her of consciousness. The way she'd gone still, and terror like he'd never known had overtaken him. *I can't lose her. I can't.*

He'd stayed with her all through the long, bleak days of her healing. Holding her in his arms as she sobbed and thrashed, willing some of his strength into her. And whenever he let go of her, she'd cried and reached for him again.

So now he was slumped against a bedhead that had been carved for looks rather than comfort, legs stretched out in front of him for Ember to use as a bolster cushion. Her foot rested on the blankets carefully slung between his legs, her arm wrapped over his thigh to clutch his hand, and Tree help him, her head was pillowed on his hip.

She snuffled and wriggled against his leg. Rhaell closed his eyes and muttered a prayer to the Tree for forbearance. He had spent some time thinking about what it might be like to have Ember's head in close proximity to his groin, but in none of his fantasies had she just had her foot chewed off.

'Buttercup?'

He still had no idea why she called him that, but nothing had ever sounded sweeter. He offered her a smile as she looked up at him. 'Hi, Sparks. Listen, don't—'

'*Fuck!*'

'—move.' Guilt burned through his gut, rose up through his

throat and swamped his mouth. He closed his eyes and concentrated on breathing as Ember shuddered and swore.

'Shitting fuckbollocks!'

A smile cut through his tears. 'Try to stay still. You're not out of the woods yet.'

Ember trembled, her voice a hoarse gasp. 'I never want to see woods again.'

'Understandable.' Her fingers crushed his, nails digging in. Rhaell stroked her hair. 'It's okay. Breathe through it. In and out. In through the nose, out through the mouth.'

'Fuck, fuck...'

She dragged in breaths and forced them out. *It's your fault. Her agony is your fault.*

Rhaell tried to make soothing noises, and eventually she calmed enough to laugh.

'What's funny?'

'You're coaching me like I'm giving birth or something.'

Rhaell felt his cheeks heat. 'Am I? Oh. Er, sorry. I've never ... um, sorry.'

'Never attended a childbed? You surprise me, Buttercup. They don't teach you that at the barracks?'

'Um, no.'

'Be glad you never had to learn.' Bitterness laced her voice.

'Did you?'

She nodded against his hip. 'Against my will, I might add. But Pa was useless, and the midwife said Ma needed someone, so...'

She'd never mentioned her mother before. She had a father and two brothers. Clearly, a mother had been involved at some point, unless the Iron World reproduced in a significantly different manner than he'd been led to believe, but he had to assume she was no longer in the picture.

As if he didn't feel guilty enough. He'd nearly got her killed, and for what? She'd never see her family again.

'You helped deliver your brothers?'

She nodded again. 'And all the rest.'

'The rest?'

'Yeah.' She yawned. 'I lost count. I think there were more when I was little, but she did a better job of keeping it from me then. I remember once being brought in to meet my new little sister. Weird little squashed pink thing, she was. I wanted to name her.'

'What did you call her?'

'Don't remember. Didn't matter anyway, she was cold in the ground two days later.'

Rhaell squeezed her fingers. 'She died?'

Ember sighed and looked up at him. 'They all died, Buttercup. Most of 'em never took breath. The rest barely breathed at all. I buried 'em in the dunny yard. Lords, if anyone ever dug it up, they'd lock us up and throw away the key.'

'Dunny yard?' said Rhaell.

'You know. Behind the house. Where the necessary is.' At his blank look, she clarified, 'The privy.'

She buried her mother's babies in the privy? That was – it was—

'Don't look at me like that. Burial fees at the temples are expensive and she lost at least one a year. There wasn't any point getting sentimental about it then and there ain't now.'

Rhaell didn't know what to say.

It wasn't a new story to him, exactly. He'd paid his respects at the Heirs Memorial just like everyone else. He'd heard the terrible, sorrowful whispers from the ladies of the court, aye, and their husbands too. Of a great, joyous hope dashed into pain and blood, of a sorrow too terrible to name. He had, in years past, stood vigil over the bodies of the king's ill-fated young wives and the awful, tiny coffins that were all they ever produced. On those days, the court had stood still, walls and turrets draped in black.

Ember spoke of it as though it happened every day, and was no more tragic than losing one's favourite boots.

'I used to wonder, you know,' Ember said quietly. 'Why she

never tried to stop it. The older I got, the more I realised there was stuff you can do, I wondered why she never did. When it was killing her. She never recovered properly after the twins. The midwife said she'd never have another one. And she kept trying, over and over. Like the three of us weren't enough for her.'

'Three children is a great blessing,' said Rhaell. Unimaginable, these days.

'It is if you can afford to feed 'em and don't have to take the oldest out thieving,' said Ember. She shifted against him, wincing. 'That's why I—'

'Why you what?'

Ember's hand left his and slipped down to her belly. Her face turned away, pressing into his hip.

'She warned me,' she muttered. 'That woman. She said it might—'

'Who warned you?' Rhaell said, a hollowness carving its way through his stomach. 'About what?'

Rhaell wasn't sure when exactly the king had become convinced that his lack of heirs was a deliberate conspiracy. His daughter had died birthing the monstrous prince, and his first wife had given him no other children. Was that the Tree's magic failing? Or did the Tree disapprove of the loveless, political match between the king and his first wife? Or had the queen taken steps to ensure she would birth no other heirs?

Either way, the king had become paranoid that his subsequent wives were trying to cheat him of the heirs he so desperately wanted. Draconian new laws had been passed restricting the sale and even harvesting of certain herbs, and anyone found to be performing, assisting, or even enquiring about the termination of a pregnancy was thrown in the cells to await a trial that would never, ever go in their favour.

What Ember was saying would have her before the axe.

No. It wouldn't. Rhaell protected as many people as he could from that. Sometimes he loaned cash. Sometimes he provided an alibi or an escort. Sometimes he simply supplied a large, innately dangerous presence that put off the city guards. Nobody ever questioned his presence at the Spreading Branches.

He couldn't save everybody. But he could save some.

Ember's fingers curled around his and he squeezed them gently. He'd kill half the city to keep her safe.

As if she'd suddenly realised what she was saying, Ember shook her head rapidly. When she looked up, the smile she gave him wasn't convincing in the slightest. 'Oh, don't listen to me. I'm probably delirious.'

'Trust me,' said Rhaell, glad for the subject change, 'you're past the delirium stage.'

'I am?' She twisted to look up at him, dread filling her expression in a way he wanted to banish forever. 'Lords have mercy, what did I say?'

Don't let me go. Don't leave me, Buttercup. 'Mostly nonsense. You called Phoebe a few names.'

'I did? Ugh. Was she healing me?'

'She and everyone else in the castle with an ounce of healing ability.'

Ember was silent for a moment. She moved her foot a tiny, tiny bit, and her face crumpled with pain. Rhaell held her hand and stroked her hair, guilt thrashing him with every beat of his heart.

'Is it ... really bad?' she whispered.

He slipped his hand round to her cheek and angled her face up so she was looking at him. 'It *was* really bad. It *is* getting better. And it *will* be fine again.'

Her big brown eyes held his for several heartbeats. 'You say that like a promise,' she said.

'Consider it one.'

She brought their joined hands together and kissed his. Kissed his scarred, ugly hand, where nobody had bothered to knit the skin back together every time he split his knuckles, where the palm and fingers were mostly calluses, where his fingers ached to touch her.

Kissed the hand of the man who'd nearly got her killed.

'You have scars,' she said.

He knew what she was asking. 'I'm a soldier.'

'Soldiers don't get healed?'

'Not like Promised Ones.'

'But ... your back—'

It didn't hurt anymore. Apart from all the times it did. 'My back doesn't matter,' he said, and that was as true now as it had ever been. 'Forget about it. You're safe, and that's all that matters.'

'But...' Ember glanced up at him, and whatever she saw in his face stopped her words. He tried to smile at her. Now of all times he didn't want to frighten her.

'And,' she began, then seemed to have to find her courage, 'and Caeda?'

Rhaell tried not to flinch, or to tighten his fingers around hers. The grisly, dripping bones, the tangled viscera, the violent horror of half her body simply not being there. The way Ember had clung to her, like a child with a favourite doll.

Rhaell had seen many gory sights in his time. But the ruined remains of Lady Caeda would haunt him.

'I'm sorry,' he said.

Her face crumpled. 'Couldn't you—?'

He shook his head and said gently, 'There was nothing anyone could have done. She was gone before I reached you.'

Ember trembled against him. 'I should've got us out sooner. I should've tried harder. I should—'

'Ember, no. There was nothing you could have done. It's not your fault.' *It's mine, it's all my fault.*

'Not my fault?' She stared up at him, face streaked with tears. 'If it wasn't for me, she'd have never been there!'

'And if it wasn't for me, you'd have never been there.' Rhaell stared at the far wall, which had been decorated with a frieze of roses. Guilt clawed at him like a living thing trying to eat its way out.

'She thought she was rescuing me from the prince,' Ember said bitterly. 'She was trying to help.'

His heart was a tiny, shrivelled thing. It beat pathetically in his treacherous breast. He said, 'It ends here. We won't look for any more stones.'

She twisted to look up at him again. 'What?'

'It isn't worth it, Ember. It wasn't worth Caeda's life and it damn sure isn't worth yours.'

By the Tree, he'd only known her a week or so, and the thought of losing her was horrific. If it had been Ember at the bottom of that cage, if she hadn't been able to climb, if he'd got there a moment later—

He couldn't even breathe through thoughts like that.

'No,' said Ember, and struggled to sit up. Rhaell tried to stop her, and she hissed in pain as she moved her foot, but she managed to push herself up on one arm. She glared at him.

'No? Ember – we didn't even get Gaeleath's Stone. You could have died – Caeda *did* die – and for what?'

Horror twisted her face. 'Did I lose it?'

'Lose it?'

'The Stone! I got it— I replaced it with a decoy— It's in my bag — Did I lose it?'

Rhaell stared at her. The Myr who'd helped him said the Speaker still wore his harness with the blue stone. 'Hold on,' he whispered.

Carefully, so carefully, he moved her foot to the mattress, and eased away from her, and then scrambled from the bed to the chest where her personal belongings were stored. He'd told Phoebe not to touch the bag containing the jewels, because then she wouldn't have to wonder why they were there. He hadn't even checked. He'd been so desperate to see Ember healed he hadn't given it any more thought.

Idiot. He was such an idiot.

His hands trembled as he found the small pouch, still dark and stiff with blood. Carried it over to the bed. Spilled the contents on the sheets.

Ember, half raised on her elbow, blew out a hard breath. 'There. It's fucking there. Lords above and below, Rhaell, you had me frightened there for a minute!'

He couldn't tell which one it was. How did she know? But her hand moved unerringly towards one medium blue jewel, and when she touched it, something extraordinary happened.

The pain that had tightened her face seemed to fade away, her muscles relaxing. Her lips curved in the faintest smile.

She looked up at him, something like relief in her eyes. 'Feel it,' she said, but when his fingers touched it, all he felt was cool stone. Puzzled, he met her gaze. 'You really can't?'

She really is the Promised One. Rhaell smiled at her, trying not to let his agony show. 'You're special,' he said. He closed his fingers over hers. 'And that's why we can't go on.'

'What? But I found this one – I felt it before I even touched it. I can find the rest.'

Rhaell shook his head. 'You can't. We can't. Ember,' he went on as she shook her head, 'I can't risk you. I can't.' His voice broke. 'You nearly died. Caeda did die. Nothing's worth that.'

'No. It's because of Caeda we've got to go on. Or what did she die for? Nothing? I can't have that on my conscience on top of everything else. You can't, either.'

'Ember. It's too dangerous.'

'No. I'm doing it. You can stop if you want, you coward, but I'm finding those fucking stones and I'm getting the hell out of this place. I'm going back somewhere without mad fish people and armoured horses and fucking purring trees.'

She was fierce, jabbing her finger at him, eyes shining with determination.

'And I'm not marrying that monster, who threatened to break my arms and legs if I refused to fuck him in his full suit of armour.'

'He— What did he say?'

'You heard.' She positively glowed with fury. 'What's he going to do if I can't give him a baby, huh? What's a monster like that going to do to me? I'm getting those stones and I'm getting out of here. You can't stop me.'

And Rhaell knew he was lost. That he'd follow her into any amount of Myr-infested swamps, and jewel towers, and dragon hoards. He'd swim the dark seas for her, he'd fight the Rakaa, he'd hack a thousand enemies to death for daring to do harm to her.

But he didn't say that. 'Sparks,' he said, 'I wouldn't even try.'

CHAPTER 19

By the time Ember was on her feet again it seemed her status as Promised One had become legendary.

'All I did was get a bit eaten,' she grumbled, as Phoebe checked over her trunks and cases.

'You survived the Myr. Not many people do,' said Phoebe.

'Caeda didn't,' Ember said.

She was determined to remember her ill-fated lady-in-waiting. Remember that it was her fault Caeda was dead. She'd sneaked around and lied and was quite possibly doing something treasonous, but Caeda had still wanted to help her, and for that she'd died.

Guilt consumed her. Ember hadn't even thought much about Caeda, or any of her ladies, apart from how irritatingly superior they seemed. But Caeda tried to help her. Had risked her own life to rescue Ember. If Ember had actually taken the time to get to know her properly, would she have been able to confide in Caeda? Would they have been friends? Would Caeda still be alive?

She had convinced the king to allow her to return Caeda's body to her family. He was clearly already bored with his progress, and now Rhaell's mythical golden hind had whetted his appetite for hunting. Apparently the Varalhen grasslands to the west were rife with both easy hunting and comfortable game lodges.

'I think you've spent enough time with my grandson for now,' he said to Ember, with an outrageous wink.

Yes, an hour on horseback was quite enough. But the king, of course, thought she'd been all day and night with him before she'd got lost and taken by the Myr. Or at least that was the lie Rhaell had spun, and apparently the prince didn't care enough to contradict him.

Ember said, 'Indeed. I feel we know each other so much better now.'

'His concern for your welfare has been unexpected,' said the king. 'You have clearly made an impression.'

Ember, who hadn't heard a single word from the prince since she'd woken in Rhaell's arms, gave a tight smile. 'Indeed, Your Grace. Now, I have a solemn duty to perform, but it is mine alone, of course.'

The king nodded. 'Are you sure this is the way of your people? To return the body alone?'

'Quite sure. As the last person to see her alive it is my sacred duty. I must spend time with her family, too. Surely Your Grace would not begrudge me this comfort?'

Ember shifted her weight at that point, and made sure to wince, although her foot felt fine. Gaeleath's Stone, Rhaell said. But that was surely nonsense.

'Of course, of course. We will see you in a week, then.'

A week. What with the time she'd spent recovering already, Ember was rapidly running out of time. Phoebe informed her they'd need to go straight from Caeda's family in Feynrith back to Yskara for dress fittings, and that was cutting it tight.

Not for a dress I'll never wear, Ember thought firmly. Now she watched Phoebe packing her clothes into trunks to either go to Feynrith or back to Yskara without her.

Ember drummed her heels on the bed. So far as anyone else

knew, she and Phoebe were travelling to Feynrith alone with Caeda's remains. Rhaell said he would be their coachman, and nobody would be any the wiser.

Ember had argued with Rhaell about their plans for a full day until he'd given up and gone off to do whatever had been so important he couldn't wait to leave.

Rhaell. He'd held her and comforted her, he'd looked at her with such tenderness in his eyes, and as soon as she'd been well enough to sit up he'd fucked off somewhere and she hadn't seen him since.

She'd nearly died. He'd held her in his arms after she'd nearly died. She'd cried and confessed her darkest secrets to him, secrets that could put her at terrible risk if they were discovered. And instead of opening up to her, he'd vanished.

The thought briefly occurred to her that he'd gone to tell the king what she'd confessed. But if that had been the case, she'd probably be in prison by now. Rhaell had just ... vanished. Probably horrified by all her embarrassing emotion.

Ember wanted to beg him to come back, to hold her again, to let her sink into his warmth and strength, but she didn't know how. He'd just been comforting a friend – he probably did it for any of his comrades when they were injured. He didn't need her wrapped around him like a snake or panting up at him like a love-starved puppy. It wasn't his fault he was disgustingly good-looking and smelled like bitter oranges.

Ember was plain. She knew she was plain, and she had been glad of it all her life. No one noticed plain girls, or if they did, they didn't remember them. If anyone happened to glimpse Ember picking a pocket or climbing out of a window, they'd just remember someone with brown hair and brown eyes, average sort of build, no distinguishing features. It was good to be plain when you were a thief.

But now she was surrounded by willowy goddesses with

waterfalls of shimmering tresses and tits like two tiny bee stings, and no amount of Phoebe's artistry was ever going to make her as beautiful as them. If she wasn't the bloody Promised One, Rhaell would probably never have even seen her.

'How long will it take to get to Feynrith?'

'Oh, a few hours.'

'Is that all? It's really close?'

Phoebe smiled. 'Well, no. But since it's just the three of us, and it's such an important journey, Feynrith has lent us something ... fast.'

Ember said goodbye to her tearful remaining ladies, thanked Lord and Lady Keenor for their hospitality, curtseyed to the king in a manner that only made Phoebe wince a little bit, and turned towards the hearse.

'Holy shit,' she said.

It was an odd-shaped carriage, held in a sort of frame that included strangely small wheels. Not that Ember was paying much attention to the cabin itself, because what surrounded it was quite the showstopper.

'Are those flying horses?' Ember gasped.

'Vyanka, yes. They're bred in Feynrith. Quite rare. And obviously they can't carry much, or we'd be using them all the time. But three people and a ... some luggage,' Phoebe said, not glancing at the flag-draped coffin being carefully fastened on top of the cabin. 'That will be fine.'

The horses were huge, and magnificent, stretching out their wings and prancing a little. Two were chestnut, one bay and one black, their massive feathered wings matching their manes. They were fastened to each corner of the cabin's frame, and Ember watched it bounce a little on its small wheels, which appeared to be some kind of landing gear. This thing was going in the air.

She was going to *fly*.

Ember had seen pictures of flying balloons, and heard reports of clever men in far-off places making machines for people to fly in. But she'd never thought she'd be one of them.

Then again, she'd never thought she'd live in a castle and wear jewels the size of goose eggs and be betrayed by mad fish people.

The coachman, in a many-caped greatcoat, broad-brimmed hat and a scarf that covered his face, bowed as he opened the door. Ember nodded to the assembled crowd and clambered into the flying cabin as elegantly as she could.

The coachman winked at her, his eyes very blue, and heat flashed through Ember.

'Ready?' he asked.

'As I'll ever be,' Ember replied, and his eyes crinkled in a smile as he fastened the door securely shut.

'We have food and drink,' said Phoebe, checking various pockets around the edge of the cabin, 'but I do hope you used the privy before we left.'

'I did,' said Ember, taking a seat on one of the low, cushioned benches. There were belts and buckles hanging from the seat backs. 'What are these – whoa!'

The cabin swayed as Rhaell climbed into his seat at the front.

'So we don't go arse over tit if he banks to the side,' Phoebe said, strapping herself in. 'I can't believe Rhaell is flying us there.'

'What do you mean?'

'Well, he does have other duties to attend to.' Phoebe looked Ember over. 'Mind you, I suppose you could ask him to find a Great Dragon and slay it for you, and he'd do it.'

Ember scowled down at the belt and buckle, which were being more complicated than they had a right to. 'I thought there weren't any Great Dragons?'

'There aren't. But he'd find you one if you wanted it.' Phoebe leaned forward and fastened the belt for her. She grinned at Ember's frown. 'Oh, come on. You know he'd do anything for you.'

'Rhaell?' Ember's face heated. 'Because I'm the Promised One.'

Phoebe grinned and sat back. 'Of course, of course. Look, just don't come crying to me if the prince's firstborn looks just like Rhaell,' she said, and laughed and laughed as the cabin rose into the air.

It was terrifying, at first, the lurch and the sway of it putting Ember queasily in mind of the cage suspended above the river. But after a mercifully short time, the flying horses levelled out, and Ember found herself peering out of the windows at the land below.

'That's the Skipta river, there, you see?' It was a twisting silver ribbon far below them. 'You can see how the land gets darker as we go north? That's the Myrlent.'

Smoke rose from sections of it. Rhaell had set fires to get her out, and the king had sent in men with torches to burn even more in retaliation for stealing his Promised One.

'Ugh,' said Ember. She should feel bad about it, but her foot was still sore from their horrible fish. 'That's going to come with a price.'

'Well, quite. All this land to the right, even far from the river, is their territory. Too marshy for anyone else. But over there, to the west, that's the Sacred Forest. You can't see the Tree from here but it's right in the middle.'

The Sacred Forest was a dark mass that Ember couldn't really make out. She kept her eyes away from the boggy Myrlent as Phoebe pointed out other landmarks, naming the forts that dotted the edge of the Sacred Forest. As they neared the thick mass of trees, she could see they were surrounded by trenches and walls, and she could just make out tiny, ant-sized men travelling between them.

'Have the Myr ever got into the Sacred Forest?' she asked.

'Not that I know. Long ago, there were stories of the Ancestors fighting them off there. But it's been protected for years. Look, there's the Tree now, can you see the gold?'

Ember could. The Sacred Tree of Yskara glowed like a jewel in its own clearing. Ember could see from here how the river flowed north from it, towards the Sacred Sea.

They flew over the gorge that contained Yskara's capital city, and the immense castle itself. From the sky, Ember could see how truly massive it was, dwarfing the city below it.

'We'll be back there soon enough,' Phoebe said.

'Must we?'

Phoebe sighed. 'He's really not that bad, you know,' she said.

'He said he could still fuck me with all my bones broken,' said Ember.

Phoebe's eyes flared. 'He does like to shock,' she said.

'Yeah? Well, so do I,' Ember said, because the damn prince might find it a shock to discover his bride had vanished.

They flew north and west, over another inland sea, more cities and forests, until the carriage finally began to descend. They landed amongst low hills, the cabin bumping along in a manner that had Ember clenching everything she had that would clench, and then the horses kept on running as they slowed the momentum of the coach.

They came to a stop with a bit of a lurch, and Phoebe already had her hand on the door latch as Ember retched.

Her vomit splashed over a pair of heavy boots. 'Welcome to Feynrith,' said Rhaell.

~

Feynrith was a bleak, windswept place. It felt like the edge of the world, the trees all bent sideways with the wind and the houses hunkered down low against the land. Beyond it was the World Sea, and nobody had ever returned from exploring that.

Their flying cabin was met by a hearse, both vehicle and horses draped in Feynrithian blue and grey. Even their flag was miserable, thought Rhaell, regarding the depressed fish wielding a spiky trident. He handed the reins of the flying cabin to the local stablemaster, and the three of them followed the hearse on the backs of mundane horses.

Ember gripped the reins in terror, despite the horse going no faster than a walk. He wondered if they had horses where she came from. She'd seemed completely terrified of the armoured hunters.

Lady Krislynn, the ruler of Feynrith, stood veiled and chilly in the courtyard of her family home. It was as grey and bleak as everything else here, but then he supposed they probably weren't hanging out the bunting for a funeral.

To his surprise, they were swept straight into the service, held on the shore of a lake. He stood behind and to the side of Ember as she watched Caeda's horribly light coffin being set onto the funeral pyre, as was the custom in Feynrith. A scholar offered prayers to the local gods, and then, with a glance at the Yskaran party, to the Tree. And as the coffin of her lady-in-waiting was set ablaze, Ember reached back for his hand.

That could have been her. I could have lost her.

He'd told her that the search for the next stone would be unbelievably dangerous, and she'd accepted it. Rhaell wanted to scream at her that it wasn't worth her life, that he forbade her from coming with him, but he knew it wouldn't make any difference. Was living here so terrible she'd risk her life to get back home?

Was he?

Caeda's mother comported herself with dignity throughout the funeral, but the moment the formalities were over, she excused herself, and the Yskaran party were escorted to their chambers for the night.

Lady Krislynn thought they were staying for one night. The king thought it was for a week. Now it was only Phoebe they had to lie to...

Ember was still looking a little green about the gills. *Gills. Bad choice of words.* Phoebe left her sleeping in the best bedroom the house had to offer and joined Rhaell in his room for a cup of wine.

'I don't blame her,' she said, draining her first cup and

motioning the bottle over with one hand. 'I've never liked being up in the air. I was only holding it together for her.'

Rhaell feigned surprise. 'Why, Phoebe! All those years ago when I was learning to fly, you were so quiet about it. Never a word!'

Phoebe glared at him, and he laughed.

'And speaking of never a word,' he added, and her eyes narrowed even further.

'You and Ember?' she said.

'Yes, we— Wait, what?' Something about the way she said it gave him pause. 'What about me and Ember?'

Phoebe rolled her eyes. 'Rhaell, love, I've known you all your life. There's not a lot you can hide from me, you know.'

He felt hot and cold all over. 'It's not what you think,' he said.

'No?'

'No. Phoebe— Please. You have to keep this quiet.'

Her eyebrows went up. 'First of all, thanks for your faith in my discretion, and second of all – so long as she gets a baby in her belly the king really won't care how it gets there.'

He felt his face burn. By the Tree, was it that obvious?

'Half the court thinks you're already at it,' she went on. 'You've certainly been spending enough time together.'

'She was barely conscious!'

Phoebe shrugged. 'Do you think the king cares about that?'

Rhaell knew he didn't. Faces flashed before his eyes – the king's young wives, one after another, barely grown women. Their white, tearstained faces as they left his chambers. Handkerchiefs clenched in white-knuckled fingers, skirts bloodied. No, the king wouldn't care.

'But I do,' he said quietly.

'I know you do.' Phoebe patted the back of his hand. 'Soul of chivalry, you are. Why, you hardly even stare at her tits at all.'

'I don't—' He glared at her. 'Look, there's nothing going on between us.'

'Sure?' Phoebe swirled her wine. 'She'd like there to be.'

Heat flashed through him. The memory of Ember in his arms back in Kasteladdor, faking an orgasm, writhing against him, warm and soft and lush and—

'Oh, there it is,' said Phoebe slyly.

'Shut up. No. Shut up.' There couldn't be anything between them. There absolutely couldn't.

He'd kept enough secrets from her. But if he told her the truth, she'd run screaming.

Just let her stay in my life a little longer.

'You know it can't happen,' he said, not looking at Phoebe. 'You know it. So stop talking about it.'

There was a short silence. Then Phoebe said, 'So what did you want me to keep quiet, if it's not a red-hot affair with the Promised One?'

Rhaell's fist clenched, but he kept his voice even. 'I have to go somewhere. With Ember. For a few days. Maybe only one day. You have to pretend we've gone back to the court,' he added, over her groans. 'Take a holiday or something.'

'You are fucking!' she cried.

'We very much are not.'

'Then you're planning to be,' she said, glaring accusingly at him. 'Look, I don't care. The two of you are mad for each other, get it out of your systems, I won't tell a soul.'

'Phoebe,' said Rhaell forcefully, and the cup in his hand cracked ever so slightly.

He wanted to tell her the truth. He'd agonised over it. But Phoebe would only tell him not to put Ember in danger anymore. And worse than that...

He trusted Phoebe with his life. But if he and Ember went missing, or if Ember never came back, he didn't want to land Phoebe in it. He'd got lucky last time, because the prince could say with total honesty that Ember had left him to walk back to the castle on her own, and nobody would dream of asking him how she'd ended up in the Myrlent.

But Phoebe? Phoebe was a servant. She might be trusted with Ember's personal care, but the king would have absolutely no compunction in extracting information from her. Phoebe couldn't know what they were doing, or why. She needed plausible deniability.

But if they disappeared, and the king wanted to know why... His nails dug into his palm. *It's for her own good.*

'Fine,' he said. 'But if you tell a soul, I will rip your entrails out and string my bow with them.'

Phoebe's hand clapped to her mouth, her eyes bright with delight. 'Really? Seriously?'

'I will cut your fingers off and feed them to you,' he said.

'You and Ember! I knew it. I *knew* it.' She was practically dancing in her chair.

'I will strip the skin from your bones and make it into a coat,' Rhaell threatened. 'Phoebe. I mean it.'

She made a lip-buttoning gesture. 'Not a word. Don't you trust me?'

Rhaell blew out a breath. 'Yes.' But she was the only one he did.

Lady Krislynn bid them a chilly farewell the next morning. There were no flying horses for them this time, but an ordinary carriage to take them to the shore.

'The vyanka must rest,' she said. 'The boats are swift, if you can conjure a good wind.'

'We thank you for your hospitality,' Rhaell said, with a bow. Phoebe curtsied.

Ember gave a curtsey, too. 'I'm so sorry for your loss,' she said, and Lady Krislynn gave a brittle nod before stepping forward. She pressed something into Ember's hand. It was a ring, a simple thing of twisted silver. The one Caeda had been wearing when she – when she—

'My daughter was so honoured to serve you, Your Grace,' she said. 'She would be honoured if you remembered her by this.'

Tears swelled Ember's throat. She nodded and took off her glove to slide the ring onto her finger. 'I will remember her,' she said. 'And I will honour her life.'

Lady Krislynn watched them until the carriage took them out of view.

The carriage took them to the inland Vaestur Sea, where the coachman offered to bespeak them a boat and captain.

'No need,' said Rhaell. 'It is my honour to serve my lady.'

As soon as the Feynrith carriage rattled away, he turned to Phoebe and handed her a purse of money. 'You can get back to Yskara by yourself?'

She sighed and looked between them. 'Of course I can,' she said. 'And what will I say when I arrive alone?'

'That we've sent you on ahead to prepare for the wedding,' said Ember. 'That I wanted to stay and comfort Lady Krislynn a while longer.'

'With your bodyguard,' Phoebe said, with some undertone Ember didn't quite understand. She'd been giving her strange looks all morning.

'Yes. The Promised One can't go bleedin' anywhere alone,' Ember said, which raised a smile.

'All right.' Phoebe chewed her lip, then gave Ember a hug. 'Be careful, all right?'

'Of course,' Ember lied.

'Don't break him. He's my favourite person. Next to you,' Phoebe added.

'What do you think we're going to be—' Ember began, and then she realised and heat flooded her face.

Rhaell took her hand as she spluttered. 'Phoebe is the soul of discretion,' he promised. 'She won't breathe a word. Will you?' he added, with a glare.

'Or you'll make a coat from my entrails and wear my fingernails as a necklace,' Phoebe said, with a wave of her hand. 'I know, I know. Now be gone with you, before I change my mind and decide you need a chaperone.'

She turned and walked briskly away towards the town, and Ember snatched her hand back and turned to Rhaell, her face burning.

'She thinks we're fucking!'

He winced. 'Um. Well, yes. Look, what else was I going to tell her? She was getting suspicious.'

'What if she tells people! I'm supposed to be marrying the prince!'

'But you won't be,' Rhaell said, turning away from her and striding for the dock.

His stride was long, and by the time she caught up to him she was panting. Rhaell was paying a man who gestured them onto a small boat, and she'd barely stepped aboard before it was moving. The means of propulsion wasn't obvious to Ember – no sails, no sarel engine, and no water horses – but they sped across the water quick enough.

Rhaell sat beside her on the small bench inside the tiny cabin. 'He's taking us to Oaksthorpe, and from there we'll travel to the Dagrai Lake, where we're going to meet someone who'll take us to meet Mnorir.'

Ember chewed her lip. 'That sounds dodgy as hell,' she said.

'It is. You still don't have to come.'

Ember twisted the silver ring on her finger. 'I do,' she said.

He sighed. 'Look, this part is going to be dangerous. I can't see any other way around it. If we survive getting Mnorir's Stone—'

'We will,' Ember said firmly.

'Then the next part will be even worse. I need you to know how to get the other two stones without me.'

Ember shook her head, looking up into his beautiful, serious face. 'I won't,' she said. 'Because you'll be with me.'

'Ember...'

'How do we meet Mnorir?' Ember went on determinedly. 'Who's this person we're meeting?'

Rhaell rubbed his face. 'Oh, you're not going to like it,' he said, and he was right.

CHAPTER 20

'I don't like this,' Ember said, folding her arms.

The small Myr glared mulishly at her. 'Hesk doesn't like it either, *erlish*,' it said. 'Water up here is cold and fish taste bad. But *erlish* said Hesk could live in Sacred Sea away from Myrlent if Hesk helped *erlish*. So here Hesk is.'

'Hesk?'

The Myr tapped its chest. It wore a cloak that dragged on the floor, and Ember might have thought it was a skinny youth until it dropped its hood and revealed its brown and grey skin. She'd nearly run, but Rhaell had taken hold of her arm and said this Myr had saved her life.

'Why?' she said. 'The others seemed quite happy to feed me to that ... I don't even know what it was.'

'Thrask? Fish. Fish that will eat anything. It's an old Myr tradition for deciding if a Myr is guilty.' The Myr cocked its head. 'The thrask ate *erlish*, so *erlish* is innocent. If *erlish* hadn't been eaten, Myr would have killed *erlish*.'

'What? That doesn't make any—'

Rhaell touched her arm again. 'And our traditions don't make sense to the Myr. But Hesk came and told me what Neris had done to you.'

'Why?'

The Myr blinked its huge pale eyes at her. It was so dappled and shaded it nearly faded into the shadows, which was probably just as well.

'Because Neris is bad Myr. Neris's people are bad Myr.' Hesk looked down and scuffed a webbed foot in the dirt. 'And now Neris is in charge.'

'I see.'

'This is what I've been doing the last couple of days,' Rhaell said. 'Gaeleath's writings said the Myr had dominion over other water creatures. I wanted to know if that was true, and how to harness it. Hesk has been helping me.'

Hesk looked up, big eyes sorrowful. 'Hesk does not like feeding people to the thrask. Hesk is sorry about other *erlish*.'

Ember rubbed Caeda's ring on her finger. 'So am I,' she said. 'So, what do we do to meet this Mnorir?'

'You won't like this, either,' said Rhaell, and he was right about that, too.

∼

Dagrai Lake emptied into the Sacred Sea by means of the Dagrai Falls, which tumbled over and over into a churning foam several hundred feet below. The edge of the lake was a swirling mass of water being sucked towards the precipice, a few rocks sticking up like rotten teeth gathering debris behind them.

Ember watched it for a moment, then picked up a bit of rotten wood and chucked it at the churning water. It vanished below, bobbed up much closer to the precipice, then smashed to pieces on the rocks before being thrown over the edge in fragments.

'Absolutely not,' she said.

'This is how to meet Mnorir,' said Hesk.

'What, to literally die?'

'We won't actually die,' said Rhaell, with more confidence than he felt. The old scrolls had been clear on this: you cast a token of the dead into the water and Mnorir would grant you an audience. It was getting back out again that would be tricky, and that was why he'd brought Hesk.

What was it Ember had said? No sense getting in if you can't get out.

'I can't swim,' Ember said, her eyes getting all big and panicked.

'That won't be a problem,' said Rhaell, and didn't add that this was because if the tokens didn't work, the current would smash them to smithereens even if they were the best swimmers in the world.

She frowned at the water again, chewing her mouth to one side. The wind whipped at her cloak, moulding it against her legs. Phoebe had found her some more plain, practical clothing, and her dark trousers and jerkin fitted even better than the ones Rhaell had got her. Dammit.

'All right, fuck it,' she said. 'So what are these tokens of the dead?'

Rhaell unhooked a pouch from his belt and from it took three small bones.

'Tell me they're animal,' Ember said.

Rhaell looked down at the bones. He'd never seen an animal with fingers like this. 'Sure.'

She covered her face and moaned. 'Tell me they're not Caeda's!'

'*Erlish* was missing half *erlish*'s body, *erlish* won't mind,' said Hesk, taking one of them.

Rhaell winced. Ember looked appalled. But right then, Hesk threw their bone into the water, and shouted, 'Hesk wants to see Mnorir!'

For a long, tense moment, nothing at all happened. Then the water that thundered towards the falls parted in the middle.

The rocks sticking up above the surface were revealed to be the top of a doorway. Below it, dripping, was a staircase, twisting down into darkness. Either side of it, the water parted calmly, leaving a rocky valley between.

'You've got to be kidding me,' Ember said.

Hesk, unconcerned, waded out into the water, into the eerie waterless valley before the doorway, and trotted out of sight.

Rhaell exchanged a look with Ember. 'Well, nothing ventured,' she said, and stepped off the bank.

'Wait—' Rhaell lunged for her.

But the water had already snapped back into place, the current sucking her down. It grabbed her by the feet, and she went under shockingly fast.

'Ember!' He nearly leapt after her, then remembered himself and tossed his bone into the water as he dived in. 'Rhaell wants to see Mnorir!'

The water parted for him so quickly his knees smacked into the rocks on the riverbed, and he saw Ember's arm flailing. He grabbed for it, and hauled as hard as he could to get her out of the water that churned only for her.

He got her face free, her eyes huge and terrified. She was breathing, thank the Tree, but the water was pulling her hard away from him. Her hand grasped his wrist, and he braced himself to pull harder against the wall of water.

'Say it,' he gasped. 'You have to say it!'

'Say what?' she screamed above the roar of water determined to follow gravity and take Ember with it.

'You want to see Mnorir!' The last fingerbone was— *No.* He'd had it in his hand as he grabbed for her and now the water had taken it. 'Say it!'

'I want to see Mnorir!' Ember yelled, but nothing happened. The water continued to churn and suck at her body. She hadn't thrown the token herself. 'Ember wants to see Mnorir!'

Her eyes met his, huge and terrified. 'You need a token of the dead,' Rhaell shouted above the roar of the water.

'I don't have it!' she cried, and Rhaell tried even harder to pull her to him. *I can't lose you.*

Then suddenly, she snatched her hand from his arm, and he screamed as the water took her, and she screamed something, too – then she was collapsing against him as the water abruptly subsided, and she clung, panting and desperate, to him.

Her hand rubbed her bare finger. Caeda's ring. She'd sacrificed it to the water.

'What the fuck,' she gasped against his chest. 'What the *fuck*.'

Rhaell wrapped his arms around her, his heart hammering. *I didn't lose her. I won't lose her.* 'I've got you,' he said. 'I've got you.'

Ember clutched at him, hands clawed on his shoulders, around his neck. Her fingers dug into his skin. Her chest heaved against his as she gasped into his neck, and then she looked up at him. Her eyes were blown wide, face pale, lips parted.

'You saved me,' she gasped. 'Again.'

He could only nod. She was all right. She wasn't hurt. His fingers tangled in her dripping hair.

And suddenly her mouth was on his.

Rhaell was too stunned to react at first, freezing in place as she kissed him. And then her body surged against his, so much softness against his hardness, and her tongue parted his lips and he groaned and dived into the kiss.

It wasn't elegant and it wasn't sophisticated. It was a desperate kiss, both of them clutching at each other, teeth clashing, staggering from the impact. Ember's fingers dug into his hair, holding his head captive so he couldn't escape from her onslaught, and he dragged her closer against him until there was no space between their bodies at all.

There was no thought, no plan. Rhaell needed her like he needed air to breathe. The rest of the world ceased to exist around them, and it was just him and Ember, her tongue inside his mouth, her breasts against his chest, her fingers curling against his neck. He tried to drag her closer, only there was no closer, and he was just filling his hands with her lush roundness.

He fed on her like an addict, only she was brand new to him and he needed to discover all of her. Needed to learn her taste and commit it to memory along with the softness of her under his hands. Where she was firm and strong, where she was soft and giving, where her body felt exactly right as he ground his own against it.

His cock throbbed, all the blood in his body rushing to his groin as his libido roared into life. Lust consumed his body like an inferno.

And then he heard a voice saying, 'Are *erlish* coming? Ugh. What are *erlish* doing?'

He froze, and a split second later so did Ember. Her eyes, which had been half closed, opened and guiltily met his.

Suddenly it felt completely wrong to be this close to her, to be manhandling her like this, hauling her around like she was a sack of flour. He released her, stepping back, dropping his gaze.

You can't have her. She doesn't belong to you.
When she discovers the real you, she will despise you.

'Uh, just, we were just... Let's go,' said Ember, and hurried away from him without looking back.

Stupid, stupid! What the hell had she been thinking?

Well, she hadn't been thinking. That was the problem. She'd nearly got herself killed, again, and he'd saved her, again. And he'd held her in those big strong arms of his and looked down at her with those blue, blue eyes of his, and his lips had been right there, parted and full and so kissable, and suddenly she needed to kiss him more than she needed to breathe—

And then he'd stepped away from her, as if she was diseased, and hadn't looked at her since.

Ember stomped down the slippery rock steps as the doorway above them sealed over, and darkness filled the stairwell. Behind her, a pale werelight flared, and she remembered she could do that too.

She could do magic. It ought to make her happier. But it was poor consolation for Rhaell's clear rejection.

She conjured a werelight and continued stomping after Hesk, who didn't seem bothered by the darkness at all. Of course, Neris had said the Myr didn't need light to see.

The spiral steps were smoothly cut and evenly spaced, and there was even a handrail of sorts carved into the side wall. Ember sped up a bit and said to Hesk, 'Can I ask you something?'

Hesk shrugged. '*Erlish* can ask. Hesk might not answer.'

'Fair enough. Is Hesk your name?'

Hesk glanced back at her as if she was stupid. 'Yes.'

'Then ... why do you always refer to yourself by it? Why not me or I?'

Hesk was still looking at her as if she was not very bright. 'Those are *erlish* words,' they said.

'Right, but ... Neris used them?'

Hesk made a sound that sounded like a cat being sick. 'Neris is a bad Myr,' they said.

'So ... it's not Myrish to use, um—' Ember flailed for a moment, her schooling not having included a lot of grammar lessons.

'Pronouns,' supplied Rhaell, behind her.

Ember glared over her shoulder at him. 'Yes. Those.'

'Hesk doesn't know what pronouns are.'

'They're— Look, are you male or female?'

'It doesn't work like that,' rumbled Rhaell behind her. 'Myr don't really have the same ideas of gender as we do.'

'But Neris was female,' Ember said, not really willing to look at him properly.

'Neris spent a lot of time around *erlish*,' said Hesk. 'Got *erlish* ideas.'

'Like murder?' Ember said.

'No, Myr knew that one already,' Hesk said sadly. 'Look, *erlish*.'

'You can call me Ember,' said Ember.

'Look, Ember,' corrected Hesk. 'It's getting lighter.'

Indeed, it was. Light crept up the stairwell, until eventually they reached the bottom, and a rocky archway opened up.

Carbonate sedimentary. Worn smooth by water, hideous to climb. Ember catalogued that as she paused, not quite close enough to see inside. Rhaell stopped behind her.

'Sparks?'

She took in a deep breath and let it out. 'We're going to see the god of death.'

'Well, not quite—'

'The Ancestor of death, then. He's associated with death.'

'Yes.'

'Does that mean... Rhaell,' she turned and looked up at him, 'is this hell?'

He shook his head and smiled. 'No. Mnorir doesn't punish the dead. He just ... watches over them. Some say he creates life, that everything is cyclical.'

'Oh.' Ember's breath rushed out of her. She'd heard that from some foreign lads at the docks, that once you died you came back as someone else. 'So ... there aren't dead people here?'

Rhaell shrugged. 'I don't know. I've never been to see Mnorir before.'

'Are *erlish* coming?' said Hesk, who had wandered to the archway and was peering through.

Ember hesitated. What if Caeda was there? What if she blamed Ember for her death? What if Ma was there?

Ember had told herself over and over that it wasn't her fault Ma died, that eventually another childbirth would have done for her, that there was nothing anyone could have done even if the midwife had been able to get there... But it didn't help.

What if that nameless man she'd knifed in an alley when he'd tried to rip her shirt off was there? What if Cracksman Jack's mangled spectre blamed her for escaping those dogs when he didn't? What if Kid Softly still blamed her for—

'Ember?' said Rhaell softly, and she found herself reaching for his hand again. He held it, squeezed gently, just like he had all those times when she'd been healing, and she nodded.

The dead couldn't hurt her. Probably.

'Let's go meet Death.'

The archway opened onto a cave, although it was a nicely finished cave, with smooth walls and niches for lighting. A fireplace crackled merrily, casting dancing lights over the wingback chairs and a table set out on a rug. There were paintings on the walls, and little tables holding ornaments.

Ember glanced at Rhaell. She didn't know what she'd been expecting, but this wasn't it.

'Come in, come in,' said a voice from one of the wingback chairs. 'Do sit down. Don't eat anything.'

This appeared to be aimed at Hesk, who had trotted on ahead and investigated the bowl of fruit on the table.

'Why is there food if Hesk can't eat it?' they wanted to know.

'Oh, you know. The look of the thing. It's rather expected.' The voice sounded elderly, but also kindly, like a jolly grandpa.

'But if we eat any we have to stay?' said Ember, who vaguely remembered seeing this in a play once.

'That's the convention, yes.'

They'd got closer now, and Ember steeled herself to look into the chair. The gentleman sitting there wore a long robe in a cheerful purple, and had a neatly trimmed grey beard. His long hair was bound into plaits and he wore spectacles on his beaky nose. Around his neck was a pendant, just like Ember's, only this one held a black jewel.

He beamed at them. 'It's so nice to have visitors! Sit down, sit down! What can I do for you today?'

Ember exchanged a look with Rhaell. 'We seek Mnorir,' said Rhaell.

'You have found him! Sit, sit. Don't give an old man a crick in the neck.'

They sat. Hesk wandered around the room, peering at the pictures.

'This is incredible,' murmured Rhaell. 'You truly are Mnorir?'

'I truly am.'

'I am speaking with one of the Ancestors,' Rhaell said, in tones of wonder. He shook himself. 'O wise and powerful Mnorir,' he began, but the old man chuckled.

'No need for those formalities. Now.' He peered through his spectacles. 'Interesting, interesting. I believe I have met your father,' he said, studying Rhaell as if he was some kind of sculpture. 'And mother. Oh dear. Yes, of course, I remember her. You never knew her, of course.'

Rhaell had let go of Ember's hand in order to sit, and now she saw his fingers clench over the damp fabric of his cloak.

'No,' he said tightly.

'Died at your birth,' said Mnorir, clucking his tongue in sympathy. 'We get so many of those. Although fewer, recently. Do you know why? Some advance in medical science, perhaps? We used to get a distressing amount of babies, but thankfully, no longer.'

'No,' said Rhaell. His fingers did not unclench. 'The birthrate has dropped.'

'Ah? I see. Well, I suppose that's to be expected.'

He looked up at that. 'It is?'

Mnorir shrugged. 'It is that time, is it not? It's so hard to tell down here, but...' He waved his hand, and Ember stifled a scream as a pale, translucent figure emerged through the cave wall, bearing a scroll. It handed it to Mnorir, who murmured a thanks, and the figure drifted away again.

'Ah, yes. Here. Twin moons, eclipse, forty-seventh year, third of his name – that's now?'

Rhaell and Ember both nodded.

'Yes. Yes, we didn't know what it would be, you see, all that time ago. But there would be a blight. The Tree would fail and falter, and with it the source of magic in the realm. I daresay it has taken the heart of Yskara first, yes? The castle?'

Rhaell nodded, mute.

'And it spreads? Strange sights have been witnessed, no doubt... Plagues, crops failing, pests perhaps?'

'The mantises,' Ember said. Rhaell said they weren't usually seen so far north.

'Mantises? Yes, could be. And it is spreading. Perhaps not fast, but it's been a few generations since things were right, yes? And now they're getting worse?'

Rhaell cleared his throat. 'The birthrate has dropped, dramatically. Magic has dwindled. We can't open portals any larger than from one end of the castle to another. I can jump a few storeys, but that's it.'

'You used to be able to fly,' said Mnorir sadly, and Rhaell flushed.

'But I can do those things,' Ember said. 'I can make werelights and those buildings I jumped over in Yskara – that's not normal. For me, I mean.'

'It isn't?' said Rhaell.

'No! We can't do that!'

'But ... you can.'

Ember raised an eyebrow at Mnorir. 'Do you know why?'

He regarded her as if she was an interesting curiosity. 'You are...' He looked her over, head to toe. 'Interesting. No parents, no grandparents ... hmm.'

'I'm not from here,' said Ember, wrapping her cloak around her as if it would shield her from his gaze.

'No-o.' His gaze was thoughtful. 'It is rare I meet a human's line fresh for the first time. It used to happen, you know. Back in my day. We visited the other realms on occasion. Backwards, primitive places, people in mud huts, that sort of thing. Is that where you're from? The mud huts?'

'Things have moved on a bit since then,' said Ember, feeling the need to defend her homeland. 'We have clockwork now.'

'How nice,' said Mnorir politely. 'What did you do to Ruvaen?'

The question came like a whiplash, out of nowhere.

'Ruvaen?' Ember touched the stone around her neck. 'I never met him.'

'Yet you wear his stone. That cannot be taken from the rightful bearer.'

That couldn't be right. She'd lifted the blue stone from the Speaker of the Myr, easy as anything. *And yet you can't take this one off.*

'She is the Promised One of the prophecy,' said Rhaell.

Ember tried to give Mnorir a defiant look.

'The Promised One, indeed? Who bears Ruvaen's Stone.'

The look the old man gave Ember was long and assessing and she didn't like it at all.

'Wise Mnorir,' began Rhaell. 'You foresaw that the Tree would lose its power?'

'Well, yes. You cannot expect to drain and drain a thing and still use its power, can you?'

'We have been draining it?' Rhaell looked aghast. 'I thought the power of the Tree was a gift!'

'It is. It was. But it has been stolen.'

'Stolen by who?'

Mnorir's gaze had not left Ember.

'I didn't steal it!' she said. 'Look, I've nicked a lot of stuff but I wouldn't even know how to nick power from a magic tree!'

'The Tree connects all things,' said Mnorir.

'So?'

'Perhaps your world is draining it.'

'What? No. That's not ... we don't have magic. We have clockwork.'

'What is clockwork?'

'It's machines that move and ... it's not magic. Listen, your Tree has a woman trapped inside it. That's probably what's killing it.'

Mnorir sighed. And it was more than a sigh, it was the sadness of eras.

'Yes,' he said, on a gust of breath. 'Dear Ephyrea.'

'Didn't think she was so dear when you locked her inside a tree,' Ember said.

'The alternative was having her killed,' said Mnorir.

'And that's worse, is it? Than being trapped forever? Not alive, never dying?'

'Ember,' said Rhaell.

'Look, I know Ysarriel was mad at her and everything, but it's been years. Decades. Centuries.'

'Millennia,' said Mnorir.

'Right. Hasn't she been punished enough?'

Mnorir merely shrugged.

'Remind me again why Ephyrea was bound into the Tree?' Ember said.

Mnorir watched her from hooded eyes. He seemed older now.

'She betrayed Ysarriel,' he said.

'By?'

Mnorir looked at Rhaell. 'Have you not told her the history of our land?'

'I have,' Rhaell said evenly. He was sitting back casually in his chair, but something about the pose told Ember he wasn't nearly as relaxed as he looked.

'Then you know why. Ephyrea betrayed Ysarriel with her husband.'

'And that's all? Ephyrea didn't ... I dunno ... accuse Ysarriel of stealing the land or anything?'

She heard Rhaell's intake of breath but didn't dare take her eyes off the old man.

Mnorir leaned forward. The firelight flickered over the hollows of his face, making shadows that brushed at something in Ember's memory.

'You have read Wynric's scroll,' he said.

'Wynric's?' said Rhaell.

'Yes.' He spoke in a language she didn't understand, but it made Rhaell stiffen.

'*Ond faegar eyattyudd us skoli,*' he repeated, leaning forward. 'What do you mean by *skoli*?'

Mnorir took his gaze off Ember for a moment, and when she followed it to Rhaell, something caught the corner of her eye.

It was Hesk, waving frantically.

In their hands was a human skull.

Ember grimaced. But Mnorir oversaw the dead, didn't he? A few skulls were surely par for the course.

'What do you want it to mean, young man?' asked Mnorir. His face seemed much sharper from this angle. Much less ... twinkly.

'Did Ysarriel steal the land?'

Mnorir shrugged. 'Steal, conquer, what's the difference? Does her descendant sit the throne today?'

'Yes,' said Rhaell.

'Are you sure?'

Rhaell's eyes narrowed. 'He wears Ysarriel's Stone.'

Mnorir waved a hand dismissively. 'What does that mean? A Rakaa wears Aywin's. And this one wears Ruvaen's Stone. And,' he cocked his head, 'Gaeleath's also. Pried it from those cold fishy hands, did you?'

'They weren't using it,' said Ember.

'No? Do you think I use mine? That's what you've come for, isn't it? You're collecting the stones.'

Ember wasn't sure why she looked around the room at that moment. At the tables against the walls, and the paintings above them. At the skulls. The bones. The jewellery, heaped in piles. Had that always been there?

At the paintings hanging on the cave walls. Each one a portrait. Each one screaming.

She looked at Hesk, who held Caeda's silver ring in one hand, and her small fingerbones in the other.

'We need to heal the Tree,' said Rhaell.

'Do you? And then what happens?'

When she looked back at Mnorir, he seemed much larger, looming over his chair. His purple robe looked more like black in this light, like the wings of a bat.

'Then the Tree is healed and whole,' said Rhaell, who had shifted his posture considerably. Ember thought his hand was near the hilt of his sword.

Mnorir laughed, and it was a sound that echoed far more than it should have. The cave was full of shadows.

'Restore the heart to the Tree, and the Tree can die,' he said. 'Is that what you want, boy?'

'The Tree cannot be whole and healthy without its heart,' Rhaell said.

'It's managed for generations,' Mnorir said. 'And trust me, I've counted them. Every one that's come to me. The children of the children of the children...'

'And the ones who come here, like us?' Ember said. 'What do you do with them?'

Mnorir smiled, and it was the grin of a predator. 'The ones who come to me before their time?' he said. 'Why, I keep them safe.'

Ember could not look at the screaming paintings.

We have to get out of here. But how? The archway they'd come through had vanished, replaced by smooth rock. The room had no exits, save for maybe the fireplace, and Ember knew that had to be magical because how the hell did a fireplace exist under a waterfall?

'Threw your tokens into the water, did you?' said Mnorir, and laughed that dreadful laugh. He was twice their height now, skin stretched right over his skull, shadow filling the room. 'I knew that wheeze was a good one.'

'Why?' Ember said. 'Why do you want people to come down here?'

'I have been here thousands of years. Sometimes they plead prettily. Sometimes they make interesting bargains,' said Mnorir. The black stone at his bony chest glittered.

'And what kind of bargain do you want from us?' said Rhaell. He was on his feet now, hand gripping his sword hilt harder.

'Me? I was not the one who started this,' said Mnorir. 'I want nothing from you.'

There had to be something. What did they have? The stones? Rhaell's sword? Did Hesk have anything?

'Would it be so bad to stay here?' Mnorir murmured. 'You have family,' he said to Rhaell. 'You have friends,' he added to Ember.

Caeda. Guilt swamped Ember. What if she could see her again? Apologise to her? Beg her forgiveness?

'I have no need to raise the shade of my mother,' said Rhaell coldly.

'Nor I mine,' said Ember.

'No? Not even to ask her why you were never enough?' Mnorir said softly, 'All those births, all those losses, making her weaker and weaker. Why didn't she stop? Why didn't she thank your Lords for the healthy children she had and stop trying to have more? Why,' he said, eyes glinting in their sockets, 'weren't you good enough?'

Ember clenched her fists, the old hurt burning through her. How did he know? Was her mother here?

'Of course, you made sure that would never happen to you,

didn't you? Dead on the inside. No life will ever come from you, will it?'

Her jaw clenched. How could he know this? Her darkest, most awful secret? How did she stop him talking? 'Shut *up*.'

'That woman and her sharp little tools...'

'Gaeleath's Stone,' Ember blurted, and Mnorir cocked his head.

Rhaell lunged for her. 'Ember, no—'

She shrugged him off. 'What use is it to us if we're dead? If I give you Gaeleath's Stone, will you let us out of here?'

Mnorir cocked his monstrous head. The shadows around his eyes were fathomless holes. His face was little more than a skull.

'Why would I want Gaeleath's Stone? What have I to heal?' He spread his skeletal hands.

What have I to heal?

When she'd held Gaeleath's Stone as she lay in bed with half her foot chewed off, she'd felt its warmth. And more than that, she'd felt its power. The throb and ache in her foot had eased, the burn had quietened, the prickle of pain had soothed. Gaeleath's Stone healed, because Gaeleath had been a healer.

So Ruvaen's Stone...

You move silently for an erlish.

Ember took the biggest gamble of her life.

'You want this?' she said, unfastening the top of her jerkin and pulling on the chain around her neck.

The dark eye sockets gleamed.

'Ember,' said Rhaell, anguished, and she held out her hand to shush him.

'This for our freedom,' she said, not taking her eyes off Mnorir. 'You let us out of here, back to the surface world, whole and unharmed. All three of us.'

Mnorir glanced around, having apparently forgotten Hesk was there, and Ember lunged.

She could climb anything. Always had. Since she was a tiny tot. Her mother had found her hanging off furniture and walls and trees. It was why she'd taken Ember out thieving in the first place. *You can do it, little ferret.*

She grasped Ruvaen's Stone in one hand and leapt as she could only leap here in Yskara.

Mnorir's robes were gritty and dusty, and the body beneath them was truly no more than bones. But bones were excellent for climbing. Ember flew up to his chest and grasped the black stone, which pulsed coldly in her hand.

Mnorir let out a roar and grabbed her off his chest.

'Rhaell, now!' she yelled, and Lords bless every inch of him, he understood what she meant.

He smashed his sword into Mnorir, and that towering skeleton crashed down like a bag of bones. Ember, still clinging to the black stone as if her life depended on it – which it probably did – kicked off his sternum and was suddenly yanked back.

'You think you can steal from me?' Mnorir roared, and grabbed Ember's body in one huge, skeletal hand. He squeezed, and she screamed. Rhaell swung his sword at Mnorir's wrist, but the pressure didn't let up.

Her free hand scrabbled desperately at her neck.

'You think Ruvaen's Stone can help you?' cackled Mnorir. 'Even he could not take my stone from its rightful owner!'

But it wasn't Ruvaen's Stone Ember grabbed from her jerkin. It wasn't the thief's charm she pressed against the bones of Mnorir's neck.

It was Gaeleath's Stone, the stone of healing, the stone that had knitted the flesh of her foot back together far faster than Phoebe and her sacred water. And it began to heal Mnorir.

Flesh began to creep back across his bones. Muscles, veins, skin. But it wasn't the flesh of a living man. Mnorir hadn't been alive for centuries. Something had been keeping him in this state of undeath, something had been perverting the natural order of death. Something rotten. Something wrong. Something that Gaeleath's Stone healed.

His jaw opened on a scream that dried into a dreadful death rattle, and the breath that washed over Ember's face stank of decay.

His huge, powerful skeleton shrank down and down, to the size of a man, and smaller. His corpse shrivelled to bones and then to dust, crunching and crumbling under Ember's knees.

Until she knelt in a pile of rotten, dusty cloth, clutching the black stone in her hand.

'Leaves and branches,' Rhaell whispered.

Ember looked up at him and sneezed.

'Did we just kill Death?' she said.

'There's no "we" about it, Sparks.' He gave her his hand, and she stood, peering at the black stone and then back at the pile of dust that had been Mnorir. 'By the Tree, Ember. How did you know what would work?'

A sob of laughter escaped her. 'I didn't. Oh Lords, Rhaell, I thought Ruvaen's Stone would let me steal it!'

He stared at her, incredulous. 'That was your back-up plan?'

'No!' She laughed hysterically. Ma would be appalled at her lack of foresight. 'That was completely made up on the spot!'

'Right,' said Rhaell faintly. He looked around. 'Now, how do we get out of here?'

'Those magic stones, *erlish*?' said Hesk.

Ember looked at the three of them, trying to sober herself. 'Well, we've got thieving, healing, and death,' she said. She went to the nearest wall – and paused.

'What?'

'The paintings.' Ember gestured at the black frames. 'They're all empty.'

The canvases were blank. The screaming faces had gone.

'The tokens,' said Hesk.

The skulls were crumbling. The bones were turning to dust. Some of these things must have been here for millennia.

Ember reached out and picked up a gold torc. Gold didn't crumble with age. It gleamed bright and strong in her hand.

'A keepsake?' said Rhaell, and Ember looked at the bright, warm gleam of it. All around her were heaps of stones and precious metals.

She put down the torc, strode over to Hesk and took Caeda's ring back.

Then she pressed Mnorir's Stone to the cave wall, and a door opened.

And the sea flooded in.

CHAPTER 21

'Deep breath!' Rhaell shouted, and grabbed Ember's hand. His other hand grasped Hesk's cloak, and the Myr leapt forward into the torrent of freezing water filling the cave.

Ember couldn't swim. And her last experience with water had nearly killed her. So, too, had the one before that, come to think of it.

As the water smashed into them like a fist, Rhaell grabbed Ember to him and clamped her against his body. *I won't let go of you.*

Hesk didn't look particularly large or powerful, but they swam up with more strength than Rhaell could have managed. He kicked off, too, propelling them upwards as Ember thrashed against him in panic.

He couldn't blame her, but it wasn't exactly helpful.

The water was dark, and full of ... things that brushed against him, grabbed and tangled. The pressure of it against him was immense, like a giant fist squeezing him. His lungs started burning before the first rays of light even penetrated the darkness, and he felt Ember kicking in panic in his arms.

Hesk had promised to get them safely out of the water. But how, when they appeared to be at the bottom of the Sacred Sea? He didn't even know how deep that was. Too deep to hold his breath for. So deep the weight of the water was crushing him.

Something nudged him from beneath, and he kicked feebly at it. It pushed again, and he tried to look down but all he saw was blackness. And then he saw teeth.

Teeth that lined a massive mouth, a mouth the size of a cave, a mouth so gigantic he couldn't even take it in. Teeth that snapped over him.

They were being *eaten*.

Rhaell kicked out at the teeth, but his lungs were bursting and what vision he had left was going dark. They were going to die. He'd so nearly saved them both, and now they were going to be eaten by some huge animal.

He clutched Ember to him. *I'm sorry. I'm so sorry.*

Then Hesk's clammy hands were shaking him. '*Erlish*? Breathe. *Erlish* is strange shade.'

Rhaell looked around wildly, but his lungs made the decision for him, sucking in gulps of air before he'd even had the chance to decide if it was safe.

He coughed and spluttered. 'Ugh! What is that smell?'

'The mouth of the kingbeast. Kingbeasts breathe air. Erlish breathes it, too.' Hesk sounded pleased, although Rhaell couldn't see them.

'It's going to eat us! We have to get out!'

Hesk shook their head. 'No, *erlish* are safe. Hesk has command over the kingbeast.'

Rhaell looked around him, panting, his lungs feeling like they'd been flayed from the inside. The huge mouth didn't actually seem to be chewing or swallowing or moving. They were being held still. In a cage of teeth. Endless, endless rows of teeth.

Rhaell had only glimpsed the kingbeast from a distance, a vast creature of scales and fins occasionally breaking the water, or as a shadow deep below the waves, but he figured its mouth must be large enough to swallow an average-sized house whole.

And the smell. Like rotten fish and old meat and sewage and bad eggs. But it was the sweetest air he'd ever breathed.

He realised he still had his arms around Ember. And that she was lying horribly still.

'Ember? Sparks? Wake up. There's air here. It's foul, but it's air.' She didn't stir. 'Ember. Ember!'

Fuck, fuck. He fumbled her in his arms, grabbing at her face and pressing his mouth to hers. He breathed out hard, three times, four, five. Felt at her chest. It wasn't moving. He breathed into her mouth again, pinching her nose so hard it would probably bruise. Not that bruising would matter if she wasn't breathing.

Come on, Ember. Come on.

He locked his hands together and pumped them against her chest. Over and over. Breathed into her mouth. Pumped her chest.

No. *No.* They couldn't escape Mnorir, death himself, for her to die like this! Rhaell tore at her jerkin, freeing her to breathe, and something hard nudged his hand.

Mnorir's Stone. He tossed it aside, and pressed his mouth to hers again, and suddenly she surged against him.

Breath filled her lungs. Wonderful, wonderful breath. Rhaell pumped her chest and thumped her back and she vomited up sea water all over the floor. Well, not the floor, because they were in the kingbeast's mouth. Its tongue, probably. Ugh.

'*Erlish?*'

Rhaell pushed Ember onto her side and grabbed her hand, massaging her back as she spat out more water. He wanted to collapse beside her, to gather her into his arms and promise he'd never let her come to harm again. But he made himself calm down. She was alive. Everything else could be fixed.

He held her hand like it was the only thing keeping her alive.

'Almost there, *erlish*. When kingbeast opens mouth, swim, yes?

Kingbeast can't reach shore. Also, Hesk can't control kingbeast's hunger for too long.'

Rhaell nodded, exhausted. 'And you?'

Hesk sounded delighted. 'Hesk has whole Sacred Sea to discover! *Erlish* can get to shore, yes?'

'Yes.' He didn't care how far it was, he'd get Ember to safety.

'Be ready,' said Hesk, and then the great mouth was opening, and the sweetness of fresh sea air filled Rhaell's lungs.

By the light of the moons he could see Ember, lying on her side and coughing, her skin silvery pale and her hair in wet tails across her face. He didn't look at the giant maw that held them, the rows of teeth and the horrifying blackness behind them.

'Ember. Can you put your arms around my neck?'

She stirred a little. Hesk said, 'No time! Go! Go! Kingbeast is hungry!'

With that, Hesk leapt out into the water, and was gone.

Rhaell glanced up, saw the mighty jaws begin to close, and grabbed Ember. Lurched across the spongy tongue – eurgh – and threw Ember ahead of him into the water. The teeth snapped down as he used all the strength he had to dive out between them and hit the blessedly clean, cold water.

The snap sounded behind him, water heaving over him in a wave. A few feet away, Ember spluttered and struggled in the water.

Rhaell hauled her into his arms and eyed the kingbeast. It snorted water, eyes glittering at him. Its snout barely broke the surface, but from nostril to eye was about the size of the throne room in the castle.

He glanced the other way. The shore was visible. They could make it, so long as the beast didn't change its mind.

'We have to go. Now. Put your arms around my neck.

She blinked at him, apparently barely awake. The kingbeast opened its mouth.

Then a whistle sounded, and the gargantuan head turned away from him, vanishing under the surface. Hesk. Thank the Tree.

'Ember! Hold onto me.' He dragged her over his back like a cape and tucked her hands into the straps of his pack. Then he set off for the shore, arms cutting through the dark water one stroke at a time.

It was hard work, and he was already exhausted. His lungs burned with the effort, and his muscles protested every stroke. Rhaell swam grimly on, Ember a heavy weight on his back.

'Still with me?' he asked, and she made a small noise. 'Sparks?'

'Yeah?'

'Stay awake for me, yeah?'

'Yeah,' Ember agreed, but he was fairly sure she wouldn't.

The moons shone high above, their light silvering the water. Rhaell began to imagine he could see shapes in it. Things moving under the surface. Leaves and branches, there had better not be any hafmey on this side of the Sacred Sea! He couldn't fight them off and keep Ember safe at the same time. But nothing emerged, and he figured he was just exhausted and seeing things.

Until something grabbed his ankle and yanked him down.

Rhaell kicked out in a panic, water shooting up his nose. The weight from his back floated free, and he realised in horror he had lost Ember. She was unmoored and *unable to swim*.

Something slashed at his thigh, and he kicked out, desperate to take a breath. He could barely see in the dark water, but the thing streaking towards him was pale, dark hair floating about its head like ink in the water.

He kicked out hard and shoved up to the surface, sucking in as much air as quickly as he could, casting about desperately for Ember. But he couldn't see her.

Something dragged his arm: sharp teeth or claws raking his flesh. Rhaell grabbed a knife and hacked at it, and it fell away, but something else was back, seizing his ankle. He kicked hard and slashed blindly at the water.

He formed his hand around a werelight, ducked it under the water, and suddenly shapes appeared.

Fucking hafmey!

Rhaell was a decent swimmer, and a decent fighter, but doing both at the same time wasn't on his list of skills. He stabbed and slashed, snapped bones and slit throats, and all the while kept ducking below the surface desperately to find Ember.

There she was! Bobbing above and then under the surface, cloak billowing around her as she thrashed and fought with a long-limbed Myr that was trying to drag her down. It was pale, its slitted nose flat, and suddenly he realised he recognised it. What the fuck was Neris doing here?

She was grabbing at Ember with clawed hands, and Ember was fighting back, but he could see her struggling. He stabbed the nearest hafmey in the eye, kicked another in the chest and darted under the surface to grab the Myr, shoving Ember upwards with his other hand. Neris turned on him, eyes big and black with hatred. *Neris is a bad Myr.*

Well, he was no saint himself. Rhaell punched out, but underwater the blow lacked force. Neris grinned, her mouth full of teeth, gills working on her neck. She launched herself at him, teeth first, and Rhaell brought his knee up into her chin. He grabbed her wrist and yanked it savagely, and while the crack of her bones was silent under the water, he felt it.

The sound of her scream was nightmarish. Rhaell needed to surface again, but she swam down at him, blocking his exit, diving with a knife in her unharmed fist. He arched away, the knife catching his arm, but he was too big and clumsy against her. Neris darted around like a fish, rounding his side and stabbing up at his ribs. Rhaell tried to defend against her, but his sight was beginning to dim around the edges and his lungs were burning.

He prayed to the Tree that Ember had been able to get away.

Neris's knife abruptly stopped, and as Rhaell's eyesight faded, he thought he saw her stab herself in the chest. No. He must be hallucinating. Someone had got Neris from behind, arms wrapped around her neck, and the Myr was jamming her own knife into her chest over and over, dark blood billowing out into the water.

He burst through the surface of the water, dragging in desperate lungfuls of air, and before he could go back down to see what the fuck was happening, Ember popped up beside him.

'We'd better go,' she said, 'that blood's gonna attract something.'

All around them were the corpses of hafmey, bobbing on the surface, some with their own claws still embedded in their throats.

Rhaell gawped at her as she trod water very badly, beginning to sink under the waves again. He grabbed her.

'What?' he spluttered. 'How? What?'

Ember raised the black Stone around her neck. 'Figured this was worth a try,' she said.

Mnorir's Stone. The Stone of Death. It had made Neris kill herself. And she had dominion over the hafmey, so they'd followed suit.

'Fuck,' Rhaell breathed.

'Yeah. Can we go? The shore ain't far but it's also too far, if you know what I mean.'

He nodded, hauled her onto his back again, and swam, the weight of Mnorir's Stone pressing through his clothes, heavy against his spine.

~

Ember would have kissed the ground, but she wasn't sure she had the energy to move. She lay on her back beside Rhaell, sodden and shivering, her mouth full of bile. Above her, one moon shone brightly, the other a mere crescent. Funny how that seemed perfectly normal now.

Rhaell's chest rose and fell with mighty deep breaths. He

looked as if he could barely move. But he did, sitting up with a groan and rubbing his head.

'Are you okay?'

She nodded. 'You're the one who just swum us here.'

'You said you couldn't swim.'

'I can't. And I think I swallowed a lot of water.' She spat some out, grimacing. There was a canteen hooked to her pack, but as she wrestled it off her back, she realised it was probably the only thing that had survived the sea water. Her change of clothes would be soaked and the food they'd brought from Feynrith would be ruined.

She gulped some blessedly cool, clean water and offered it to Rhaell. He drank some, too, looking around the rocky shore they'd washed up on. Rocky cliffs rose not far behind them, topped with dark trees. In either direction, rocks and trees were the only things visible. That, and the dark, lapping sea.

'I don't suppose we're half a mile from the castle?' Ember asked hopefully.

He shook his head, handing her back the canteen. 'We're a long way from the castle. We're a long way from anywhere. That,' he pointed, 'is Bronavon Point.'

Ember followed the direction to a peak of rocks guarding a dark cleft in the land where the moon didn't shine.

'And what's Bronavon Point?'

'The entry to a canyon, where a river flows from the mountains into the sea. It used to be called Gluyver's Point, but many Yskarans fell there during the war with the Rakaa. Bronavon means "River of Sorrows",' he told her.

'Rakaa again. Mnorir said – wait – Mnorir said—'

Rhaell smiled, his white teeth glinting in the darkness. 'That Aywin's Stone is worn by a Rakaa.'

Ember glazed at the canyon, beyond which the sky was black, empty of stars. Mountains? Or something more sinister?

She shivered. 'Hesk brought us here on purpose?'

'Well, I asked them to bring us out on the north shore, because if we're going to go searching for Wynric's Stone among the dragon caves, that's where we need to go. But, uh...'

'Uh?'

He ran a hand over his square jaw, now rough with a day's stubble. It just made him look more handsome. 'This,' he said, 'might be one of the more dangerous stones to retrieve.'

Ember threw up her hands. 'More difficult than the one where I nearly died or the one where we both nearly died?'

He winced and nodded.

Ember wrapped her arms around herself. She was soaking wet, and it was freezing up here. 'Okay,' she said. 'Okay. First things first. We find shelter, we get warm, and then you tell me what the fuck your plan is to steal a stone from some barbarians. 'Cos last time that didn't go so well. We need a proper plan, Rhaell. A proper plan. To get out, as well as in.'

'Of course,' he said. 'Would I take you into enemy territory with no plan?'

It wasn't that Rhaell didn't have a plan to get out. It was more that the plan he had really just involved only Ember getting out.

But he didn't tell Ember that. Instead, he got to his feet, taking in a deep breath of the blessedly clean air, and scanned the cliffs. He'd been here once or twice before, and he recalled there were caves in Bronavon Canyon. They could probably find shelter there.

'Can you walk?' he said.

Ember nodded and got to her own feet. She was shivering.

'Look – there's no sense walking in wet clothes. Perhaps we should get changed.'

'Into what? I dunno if you noticed but we just got soaked through and so did all our stuff.'

Rhaell blinked. 'Did the charm fail?'

'Charm?'

He took off his own pack and opened it. The contents were bone dry.

'I put a charm on them to keep them dry. What with us going under the sea and all.'

Ember gaped at him, and grabbed her own pack, peering in. 'You're joking! How?'

'It's a pretty simple charm...'

'One you're going to have to teach me.' She threw her pack to the ground and began stripping off her jerkin. 'Can I do charms? I opened the portal, and I could jump and stuff, so can I do the other stuff?'

'I don't know.' Rhaell averted his eyes from her clinging wet shirt. 'We can try.'

'Cool. Because keeping shit dry would be so useful. Couldn't you have charmed the clothes we were wearing?'

'Not without suffocating us. Um. Are you getting changed right now?'

Ember cast a withering look in his direction before she dragged her shirt over her head. Rhaell spun around.

'No need to be coy, Buttercup. I've seen you with your shirt off.'

His hands clenched into fists, shame burning at him. Yes. She'd seen the ruin of his back. He should have been more careful. But she got under his skin, this Promised One, this thief, with her wit and her defiance and her exceptionally lovely curves—

'Come to think of it, you've seen me in just my chemmy before.'

He could hear the wet splat of more clothing hitting the rocks.

'Yes, but not on purpose,' he said, anguished. Oh, the moonlight would turn her skin to silver...

'Well, suit yourself. But just so you know,' Ember said, and paused long enough that he almost turned around. 'Any time you want to see me naked? You just say so.'

Rhaell actually felt his eyes bulge.

''Cos that kiss?' she said, and whistled, 'we can do that any time you want, too.'

By the Tree. Rhaell wanted that with everything he had. He closed his eyes and indulged in the fantasy of turning around and taking her naked body in his arms and kissing her mouth thoroughly. And then he'd kiss the rest of her thoroughly. All over. Until she squirmed and screamed and he—

He cleared his throat. 'Are you done?'

'I'm decent, if that's what you mean.'

It wasn't. But he risked a look over his shoulder to see her in clean, dry trousers and shirt, pulling on a thick sweater. It mussed up her hair, and his fingers itched to go and smooth it.

Instead, he said, 'Would you mind turning around?'

Ember looked like she wanted to say something, but she threw up her hands and turned to sit on a rock to lace her boots up.

'Rhaell?'

'Yeah?'

Rhaell got his clean shirt ready before he stripped off his wet one.

'Do you think... He was lying about my mother being there, wasn't he? And yours.'

He paused, dripping. 'I don't know.'

''Cos the other thing he said ... about me being ... dead inside...'

'You're not dead inside,' said Rhaell firmly, taking a deep breath and stripping as quickly as possible, leaving his back uncovered for the merest fraction of a second. The scars there hadn't hurt for years, but he felt them burning now.

Ember was silent for a long enough that he nearly turned around, then she said quietly, 'No life will come from me. That part's true.'

He hesitated with his clean shirt over his head, and then pulled it on. 'Is it?'

'Yeah. I think so. Yeah.' She hesitated for a moment, and he heard her sigh. 'I was young. Not long after my mother died. And I ... got into trouble.'

Trouble. That was an old expression. Yskaran women didn't talk about 'getting into trouble' anymore. Not out loud.

'And I knew I couldn't have a baby – I had a crippled father and two baby brothers and I could barely put food on the table for us, and I was alone, and...'

Her voice rose with panic. Rhaell said, 'It's okay. It's okay.'

'So, I asked around – upside of being a thief is you know plenty of criminals – and went to see this woman. She had ... sharp metal things. She warned me.'

Rhaell fastened his trousers. 'Warned you?'

'That the consequences could be ... permanent. And I thought, well that's okay, 'cos I saw what childbearing did to my mother and how hard being a mother was and I thought, I don't want to ever do that. Ever. And it's just as well, because now I ... can't. Mnorir was right.'

Rhaell sat down to do up his boots, his back to her, when really he wanted to go and take her in his arms and reassure her everything was all right. 'That must have been hard,' he said.

'I never knew pain like it. And I've had my foot chewed off by little fishes. I bled and I bled, until I thought I was gonna die. And then after that, I never bled again.'

He had heard of such things. Merelle and her girls had horror stories they didn't tell him, but Rhaell knew how to listen to what people weren't saying. To the king and the court, a child was greatly sought after, a blessing from the Ancestors.

Was it still a blessing if you didn't want it?

I was alone. 'What about the father?' he said, trying not to think about any other man getting his hands all over Ember.

Ember snorted. 'Absolutely none of the candidates were even worth telling about it.' She sniffed, and said, 'In Coldonia you can go to jail for it. Here ... I'd be executed *by my own fiancé.*'

His fists clenched. 'That won't happen.'

She gave a desperate laugh. 'You sure?'

'Ember. I will kill anyone who even tries to harm you.' He meant it. He'd have killed that bastard Mnorir if he could, and as for the Myr he'd burned, he was glad of it. He would burn the world to keep her safe.

Ember was precious. Ember was his.

'Thanks,' she said after a moment, and he heard her push out a breath of relief. 'I wasn't sure if you'd understand.'

His heart ached. How could he condemn a scared girl who was already drowning under responsibilities she'd never asked for? *Do you think she became a thief by choice?*

'Not everyone in Yskara feels the same way as the king,' he told her gently.

'Glad to hear it. Between you and me, I think he might not be a very nice person.'

Rhaell snorted. 'You have no idea.'

'You won't ... um, tell him, will you? Or anyone?'

'Of course not.' He should tell her about what he did for Merelle and the others. Rhaell opened his mouth, but she got there first.

'Or I'll ... I'll turn around and look right at your back,' she said, 'and then tell everyone about it.'

His reaction was involuntary and violent, a shudder ripping through him, a snarl coming from his throat. He whirled towards her, hands moving to weapons he hadn't yet fastened at his hips.

Stand down, you stupid animal. He forced himself to relax his muscles, turn back to his clothes and finish dressing. Ember was not a threat. And he was in control of himself.

'Lords, Rhaell, I won't,' she said. 'Mutually assured destruction, yeah? Your secret's safe with me. Even if I don't understand it.'

I pray you never will.

These weren't wounds he'd received defending his own life or anyone else's. They weren't the honest scars of a soldier. They were his shame and his disgrace, and he had spent his life hiding them from everyone.

He paused, hands gripping a clean jerkin. She'd find out soon enough what they meant. When they strode into a Rakaa camp and he told them the truth he'd kept from her. Then he'd see her anger, her disgust, her hatred. Because she would hate him. He'd betrayed her trust. He'd *lied*.

But once he told them the truth, they'd be distracted enough for her to steal the stone.

It was a terrible plan, but it was the best one he'd got.

His throat was thick with self-loathing as he finished dressing and bundled his wet clothes into his cloak. 'When we find shelter, I'll make a fire and we can dry these out,' he said.

'Sure.' Out of the corner of his eye he saw Ember get to her feet. Her voice was entirely neutral. 'Are we both decently covered? Let's go.'

~

'Never?' said King Onas, his anger mounting. 'Not once?'

His informant remained kneeling, image translucent and flickering up from the charm bracelet he'd placed on the floor. 'No, Your Grace.'

There was a bottle of Feynrithian ice wine on the table. The king's hand curled around the neck.

'Do Yskaran women bleed?'

'Rarely, Your Grace.'

'Yet, it's necessary? If she's to be fertile?'

'Usually, Your Grace.'

And the treacherous, lying, common little bitch wasn't.

'She lied!'

Onas's roar echoed off the chamber walls as he hurled the bottle at the informant. It passed right through their image, hitting the wall behind, smashing into a tapestry ten generations old and soaking it in purple.

The prophecy had said she would bear fruit! How had she tricked them all?

Onas needed that heir. He had to secure his legacy. The Tree was dying because his successors consisted of one monstrous whelp and no one else. A dynasty needed to last for generations, to have a strong future as well as a grounded past. The more heirs you had, the fewer questions people asked.

Wine dripped down the wall and puddled on a priceless carpet.

The wedding was in less than a week. A few days more and that vulgar bitch would be a princess, a member of the royal family. The future queen. She could bump off Bronadyr and seize power in her own right. Was that her game? Seduce him, flatter his obscenity until he was cuntstruck and would follow her anywhere. Look how he'd mooned over her in Valoris! And then when she'd said her vows beneath the Tree, when her blood was truly bound to his, she'd lead a coup against him.

He could see it now. She'd faked her arrival into the Great Chamber, given herself a few superficial wounds to distract them into asking the wrong questions, and now she planned to overthrow him.

Onas paced, his slippers squelching lightly on the soaked carpet. What if she hadn't gone to Feynrith after all? What if she'd bumped off Cadia or Caedis – or whatever her name was – in order to have some excuse to leave the progress? She could be gathering troops right now. She could be in league with the Myr. He didn't buy the boy's story about her straying off course. Of course not! Another faked injury, no doubt, or perhaps that Cadis girl had fought back before the usurper violently murdered her.

'Where is she?' he demanded. 'Did she go to Feynrith?'

His informant said, 'Yes, Your Grace.'

'And? Is she still there? Or was staying a week a total bluff, too?'

The informant hesitated. 'It was, Your Grace.'

Onas howled and threw his wineglass after the bottle. 'Where is she now? Gone back to the Myr? Are we to expect an invasion from the sea?'

'I ... don't think so, Your Grace. I think...'

The informant looked away. Onas knew this reluctance. Knew from experience that no amount of honey would sweeten the deal. Threats were the only thing that worked.

'I think your mother would want you to tell me,' he growled softly.

Ah! Such a delicious capitulation.

'North,' whispered his informant. 'The Shadowed Mountains.'

~

Ember didn't know how long she slept for, but she woke up aching and stiff. And warm. And breathing in ... bitter orange?

Right. The canyon, the cave. They'd trekked until she could barely put one foot in front of the other, but Rhaell had found a shallow cave for shelter, and lit a fire, and Ember had dozed off...

And now Rhaell held her cradled in his arms, his whole body wrapped around hers, the two of them covered by his jacket. Both of them were otherwise fully dressed, but she could feel every inch of him. Every rock-hard, magnificent inch.

Well, well. For a man who pleaded disinterest, there was a lot of ... interest ... pressing against her stomach.

Should she try to kiss him? Early-morning light stole in from the mouth of the cave, lovingly gilding his beautiful profile. His chest rose and fell evenly against hers, skin warm through his shirt. His chiselled jaw was dark with stubble, his lips softly parted. Ember remembered those lips, remembered the desperate hunger he'd kissed her with.

He'd wanted that kiss just as much as she had. He'd been just as devoured by passion. If Hesk hadn't interrupted them, they'd probably still be naked on that riverbed, frantically fucking each other's brains out.

The thought had her shifting against him, letting her body shamelessly memorise the feel of his. Oh *yes*. His body wanted this, even if the rest of him didn't know it.

She couldn't actually kiss him while he was sleeping. That was a bit of a shitty thing to do; she wouldn't think much of him if he tried it on her. But she could try to wake him up.

She stretched up to his neck and breathed in his scent. By rights, he ought to smell terrible, damp and sweaty and salty from the sea. And somehow she was still breathing in bitter oranges. His skin smelled so good she wanted to lick it. Would he taste like he smelled? Would there be bitter oranges on her tongue, or salt and sweat?

A tiny whimper escaped her throat. She couldn't help it. But Rhaell didn't wake, just squeezed his arms around her a little, sighing in his sleep.

Please wake up. She was beginning to get desperate now, thighs pressing together with need. Except his leg was between hers, and dear Lords, if he didn't wake up soon, she was going to start humping his thigh.

'Rhaell.' She let her fingers caress his cheek, and he nuzzled into her touch. 'Wake up, Buttercup.'

Her lips grazed his jaw, and his eyelids fluttered.

'Rhaell.' It was a whisper and a plea. 'Can you hear me?'

'Mmm.'

'Can I kiss you?'

Those delicious lips curved in a smile. 'Yes.'

Oh, thank the *Lords*. Ember touched her lips to his, willing him to wake further. She let her tongue trace the fullness of his lower lip, and he groaned and tightened his arms around her.

'Ember.'

Yes. *Yes.* Ember sucked gently on his lower lip and he groaned again, his mouth opening under hers.

His eyes opened.

And he kissed her back.

Ember made a desperate sound against his mouth and surged against him, hand going to his hair and tangling there. Her leg slid over his, wrapping around his hip, holding him against her.

He felt so *good*.

She kissed him with wild hunger, scarcely daring to breathe. She needed him, needed to taste him and touch him. Her hands roamed his magnificent body, pushing at his leather jerkin, and she shamelessly arched her back to press her breasts against his chest. His hands slid over her, holding her to him, fingers grasping at her shoulders, her neck, her back, as if he couldn't believe she was real.

Between her legs, she felt him grow harder, and she rubbed herself against him, trying to get the right friction. His cock felt amazing, even through layers of clothing. What was it going to be like against her bare skin, gliding against her slippery wet folds, nudging her clit, pushing inside her? He was big, she could already tell. He'd stretch her, press hard against all those places inside that rarely got the stimulation they needed. He'd fill her right up, until there was no space inside her for anything but him. Until she consumed him, and he consumed her right back.

Ember moaned at the thought. Lords, she had to feel him. She needed to grasp his hot length in her hand, see if her fingers even fit around it, feel it throb against her palm. She wanted to taste him, feel him against her tongue, lick up his flavour, swallow him down.

There were too many clothes between them, too much separating her skin from his, and she growled in frustration, worming one hand between them to fiddle with the fastening of his trousers.

And suddenly she found herself on her back, cold air rushing in as Rhaell leapt away from her like a scalded cat.

'Wha—?' Ember gazed up at him, lust-dazed, as he plastered himself back against the opposite wall of the cave. His blue eyes nearly glowed, but it wasn't with desire. It was shock. Anger. Fear. 'Rhaell?'

'I don't—' His fists clenched. 'That was—'

'Amazing,' Ember moaned, arching her back and thrusting her breasts in his direction. Her hands reached out to him, and he shrank back.

'A mistake.'

He shoved away from the wall and was outside, away from her, in seconds.

Ember lay there, cold, panting, her whole body throbbing with frustration. What had she done wrong? One second he'd been kissing her like his life depended on it, the next he couldn't get away fast enough. Had she moved too fast? Maybe she'd gone for his cock too soon. Maybe he wanted more ... wooing.

'First time for everything,' she muttered.

But he'd pulled away from her before, hadn't he? At the waterfall, when she'd kissed him the first time. The look on his face then had been ... almost fearful.

Was he rejecting her because he didn't want her? Or because he was afraid of what would happen if he had her? She was, technically, engaged to the prince. Was Rhaell afraid of him? The Beast would probably be a fearsome rival in love, but then he didn't actually love her. The Beast seemed to either forget about her or despise her.

You could give me heirs with all your arms and legs broken.

Maybe Rhaell was afraid of him. Ember knew she was. But she'd have thought he'd have more balls about it. *Don't think about his balls.*

Her fingers clenched with the need to touch him. To feel those calloused hands on her, to learn all the planes and valleys of his body. To search the canyons of the scars on his back.

She sat up. Was that it? He was ashamed of his scars? He'd been horrified at the idea of her seeing them as he was getting dressed; she'd only meant to joke about it last night, but had he really been hurt?

Surely, he didn't think those scars made him ... ugly?

Ember sighed. How the hell did she get him to talk about this?

'Hey, you know those scars on your back that are clearly from some horrific injury and you're appalled by the very idea of me seeing them? No worries, it's cool, I think they're sexy.' No. He'd think she had some kind of weird fetish.

She shook herself and got to her knees, trying to ignore the various aches that were making themselves known. She was in a shallow cave, and nearby was the remains of a fire. Their wet clothing had been staked out on sticks and twigs and was mostly dry, so she bundled it up and repacked it. And while she did that, she had a tiny peek at what Rhaell had deemed necessary to bring with him on this little trip.

Socks. Bandages. Various salves. Bags of jewels, which briefly excited her until she realised they were more fakes to substitute for the stones. Notebooks with details of the Ancestors' legends copied out in neat script.

A small carved wooden dragon, the paint mostly rubbed off. It had been wrapped in a stained piece of fabric, the silk once fine and patterned.

The scarf he'd tried to return to her after the hunt in Addor. He'd kept it.

Ember knelt there with it in her hand, staring at the cave wall. He'd kept her scarf. And he'd washed out the mud, and he'd used it to wrap what looked like a child's toy.

What the fuck was she supposed to make of that?

She carefully packed the keepsakes away, frowning, and put on her cloak. Outside, a light rain was falling, and she'd had enough of being wet for now. There was a little food left, so she ate some dried meat and berries while she waited to see if Rhaell would come back, decided he was sulking, and set out to refill her water canteen.

The stones she wore under her shirt vibrated slightly. That was odd. Maybe they were reacting to her mood.

She'd got a couple of steps outside when something grabbed her arm and a voice snarled words she couldn't understand.

'Lemme go! I'll scream!'

The voice snarled some more at her. It sounded like a bear would, if bears could talk, but it was definitely saying words. The hand that gripped her arm felt pretty human, albeit much larger than usual. The intonation of the voice was asking her a question.

'I'm sorry if I ain't supposed to be here,' she said. 'I got lost?' And then, because like most Coldonians faced with a foreigner her response was to speak her own language more loudly, she repeated, 'Lost, yeah?'

The person behind her growled. Ember really, really wished she'd fastened on her belt with her knives, but all she had was her fists and the three stones on pendants or in her pocket. They pulsed, and some impulse was telling her to turn around, to reach out—

Healing was no use to her. Death was too dangerous. But Ruvaen's Stone? If she could reach that, she could maybe slip away from the creature, unnoticed?

But she couldn't move her arms. Ember tried to think. She wasn't much of a fighter, but she was strong. Maybe she could twist away, or kick her captor's legs out from underneath them, or—

Well, the old ones were the best. She smacked her head sharply backwards, connecting satisfyingly with bone. She made to kick back into his balls, but she was thrown heavily to the ground, and kicked hard in the ribs.

Curling over, she glanced up, and all the breath fled her body.

The creature standing over her had two legs and two arms and a head and was ... roughly man-shaped, but it sure as hell was not a man. Men didn't tend to be eight feet tall with shoulders like an ox, and they certainly didn't have horns. Or tails. Or wings.

Wings he's got wings he's got wings—

The massive, winged man snarled something at her, then leaned down, grabbed her in his huge hands, and took to the sky.

CHAPTER 22

Rhaell was a fool and he knew it.

He waded deeper into the freezing water of the river, willing it to cool his ardour. Every part of his body seemed to feel the imprint of Ember against him as if she was still there, writhing in his arms as she kissed him like her life depended on it.

Can I kiss you?

A sane, sensible man would have said no. Would have told her he wasn't interested and walked away before he did anything stupid, like inhale her mouth and grind her against his cock and moan her name like he did in his fevered dreams.

But he wasn't a sane, sensible man, and he'd kissed her like he wanted to, grasped her delicious body in his big stupid hands and filled his senses with her. Relaxed into the fantasy that he could have her. Until she'd palmed his cock and the shock of someone else's hand there had jolted him back to reality, and the reason why he couldn't.

If she saw him naked, she'd run screaming.

She'd caught a glimpse, back in the barracks. She hadn't

screamed. It was worse than screaming. She'd looked at him with pity. But that was only a glimpse, and not even the worst of it.

She must have forgotten that, or she'd never have tried to get his clothes off this morning.

Savagely, he scrubbed himself with the sweet leaves that overhung the river. He needed to scrape the scent of her from his skin, so he didn't go mad from it.

At least he only had a few more hours of this. Of her looking at him like he wasn't her worst nightmare, of being tempted to give in. Because once he walked into the Rakaa camp and told them who he was, she'd never look at him again.

It's for the best. He told himself this as he dried himself off with his shirt and got dressed. He told himself it as he started back up the rocky scree to the cave where he'd woken with her in his arms and given into temptation. He told himself over and over, until he heard a sudden cry and rushed up the slope to see a huge creature taking to the sky, holding a limp figure in its monstrous arms.

On the ground outside the cave lay an empty water canteen, and a smear of blood.

~

'... expect us to do wi' her?'

'Ransom her, he says.'

'Ransom?'

'Aye, to the humans.'

A tutting sound. 'Have not I always said Ikrai were a wazzock?'

'Aye. Worse and worse these days. Has tha heard him wi' his "language of the bloodline"?'

'Bloodline!' There was a cackle of laughter. 'Who's he think he is, Dlorroch the Dragonrider?'

'Oh aye, hasn't tha heard him? "Seventeen generations ago..."'

'Seventeen? Lad thinks he's the Lost Prince of Damholm, but I knew his father and he weren't no prince.'

'Oh, he's a *pillock*. And tha knows— Oh, she wakes.'

Ember's head was pounding. She could smell woodsmoke and hear the chatter of voices, and for a moment she couldn't work out where she was at all. Not home, in the castle, with Phoebe. Not in any of the rooms she'd had on their stupid progress.

Guiltily, she realised home was supposed to be with Pa and the boys, and she hadn't even thought of that.

I need to get back to the Clockwork City, she told herself, but increasingly it sounded like an obligation rather than a desire. Get home. Get Pa his medicine. Would the boys even remember? Pa wouldn't, not until it was too late, and they'd have spent all their money on drink and girls, because despite being quite old enough to look after themselves they never did—

'Can tha hear me, littlin?'

Ember didn't want to open her eyes. These women were speaking weirdly, and she'd really had enough of weird for now.

'I can hear you,' she said wearily.

'Can tha open thi' eyes?'

Ember probed at her head and found a sticky wound on her scalp, already half-healed. 'Why are you talking like an old play?' she said.

There was a pause. 'Old play,' said one.

'Old play?' said the other.

'Never mind.' Ember shaded her eyes and opened them.

She yelped and shut them again.

'Tha's never seen one of us before,' chuckled one of the women.

No. People – *things* – that looked like that didn't chuckle. And they weren't women, because women implied humans, and humans didn't have *horns*.

Scrunching up her face, Ember muttered, 'I've seen one before. I think it kidnapped me.' She squinted through one eye. Yes, there they were, horned monsters peering down at her, their features strong and harsh, their backs framed by furled wings.

Wings. Oh Lords.

'Oh, aye. That'd be Ikrai. He's a right wazzock,' said one of them, and it was such an un-monster-like thing to say that Ember opened her eyes fully.

'A ... wazzock?'

'Stupid, littlin. Soft in the head.'

'I reckon that blow he took winning the Championship addled his pate,' said one.

'Dented the crown right onto it,' agreed the other.

'Oh, is what why he never takes it off?'

'Nay, that's because he's a wazzock.'

Ember took stock. She appeared to be lying in a large, cosy cabin bed, covered by a striped blanket, and she was inside a house with a steeply sloping ceiling that came right down to the floor. There was a fire crackling away merrily in a stone fireplace, and a large door thrown open to the mountain air. Beyond it, she could see other thatched-roof dwellings.

And then there were the two ... women? Probably women, sitting nearby. One was spinning yarn on some kind of drop spindle, the other carefully winding it into skeins. They were large, much larger than any women Ember had ever seen before, and they were fearsome looking, but they were also ... not.

It was hard to look particularly scary when you were spinning yarn.

They wore long tunics and trousers of fine woollen fabric that had been embroidered around the edges and trimmed with fur. One had a knitted shawl in bright colours over her shoulders, hitched up at the back by her wings. Their long hair was tied in intricate braids that looped around their horns.

Their wings were, she had to admit, really beautiful. One had tawny wings, brown and white in stripes and speckles; the other's were shaded from mid to dark green, gleaming like emeralds. Their horns were curved back, glinting in the light as if polished.

'Aye,' said the one spinning. 'Always said he'd get hisself killed, and he will when he takes thee down to Addor for a ransom. That's where tha's from? Addor?'

'Uh, sure,' said Ember. She had no idea if these people might have heard of the Promised One and really didn't want to fuel any ransom fantasies.

'What was tha doing all the way up here?'

'Um,' said Ember, who hadn't worked out any lies yet, 'where is here?'

'Oh. Tha's in the Jolvista village. Don't worry, littlin, we won't hurt thee.'

The other one made a so-so face.

'Zikol needs to thump some sense into that halfwit Ikrai, and then we'll work out what to do with thee.'

'Do with me?' said Ember. 'Um, I'd quite like to go, if you don't mind.' She sat up, head swimming a little, and made to stand. Her ribs ached.

Firm hands pushed her back down again. 'Nay, lass. First off, tha's taken a few thumps, and I don't know how littlin's heal but I reckon tha needs a good rest.'

'And second, Ikrai's taken thee as a prisoner of war. We can't let thee go until that's resolved.'

'Prisoner of— But I'm not at war with anyone!'

The spinning woman sighed. 'Mebbe not thee, but thi' people are.'

'Perhaps thee hit thi' head harder than we realised,' said the one winding the yarn.

'My people?' said Ember. 'Look, I'm sorry, but I don't even know who you are.'

The two women exchanged a look. Then the one spinning put down her spindle and leaned forward.

'We're Jolvista, of the Moonlit Highlands,' she said. 'We're Rakaa.'

The foothills of the Shadowed Mountains quickly grew into monstrous peaks that demonstrated quite clearly how they'd got their name. The terrain was beyond rough, with barely a goat track to follow up near-vertical slopes. More than once Rhaell had to turn back and find another route, as a chasm opened up, or a rock fall blocked the way.

But he did not stop.

Shouldering the contents of both his and Ember's packs, wearing most of his spare clothes against the cold, he trudged on and on towards the last location of a Rakaa camp marked on the old maps. He hunted along the way and forced himself to take brief rest breaks, strict with himself because he knew a starving, exhausted man would be no good at killing Rakaa.

And he intended to kill a lot of Rakaa.

If they'd harmed Ember in any way, he'd slaughter every one he could. Even if they hadn't harmed her, he'd slaughter them anyway. Images of those mighty wings beating the air, Ember's limp body hanging in its arms, haunted his every waking moment. The cry she'd made as he raced up the slope. The smear of blood on the rocks. Too late, too late!

He'd almost been too late to save her last time. He wouldn't allow that to happen again.

So Rhaell trudged on, fear and guilt weighing down his every step. He walked at night by werelight. Napped for no longer than it took to roast the small creatures he hunted along the way. And some time after dawn on the second day, he heard voices.

They were not bothering to conceal themselves. Rhaell could see their hulking forms through the trees. Massive, ugly creatures with huge hideous wings, like monstrous bats. They were taller than him, and he wasn't a small man. He glimpsed one draw back a bow and heard a thump, and then a jeer.

'That were miles off, tha wazzock!'

Rhaell paused.

'All right, then, let's see thee try!'

Another thump, and a cackle of laughter. 'Try aiming for the sky Ivvo, tha might hit it!'

They sounded ... juvenile. Rhaell's fingers flexed on the hilt of his sword. Aye, and he'd been a juvenile the first time he'd slit a man's throat. He crept up behind the nearest one. It wore leather leggings and a sort of tunic that fastened at the back, around its wings. It raised its bow.

'Has tha seen the human yet?'

Rhaell froze.

'The littlin? Aye, I went for us bread this morning.' The Rakaa loosed the arrow, missing a target set up at the other end of the clearing. 'Right funny little thing. Not locked up or nowt.'

The first voice snorted. 'And they've allus told us of the dangers!'

'My babby sister's more dangerous than that'un, and she's no horns yet.'

The two of them laughed, and the one nearest Rhaell nocked another arrow. He squinted down the length of the bow, and then froze.

This was because Rhaell had his sword at the youth's throat.

'It's too small for you, lad,' he said conversationally. 'You need to aim lower with a bow that much shorter. Has no one told you how tall it should be?'

The other Rakaa had his bow aimed at Rhaell, glowering at him from beneath a heavy brow.

'Short or not, I could hit thee from here,' he said.

'And your friend would be dead. Now, put it down, and tell me where you're keeping her.'

The bow didn't move. 'Who?'

'The human. The,' he ground his teeth, 'right funny little thing.'

'Ah.' The one with the bow lowered it. 'Has tha come to negotiate for her?'

'No,' said Rhaell. 'I've come to slaughter everyone who keeps me from her.'

'Oh.' He scratched his neck. 'We'd really prefer it if tha negotiated.'

Rhaell frowned, because this wasn't quite right. Why were these two Rakaa not fighting him? He'd just said he was going to slaughter them, and they were asking if he'd like to rethink it?

'Take me to her,' he growled.

The Rakaa exchanged a glance. 'Er, now?'

'Yes, now!' He pressed his sword closer to the Rakaa's throat.

'Only, it's just, Thrala said she were going to take her to the hot springs to bathe and we weren't to go near, on account of her being, you know. Female.'

Hot springs? 'Take me there now,' Rhaell growled, and the Rakaa dropped their bows.

Ember had just got dressed in what appeared to be children's clothes – with slits and fastenings at the back for wings and a tail she didn't have – and was combing her wet hair when she heard the bellow from outside the longhouse. The words didn't make sense, but the voice made her freeze, because it was the one that had kidnapped her.

'Enough of that bloodline nonsense, Ikrai,' said another voice wearily. 'Speak in the common tongue.'

'I demand a price in blood!' the first Rakaa growled.

The Rakaa with the tawny wings, who'd identified herself as Thrala, rolled her eyes.

'Is that the wazzock?' Ember said.

'Aye, and it sounds like negotiations have been opened. Stay here, lass, tha'll just rile him up.'

She strode for the open door, and Erli, the other Rakaa, flared her emerald wings to stop Ember from following.

'Negotiations with who?' she said, trying to peek around them.

The damn things were each as wide as Erli was tall. Her heart pounded. 'With who?'

'Then blood you shall have,' roared an all-too-familiar voice in return. 'But it shall not be mine!'

Relief surged in Ember, crashing over her in a dizzying wave. '*Rhaell*,' she gasped, and Erli had to grab her by the arm to keep her from running outside. 'He came for me, I knew he would—'

'Stop inside,' said Erli. 'Ikrai's all riled up, no telling what he might do.'

'But—'

'I said stop,' said Erli firmly. 'We've not healed thee to get thee killed, lass.'

'I'll slaughter thi' weak and feeble corpse and feed it the pigs!' screamed Ikrai.

'You said Rhaell could pay him a ransom,' Ember said desperately. 'He's got jewels.' Fake jewels, but that wasn't important now. For the safe return of the Promised One, the king would surely pay whatever price they wanted.

'What need have us of jewels, lass? We trade in meat and furs and wheat. Only jewels we have are the ones we've won in war, and they're worth nowt to us other than trophies.' She sighed. 'I do wish it hadn't been Ikrai who found thee. Pride's swelled his head since he won the Championship.'

'What Championship?' said Ember, still trying to see around the huge green wings, but Erli kept moving them to stop her.

'Annual tournament. Used to be for finding the best warrior, but these days it's a bit of fun for the lads and lasses. Ikrai won it last three years and now he thinks he's a fabled hero.'

'A hero who knocked out and kidnapped someone half his size,' Ember grumbled.

'Spoils of war,' said Erli.

'But we're not at war,' Ember insisted. 'That was generations ago!'

Erli looked down at her, puzzlement written over her broad face. 'Two dozen winters is generations ago?'

For a moment Ember could only stare. She stopped struggling to see outside. 'What did you say?'

'Two dozen winters, mebbe more. Less than thirty. Since the massacre at Gluyver's Point,' said Erli. She peered down at Ember. 'Tha didn't know? Thi' people killed so many of ours we retreated to the Moonlit Valley and beyond. No Rakaa has ventured out of the mountains since. Only fools like Ikrai go so far as the canyon now. He says he were called there to thee.'

Two dozen winters. But the way Eletha and the others had talked when they arrived in Addor...

'I thought it was longer ago than that,' she mumbled.

'Nay, lass. We all lost people then. My mother, Thrala's brother, Ikrai's father. He were nobbut a bairn at the time, horns barely grown in, but he's vowed vengeance all the days since.'

'On us? On humans?'

'Aye. Tha were the first he found. He were talking about making thee a slave, or sending back thi' body in pieces. Don't worry, lass, Zikol's a leader with a brain in his head. We don't keep slaves and we've no reason to murder thee. Thi' mate, however...'

She stared out into the village square, where the shouting had gone ominously quiet. Footsteps sounded, and Erli dropped her wing as Thrala came back into the house.

'Thi' mate's here,' she said to Ember. 'Waving his sword around like Ikrai. Does he know how to use it?'

'Yes,' said Ember, who could only assume as much, because Rhaell was a soldier. He had those scars. He'd seen combat.

'Good. Because Ikrai's set the price for your freedom: a fight to the death with thi' mate.'

He was allowed to see Ember before he died.

They were keeping her in one of the Rakaa houses, which were steeply roofed and built into the mountainside. The doors were huge, to accommodate the Rakaa wings, and Ember looked very small as she stood inside by a bed large enough for half a dozen men.

Her eyes lit up when she saw him. 'Rhaell!'

He dropped his sword and swept her into his arms. She clung to him, sobbing, and he wrapped her up as close as he could get her. She was alive. She wasn't badly hurt. She was whole and in his arms.

'Are you hurt? Have they mistreated you?' *I'll kill them all if they've harmed you.*

She shook her head. 'I'm fine. They've actually been really kind. They're very civilised,' she said, looking around the cosy house with its woven rugs and carved furniture.

They weren't civilised. Rhaell had heard all his life that the Rakaa were barbarians, little better than animals, who fought and killed simply because they wanted to. The children playing on the green outside, the intricate patterns on Ember's clothing, the smell of baking bread – all of these things were just a confusion. How could they be civilised?

'So civilised I've been challenged to a fight to the death,' he said. He wanted to memorise the feel of Ember in his arms, the softness and the curves of her.

'Erli said it's a stupid old tradition they don't do anymore, but this Ikrai's obsessed with some ancient warrior ways or something.'

Rhaell just grunted, pressing his cheek to Ember's hair and breathing in her scent. Under whatever primitive soap these people used, she was still there, still his Ember. Her hair was soft against his grizzled cheek, her breath warm against his unshaven neck. *I won't let go of you.*

'But you can take him, right? I mean, he's big, but you're fast. Right?'

'Sure,' said Rhaell. His fingers clenched in her hair. 'Ember. I—'

He wanted to say so many things to her. Practical things, like how to find her way back out of the canyon when this was over. Lustful things, like how much he regretted not taking up her offer when they were in that cave.

Sentimental things, like how desperately he cared for her. Might even love her.

'You should take this,' she said, rearing back and reaching for the pendant around her neck. 'Mnorir's Stone. Maybe you can use it to kill him. Or make him kill himself.'

'You don't think that might be viewed somewhat suspiciously? Rakaa can't do magic. They used to accuse Yskara of sorcery.'

'Does it matter, if he's dead?'

'It does if they kill us for it.'

She grimaced. 'Okay, then this. Take the Healing Stone. What harm can that do you, huh?' She took the little pouch from her pocket and held it out.

He tucked the stone into his pocket. A token from his lady, like the scarf he'd taken from his pack and wept into on his way up the mountain.

Ember looked up at him, brown eyes full of emotions he couldn't read.

'Please don't die,' she whispered.

'I'll try,' he promised, and attempted a smile. It didn't even convince him.

'Try very hard,' she said, her voice breaking on a sob that almost destroyed him, and threw her arms around him again.

He hugged her close. 'Ember,' he said into her hair, because it was easier if he wasn't looking at her. 'The Rakaa have Aywin's Stone. Wynric's Stone is with the dragons. I don't know where the dragons lived, but maybe the Rakaa will be able to tell you. Be really careful heading north, the mountains can be absolutely treacherous. Stay well-armed and dress as warmly as you can.'

'Rhaell—' she began, but he didn't let her speak. He focused his eyes on the weave of a curtain over the bed.

'Ysarriel's Stone is in the crown, so you might need Ruvaen's Stone to get it. When you've got all the stones take them to the Tree. Ephyrea's Stone is in the Tree. As soon as you've united them make a portal to take you home. But remember not to take the first two.'

'Stop it,' she mumbled against his shoulder.

But he couldn't. 'If you can't find the Dragon's Stone, don't get yourself killed looking for it. Find somewhere, maybe in the north, and live out your life there. Don't go back to the court. The king will—' He choked off the rest of that sentence.

The king might do a lot to Ember. He might throw her in jail. He might take her as his own wife. He might find out she couldn't bear children and execute her.

He held her tight so she couldn't see his tears. 'May the Tree protect and shelter you. Live a really good life, Ember.'

She pushed back from him, hard, and glared tearfully up at him. 'I'm going to,' she said. 'After you and I get all the stones. Together.'

He nodded, not able to speak when she looked at him like that. Like he could save her, like he could save them both. Like he was a hero, and not just some bastard who'd always been bigger and meaner than whoever he was fighting.

That wasn't going to help him this time. The Rakaa was twice his size and psychotic with it, and he wasn't exhausted from trekking through the mountains for two days either.

'You'll just fight this bastard, and kill him, and we'll go on our way.' She nodded decisively, as if this was how it would definitely go.

He nodded again, his heart breaking into pieces.

'Time to go,' said one of the Rakaa at the door.

'Fuck off,' said Ember. She touched Rhaell's lips with her finger. 'That was a really good kiss,' she whispered. Her eyes were wet with tears.

'Which one?'

'Both. We need to do it again. We need to do a lot more than kissing,' she said, and Rhaell cursed himself as a fool for not taking what she'd offered the first time. He could have still been lying in that cave with her, naked and sated, drowsily considering another round of stupendous sex, while that damn fool Ikrai flew on by with no idea of their presence.

He could have had Ember. Could have kissed her and undressed her and weighed those wonderful breasts in his palms. Could have explored the softness of her skin, the dips and swells of her body, the softness and the strength of her. He could have learned her taste with his tongue, fed on the nectar between her legs, licked the sweat from her skin. He could have buried himself inside her, eased the desperate need for her that throbbed through his entire body, could have—

Except he couldn't have, because Ember didn't really know what she was asking for. What secrets he kept from her. How unworthy of her he really was.

And now he was going to die.

He knew what happened when one man was weak, disadvantaged, exhausted, poorly armed, and up against an opponent with every advantage of size, strength and weaponry, not to mention the bone-deep certainty that he'd win. He'd memorised this tune, and he knew how the ending went.

Rhaell knew he was going to die.

'Ember, if I survive this, we'll do whatever you want,' he said.

'That a promise?'

He cupped her face in his trembling hands and leaned down to kiss her softly for the last time. 'Yes,' he said. Because it was a promise he knew he'd never have to keep.

Ember watched him walk away from her and told herself it would not be for the last time. Rhaell was the Captain of the Guard, and you didn't get a position like that if you couldn't fight. Besides, he had to win. There was no 'if' about it. He had to win, and then they'd get this stone from the Rakaa and go on their way.

They'd get all the stones and heal the Tree.

And then they'd open a portal and she could go home.

The thought made her stomach hollow, and she told herself to stop being so ridiculous. Home was what she wanted. Pa and the boys needed her.

It *was* what she wanted.

The Rakaa village was loosely built around a central green, where children had been playing most of the morning, and women sat knitting and rocking cradles in the autumn sunshine. Now it had been cleared apart from a dwindling stack of hurdles, which were being set out to contain what Ember now realised was an arena.

'Is't ready, lass?' said Thrala gently.

Ember pressed the heels of her hands to her eyes and swiped at her nose before she turned around. 'To see Rhaell kill the bastard who kidnapped me? Sure. Question,' she went on recklessly. 'Do you have laws here? Like, against kidnapping?'

'It's against our creed,' said Erli, 'but tha weren't kidnapped. Tha's a prisoner of war.'

'But we're not at war!'

'No peace were ever declared, lass. Ikrai were within his rights.'

'Then they're stupid rights!'

'Agreed,' said Thrala, 'but that's the creed we have. Tha could fight him thyssel, if tha wanted.'

Ember stood in the doorway of the cosy Rakaa house and gazed out at the village green, where every single Rakaa was twice her size. Even a single lash of their tails could probably knock her out.

'Rhaell's a good fighter,' she said, on the basis of absolutely no evidence whatsoever. But surely the Captain of the Guard had to be. 'Doesn't it bother you he's going to kill Ikrai?'

The two Rakaa exchanged a glance, and suddenly Ember remembered the king telling her so confidently, 'They never win.'

Oh, Lords above and all their little children – was Ikrai their Prince Bronadyr?

The two Rakaa shepherded her out of the house and across to the green, where a crowd had gathered around a sort of maypole to watch the fight. Ember saw a few older children, but none of the younger ones who'd been playing earlier. She supposed nobody wanted to see their playground turned into a bloodbath.

A Rakaa with large, dark wings turned as they approached. Zikol, their leader, who had briefly visited her earlier. 'Tha's said thi' farewells?'

Ember raised her chin. 'Farewell for now. He'll win.'

There was pity in Zikol's eyes, but he nodded. 'The heart of a warrior. Tha'll do, littlin.'

The crowd murmured as Rhaell entered the ring, escorted by two burly Rakaa. He didn't look around, didn't look for her. Just swung his sword and rolled his shoulders as if this was an ordinary day in the training ring.

He doesn't even have any armour. But neither did Ikrai, when he flew down into the arena with what Ember could only call swagger. Ember expected the crowd to cheer, but there was only a murmur.

It was just like that day in the arena. Everyone knew who the winner would be, and once again Ember was backing the underdog. Only this time he wasn't a stranger she was rooting for on principle, but Rhaell, who was so important to her she didn't even know how to describe it.

He had to win. He *had* to.

'Is Ikrai not popular?' she said, looking over the large Rakaa with his dark red leathery wings and gleaming black horns. A battered tin crown was squashed onto his monstrous head.

Thrala snorted. Erli said, 'As popular as a dose of the itch.'

'He's a troublemaker,' said Thrala.

'A bully,' rumbled Zikol. In the arena, Ikrai shed the wrappings on his upper body. The sunlight gleamed on his reddish skin as he posed with his double-headed axe. Oh Lords, that thing was *so* big.

'Then why are you letting him fight Rhaell like this? Shouldn't you be ... I dunno, locking him up?'

'On what charge?'

'I dunno, inciting violence? He clearly kidnapped me just so he could kill a human!'

Zikol folded his arms. They were each like tree trunks. 'Those are the rules of war,' he said calmly.

'We're not at war,' Ember nearly screamed.

'Ikrai is,' Thrala said quietly. 'He has been since his father were killed.'

Before Ember could say any more, Zikol grabbed a large staff and thumped it hard against the maypole three times. The ground reverberated.

'Stand tha ready?' he roared.

'Aye!' roared Ikrai. He shook his huge axe. Sunlight glinted off the thick, jewel-studded metal cuff he wore on one arm.

Jewel-studded...

'Yeah,' replied Rhaell. Good lords, Ikrai was a big bastard. Rhaell was a big man himself, but the Rakaa absolutely towered over him.

'Tha'll not leave the area marked out by these hurdles. Tha'll not harm anyone but each other. Nobody shall interfere once tha's started. The fight shall end when one dies and not before. The prize is the freedom of the humans. Does tha ken?'

'Aye,' roared Ikrai again. The sun glinted red off the stone in his cuff.

Rhaell rolled his shoulders. 'I understand,' he said, voice soft. He still didn't look at Ember.

Ruvaen's Stone pulsed at her chest.

Ikrai wore Aywin's Stone. The War Stone. Ember surged forward in panic, but Erli's strong arm held her back.

Zikol smacked the post with his staff again. 'Begin!'

Ikrai wore only leather breeches, his chest and feet bare. His hands and feet were tipped with claws. His wings were red, his skin was tinged red, and even the markings that flowed over his shoulders were dark red.

But none of that mattered, when the big bastard in question was wielding a fucking war axe.

Rhaell had faced such an axe before, but not often. Generally, they were only wielded by very large men because they took huge strength. But with that strength usually came slowness, and because a big bastard has long arms, a weak spot. Rhaell had to be quick.

He really wished he'd had more sleep.

Ikrai came at him with a roar, swinging the axe down with such force it left a furrow in the earth. Rhaell dodged it easily and hacked his sword into Ikrai's arm. It left a slice of red blood, but the Rakaa didn't even seem to notice. He lifted his huge axe again and whirled it around in an arc that would have cleaved Rhaell in two if he hadn't dived to the side.

He rolled to his feet and cut upwards, but Ikrai stepped away. They circled each other.

'I have been waiting for this,' Ikrai growled.

'Sorry to have kept you.'

'Thi'' father killed my father!'

'I doubt that,' said Rhaell, watching the Rakaa's feet. They were large, and bare, and his toenails were sharpened to claws. *Poser*.

'All humans were thi'' father,' Ikrai sneered.

'Is that you calling me a bastard? Because I'm okay with that.' He'd never known his father and he was glad for it.

Ikrai leaned in. 'When I've killed thee, I'll kill thi'' mate,' he leered. 'I'll revel in her blood.'

Rhaell didn't react. He didn't look over at Ember. He couldn't afford to be distracted.

Ikrai struck, with greater speed than Rhaell had anticipated. He leapt into the air as the axe whistled a few inches below where his knees had been.

The crowd murmured. Maybe they'd never seen an Yskaran jump before.

Unfortunately, they'd seen a Rakaa fly, and there didn't appear to be anything in Zikol's rules about Ikrai not using his natural advantage. The mighty wings flapped, and the force of them sent Rhaell back on his heels. He recovered, and lunged forward, swiping at Ikrai's feet.

The huge Rakaa didn't seem to notice, flying up and then swooping back down, swinging his axe with terrifying force. Rhaell rolled to the side, and then backflipped as the axe swiped into the space where he'd been.

A sword against an axe. He should have clarified the rules on weaponry before they started. He had a knife or two, but reaching for them would cost him too much time and signal his intention too clearly.

Ikrai beat his powerful wings and backed out of Rhaell's range. When he swiped again it was with the axe at the fullest extension of his arm, keeping his body far away from Rhaell and his blade.

But flying was a slow, cumbersome business. The momentum of it cost Ikrai too much time to recover from, and Rhaell could use that. He moved as soon as the Rakaa dived, jabbing upwards and slicing deep into Ikrai's bare foot.

Serves you right for not protecting yourself, you cocky bastard, he thought savagely, as blood spattered him and the Rakaa howled. And then, *Damn, I wish I had my armour*.

He didn't let Ikrai recover, but used the momentum of his sword to swing it round and hack at the Rakaa's leg. More blood spurted.

Well, he was causing damage, but he just couldn't kill someone who kept hovering overhead. Rhaell's sword was sharp, but he didn't think he could hack off a limb to make the bastard bleed out.

If I only had wings.

A spear would have been helpful, but Rhaell didn't want to throw his sword and risk losing it. He waited for the next dive, then leapt over Ikrai's back, hacking down with his sword to cut into the Rakaa's wing.

The crowd gasped. Ikrai bellowed.

But Rhaell hadn't disabled him enough to keep him from flying. Ikrai beat his wings, one harder than the other, and rose for another dive. Then another. Another. Rhaell cut into his feet, his legs, his wings. He sliced off half the creature's damn tail. He rolled and he jumped, but the Rakaa didn't tire.

And Rhaell, who had barely slept for a day and a half, did.

Ikrai was beginning to get wise to his tactics now and twisted as he dived, so that the next time Rhaell attempted to land on his back, he was grabbed by one huge, muscular arm and tossed up in the air.

Rhaell braced for the fall, trying to roll into a ball, but he had no time. He hit the ground with a crunch, and pain shocked through his entire body.

It was only instinct that had him rolling away from the axe as it came down, but he wasn't fast enough, and the blade sliced deep into his arm.

Ember's fist was stuffed in her mouth to keep her from crying out. Rhaell rolled to his feet, but the movement was all wrong, like a puppet with half its strings cut. Blood cascaded down the back of one arm, and he held it close to his body. Lords only knew what that fall had done to him. She'd heard a crunch, but he wasn't giving away where he was hurt.

He merely swiped the sweat from his eyes and beckoned the Rakaa to try again.

'Weak, puny little thing,' sneered the Rakaa flying above. His wings were sliced and slashed, and his movements were off-balance. She had no idea how he was staying in the air. Rhaell had hacked at him, over and over, but the mad beast just wouldn't stay down.

Was it the stone on his arm? Was it giving him power? Was Gaeleath's Stone healing Rhaell? If one was true, then the other must be.

She watched in horror as the great axe swung at Rhaell and he narrowly avoided it.

She had Mnorir's Stone. Could she use it? Was Rhaell right and they'd condemn her for sorcery? It would look pretty suspicious if Ikrai simply turned his axe on himself.

Rhaell worked his arm a moment, then switched his sword into his other hand and attacked Ikrai's legs. The Rakaa was red with blood from the thighs down, and probably couldn't stand any more. If Rhaell could just get him to the ground...

But the Rakaa was refusing to land. He kept diving and swiping, and sooner or later that axe was going to do some damage Gaeleath's Stone couldn't repair.

Her hand clutched Ruvaen's Stone beneath her tunic. *You move silently for an Erlish.* Mnorir hadn't seemed to see her coming. Did the Thief's Stone make her invisible?

She watched Rhaell roll away from another devastating blow, barely missing it at all. He was tiring, his movements becoming sluggish. She couldn't let him go on.

Ikrai was going to kill him.

Fuck it.

Ember clutched Ruvaen's Stone in one hand and willed herself to become unnoticeable, the same way she willed a light to exist when Rhaell taught her how to make a werelight. She slowly ducked down, moved towards the hurdle that stood at shoulder height, and paused, looking very carefully around.

No one had noticed. No one could see her! Ember sneaked forward, easing Mnorir's Stone over her head. Perhaps if she concentrated hard on weakening him, rather than him turning the axe on himself? Or tripping over his own axe? Yes, nobody would be suspicious of him stumbling when Rhaell had hacked at his legs so much.

The two men swung at each other, and Ember darted back, slipping on the bloody ground and going down. She rolled, barely missing Ikrai's massive, clawed foot, and Mnorir's Stone slipped from her grasp. *No!*

Ikrai raised his axe in one powerful arm, and then bellowed, axe stilled above his head.

On his back, Rhaell was doggedly, determinedly cutting down into the red, bony joint of Ikrai's wing, severing it from his back bit by bit.

Ember lay frozen like a rabbit, watching Ikrai thrash and try to throw Rhaell off. He swiped with his axe but couldn't reach something that close. His free hand went back and grabbed at Rhaell, who wrenched his sword up, hacking into the Rakaa's wrist.

Ikrai roared and tried to take to the sky, but Rhaell had done too much damage to his wing. The Rakaa reached back with his undamaged hand to try to dislodge Rhaell. When that failed, he threw himself on his back, and there was another awful crunch.

Ember sprang to her feet, heart hammering so hard she thought it would break her chest. But Rhaell was not crushed beneath that mighty back. He was on his knees a few feet away, and he brought his sword down hard into Ikrai's neck. The stab wasn't enough to kill him, but it pinned him, and he writhed.

Ember moved without even thinking, drawing a knife from her boot and racing forwards to hack down at Ikrai's hand where it grasped his axe. He howled, and she did it again. And again. Blood spattered her hands. The axe fell from his fingers.

She glanced to the side, where Rhaell had one knee on Ikrai's shoulder and was hammering his sword down for another stab. The Rakaa reached out with the hand Ember had been stabbing and she leapt back out of the way as he grabbed Rhaell by his injured arm and wrenched it back. They couldn't know she was here.

Rhaell's teeth bared in a snarl, but he didn't stop, not until Ikrai's other hand came up and swiped claws down his face and chest.

Rhaell vaulted back, off the Rakaa's chest, but he landed unevenly and fell to one knee. Ikrai sat up and sneered at him.

'You think I need my wings, puny human?' he growled.

Blood poured from his neck, but he barely seemed to notice. Rhaell's blows to the neck should have incapacitated him.

'Where's the littlin?' said someone, and Ember realised she was just standing there in the middle of the arena.

If they thought she had intervened, that she'd used magic, what would they do? Lock her up? Lock them both up? Kill them? It was a fight to the death, after all. Ikrai would probably be within his rights to kill them both.

And he was a fanatic who only wanted the death of any humans he found. He'd kill them both in a heartbeat.

She'd missed her chance to help Rhaell. If he died now, it would be her fault; Mnorir's Stone was trodden down into the mud; there was no way she could retrieve it. And if they realised she was missing...

She scuttled back under the hurdle, hiding her knife and bloodied hands under her too-long sleeves.

She let go of the Thief's Stone. 'I'm here,' she said. 'You think I'd go anywhere?'

Zikol gave her a long, inscrutable look, then turned his attention back to the arena.

Ikrai was on one knee, shaking out his bloodied hand. Rhaell was a few feet away, crouched and ready to fight, but his chest was heaving. Blood dripped down his face and his arm. Ember saw his sword tremble.

Ikrai fumbled for his axe, but Rhaell dived for it, flinging it far away, then rolling and stabbing upwards at the same time, in a move so fast Ember almost missed it. He got the Rakaa on the underside of his arm, but the sword lodged, and as Ikrai moved off, Rhaell's hand gave way.

Ember gasped, clutching hard at her knife. Rhaell had lost his sword. He was unarmed.

Ikrai plucked the sword from his arm and laughed.

Just like the Beast and the prisoner. Ember couldn't breathe. It had to end differently, it had to.

But Rhaell wasn't done. He drew a knife from a sheath on his thigh and stood for a long moment, hair blowing in the breeze, before he charged.

Ikrai hacked at Rhaell with his own sword. The blade came down on his shoulder, his arm, his chest. He took a slice to the thigh whilst managing only to get in one shallow stab to Ikrai's ribs.

They circled, and circled, and Ember stood frozen, fingers clutched so hard on her knife they hurt. Her other hand hovered over Ruvaen's Stone. Her gaze darted to Mnorir's Stone, half trampled in the mud.

Ikrai swung the sword in an arc that sliced into Rhaell's chest and he went to his knees; Ikrai stood braced above him, sword raised.

Ember grabbed the Thief's Stone.

Rhaell smiled.

He reached out one hand, and the axe flew into it. *He's been circling towards it*. Without breaking momentum, Rhaell swung the mighty, double-headed war axe into Ikrai's side.

The blade lodged deep, but Ikrai was already bringing his sword down in a wide arc. Rhaell whipped his head to the side, the sword barely slicing into his neck. But he carried the momentum through, rearing back and kicking out with his foot to shove the Rakaa off the blade of the war axe.

Then he swung it up, right between Ikrai's legs.

Then, as blood poured from the Rakaa's groin, Rhaell swung the axe one more time, into Ikrai's right arm.

The blow nearly severed the limb, but Rhaell had hacked at it enough already that only a few sinews remained. He grabbed at Aywin's Stone with his free hand, and with a terrible, wet, tearing sound, the cuff and half of Ikrai's arm came with it.

The Rakaa fell to his knees, mouth open, eyes staring in disbelief at the place where his hand had been. But not for long. Rhaell's next blow went into his neck. Ikrai slumped to the side, and Rhaell followed, standing over the Rakaa and hacking down with the axe again, and again, and again. Blood sprayed his face, soaked his clothes, flew from his hair as he swung, over and over, blue eyes blazing grimly.

Then he faltered, axe lodging in the blood-soaked ground. He let go of it and straightened, chest heaving. He clambered over the Rakaa, stumbling a little, and his whole body was red with blood as he reached down and grasped Ikrai's braided hair.

He raised the Rakaa's severed head in the air, and stood for a moment, utterly still, blood dripping from every part of him.

He swayed. He was going to fall. He did not take his eyes off Zikol.

Ember clutched the hurdle in front of her, blood threatening to soak through her tunic sleeves. Her heart felt like it was about to break her chest wide open. She couldn't breathe.

Zikol's staff hit the maypole with a thump that shook the

ground. 'Rhaell of Yskara is the victor,' he declared. 'The humans win their prize.'

Ember ducked under the hurdle and ran to Rhaell, not caring this time who saw her.

Rhaell staggered towards her, the Rakaa head rolling, forgotten, on the ground, and grasped her face in both gory hands. His eyes were the only thing in his face that weren't red, and they burned at her with blue fire.

Then his mouth was on hers. Ember threw her arms around him and kissed him back. He'd won. He'd won the fight and won their freedom and he was alive, he was alive in her arms and he was kissing her.

Blood ran down his face and into her mouth. She didn't care. Her clothes, her hair, all of her was soaked with the blood that cascaded off Rhaell in rivers, and she only pressed herself closer to his body.

Ember didn't realise she was crying until Rhaell drew back, concern filling those blue eyes. His thumb swiped unsteadily across her cheek.

'Don't cry,' he said. 'I've got you.'

Then he collapsed in her arms.

CHAPTER 23

Ember was no stranger to blood, or emergency wound care. She'd seen her mother through countless miscarriages and stillbirths, she'd fixed up her own wounds when a job had gone wrong, she'd even wrenched Three-Finger Steve's shoulder back into place that time they'd had to leap out of a window to keep from being caught.

But she'd never seen anyone as hacked to pieces as Rhaell. He was more blood than skin, torn flesh hanging off him in strips and lumps. In places, she thought she could see bone. But he had to live. He had to be all right. Or what was this all for?

'Fret not, we'll patch him up,' said Thrala, as Erli gently tried to prise Rhaell from Ember's arms.

She clutched him tighter like a grotesque ragdoll. 'No—'

'We'll not hurt him, lass. We're practised at healing.'

'Does tha need owt?' Zikol asked, as Ember tried to brush the blood from Rhaell's face. But there was so much of it, soaking into his eyelashes and his hair and between his lips. His cheek had been torn open and his eye was pouring blood.

Come back to me, please come back to me.

'Some bandages, mebbe,' said Thrala. 'Someone to heat the water. We've plenty of thread and salve.'

'Ivvo, get to it.' A Rakaa youth raced off.

Ember somehow heard them. She gazed between the Rakaa, feeling not unlike she'd taken another blow to the head. 'You're ... going to heal him?'

'Aye.'

'But he's your enemy.'

'He won the challenge, fair and square,' said Zikol. He glanced at the pile of meat that had once been Ikrai. 'We'll set a pyre for that one. Go on, lass, see to thi' mate. I know I'd not rest if he were mine.'

Erli stepped forward again, and this time Ember let her take Rhaell from her, so carefully, fretting over him like a mother with a newborn. 'Careful! He's really hurt,' she said, and her voice broke on a sob.

'We'll look after him, lass,' said Erli, and then she was carrying him away.

Ember did not stop and ask if she was in trouble, because she'd interfered with the fight, and she really didn't want anyone to think about whether she'd been beside them the whole time. Zikol's face was like stone, and Rhaell was being carried away, so there was really only one choice for her.

She marched out into the arena and retrieved Mnorir's Stone, defying anyone to comment, and followed the healers back to their house.

Erli took Rhaell to the curtained alcove where Ember herself had slept, and the two Rakaa women wasted no time in stripping him of his tattered clothes, simply cutting through what was left until it fell away.

Ember's hand went to her mouth, but it didn't stifle her cry. His skin had been sliced open in so many places it looked like ribbons. His shoulder was at entirely the wrong angle, and the claw marks on his face had left his eye pouring blood. His chest rose and fell with ragged breaths.

'I've got the water boiling,' said another voice, but Ember didn't really look around. 'Here, help me sterilise the needles.'

'No, let me help—'

Thrala nudged her away. 'Lass, we know what we're doing. Tha'll be more help to him if tha goes and supervises Ivvo with the water.'

'But—'

Erli pinned her with a look, her horns glinting in the lamplight. 'Be practical, Ember,' she said. 'That's no help if tha gets in the way.'

And Ember remembered saying the same to Pa, all those times Ma had been drowning in childbed blood. *Hovering around worrying isn't going to help anybody. Either help or fuck off.*

'Ember?'

She tore her gaze from Rhaell's mutilated body and saw a Rakaa youth watching her, gangly and short-horned.

'But he's my...' she began, and didn't know how to finish that. *Everything. He's my everything.*

'I know,' said the young Rakaa gently. 'Thrala and Erli know what they're doing. I'm Ivvo. Come and help me with the water.'

Erli shooed her away, so she went, reluctantly, and was just picking up a metal needle with a pair of tongs when she heard two sharp intakes of breath from the bed.

'Mother of us all,' gasped Thrala.

'What?' Ember was by the bed before she even knew she'd moved.

Rhaell lay on his side, his back bared to them. The two deep scars she'd seen before stood out in shocking relief, long canyons carved either side of his spine. They were ragged, uneven, and clearly very old. Around them were the remains of the tattoo she'd glimpsed, partly destroyed by whatever had made those scars, partly hacked away at with smaller cuts. And below, at the base of his spine, was another ugly mass of scar tissue.

'By the Mother,' breathed Erli. 'He's Rakaa.'

CHAPTER 24

Deer and Rainbow ran through the attics, the tiny dragon looping in the air ahead of them. Well, Rainbow ran; Deer soared through the air, nearly catching the dragon but holding back, because catching it wasn't the point.

'It's from Addor!' Rainbow cried as she dodged around an old crate.

'How do you know that?'

'Because it's on their crest! Durr! Haven't you seen it?'

'That doesn't mean that's where it's from! The Lady of Sehari has a pet dragon!'

A sudden bang had them both faltering and turning, Deer in mid-air. Running footsteps came closer.

Mama appeared in the doorway, clutching the frame, her face white. 'Hide,' she gasped. 'For the love of the Tree, hide, Deer!'

'But we were chasing—' Deer said, glancing back at the dragon, which had vanished.

'This isn't a game.' Mama ran closer and pulled him out of the air. 'You have to hide, now. Men are coming. Bad men. I don't care where, just don't let them—' She glanced back over her shoulder. 'Go!'

Deer had never seen Mama like this, and it terrified him. He nodded and flew away, but he didn't know where to go. He and Rainbow played hide and seek all the time, but they didn't hide too hard because it got boring just waiting all by yourself.

'The armoire,' hissed Rainbow.

His heart pounded as he flew into the next room and prised open the door of the large wardrobe, tumbling to the floor of it and wincing at the noise. He eased his fingertips under the edge of the door and pulled it back, darkness settling around him. Mama's clothes fell around him like drapes.

For a long moment he heard nothing. And then the tread of heavy boots, people who didn't care how much noise they made. He heard things crashing and Rainbow crying. Mama was shouting at them, but he couldn't make out the words.

Then the footsteps came closer. Deer huddled as small as he could inside the dark space and tried to breathe as quietly as possible. His tail curled around his knees.

'... tell me where he is, or I'll send men up here with axes and destroy everything.'

'We have very little to destroy.' That was Mama.

'And you'll have even less. You can't hide him up here forever, Nykisa. You knew I'd come and claim him.'

'You don't need him,' pleaded Mama, and then there was a smacking sound and she sobbed.

'Don't presume to tell me what I need. Bring the boy to me. We will have to make him look as human as possible.'

Mama made a terrible keening sound. 'Please, no. He's just a child.'

'A monstrous child with wings and horns.'

Were they talking about him? Mama said his wings were beautiful, not monstrous. Rainbow was always dead jealous of them.

'Please, let him stay, he can—'

The man sounded bored. 'Nykisa, if you stall me any longer, I shall be forced to hurt you.'

'Do what you will,' Mama said. Her voice trembled.

'Or the girl.' There was a pause, then in a tone Deer could only describe as gloating, 'Yes, that's better. Guards!'

'Don't you touch her!'

'Mama!' cried Rainbow, afraid.

Deer trembled. Should he go? Should he burst out and let them take him? But what were they going to do to him? He was too afraid.

'Hold her,' said the man, and Deer heard a scuffle. Mama screamed obscenities she'd always told them off for using. Rainbow screamed and cried out, sharply.

'It hurts, it hurts!'

Deer clapped his hand over his mouth. It was his fault. Rainbow was hurt because he was hiding.

'Good. Next... Oh, say, a finger?'

'He's in the cupboard,' burst out Mama, and then she made the most terrible sound Deer had ever heard. It was like sobbing, but with a howl inside it. Deer had to stop it. He burst out of the armoire.

'Don't you hurt my sister!'

The man in the doorway looked him over, sneering. 'She's not your sister, boy. If she were I'd take her instead. She's not deformed. Guards.'

The large men came towards him, and their swords glinted at their sides. They wore armour that gleamed and their helmets had spikes on the top of them. They were large men, made of hard, spiky things, and Mama was on her knees keening like the world had ended, and Rainbow was—

'What did you do to her?' Deer demanded, as Rainbow clutched at her bleeding face.

'Oh, nothing. It'll heal. As will you, boy. Now, don't struggle, it'll be easier that way.'

The large men seized Deer, one grabbing each arm. Deer was bigger than Rainbow, but he was still a child, and no matter how much he struggled he wasn't strong enough to get free. So he did what Mama had always told him not to do, and used his horns to strike them.

'Ow! Little bloody monster,' swore one of the guards.

'We'll cut those off, too,' said the man who stood in the doorway. He wore fine clothes, like the lords at court, and he looked at Deer like he was something disgusting he'd scraped off his shoe. 'Wings, tail, horns. Who has the saw? Ah, there...'

Mama sobbed. 'No. Please.' Her face was bruised. Guards held her by the arms.

A man was advancing on Deer with a large saw. It was the kind of thing he'd seen men using in the gardens. It was huge, and the teeth on it looked unspeakably violent.

'Mama, I'm scared,' Deer cried.

Mama lunged towards him, but two guards held her back easily. 'I'm sorry,' she whispered. 'I'm so sorry, my love.'

Deer didn't understand. Were they really going to cut his wings off? But why? Mama said they were special. She said they made him special.

'But I won't be able to fly,' he said, as the blade came closer. More men crowded in, grasping his wings and wrenching them out, holding them tight. 'That hurts!'

'It's going to hurt more,' said the man with the saw.

'No, you can't, you can't!' cried Rainbow, and she raced over the floor to him, evading the clumsy guards, and threw herself in front of Deer. She spread her skinny arms and legs out wide and glared at the man with the saw. 'You can't take his wings!'

The man in charge strode over and stood looking down at her. 'You've got moxie,' he said. 'We'll soon beat that out of you.' Then he struck her so hard she was flung to the side, and Mama screamed.

'Hold him,' said the man with the saw dispassionately, and Deer squeezed his eyes shut on the sight of Rainbow lying still on the floor. The saw bit into his wings.

CHAPTER 25

Rhaell woke from a nightmare of blood and pain, and found cosy, lamplit warmth.

That was strange, because he'd really rather expected to be dead.

He was in a large bed, surrounded by thick curtains and carved wooden panels. A lamp burned merrily from a bracket on the wall. It illuminated Ember, curled up at the foot of the bed, eyes closed and head resting on a pillow she'd wedged into the corner. Her tunic and trousers were too big for her, and they were stained with blood.

Rhaell jolted towards her – and fell back, wordless with pain. Everything hurt. Everything.

'Whassa?' Ember woke, blinking, and winced. 'Rhaell. Stay still, love. Don't try to move. You're in a bad way.'

She crawled closer to him, swinging the lamp down so she could peer at him. Rhaell realised in horror that he was shirtless, only a blanket covering him to his midriff. He snatched at it, and she smacked his hand like he was a child with bad manners.

Mama used to do that.

'I said lie still, Buttercup! You're mostly held together with thread right now. Let me look,' Ember said, and Rhaell tried to move away from her, pain making him gasp. 'You're being silly. I just need to check how well you're healing.'

'Don't look at me,' Rhaell gasped.

'It's going to be quite hard to do this by touch,' Ember said. She peered at his face, which throbbed as much as the rest of him. He touched it gingerly and found a bandage over one eye. 'They said keep that on for a few days to be on the safe side. I don't think it damaged your eye, but who wants to risk it?'

Great. He might end up with an eye patch. As if he didn't look reprehensible enough.

'But the rest of it is looking *so* much better.' She sounded pleased. 'The stone is working.'

'Stone?' said Rhaell, dragging the blanket up to his chest. Ember tutted and tugged it back again.

She nodded to his chest. 'The Healing Stone. I had the blacksmith make a holder for it. It ain't elegant, but it's doing the job.'

Rhaell craned to see his chest. Mostly it was covered with bandages, but amongst them nestled a blue stone in a crude iron frame, fastened to a narrow chain that ran around his neck. Gaeleath's Stone.

'Honestly, you should've seen the state of you a few hours ago. I thought you'd be in bed for weeks. Now it looks like you already have been.'

As she spoke, she was carefully lifting a bandage on his arm. Rhaell let her. His arms weren't so bad. They were unattractively large, like those of a labourer, but they weren't as hideous as the rest of him.

'Wow, that's miles better. Let me look at the ones on your chest—'

'No!'

Ember frowned at him. 'Rhaell, honey, I've seen them already. I've seen all of you. They really can't be worse than when we first got you in here. I just need to check there's no infection—'

'Just leave it,' he said.

'Oh, you want to be all maggoty, do you?'

'You said the stone was healing me. I feel better already. You don't need to look.'

Ember sat back on her haunches and regarded him through narrowed eyes. 'Did you whine like this when army surgeons patched up the scars on your back?' she said.

Rhaell flinched. He closed his eyes. 'Yeah,' he mumbled.

'You fucking liar,' said Ember, and he went cold. 'I know exactly what those scars are. Thrala and Erli told me.'

Ember knew what he was. Who he was.

He went hot, then cold. This wasn't how she was meant to find out. He'd have had to tell her eventually – especially once they got back to Yskara. He'd managed to get away with it for weeks now, but she'd caught up to him. She knew, she knew—

'You're Rakaa, Rhaell. Those marks on your back – they're clan markings. The Jolvista say you're not one of them—'

'No,' Rhaell whispered. She knew. She knew, and now everything was over. His muscles drew tight, his wounds screaming in protest. He'd thought he was in pain before, but it was nothing to this. Nothing.

'You didn't want me to see you...'

He could barely hear her. The blood roared in his ears, shame and horror pulling him under. He was on his side now, uncaring of how much it hurt. 'Stop,' he whispered, pulling the blanket over his bare back so she wouldn't have to look at his shame. So he wouldn't have to look at her, either.

'I'm horrified,' said Ember, and he heard the tremor in her voice.

She'd hate him now. There was no way she wouldn't.

Her hand touched his arm, a rare bit of skin not covered in bandages. He flinched away.

His treacherous memory replayed her voice in his head. *We need to do a lot more than kissing.* Well, that was never going to happen now, was it? He mashed his hideous face into the pillow, pain throbbing under the bandage.

'At least you're healing quickly now. I dunno if that stone will leave scars, but that's okay. Scars are sexy.' She sniffed, and there was a hitch in her voice as she added, 'I could kiss them all better for you if you like.'

Kiss them—

Wait, what?

Rhaell rolled slowly to his back. 'You want to—' he began. 'What?'

'I mean – like, when you're ready and everything. But I'm on a promise here, yeah? The minute you're not dying of blood loss I'm gonna climb you like a tree.' Her brow creased. 'Unless you've changed your mind?'

Changed his mind? How could he ever change his mind about being with her?

How hadn't *she* changed her mind about being with *him*?

'Of course not,' he said, searching her face. 'But...'

'But?'

Emotions trembled across her face. Her eyes were damp, her smile unconvincing. But the way she looked at him, running her gaze all over his body – that wasn't hatred. It wasn't loathing. It wasn't disgust. It was ... worry? Hope?

She didn't hate him.

'You,' he began slowly. 'You think I'm Rakaa?'

She nodded. 'And I know that's super weird to you 'cos you've grown up hating them and all; but look, they're really not bad. They're just people. They've actually been really kind.' She shuddered. 'Apart from that Ikrai.'

Rhaell felt his face darken. 'Did he hurt you?'

'No. And if he had I'd have stabbed him in the balls. No wait, you did that.'

'Are you okay?'

'Um, am *I* okay? I'm not the one who just nearly died.'

'Yes, but you are the one who got kidnapped.'

She pulled a face. 'Yeah, and that's really fucking embarrassing.'

Rhaell's head hurt. He couldn't keep up. 'Embarrassing? Why? You were the victim. It's not your fault.'

Ember laughed bitterly. 'Sure. Sure.' She took his hand. 'Then explain to me why you're so ashamed of those scars on your back?'

He fell back against the pillows, and winced, because everything still hurt. She had no idea.

'Rhaell, who did this to you?'

He turned his face away and shuddered.

'All right. You don't want to talk about it. That's fair.'

He couldn't. The memory of it sliced into him, hacked him down to childhood, a small, terrified child who had no idea how much worse things were going to get. The pain of it stuck in his throat.

'But don't you ever feel ashamed of it, you hear? Someone *mutilated* you. They cut away—' She broke off, shaking her head, a blur on the edge of his tearstained vision. 'If I ever find the person who did this to you,' she vowed, voice trembling, 'I will mutilate them right back.'

Rhaell blinked up at her. Ember's face was wet with tears, her eyes swollen, and he realised she must have been crying quite a lot. Her mouth trembled, her chin stubborn. Now she looked furious. But *not at him*.

She didn't look disgusted, or appalled, or even pitying. She suddenly let out a sob and threw herself over him, pressing her face against the unhurt side of his and keeping her body carefully clear of his wounds.

Well, most of her body. Her breasts brushed his chest. Rhaell could never mind that.

'You're not...' he began, but didn't know what else to say. She'd kissed him three times now – was it four? Had he kissed her just before he'd passed out? – and she'd seen him with his shirt off and she was still touching him.

She said she'd seen ... all of him. And she wasn't running screaming.

Carefully, he reached around her and patted her back. Ember very carefully hugged him a bit tighter, kissed his cheek, and sat back.

By the Tree, she was lovely. Even pink-eyed and teary, hair dishevelled, clothes filthy, a smear of blood on her cheek, she glowed in the lamplight.

He was so hopelessly in love with her.

'Ember, you're not ... horrified by me?'

She looked baffled. 'Horrified? No. Rhaell, in case you hadn't noticed, I think you're fucking gorgeous. I literally can't wait for you to be well enough for us to bone each other's brains out.'

He closed his eyes.

The way people stared, and whispered, the scornful looks they gave him, the disgust in their eyes. The pity. The girls who recoiled as if he'd infect them with his ugliness. The ones who screamed when they saw him unclothed. The whores he paid handfuls of golden leaves to and came away untouched because there was no money in the world that would overcome his monstrosity.

And Ember still wanted him.

'You've seen all of me?' he whispered, eyes still closed.

'Yes. And I liked all of it. Well, not the bits where you were bleeding, but...' Her hand skimmed down over his chest, to his hip. His thigh. Rhaell was naked beneath the blanket, and that was going to become very obvious if she didn't stop. 'Not to perve on you while you were unconscious, but ... yeah. I want you, Rhaell. A lot.'

A tear leaked from his eye.

'Don't cry,' Ember said, and curled up against his side. 'I've got you.'

CHAPTER 26

Rhaell healed rapidly, but after that first night, Ember could not get him to talk about being Rakaa. He wouldn't tell her which of his parents had been Rakaa, or what had happened to them. He wouldn't even wear Rakaa clothing, with its back-fastening to accommodate wings. He shut down the conversation entirely, turned the subject to something else, or sometimes just pretended to go to sleep.

'But it's important,' Ember exploded one afternoon. 'Don't you want to know where you came from?'

'No! I don't want to know which of these monsters I'm related to.'

'They're not monsters! They're people. People who've taken us in and fed us and incidentally saved your life!'

'Which wouldn't have needed saving if it hadn't been for them in the first place!'

Ember threw up her hands. 'Oh my *Lords*, you are being impossible today.'

She knew he was bored. He was sick and tired of resting. Rhaell wasn't the sort of person to whom resting came naturally. But if she spent one more minute with his stubborn body, she might undo all his healing.

She got up. 'I'm going to see the blacksmith. I promised to help him work out a new cog design for the water wheel.'

'Cogs? What?'

'My father was a clockmaker,' Ember said, and it was only after she'd stalked out that she realised she'd used the past tense.

She was already thinking of Pa and the boys as long gone. Already behaving like she'd never go back.

Did she want to stay?

I want to stay with Rhaell.

The thought slowed her steps. Even if right now he was being incredibly annoying, she actually did want to stay, specifically, with him. The events of the last few days had made it pretty clear to her how desperately she felt about him.

Am I in love with him? Is that what's happening here?

Ember had never been in love. She'd never expected or even wanted to be. She knew she'd be taking care of Pa and the boys for the rest of her life; she already had a family to take care of, she didn't need a second one. Not to mention the other thing.

'Is't well, lass?' said a Rakaa, pausing and looking her over. 'Tha's the shade of old milk.'

'That's my normal colour,' said Ember.

The Rakaa shrugged as if this was a weird human trait, and went about his way. Ember shook herself and went on to the forge. She'd chatted with the blacksmith a bit on that first day, before Rhaell came for her; she suspected he was sweet on Thrala, but she also suspected Thrala only had eyes for Erli. But he was pleasant enough, interested in her talk of clockwork, and had made the pendant for the Healing Stone quickly and with very little fuss.

The forge was incredibly hot, even open to the mountain air, and so noisy it took a moment for the blacksmith to notice her. He was large even for a Rakaa, his biceps the size of Ember's torso, and his leathery wings were the colour of clay soil, his skin only a few shades lighter. When he saw her, he motioned her over to look at the mould he'd been making.

'I were thinking about what thee said, about turning the mechanism sideways,' he said. 'Now, the teeth will have to connect like this, see thee? Which makes them a different shape on the edge. Now, does tha think this will work?'

It had been a while since Ember had helped Pa in his workroom, but she'd always enjoyed it. She managed to forget about Rhaell for the rest of the afternoon, helping the blacksmith make a prototype and testing it against the existing wheel.

'It's gone dark, lass,' he said eventually. 'Tha ought to get back to thi' mate.'

'Why does everyone keep calling him that? I don't even know what that means, but we're not...'

The blacksmith raised an eyebrow.

'We're not anything. He's not my boyfriend or sweetheart or anything. He's definitely not my husband. I don't think he even likes me very much right now.'

'I like you,' came a voice from behind her, and she turned around guiltily.

Rhaell stood there, for once not the largest presence in the room. He had on a clean shirt and trousers, and his hair was wet, and he smelled of soap. Around his shoulders he wore a woollen wrap against the night air – not quite as the Rakaa did, but more like a sort of cloak, spilling over his back where his wings would have been.

The bandage had come off his face, his eye healed beneath it, although the scratches still stood out pink and livid against his skin. He looked strong, tired, human and inhuman, indomitable and weary. He looked perfect.

I really am in love with him.

'Can I talk to you?' he said.

The blacksmith made a shooing gesture, and Ember found herself following Rhaell outside. It had indeed got dark, and the path back to the village was quiet. Rhaell still walked her away from the forge and into a small stand of trees. He looked around nervously before he spoke.

'Look, I'm sorry I yelled. It's ... an emotive subject for me.'

'No kidding.'

He ran a hand through his hair and winced. And then he reached for her hand and touched it to the top of his head.

'Feel there? Those bumps?'

She did. Covered by the wild mess of his thick hair, they were invisible, but obvious to the touch.

'Were they your horns?'

'Still are,' he said. He swallowed. 'They grew back after ... after. I cut them back every now and then. File them down.'

'Why?' The horns on the other Rakaa looked magnificent. She bet Rhaell's would, too.

He looked incredulous. 'Why do you think, Ember? You think I could just walk around Yskara with horns growing out of my head? If anyone thought there was a Rakaa on the loose they'd shoot first, ask questions later.'

She kept petting the two hard stumps beneath his hair. Her eyes felt hot with tears. 'I'm sorry.'

'Yeah.' Rhaell blew out a breath. 'Me too.'

'Does it hurt?'

'When I cut them? Yes. To touch now? No.' He closed his eyes briefly. 'It's really the opposite.'

'You like this?' She read it in his parted lips, the rise and fall of his chest. 'Oh. You *like* this.'

He shrugged awkwardly.

Ember caressed one stump and he exhaled. 'Want me to stop?'

'Very much not.'

Ember smiled. She was standing pretty close; she had to be, to reach up to the top of his head. To her he was a large man; to the Rakaa he seemed small.

'Did you really think I'd think less of you if I knew?' she said.

'Everyone else has.'

'Then everyone else is a dick.'

He smiled a bit at that.

'You can see they're not bad people.'

'I can,' he said slowly. Reluctantly. 'But it's hard. Ember, I've been told all my life they're savage beasts. Little more than animals. That *I'm* little more than an animal.'

Ember slipped her other arm around his waist and pressed her body against his.

'My mother was kidnapped,' he said quietly, looking out over the top of her head. 'During the war with the Rakaa. She was kidnapped, and when she was rescued, she was pregnant.'

'With you? Your father was Rakaa?'

He nodded silently. Ember flinched. She had heard enough of wars to know that rape was used as a weapon.

'And when you were taken, all I could think was ... Ember, I thought he'd taken you to—'

Rhaell was trembling. Ember stroked her thumb over the stump of his horn and kissed his cheek, and his arms tentatively came around her.

'He didn't touch me. Apart from to bring me here. I was a hostage. That's all. To be honest, he seemed pretty disgusted by me.'

'Thank the Tree.' When she looked up, annoyed, he clarified,' That he didn't touch you. I'd have killed him all over again if he had.'

Ember narrowed her eyes. 'Is that why you stabbed him in the dick?'

Rhaell coloured slightly. 'Well – that, and it's a really good place to stab someone.'

She probably shouldn't find that sexy, but she did. 'Well, I'm untouched. I mean – by him. Not in general. That's not a problem, is it?'

She didn't know why she was asking. It wasn't as if they were getting married and he expected a virgin bride. Even the king knew she wasn't a blushing maiden.

'Of course not,' he said. He swallowed a couple of times, and she watched the muscles of his throat work. She wanted to kiss him there. Wanted to taste his skin, clean and fresh; wanted to taste it salty with sweat and sour with blood. She wanted to taste all of him.

'Ember, you said you'd seen me. All of me. And you still want...?'

She used the hand she had on his head to force him to look at her. 'You, Buttercup. I want you. All of you.'

'But I'm...'

He looked completely desolate, only the tiniest spark of hope in those lovely blue eyes. Ember said firmly, 'Let me make this really clear, so there's no misunderstanding. I've seen every bit of you, and I think you're fucking gorgeous, and I want to fuck you. A lot.'

His breath was hot as he exhaled, hard.

'And if you don't want to, then tell me, and I'll drop it, but if—'

His mouth cut her off. Ember melted against him, twining her arms around his neck as she sighed into his kiss.

'That's a yes,' he mumbled against her lips. 'I do. I do want to fuck you.'

'Thank the Lords for that,' Ember groaned. 'And are you – do you feel – I mean, are you healed enough?'

'Leaves and branches, yes.'

Ember kissed him some more and backed him against the nearest tree. She wanted to feel all of him, wanted to press as much of herself against him as possible. Her body pined for him. She felt desperate.

She had one leg hooked around his waist before she even knew it, grinding herself against him. Oh yes. She'd been trying not to perve over him while he was naked and bleeding, but it had been hard not to notice how very ... well, how very *much* he had to offer.

And all that muchness was thickening and hardening as she rubbed herself shamelessly against it.

Rhaell groaned, one large hand sliding down her back and slipping between the slits in the back of her tunic.

'Yes, touch me,' she gasped. They were both still dressed, and that was entirely wrong. She shoved away his wrapper, tugged at the neck of his shirt, and applied her lips to the skin she found there.

'We should go back,' he gasped. 'The others—'

'I don't want an audience,' Ember said, drawing back enough to tug his shirt up. The fabric caught between their bodies, and she growled in frustration.

Later, when everyone else had gone to bed, she'd take him to their nook and close the curtains and light the lamps and fill her senses with him. But right now, she thought she might go mad if she didn't get to feel his skin against hers.

She stepped back and pulled and tugged his shirt up, over his head, until his chest was bared to her.

Moonlight showed his healing wounds, his dark hair, his clearly defined muscles. Showed his chest heaving with each breath. The blue Healing Stone glowed faintly against his skin. He watched her intently.

Ember stripped her own tunic off, wrestled herself out of her undergarment and palmed her own breasts. Her nipples were tight and aching.

'Touch me,' she said, taking his hand and pressing it over her breast. His palm was large and rough, and she arched into it with a gasp. 'Yes. That. More.'

She showed him what she liked, kneading and rubbing, and went back to the serious business of kissing him. Rhaell didn't kiss demandingly, but he did kiss hungrily. His finger and thumb gently pinched her nipple as his tongue delicately fought with hers, and she let out a whimper.

All of a sudden, she was spun around, her back against the

rough bark of the tree, and it was a shock that stole her breath. But she forgot about it in the next second as Rhaell bent his head and sucked her nipple into his mouth.

Her eyes closed in bliss. Her hand went to his head, groping blindly through his hair until she felt the stub of one horn and rubbed it with her thumb. Rhaell growled and did the same to her other nipple.

It was delicious, it was torture, and it wasn't enough. Ember's hand grasped at his neck, his shoulder, his back – and her fingers hit the edge of one of his deep scars.

His back flexed, and for a second, she thought he might stop, but all he did was switch breasts, and she let a whimper escape her.

'Rhaell, yes. So good,' she murmured, and it was good, but it still wasn't enough. Between her legs she ached, squirming and writhing to no effect. Eventually, she dropped her hand from his back and slid it down her own body, swearing and squirming when she remembered her trousers fastened at the back over a tail she didn't have. She wrenched open the tie and wormed her hand back around to the front.

'Fuck,' Rhaell gasped, and lifted his head. His lips were swollen, wet from sucking her, his blue eyes molten with desire. 'Are you touching yourself?'

Ember slid her fingers lower and moaned at the relief. 'Yes.'

'Show me.'

It was nearly unbearable. He drew back from her, pulled her trousers down to her ankles, and put his hand over hers.

'Show me what you like,' he said, and Ember whimpered. She touched herself, and his fingers followed hers, sliding into her wetness until she slipped her hand over his and guided his fingers where she wanted them.

There— 'Yes,' she gasped, and he gave her a wolfish grin before repeating the motion, then swooping in to kiss her again.

He fingered her against the tree, his tongue in her mouth, his other hand pinching her nipple. It was filthy and glorious, being spread out in the dark, on the mountainside, where anyone might come across them.

Ember writhed and whimpered, clutching at his neck, forgetting all about his horns. Rhaell bit softly on her lip, then murmured, 'I want to put my mouth there, too,' and did something with his fingers that made her cry out.

'Again, again,' she panted, and he smiled against her lips and kissed her sweetly as he frigged her to an orgasm that had her shaking and spasming in his arms.

'Yes, Ember, yes,' he groaned, and then he was stepping away from her, reaching into his trousers and taking out his—

'Dear Lords and all their little angels,' Ember gasped, as Rhaell wrapped both hands around his cock. Engorged wasn't even the word. That thing was massive.

Her fingers went between her legs again and he groaned, stroking himself frantically, his eyes on her moving hand.

'Yes – yes—' he gasped, and then he moaned and spurted all over his hands, onto the floor, even onto her.

There was a lot of it. There was a lot of him. If Ember hadn't just come her brains out all over his hand, she'd be having second thoughts right about now. But she was high on pleasure, so all she did was stumble towards him and kiss him, reaching down to take his shaft in hand and feel it throb.

He moaned her name, and she nearly came again at the power of it.

'Oh, the things I'm gonna do to you when everyone else is asleep,' she whispered wickedly.

Rhaell huffed out a laugh. 'They've gone out,' he said, rocking into her fingers. She couldn't close them around him. 'That's what I was trying to say. They've gone to the mead hall.'

Ember felt laughter escape her. 'Fuck's sake,' she groaned. 'We could've been doing this in a bed?'

'We still can,' said Rhaell, his hands grasping randomly at her as if he didn't know what to do with himself. 'If you want.'

Her eyebrows went up. 'Another round?'

'If you— Whoa! Ember! Clothes!'

She'd begun to drag him down the mountain, but he was right, they should probably restore some semblance of order first. She nearly tripped over her own trousers, tied them carelessly, and dragged her tunic on. Rhaell picked up the brassiere-like garment Phoebe had made for her and raised an eyebrow.

'Less to take off,' she said, and grabbed his hand.

Thrala and Erli had seemed to know what was on Rhaell's mind earlier when he left to bathe. They had informed Ivvo he needed some mead, and that the house would be empty when Rhaell returned.

His heart had hammered in his chest all the way to the blacksmith's forge. What if she was angry with him, what if she'd changed her mind, what if once she saw his obscenity she ran screaming?

Or worse, laughed?

And now here he was, being stripped and pushed down onto the bed by Ember, who threw off her clothes before climbing in after him and pulling the curtain closed.

'Lamps,' she said, stretching up, and Rhaell made a werelight. 'Fuck, I keep forgetting about those.'

'But don't let me keep you from doing that,' he said, dreamily watching the curve of her breast as she moved.

She grinned and made a light, and then another. 'I want to see you,' she explained.

He didn't understand why. He was scarred, lumpen, misshapen. He was ugly. He'd been told so every day of his life. And yet Ember was looking at him as if she was starving and he was made out of cheese.

'Look at you,' she said, as Rhaell fought the urge to cover himself. There was longing in her voice. 'You're a fucking banquet.' Her gaze flickered down to his obscenity. 'Can I eat you?'

Rhaell couldn't speak. And when he managed to, it came out scratchy. 'Are you sure?'

'Oh yes. I've been dreaming about this,' she said, crawling over him, 'since that morning in the cave. Remember?'

Remember? It was seared into his memory forever. Rhaell had kept that memory and used it to keep warm when he was climbing the mountain to find her.

She leaned in and kissed his mouth, her lips sweet and swollen, and then she moved to his chest. He was still sore in places, the Healing Stone apparently working from the inside out, but the touch of Ember's lips on his healing skin was like the kiss of an angel.

'Is that okay?' she whispered, and he could only nod.

She found other scars on his ribs and belly, tonguing them in a way that made him squirm, and then she ran out of torso and arrived at his groin.

Rhaell's body proclaimed his Rakaa heritage everywhere, but nowhere was the shame more acute than his cock. No decent woman would take it. No indecent woman, either. He'd had whores shove handfuls of money back at him because the mere sight of it terrified them.

And yet Ember leaned down and nuzzled it, as if she'd never seen anything more enticing.

She settled between his legs, where the view had to be even worse, and stroked his cock, which leapt up enthusiastically to meet her.

'Well,' she purred. 'What do we have here?'

Rhaell wanted to apologise. He wanted to warn her. And he desperately didn't want her to stop.

'It's too big,' he gasped, unable to help himself.

Well, that was a nice move, half-wit. Put her off, why don't you.

Ember gave it an assessing look. 'Look, I'm not gonna lie to you,' she said, 'it is fucking massive. But *too* big? Rhaell, honey. There ain't no such thing.'

'But...'

Shut up, shut up.

'Shh.' Evidently, she agreed, reaching up and putting a finger against his lips. Her breasts grazed his hip. 'I want to suck your cock. Do you want me to suck your cock?'

Rhaell nodded helplessly.

'Then we are in accord,' said Ember, and lowered her head.

The first lick robbed him of his breath. She mouthed up and down his length, and his fingers fisted in the sheets.

Then she sucked the head into her mouth, and looked right up at him as she did, and Rhaell bit down on his own lip so hard he tasted blood.

'Ember,' he gasped. 'I don't – I don't want this to be over too soon.'

She ran her lips over the head, and he whimpered. 'Been a while?'

'You have no idea.'

'Well, you're a healthy young man,' she said cheerfully, 'I'm sure there's more where this comes from.'

Then she sucked on him again, and Rhaell gave up trying to resist her.

She sucked. She licked. She moaned around a mouthful of him. Her hands came into play, stroking him up and down, cupping his balls, feathering wickedly light touches over the head until he whimpered. She showed him no mercy.

And when he came, as he knew he would, she sat up and aimed his cock at her tits, spreading his seed over her bountiful, beautiful body.

'Fuck, Ember,' he cried, nearly sobbing, and she just smiled at him and massaged some more out of him.

'You looked like you needed that,' she said, when he was finally done, and slid up his body to kiss him. She was wet and sticky with his release, and he could taste it all over her mouth. He fed on her ravenously.

'I want to taste you,' he mumbled, and she nipped his lip with her teeth and said, 'Are you sure? "Cos I'm good to go here.'

'Please,' he said, and she made a sound of capitulation.

'Well, if you're going to ask so nicely,' she said, and allowed him to tumble her to the bed.

He wanted to kiss her everywhere. Take mouthfuls of her, fill his hands and mouth with her. He tongued her collarbone, letting his fingers explore her shoulders and arms. She was so strong here, Ember the thief who'd climbed down the castle wall and out of the Myr cage. The king wanted her to be a dolly in a dress, caged and imprisoned in frills and jewels, but Ember was a fighter, fearless and powerful. Her forearms were exquisite. Her hands were works of art.

The purple stone, Ruvaen's Stone, glowed between her breasts, clinking softly against the unshining, fathomless black of Mnorir's Stone.

'The blacksmith's remaking the vambrace for you,' she said, as he moved the two stones aside. 'I figured it should go on your wrist. You're the one who won it.'

'Mmm.' He didn't care about the stones now. He had Ember naked and willing in his arms. He didn't care about anything else in the world. He cupped her breasts in his hands, weighing their fullness. The ladies of the court didn't have tits like this. They were slender willows, elegant and sexless. They wafted around the place in gowns slashed to the navel – and they held no interest for Rhaell.

Ember merely had to take a deep breath, and she had his full attention.

'You like them, huh?' she said, as he played with them.

'Like isn't nearly strong enough a word,' he said, and swiped his tongue lewdly over her nipple. He was rewarded with a gasp, and her fingers going into his hair. She'd learned now how to play with his horns – an area he had not previously thought of as erotic. Maybe because it was Ember. Everything she did was erotic to him.

But her breasts, fascinating as they were, were not his goal right now. He slid one hand down, over the roundness of her hip, and squeezed one buttock. She was soft here, flesh giving beneath his fingers, but her thighs were strong. Her muscles tensed as he trailed his fingers over them.

'Stop teasing me,' she said.

'Hmm?'

Ember tilted her hips and rocked her core against him, and Rhaell's breath left him in a rush. She was hot and slick there, and he was wasting damn time stroking her thighs when there was a feast to be had.

He'd touched her there, but he'd been in a desperate rush, hardly paying attention, and now he wanted to see, to taste, to savour. He parted her legs, and looked up at her, slightly surprised.

'What?' she said. 'Oh. Yeah, Phoebe said the court ladies don't have no hair down there, but I said she wasn't taking it off me. I let her do my legs though. Is it weird?'

She grabbed his hand and stroked it up her calf. Rhaell turned his head and kissed the inside of her knee.

'It's perfect,' he said. 'You're perfect.' And he licked a stripe up the centre of her.

Ember let out a guttural cry, and those thigh muscles tensed under his hands. Rhaell slid his palms down under her buttocks to lift her to his mouth, and slid his tongue between her folds.

He knew how to do this, although he wasn't about to admit to her why. Before he'd learned he couldn't even pay a woman to take his cock, he'd held out hope one might come around if he pleasured her first. There were plenty of nights he'd paid for the privilege of eating out a woman, and got nothing in return but satisfaction at his own hand.

With Ember, though, the pleasure was all his. He used his tongue to explore her, discover where she was most sensitive, where made her arch her back and whimper. He kissed her, ripe as a peach, and sucked on her nectar. He found her clit, swollen and begging for attention, and gave it what it wanted.

Ember's gasp was wordless, her fingers clutching at his scalp, her toes curling against his back.

Well, maybe the pleasure wasn't *all* his.

She made delicious, filthy sounds as he licked her, as he circled and thrust and sucked. He tasted her deep inside, drank down her whimpering cries, and gorged himself on her flesh.

'Fuck, I'm gonna—' She gasped, hips bucking, her fingers clenching in his hair. The way she pressed her thumb down on the stub of one horn made Rhaell growl, and that was, apparently, what sent her over the edge.

She cried and yelled filthy nonsense, grinding herself into his mouth, flooding his tongue. Rhaell looked up at her as she writhed, and pushed his fingers deep into her grasping, spasming channel.

'Fuck, fuck!' She tightened around him and rode him to another peak, finally pushing his head away with a cry of, 'Too much, too much.'

Rhaell kissed her inner thigh. His fingers were still inside her, and he flexed them a little as she moaned, one arm over her eyes.

'Lord Ruven and all his little thieves,' she gasped, 'where did you learn to do that?'

Probably best not to say. He gave her one more little lick. He couldn't help it. Then he kissed her mouth, as she'd kissed him, and she sucked on his tongue.

'I want you inside me,' she gasped. 'Now. Please.'

Rhaell suddenly realised he was so hard it hurt. Ember squirmed against him, and that was a test of his self-control. 'Are you sure?'

'Yes. I need— Please ... I need—' She rolled against him, one leg going over his thigh, her hand going down beneath them to grasp his throbbing cock. 'This.' She rubbed the head of him against her entrance, all slick and wet from what they'd been doing.

Rhaell could hardly breathe. She wanted it – he had never seen anybody want anything more in his life – but once he gave her what she wanted, would she beg him to stop?

His cock had its own ideas, eagerly surging against her hand, and she lodged the head of him against her entrance. Her hips sank against him, and he hissed out a breath. Just the tip—

But she kept on moving, taking more of him, moaning low in her throat as she did. 'Lords ... fuck ... yes—'

And then he was inside her tight, wet heat, and her leg curled around his hip and thigh to pull him in closer to her. Her mouth was hot against his throat, and then she grabbed his head and kissed him.

They were on their sides now, which meant there was nothing to stop Ember rocking herself against him just as she liked. Her leg tightened around his, as if refusing to let him escape. *What sort of fool would ever want to escape this?*

'Fuck,' she moaned against his mouth, 'you feel so good inside me.'

'You like it?' he asked, in disbelief.

'Like isn't nearly strong enough a word,' she said, and from somewhere he found a laugh.

Ember laughed too, grinning up at him, sweat gleaming on her skin, eyes bright. Her laughing mouth met his, and the smile in her eyes nearly undid him. Then her eyelids fluttered, and she shuddered, rippling around him. Her fingers gripped his back, and they caught the edge of one of his wing scars, and Rhaell realised he didn't mind at all.

She'd seen all of him, his scars and his ugliness, his hideous deformities, and she *liked* it. She plunged and writhed on the cock he'd been told all his life was an obscenity, grasping him with her strong thighs to pull him deeper. She was a miracle.

'More,' she muttered against his neck, mouthing at his throat. 'There's more.'

'There is?' Rhaell said, and then she rolled him to his back and sank deeper on him and as his senses overloaded, he realised what she meant. She wanted more of *him*.

She sat up, working her hips, rocking herself down until she was grinding her clit against his root. 'Fuck,' she gasped. 'Yes. All of you. Holy shit.'

Her hands were on his chest, fingers kneading helplessly into the dark hair there. Her hips rolled, apparently of their own volition, her head falling back in bliss. The sounds she made were wordless and desperate.

Rhaell could only gaze up at her as she took her pleasure from him, on him, shuddering and quivering above him. Her hot, tight cunt squeezed and shivered around him, and Rhaell really thought he was going to lose control.

Ember crashed down against him, clumsy with pleasure, and mouthed at his lip. 'That was so good,' she gasped.

'Yeah?' Breathless, all he could do was hold her, stroke her back, caress her as she came down from her high. 'Ember— I need you to ... I think I might—'

'Mmm,' she purred, wriggling against him, plastering herself all over him so he couldn't move. 'Go on, then.'

'No, I need you to— I can't ... not inside you,' he said desperately.

'Oh.' She kissed sloppily up to his ear. 'Yes, you can,' she murmured. 'It's safe.'

His fingers tightened on her back. 'Are you sure?'

'Yes. I told you. You ain't gonna knock me up, Buttercup. I promise.'

His hands were squeezing handfuls of her now, grasping her

buttocks and kneading. He wanted – he *wanted* – but he was still afraid.

'Your turn,' she breathed in his ear. 'Go nuts. What do you want?'

'I – I don't want to hurt you.'

She laughed, a rich, dark sound. 'I don't think you could. Shall I tell you what I want, and see if you want it, too?'

He nodded, looking up at her as she continued to gently rock her hips against him.

'I want you to fuck me. As hard as you like. I want you to *pound* me.'

Rhaell let out a strangled sound.

Ember put her lips right next to his ear and breathed, 'I want to feel you in my cunt for days,' and Rhaell had her on her back before the sound was even out of his ear.

He surged into her, and she laughed in delight, stretching out her arms above her head. 'Yes. Like that. *Fuck* me, Buttercup.'

And he did. Rhaell grasped her hips in his hands and hammered into her, sweat flying from his skin, desperate to lose himself in her. Ember braced her hands on the wall he'd fucked her against, and arched her back, thrusting her breasts at him just in case he needed any more visual stimulation.

He didn't. He couldn't take a second more. White hot fire erupted through his veins, and he roared as he came, grabbing her to him and forcing himself as deep as he could go. And Ember wrapped her arms around him and murmured, 'Yes, yes, just like that. *Yes*, Rhaell,' as he lost control of himself, his vision blacking out.

When he came to, he lay half on her, his face pressed into her neck, chest heaving and every nerve ending alight.

'Mmm, well,' said Ember, her hands idly stroking his back. 'More than three or four times a day like that and I think I shall have to complain.'

'Three – what?' His brain felt like soup.

She patted his back. 'I'm joking. You can fuck me like that as often as you damn well want. I just might not be able to move again. Like, ever.'

Rhaell tried to laugh and found he didn't have the energy. By the Tree, he'd fought in pitched battles and slain mantises larger than he was and only two days ago he'd narrowly escaped being hacked to pieces by a monster twice his size, and yet he couldn't remember ever being so exhausted.

Or so absolutely bone-deep *satisfied*.

'That,' he began, and had to try again. 'That was…'

Ember's laughter was warm in his ear. 'Yes,' she agreed. 'It was a bit.'

He managed to lift his head and look across at her smiling face. He'd never seen anyone look so pleased with themselves. Not that he could blame her. He thought about the feeling of her coming on his fingers, his tongue, his cock, and a shiver of pleasure ran through him.

'Lords, don't tell me you're getting hard again,' she said. 'Rhaell, honey, that was amazing, but I really don't think I can go again for a while. A girl needs a rest.'

'No,' he said, embarrassed, because she wasn't entirely wrong. 'I was just … um, I should probably…'

He withdrew from her clasping heat, and Ember sighed as he did. She followed him as he flopped on his back, snuggling up against his side. Rhaell felt like a king.

'I should probably go and fetch a cloth or something,' she said vaguely. 'In a minute. I'm not sure I can move.'

'Me neither. Is it always like that?' he said, and then his whole body cringed as he realised what he'd just said.

But Ember just nuzzled his shoulder and said, 'If you're lucky.' Her thigh slipped over his, nudging his cock, which wasn't entirely convinced everything was over. 'Fucking hell, Buttercup, every woman in Yskara is a fucking moron.'

'What?'

'"Too big". What a bunch of frigid twats. Bet they wouldn't know an orgasm if it hit them in the face.'

Rhaell opened his mouth to ask what that was supposed to mean, then figured he didn't really want to know.

'Mmm. I feel drunk. I think you fucked my brains out.' She stretched against him like a cat and settled her head back on his shoulder. 'D'you know what I regret?'

He tensed. His mouth went dry. 'What?'

'Not doing this sooner.' She reached ineffectually for the blanket, and Rhaell beckoned for it with his hand, letting it settle over them both. 'I'm gonna have to learn how to do that beckoning thing one day.'

'I'll teach you.'

Ember snuggled into his side. 'D'you mind if I have a little nap?'

'Nap as much as you want.' He could think of no greater privilege than holding her in his arms as she slept.

'Cool. You should get some rest too, 'cos I reckon we're gonna be doing round two before the sun comes up.'

'We are?'

'Mmm. If you want.' She burrowed against him.

Oh, he wanted. He wanted a lot. But he held her close in his arms, and kissed the top of her head, and drifted into sleep, happier than he'd ever been.

CHAPTER 27

Ember hadn't been kidding about feeling him for days. By the time they emerged from their extremely rumpled sex den and braved the hot springs the Rakaa bathed in, she wasn't entirely sure she could walk.

'I'll carry you,' said Rhaell, but he didn't look much better off. She supposed nearly dying and then having a sex marathon would do that to you. She twined her arm around his and leaned into him as they made their way through the village. Thrala and Erli gave them knowing looks.

'That's adorable,' Ember teased.

'What?'

'You're blushing.' She nudged him.

'Well.' His ears were going red now. 'I mean ... do you think they know what we were doing?'

Ember laughed. 'What, you think me screaming "Fuck me, Rhaell" until I was hoarse wasn't a bit of a clue?'

He covered his face with his free hand.

'Why're you embarrassed? If I were you, I'd be feeling pretty pleased with myself about now,' she said, and he managed a smile at that. 'And it's not like there's any reason we shouldn't fuck each other's brains out whenever we want.'

His smile seemed to sort of freeze on his face, and cold doubt pooled in Ember's stomach as she realised why.

Technically, she was engaged to Prince Bronadyr. She was supposed to go back to Yskara and marry him. And given the time they'd lost to Ember getting kidnapped, Rhaell nearly dying and the two of them failing to stop having sex, they were rapidly running out of time to get the stones and get Ember home before the wedding.

Home. She knew she ought to want to go back to Pa and the boys. But they felt like strangers, somewhere far away. They'd probably decided she was dead by now. Maybe Dandelia had gone back to her family and told them the truth, or maybe nobody had even noticed Ember was missing until the food stopped arriving on the table and the bills remained unpaid.

She glanced up at Rhaell as they neared the hot springs. Did he want her to leave? The last few days very much seemed as if he didn't. He'd nearly died with her. He'd fought and killed for her. And he was very clearly not the sort of man to take a woman to his bed and then get tired of her quickly.

But if she broke the engagement with the prince, what would happen? The king really wanted his heirs. What if Ember told him she couldn't give them to him? Would he release her? Would he throw her in jail, or worse – onto the scaffold for the prince to behead her?

If the king found out she'd had an abortion all those years ago, he'd have her hacked to pieces.

She couldn't go back. Not to the court. Once they'd got the stones together and restored the heart of the Tree, she'd have to go into hiding. Maybe Rhaell could say she'd died, or maybe they could pretend they'd both died, and—

'Ember?'

They were at the hot springs. Ember looked at Rhaell, who was still reluctant to disrobe even though there was no one else around and they both desperately needed a bath, and her heart softened.

She wanted to stay with him. Whatever happened after they'd got the stones, she wanted to stay with him.

She kissed him, and drew him down into the warm water, and even though every muscle she had told her it was a bad idea, she made love to him in the open, riding his lap beneath the water, revelling in the glory of being with him.

It was right. It was where she was meant to be. It was—

'What the *fuck* is that?'

She was suddenly tipped into the water as Rhaell launched himself onto the rocks, reaching for his clothes and the sword belt he insisted on wearing everywhere. Ember was about to complain, but then a shadow passed overhead, and when she looked up, every word she had ever known fled her mind.

A dragon it's a dragon that's a fucking dragon—

A dragon the size of a house, its belly gleaming with pale iridescent scales and its green wings too large for her to even take in. Its head was topped with spikes, its huge jaw lined with fangs, and on its feet were claws that could eviscerate a rhino.

It flew serenely overhead, as she and Rhaell gaped up at it, and then it banked and flew back.

Rhaell grabbed Ember and shoved her behind him.

'I thought you said there weren't any Great Dragons,' she hissed, peering over his shoulder.

'There aren't.' He swallowed. 'There shouldn't be.'

With an impact that made the ground tremble, the dragon landed on the hillside. Along its neck and back were plumes of feathers, spreading out along its wings and tail into every shade of green. Its head tilted to one side as it regarded them. Steam blew from its nostrils.

We're going to die. It's going to kill us.

'I love you,' Ember whispered to Rhaell, wrapping her arm around his waist.

The stones she wore pulsed against her skin.

'What do you think you're going to do with that?' said the Great Dragon.

Ember went rigid. In front of her, so did Rhaell. 'Did the dragon just *speak*?' he said from the corner of his mouth.

'I think so, yeah.' Her voice was a squeak.

He cleared his throat. 'With what?' he asked the creature.

The dragon gave him a slow perusal. 'I meant the sword, but ... have humans stopped wearing clothes?'

Fuck, they were both naked. And Rhaell hated to be seen naked. He'd turned into an absolute statue in front of her, frozen with mortification. And the dragon sounded ... sort of ... female?

'Yeah, uh, sorry, we were ... um, bathing,' Ember said, leaving the safety of Rhaell's back to find some clothes. It would be pretty humiliating to die naked.

'Bathing?' said the dragon, as Ember covered herself with her blanket wrap. 'Is that what you're calling it these days?'

Great, the dragon thought it was funny.

Ember handed Rhaell his trousers, but it was hard for him to get into them because he wouldn't let go of his sword. Ember thought the huffing noise the dragon made might have been laughter.

She eventually wrestled the sword from him and glared him into getting dressed. 'Um, can we help you?'

The Great Dragon regarded them. She stood on the grassy hillside, in a meadow leading from the village to the hot springs. All around her was grass, and bushes, and trees of every shade of green, and yet somehow, she managed to be the greenest thing that Ember had ever seen.

'You wear Heart Stones,' she said.

Ember's hand went to the two pendants around her neck. Rhaell still wore the Healing Stone, and the War Stone shone in the vambrace on his wrist.

'We do,' she said.

The dragon's feathered tail swished, as if it was a very large cat. With spikes and a club on its tail.

'What is your interest in them?'

Rhaell had wrestled himself into his trousers and tunic now and took his sword back from Ember. She turned to pull her clothes on under cover of the blanket. 'What's yours?' he challenged.

'We were charged with the protection of one,' said the dragon. 'Our friend Wynric gave it to us. He said—' She stopped and looked them over again. 'How did you come by the others?'

'I won this one,' said Rhaell, brandishing the War Stone on his wrist. 'In a fight to the death.'

'Appropriate. Who did you kill for Mnorir's?'

'Mnorir.'

The dragon looked surprised. 'That old ghoul was still alive?'

'Well – sort of. In a feeding-off-the-dead kind of way.'

The dragon huffed hot hair from her nostrils. 'You stole Ruvaen's Stone, then?'

'Well, I tried,' Ember said. 'Long story, actually.' She winced, because there was an obvious question to come next. Could the dragon tell if she was lying?

'We were given Gaeleath's,' said Rhaell.

'You're lying.'

Well, that answered that question.

'All right, we stole that, too,' Ember said. 'But we didn't kill anyone,' she hastily corrected.

'No one at all?'

Ember darted a frantic glance at Rhaell. He cleared his throat. 'No one I didn't have to,' he said. 'They were going to kill you,' he added to Ember, who gripped his arm as the memory overflooded her.

'Well, I see how you'll get the Love Stone,' said the dragon cryptically. 'And the sixth? Ysarriel's Stone?'

Rhaell lifted his chin. 'That won't be a problem.'

'Indeed? The king is happy to give it to you?'

'I wouldn't say happy,' said Rhaell. 'But we'll get it.'

The dragon was silent a moment, tail swishing. Then she said, 'I asked you who you killed to obtain the Stone of Death. You fought for the War Stone. Stole the Thieves' Stone. Does this give rise to any questions in your mind about how to obtain the Royal Stone?'

Oh, fuck. Did that mean they had to be royal to get it? Well, that ruled out everyone but the king and Prince Bronadyr.

Who was her fiancé.

'Oh, bollocks,' Ember sighed.

'What? Look, we didn't need to heal to get the Healing Stone, it'll be fine.'

'Maybe,' said Ember, but she knew it wasn't.

The dragon studied her. 'Walk with me,' she said.

Ember looked at the clawed feet, larger than a horse, and said, 'Um, what?'

'I wish to speak with you privately. Away from the sword-wielder.'

Ember wasn't sure if that was meant to be some kind of dick joke.

'I don't like this,' said Rhaell.

'Buttercup, she could have flambéed us ten times over if she wanted to. A bit of distance won't make much difference.'

Rhaell caught her arm as she turned away. 'Ember,' he said, and there was urgency in his voice but not enough words. For a moment his eyes burned into her.

Is he going to say he loves me? Did he hear what I said? Do I want him to have heard?

'Be careful,' he said.

Ember found a smile. 'I'll be fine,' she said, and patted his arm. 'We're just going to talk.'

She walked away towards the dragon, which only seemed to get bigger as she approached. It could crush her, never mind incinerate her. The dragon lowered its great green head, dinner-plate eyes glowing a greenish yellow.

'You offered mercy,' said the dragon, voice low.

'What?'

Her huge mouth split in a terrifying grin. 'Wynric gave his Stone to us because we are the wisest of all beasts. We see into hearts and minds. And I see the prayer you offered as you took the stone.'

Fuck. She could see that? How? That was a terrifying thought.

Wait, the dragon could probably hear her thinking that, too.

Gilia's Prayer. She'd just thought it automatically, the way you did when you heard someone was sick. Because the Speaker had been dying. She'd just wanted to ease his suffering a bit.

'It was just a prayer,' she said.

'It was enough for the stone to recognise. The Speaker was going to die anyway,' the dragon added dismissively.

Ember rubbed her face. 'Are you saying we have to get someone royal to get us the king's Stone?'

'Yes, Ember Hart. I am.'

Shit. Shit. There was a way. And Ember really, really didn't want to do it.

'I ... have to ask for the prince's help?' she tried.

The dragon gave her a knowing look.

Ember rubbed her hands across her face. The prince wouldn't help. He didn't care about her. But if she married him...

Could she take the stone then? Would that be enough?

'You're really sure I'd have to actually be a royal?' she said.

The dragon huffed in amusement. 'This seems to be the way of things,' she said.

Ember narrowed her eyes. 'Is that actually true or are you saying it to sound wise?'

The dragon huffed again. 'Perhaps you may yet win the final stone,' she said.

'Wynric's Stone? You have it?'

The dragon blinked slowly.

'Is that a yes? Look, if this is a test can you at least tell me?' She was the least wise person in the world. Rhaell had read all those books and scrolls, he'd have to pass the wisdom test.

'Ah, then, Ember Hart, would it even be a real test?'

Ember scowled. 'They told us about spelling tests at school and they were definitely real.'

This time the sound of the dragon's laughter was clear. 'There are many ways of proving your wisdom. Find out the truth at the heart of the prophecy, and perhaps I shall consider giving you what you desire.'

'You'd give us the stone? For real?'

The dragon made a head movement that was not particularly easy to interpret. She turned as if to go.

'Wait! The prophecy. It can't be me. It can't be true.'

The dragon looked back. 'What do you mean?'

'I mean, it says I've got to have babies. And I can't.'

The dragon cocked her huge head. 'Are you sure?'

'Yeah.' The memory of that night would always be vivid in Ember's mind. 'I'm really sure.'

'Well, you know best, then,' said the dragon mildly. 'My regards to your mate,' she added. She stepped away, her huge feet making the ground vibrate a little, then she said, 'Do something ... smart, Ember Hart.'

And then the green Great Dragon gave a huge leap, her wings beating, and Ember was thrown to the ground as the dragon soared away.

'Ember! Are you all right?' Rhaell was there before she'd even taken her eyes off the dragon. 'Did it hurt you?'

'No. Just the ... you know. Wind.' She let him help her to her feet.

'What did it say?'

Ember watched the large shape vanish off to the north. *She said I have to marry Bronadyr.*

'It was cryptic,' she said. 'I'll have to think about it.' She shivered. 'Let's get dressed properly and go back somewhere warm. We've got to think about getting back to Yskara.'

Rhaell sighed. 'Yeah, I know. But without the Dragon's Stone?'

Ember stared at the sky, where the dragon had vanished into the clouds. 'We still might,' she said.

They went back to the village, but it was clear even as they approached that something was wrong.

'What is it?'

Ivvo, the healers' apprentice, gave them a distracted look. 'Summat's happening in the canyon. I don't know. They've just told me to pack for casualties.'

Rhaell and Ember exchanged a look, and then they started running for Thrala and Erli's house.

'We'll get our packs,' said Ember, 'and make our way—'

Two large shapes blocked their path. 'I'm afraid,' said Zikol, shoving her pack at her, 'there's no time for that.'

Then he grabbed her, and another Rakaa took Rhaell, and they were being jerked high into the sky. Ember screamed, because this had happened to her before, and she really hadn't liked that.

'What's happening?' she yelled, wrapping one arm around his muscular neck and trying not to look down.

'Littlins. Humans,' said Zikol, his voice snatched away by the wind. 'Marching into the canyon.'

'But – which humans? From where?'

'I don't know! Tha don't have clan markings!'

'No – I mean, are they in uniform?' Wincing, she asked, 'Green and silver?'

'I don't know, lass. Angaa sent word of a sighting of a group of humans – and not a few lost or exploring, neither. Men on horseback, lots of them. Carrying spears and bows.'

'An army?' said Ember.

'Aye. We sent out a few more scouts – they shot down Dotan.'

'Is he alive?'

'I don't know,' said Zikol grimly. 'That's why we're taking thee. Before they get any further, before they find our village, before they kill any more.'

'You think they want us?'

'I hope so, lass. Listen, it's nowt personal. Tha's been a pleasant guest, and thi' mate … in't as bad as we feared. But we can't risk them coming to our home and destroying it. Or anybody else's.'

'I understand,' said Ember, and she did. Why would humans be entering Bronavon Point, knowing it led to the Rakaa lands? Had they come to attack, to invade? But they had no reason, apart from perhaps believing Ember had been taken hostage by them.

But how would they know that? Hesk was the only one who knew they'd even gone to the north shore of the Sacred Sea, and she didn't think Rhaell had told them where they were headed after that. Had he? Was Hesk a spy?

'Here,' said Zikol over his shoulder, to the Rakaa carrying Rhaell, and they swooped downwards into a side canyon.

'I don't see any troops?' Ember said.

'No. They're around the next bend. We do not wish to be seen.' Zikol set her down carefully on the ground. 'I am sorry it has to be like this,' he said. 'But I must protect my people.'

'I understand,' Ember said again. She reached out to Rhaell, who was gaining his feet nearby, looking slightly green around the gills. 'Are you okay?'

He nodded, shouldering his pack. 'Our friend here says humans have been sighted? They're coming to attack?'

'Sounds like it. You want us to go and tell them … what? There's no one here?'

Zikol looked grim. 'They know we're here, lass. They don't know where, but that don't matter to them. They'll find us. We need to give them a reason not to.'

Rhaell nodded in understanding. 'You don't want us to mention you at all? We just … got lost in the canyon?'

'And then they'll ask why tha's in the canyon,' said Zikol. 'Tell them tha saw Rakaa and came here to hide.'

'There goes my reputation as a brave warrior,' Rhaell grumped, but he nodded. 'Boat blown off course, didn't know where we were ... sighted the fearsome Rakaa, needed to protect my lady, hid out here ... relief to see humans, thank goodness they're here, et cetera.' He narrowed his eyes at the distance. 'Why are they here?'

'We don't even know who they are,' said Ember. She looked at Zikol. 'What if they're not here for us? Another invading force, come to ... um...'

'Slaughter us all?' said Zikol. 'Then we fight, littlin.' He bared his teeth. 'Tha might tell them tha saw Rakaa in the woods off to the north. There's no one there,' he explained. 'But there's a fair few things with teeth, and I'm not just talking about the plants.'

'Good to know,' Ember said faintly. She hesitated, then gave Zikol a hug. He was so massive her arms didn't go around him and her head barely reached his chest. 'Thank you,' she said, looking up. 'You've been so kind.'

'If I'd died, they'd have kept you as a slave,' Rhaell pointed out. Ember released Zikol.

'Nay,' dismissed Zikol. 'A pot maiden, perhaps. And tha didn't die, lad, so don't go thinking about it as if tha did.' He looked Rhaell over. 'Tha might have living relatives, tha knows.'

'I don't want to know them.'

Zikol looked thoughtful. 'I hope tha changes thi' mind, Hraeul-fr,' he said, and clapped Rhaell on his wingless back. 'Now go. If tha really wants to pay back our kindness, pretend tha never met us. Aye?'

'Aye,' agreed Ember, and took Rhaell's arm. 'Let's go.'

When they were out of earshot, she asked, 'What was that he called you?'

'Hmm? Oh. He says it's the Rakaa version of my name. Which sounds like a reach, frankly. My mother named me, and she was definitely human.'

She slipped her hand down to his. 'I think it's nice. Like they're letting you into the family.'

Rhaell gave her a sideways look. 'You really want me to be a part of this, don't you.'

'They're nice people! You were lied to, Rhaell.'

He sighed. 'Sparks ... they're the enemy. And don't you start – I mean when you're at war, when you have an enemy, you can't afford to go around thinking of them as good people, because that makes it really hard to kill them. So yeah, obviously we were told the Rakaa were terrible, violent beasts. It's easy to kill those.'

'But now you know different?'

He nudged his head against hers. 'Yeah. Although don't go asking me to like Ikrai ... or the Rakaa who sired me.'

'I suppose Rakaa are allowed to be shitty, just like humans are,' Ember said.

'Ha.'

They neared the end of the side canyon, sunlight flooding in, and he squeezed her hand, and slowed.

'Buttercup?'

He tilted his head. 'Why do you call me that?'

Ember didn't know if actual buttercups existed here. 'It's after this fierce guard dog I knew,' she said. 'Had a reputation for tearing people's legs off. But if you didn't offer a threat, he was the sweetest thing.'

Rhaell cocked an eyebrow at her. 'I'm a guard dog?' he said.

'A nice one,' she emphasised.

'Who still tears people's legs off?'

She shrugged. 'Hey, I saw what you did to Ikrai.'

'Fair enough. Nothing to do with the flower, then?'

His eyes sparkled. Ember groaned and stretched up to kiss him. 'They're very nice flowers,' she said.

'Yeah, yeah.' Rhaell kissed her some more, then he cupped the back of her neck and said, 'Sparks? I don't know what's going to be out there.'

'Me neither. You think it's Yskaran forces?'

'How would they know we're here?'

'I don't know. Maybe Hesk spilled the beans.'

'Spilled the—?'

'Told them. Look, whatever it is, we've got these stones, right?' She tapped them, hidden under his clothing and her own. 'War and healing and thieving and death. We can face it together.'

She smiled bravely at him, but that was a lie, wasn't it? She was going to have to marry Bronadyr. It was the only way to get Ysarriel's Stone.

Marry him and then run away with Rhaell. Open a portal and take him home with her. Or just stab Bronadyr in the dick on their wedding night and take the Captain of the Guard as her lover.

Either way, it felt like a betrayal. Even if she knew she wouldn't mean a word of her wedding vows.

Rhaell was silent a moment, then he said, 'Whatever it is, we've got each other. I...'

Ember looked up at him. The sunlight cast his face half into shadow.

'I need you to trust me,' he said.

'I do trust you.' *I love you.*

Rhaell looked like he was going to say something else, and then he kissed her, took her hand, and walked with her out of the canyon.

CHAPTER 28

The mouth of the canyon was flooded with Yskaran soldiers, horses and wagons, a sea of green and silver with the red and gold of Addor like a landmass beside it. A flag bearing the Sacred Tree stood proud of the crowd, the peak of a hastily erected command tent beside it.

Ember slipped her hand from his as they approached. 'Remember, I'm still engaged to the prince,' she said, and there was a strange note in her voice. 'Can't let them think I've just been banging my guard all week, can I?'

His empty fingers flexed. He wanted to grab her hand and tell her that yes, they should be letting people think that because it was the fucking truth, but he needed to just hold onto the lie for as long as he could.

His heart beat hard in his chest. How the hell was he going to do this? Address everyone first, so they didn't get to it, and maybe—

You've got to tell her some time.

But not now. Please, not yet.

'Your—' began a man in captain's insignia, and Rhaell held up a hand.

'Captain Tyvin. Who is in command here?'

'Well, sir, in your absence it's Colonel Datris, but—'

'Good, good.' Datris was a solid man. 'In the command tent?'

'Yessir.'

He could feel Ember turning to give the man a curious look as they passed, and his stomach clenched.

'What did he mean, in your absence?'

'Oh.' He could tell her this. 'I'm, er, a bit more senior than I might have led you to believe.'

'Really? How senior?'

Almost as senior as you can get. 'I'm kind of the general,' he told her, wincing.

'The general? Of the ... army?'

He nodded guiltily.

'But ... you just mooch around the barracks like an ordinary soldier!'

Rhaell shrugged. 'We're not at war. It's really a ceremonial sort of position in peacetime.'

Ember narrowed her eyes at him. 'Is it?' she asked doubtfully.

'Sure. Look, let me talk to the colonel, okay? There's probably been some kind of misunderstanding.'

But then the men ringed around the command tent moved aside to let them in, and Rhaell's stomach dropped. Colonel Datris was there, all right, and so was Lord Addor and several high-ranking officers. Their breastplates were very shiny. Their helmets plumed. Their swords very, very sharp.

Because they were guarding the king.

'There you are!' he said, turning to face them. 'Where the hell have you been? I told you to bed her and breed her, Bronadyr, not to fucking kidnap her!'

Rhaell had wondered, once or twice, what it might feel like to be dealt a killing blow. Whether he'd be aware he was dying or if he'd think he'd be all right. Would it hurt so terribly, or would dying end all the pain?

Now he knew, with shocking clarity, exactly what it felt like to have his heart ripped from his chest and crushed in front of him.

Rhaell couldn't look at Ember. He wasn't sure he could breathe.

'Not that it matters now,' said King Onas, pointing at Ember. 'Little bitch has been lying to us. Murderer! Liar! Traitor! Arrest her!' The soldiers stepped forward. One carried manacles.

The sound that came from Ember was the merest whisper, like the final breath of a dying animal.

'Bronadyr?'

'No,' said Rhaell, stepping in front of her. His voice shook. *It's ruined. It's over. She knows. She knows!*

'Oh, fond of her, are we? Good fuck, was she? Tree only knows how she took that obscenity of yours. For all the good it's done you, anyway.'

'Come one step closer and I will end you,' Rhaell growled, but the soldiers surrounded them now. His own men. He knew how highly trained they were because he'd damn well trained them himself.

He'd trained them to be fighters. To attack, to defend, to work together. To kill. Because that was all he was good at. *Don't get in if you can't get out,* Ember had said, and she was right, because he'd got himself into this and he'd got no exit strategy, none at all. He was as dumb as the beast his grandfather called him. Good for violence and nothing more.

'Thought you were being clever, did you?' sneered the king, sauntering up to Ember. Rhaell flinched to protect her and was pushed aside. 'Get the coronet on your head before you told us, eh?'

'Told you what?' said Ember, and he couldn't read her voice.

The king's face was twisted with hatred. 'That you're as barren as an old stone,' he spat. 'And you knew it.'

'Not for sure,' Ember tried, voice trembling. Rhaell turned instinctively to wrap his arms around her, and she pushed him away, violently.

Fuck. Fuck, he'd messed this up.

'No? Not even after you paid a woman to make sure? With her metal *things*?'

The intake of breath around them came from everyone. The soldiers looked horrified, disgusted. Lord Addor spat on the ground.

Ember clutched at her stomach, her face white. 'How – how did you know that?' she stammered.

The king smirked at her, an unpleasant twisting of his smile. 'I know everything that happens in my court,' he spat. 'Arrest her,' he said. 'For murder, for impersonation, and for conspiracy against the Crown.'

'No,' gasped Ember.

'Belay that order,' snapped Rhaell, and they paused.

'Obey that order,' said the king, his gaze on Rhaell. His smile was smug and cold. No, not a smile. A smirk.

Rhaell turned to Ember and wrapped his arms around her. His monstrous, ugly arms. She alone hadn't seen him as a monster. She'd found beauty in him. Made him feel desirable, wanted, cherished.

She looked at him with absolute hatred and spat, 'Get off me!'

Shocked, he let her push him away and watched them grab her arms, hard enough to bruise. The soldiers moved forward.

'I am your prince and your general,' Rhaell said, bracing himself in front of Ember.

'And I am your king,' purred King Onas. 'Arrest her.'

And Ember moved away from Rhaell's protection, as if she preferred getting arrested to being near him.

'But she's the Promised One,' he said brokenly, as they shackled Ember's wrists. He jolted forward, unable to stop himself, and found spears crossed in his way. *I could kill the lot of you.* The War Stone glowed on his wrist. 'She's still going to save Yskara.'

'Her? You've been lying since you got here, haven't you, you little bitch? You stole someone else's place, didn't you?'

She'd been telling him all along. That she'd saved some other girl and come here in her place. Rhaell hadn't thought it mattered. He still didn't. He didn't care about heirs – he cared about Ember.

'I could still help,' she said. 'I'm more than just a walking womb.'

The king spat at her, and Ember recoiled, spittle dripping from her hair. Rhaell lunged forward, and hands grabbed his arms. His own men. He wrestled them off, but more grabbed him, and then Colonel Datris was aiming a sword at his throat, though there was a hint of apology in the man's eyes.

'Not to me you're not,' said the king. 'Put her in the wagon. Bronadyr. You're with me.'

He walked away, clearly expecting Rhaell to follow.

'Ember,' Rhaell said, struggling against the hold of his bloody well-trained soldiers. 'I'll sort this out. It's a misunderstanding. I'll talk to him.'

She didn't look at him. 'Really? A nice cosy chat with your grandpa?'

That cut like a knife. 'I was going to tell you,' he said, but it sounded so weak even to his ears.

'You're the Beast,' Ember said, and she turned slowly to look at him. Her eyes were so cold they could have frozen fire.

Yes, this was what it would feel like, if some bigger, meaner bastard reached into his chest and tore out his heart. Rhaell could almost see it lying there on the grass, feebly trying to beat, mashed into the ground under a heavy boot heel. His whole chest was an agony of emptiness.

Except it hadn't been some bigger, meaner bastard who'd torn out his heart. He'd done it himself and handed it to Ember for her to leave it, bleeding, on the ground.

He stopped struggling.

'You're the prince.' Her lip curled. 'All this time, you've been lying to me. Laughing at me.'

'I never lied,' he said, as the soldiers began leading her away. To his men, he added, desperately and without much hope, 'I order you to stop.'

'King's orders,' said the Colonel. 'I'm sorry, sir.' To the soldiers, he said, 'Take him to the king.'

Rhaell raised his voice, fighting against the men taking him away from her. 'Ember. I'm sorry. I never lied. I never laughed at you!'

She glanced back at him and spat at his feet. 'You told them,' she said. 'About the abortion. No one else knew. *No one.*'

'I—'

'I hate you,' she said, and the fire of it burned in her eyes. 'I *hate* you. I wish I'd let you die. Fuck you, Bronadyr.'

The trip back to Yskara was quick, thanks to flying horses and sea horses and Lords only knew what else. Ember spent it shackled in a wagon, a ship's cabin, and then another wagon, this one with extra bars. They weren't necessary. She wasn't going to escape.

Bronadyr was going to kill her.

No, not Bronadyr. Rhaell. The man she'd fallen in love with, and who had lied to her.

She thought about the first time she'd seen the prince, massive in his spiked armour with that terrifying helmet. *To hide his face.* Not to mention his voice. Every time afterwards that she'd met the prince, he'd been wearing that helmet and growling at her, his voice distorted and metallic.

She'd watched Rhaell fight, for sure, but without his armour, and against an opponent twice his size.

He'd hacked off the Rakaa's arm. He'd hacked off his head. He'd even made the same beckoning gesture!

Every time she had complained about the prince to him. Every time she had told him how afraid she was. Every time she had mentioned him, and Rhaell had said nothing, because she was talking *to* him *about* him. He must have been laughing his head off. How stupid she was, how naïve, how he'd tricked her. Stupid little Ember from her backwards little mud-hut world. It was probably some sophisticated Yskaran joke. The ladies-in-waiting were probably in on it.

Beast. The man was too gorgeous to look at and he'd convinced her he was a hideous beast. Deformed, violent, little better than an animal. She wondered how long he'd spent laughing over the whole 'cock as big as my forearm' joke.

The horns, the height. Of course the Beast was Rakaa. He must have been terrified she'd figure it out once she saw what his scars really meant. No wonder he'd kept her out of her mind with orgasms.

The King had been so pleased that she'd been spending time with the prince. He hadn't meant on their short ride out into Valoris. He'd meant Rhaell sitting by her side as she recovered. While she poured out her heart to him and told him her darkest secret. And then he'd gone and told that secret to the king.

And now she'd be executed, just like those women on the block, just like the man who'd tried to fight.

She was an idiot. A pathetic, naïve, credulous idiot. How could she have believed anything he'd said? How was she so *stupid*?

Could she use Ruvaen's Stone to escape? But where would she go? Without Rhaell by her side the whole of Yskara seemed hostile, not to mention deadly. To the Rakaa? But he'd known to look for her there; and if the king sent his army in to destroy those peaceful people, she'd never forgive herself. She'd never be able to get the King's Stone if she couldn't marry the prince, and that certainly wasn't going to happen now. And without the stones she had no hope of returning home.

Ember leaned against the wagon's rough wooden wall and stared out of the tiny grille opposite, anger building in her. Rhaell had made a fool of her, and now he was going to kill her. And that was so stupidly unfair it shoved all the sorrow out of her and replaced it with rage. And hatred. Burning, deep hatred.

I want to hurt him. To tear out his heart and stab at it until it was a bloody pulp. She wanted to humiliate him, wound him, obliterate him. She wanted to hurt him as much as he'd hurt her.

Do something smart. Somehow, she didn't think this was what the dragon had meant.

The castle was strangely silent and subdued as her wagon was led into one of the courtyards. Ember was taken from it, to a portal – a glimpse of an inviting bedchamber, a sweet grassy meadow – and into a dark, stony corridor.

The cuffs on her wrists jangled, and the guards escorting her regarded her with pity. But Ember wasn't trembling with fear. She was so incandescently angry she thought she might burst.

It didn't surprise her there were dungeons here. Ember allowed herself to be locked into a stone cell – granite, hard and cold – with one small window, a cot, and a bucket in the corner. The door was an iron grille so the jailer could see her every movement.

Do something smart. Well, what the fuck was that supposed to mean? She was in jail, and probably going to be executed by the man she'd stupidly fallen in love with. Ember curled on her side, trying not to cry. The two stones at her breast clinked against each other.

Wait. The stones.

Ember found her lips beginning to curl incredulously into a smile.

~

'Your Grace.' Rhaell hated having to kneel to his grandfather, but he did it anyway. The presence chamber smelled of stale wine and sweat and they'd only been back an hour.

The king was in a foul mood, and had been all the way home.

He threw things at servants, shouted and ranted like an angry toddler.

I don't think the king is a very nice person.

He should have damn well told her then.

He should have told her he was the prince, that it didn't matter to him if she could give him an heir or not. Let his cousin Sarea take the throne. She wanted it enough. He and Ember could just go away and be themselves. Maybe in the mountains. Maybe he should meet his father's kin. They could hardly be worse than his mother's.

'Why'd you do it, Bronadyr?'

He hated that name. It was the one the king had given him. Legend had it, he'd taken one look at the misshapen, deformed, winged thing his beloved daughter had died birthing, and named it *Beast of Sorrow*.

Nykisa, the only mother he'd ever known, had promised to call Rhaell by the name his mother had chosen. But even then, she'd called him Deer more often. It was safer that way, she said, but she'd never said what it was safer from.

'Do what, Your Grace?'

'Take her away. Fuck her. You knew it would do no good.'

Rhaell looked at his grandfather and saw a man who had lost his daughter and five young wives to the single-minded pursuit of an heir. Five young wives who had met with terrible, terrible accidents. He had no doubt that if any of those poor girls had provided the king with a son who wasn't malformed and monstrous, Rhaell would have found himself with his throat slit.

He suddenly remembered that his grandmother, the old queen, had died of a fever before he was born. It was said their marriage had been a political alliance, and that she and the king had loathed each other.

Had it been a fever?

Rhaell looked at his grandfather, and for the first time saw a murderer.

'I didn't know,' he said.

The king snorted as he threw himself into a chair and waved for more wine. 'Are you dumb, boy? I knew. Don't pretend you didn't. Or was it just the lure of a loose peasant cunny? By the Tree, it seems she'll let anyone stick anything up there.'

Rhaell's hands formed fists and his feet moved forward. He forced himself to relax. He'd be no good to Ember if he got himself executed for regicide.

He watched King Onas pick at some fruit and find it all unworthy. Ember was right. He didn't see her as the Promised One who would heal the Tree and save the land. He saw a walking womb.

'Well, it seems she fooled the prophecy. Lied her way into Yskara. I'd like to know how she did it,' Onas said, gazing thoughtfully at the fire. 'Find out, will you?'

'Your Grace?'

The king waved a hand irritably. 'Fuck it out of her. Or torture her. The Beast is good at extracting secrets.'

He was. Mostly by simply donning the fearsome mask and hefting his war axe. The king preferred more traditional methods, however, involving blades and screws and racks.

'I can try.' He was desperate to talk to Ember. To explain why he hadn't told her the whole truth. To beg her not to hate him. To tell her he loved her.

'Don't be taken in by her whore's lies. They always tell you what you want to hear.' The king looked him over disparagingly. 'What did she tell you? She likes the way you look? Men like you are handsome where she comes from? You're not disgusting?'

Don't listen to him. But it was impossible. A few days of lolling around in bed with a pretty girl couldn't erase years of truth. He was a monster.

'Eh, it doesn't matter anyway. You'll be the one executing her,' said the king, and Rhaell's stomach roiled.

If it came to that, if he couldn't stop the trial or help her escape, he'd turn his axe on the king.

'And if she's innocent?' he said evenly.

'Ha! Oh, look at you, boy, found something to dip your wick in and you're cuntstruck, aren't you? Don't tell me, you think you're in love with her? She played you!'

She didn't know who I was.

Fuck. Did she?

Rhaell froze in horror. Had she known? Was this a double bluff? Had he been so busy lying to her that he hadn't noticed her lying to him?

But before he could even work out if he believed half of that, the guards opened the door and a page ran in, panting.

'Your Grace! And... Your Grace. It's Her Grace!'

'What?' said the king.

'Ember?' said Rhaell.

'I think we can drop the title for her now,' the king sneered.

'Yes, sir, but she, er ... she's dying, sir!'

Ember had to feign sleep to get the jailer's attention off her, squinting through her lashes to see if he'd finally looked away. Dammit, why wasn't he an easily bored man?

But finally he looked down at a ledger in front of him and began to write. That still wasn't good enough. The slightest movement and she'd be the centre of his attention again.

It was agony, waiting for a distraction. Eventually another man came in and began talking to him, the two of them discussing shift rotas and other unspeakably dull things, until the first man got up and went to make tea, while the other man sat with his back half turned to Ember, his eyes on the ledger.

Ember moved fast.

With one hand she reached out under the blanket and touched the wall. With her other hand she made the sign of the Tree and concentrated hard on her destination. Yes. The stone began to give, and she carefully pushed it inwards, the sounds of hooves striking cobblestones coming to her ears. A newsboy shouting, 'Extra extra!' Too loud! She faked a snore and let the portal door close, then waited in agonised silence before she tried it a second time.

Brass lacquer. Slate blacking. Pumice powder.

Pa's workshop.

She could hear the crick-crick of a watch being carefully wound, the chime of the grandfather clock in the corner, the tap of Pa's cane on the floor.

Ember couldn't breathe. Home. That was home. She could—

Never go through on the first or second try. Never. It isn't real.

'Embla?' came Pa's voice, a name he hadn't called her since she was a tiny child. In the distance she heard the rowdy shouts of the boys coming home from the mines. 'I've missed you.'

'No.' The word was snatched from her as she pushed the door shut, her fingers trembling on the cold stone. It wasn't real. That wasn't home. That hadn't been them.

Pa would never have said he missed her.

She took in a deep breath and reminded herself where her true destination was.

Knives. She needed knives.

There would be blood.

CHAPTER 29

'Good fucking riddance!' snapped the King, but Rhaell was already opening a portal. Ember wasn't dying, she couldn't be dying—

A meadow. A cave. The dungeons.

He dashed through, not really caring if his grandfather followed. 'What happened? Where is she? Ember!'

He'd opened the portal right into her cell, where she lay curled on her side on her cot, facing away from him. There was blood on her trousers.

'Ember! What happened?'

She didn't look up. 'Go away.'

She's alive. His heart nearly fell out of his chest. 'You're bleeding.' He was on his knees beside her before he knew what he was doing. 'What happened?' Over his shoulder he shouted, 'Send for Phoebe!'

'Phoebe can't help.' She curled into a ball, wincing.

'She saved your life before, she can do it again. Phoebe!'

'My—? Rhaell, you sack of dumb muscle.' Ember glanced over her shoulder at him, her face full of contempt. 'I'm not dying. Haven't you ever seen a woman have a period before?'

'A ... what?'

'Sorry, not Rhaell, is it? Prince Bronadyr. Your Grace. I'd curtsey but right now I feel like my uterus is gonna drop out.'

'What the hell is going on?'

That was the king, striding into the cell and filling all the remaining space.

'Oh good. More men. Look, if you can get Phoebe here maybe she can get me a hot-water bottle or something. Maybe some willow bark.'

'Willow—? Ember, what's...' Belatedly, his brain caught up with him, and he sat back on his heels, feeling his face heat. 'Oh.'

'There it is,' Ember sneered. 'Fucking men. If you had to deal with this, you'd be dead.'

'How dare you threaten the heir to the throne!' thundered the king, who did it all the time.

Ember rolled onto her back. She eyeballed the king.

'That wasn't a threat,' she said. 'It was a statement of fact. Your Grace, you've been married five times—'

'Six,' murmured Rhaell, his mind reeling. Had she been lying to him? All this time?

'Six, right. Haven't any of them ever had periods? Monthly bleeds? Special moon times? I dunno what you call it here.'

'It's your woman's blood, and most of us don't have it,' said Phoebe, entering the cell through the more traditional means of the door and kneeling beside Rhaell. 'I didn't think you did.'

'Well, maybe my cycle got knocked off by, I dunno, all those times I almost died,' Ember said, glaring at Rhaell as Phoebe laid a gentle hand on her belly.

'But ... you said you didn't,' he mumbled.

'Yeah, and you were pretty quick to report that one back to Grandpa, weren't you?' She sat up, shrugging away Phoebe's hand. The manacles on her wrists clinked.

'I didn't. I didn't report anything to anyone.' How could he make her believe him?

'Sure.' She eyed him with disgust. 'Lords, Rhaell, is there anything inside that head but more muscle? Did it ever occur to you I might be lying?'

'But ... why?' When she'd known from the start what the king wanted her for? Her only purpose in his eyes was to provide heirs and she'd sworn to Rhaell that wasn't possible.

To him. She'd sworn to him it wasn't possible. Not to the king. Not to Phoebe. Not to anyone else. She'd only told him. And then she'd fucked him.

The realisation felt like ice spreading from his gut. He rocked back away from her.

Had he thought it hurt before?

'Oh, there it goes,' said Ember, with a smile that didn't match the spite in her eyes. 'Feels nice, doesn't it? Being used and lied to. Your Grace.'

The words fell like the blows of a fist.

'Oh, and by the way.' She cast a disparaging look at his crotch. 'Size of my forearm? You wish.'

'What the fuck are you two talking about?' the king demanded. 'Woman's blood? Does that mean she can be bred?'

Ember sighed. 'Yes,' she said. She didn't look at Rhaell. 'I lied. To him. I thought if I told him I couldn't get pregnant he wouldn't take precautions and I'd get knocked up, and then I wouldn't have to marry your hideous monstrous prince. The women in my family have always been too fertile,' she added ruefully.

His heart wasn't lying bleeding on the floor anymore. It was pumping hard, and strong, and filling his veins with fire.

'But he is the monstrous prince,' said the king.

'Well, I know that now, don't I? But he lied to me. He told me he was the Captain of the Guard. I didn't know what your bloody prince looked like, did I? He always wore that sodding helmet. Even his voice was different.'

No. It couldn't be. He hadn't meant to lie to her about who he was, he just ... hadn't corrected her assumptions, and he'd meant to tell her, but she—

She'd done this on purpose. Told him her terrible sob story to trick him into falling in love with her. To trick him into trusting her. She'd been all over him in that cave, and back in Kasteladdor too. She'd been trying to seduce him for weeks. Hadn't she tried it on with him that very first night, when she was trying to escape?

I think you're fucking gorgeous. And he'd believed her. He'd believed the lying, treacherous bitch.

She must have thought he was so stupid.

Desperate, naïve, gullible – and stupid. She could probably smell the lack of experience on him. Knew he was ripe for the picking. A couple of heated kisses, rub those splendid breasts all over him, and reel him in.

I thought I loved you.

'Sorry, Buttercup,' she said now, looking him over with contempt. To the king, she added, 'Well, that didn't work out so well, did it?'

'Didn't— Ha! Oh, you stupid, stupid girl.' The king clapped his hands together. 'You,' he said to Phoebe. 'Get her what she needs to clean up this ... unsavoury business. Then get that wedding dress down here and fitted. She stays locked up until the wedding.'

'The—? Wait, what?' Ember started to her feet. Rhaell reeled back, away from her, scrambling to his feet.

'Your Grace, I cannot fit a wedding dress in these conditions,' began Phoebe.

'Wedding?' said Ember.

'There's not going to be a wedding,' snapped Rhaell. He needed to get out of here, away from her.

'It is most unsanitary – the dress would be ruined—' Phoebe added.

'Dress her in fucking rags, I don't care—'

'Yskara will care, Your Grace,' said Phoebe quietly.

The King snarled at her. And at Ember and Rhaell for good

measure. 'Fine. Have her old quarters locked down – guards on every door, balcony – get the damn gargoyles down to spy on her. Keep her chained up.'

'I am not marrying that treacherous bitch,' Rhaell snarled.

'Feeling's mutual,' Ember spat. 'You can keep your obscene Rakaa cock, you lying bastard.'

He tried not to flinch. 'Trust me, that won't be a problem.'

Ember looked up at him with hatred burning in her eyes. 'Good. If you were the last man alive ... well, you'd be the last man alive.'

The king's hand slapped her, hard. Rhaell's body moved without his intention, to defend her, to assist her, to protect her. He lurched forward, and found the royal fist planted in his face.

He froze, for a second pain-free. And then it welled in his eye socket.

The king shook out his fist. 'You'll marry who I say, boy. She'll be chained to the bed until you put an heir in her.' He was grinning, the evil old cunt. 'Plenty of time to sort out your differences later. I didn't like any of my wives, boy, and I still fucked them. Think of Yskara and do your duty.'

'I'd rather die,' said Ember.

'Oh, that could be arranged,' said Rhaell.

'Children, please,' muttered Phoebe.

'The wedding is in two days! Out, everybody, out! Let the whore's woman attend to her. This is women's business,' he added distastefully. 'Get those guards up to her room. Not your men,' he added to Rhaell. 'Ones we actually trust.'

Rhaell strode from the cell ahead of his grandfather before he was humiliated any more.

~

'Well, that went well,' said Phoebe brightly, into the silence.

Ember flopped back onto the hard cot and winced. 'About as

well as could be expected. I don't suppose a cloak or anything might be forthcoming? Or do I have to parade through the castle with blood all over me?'

Phoebe gave her a long, assessing look. Ember tried not to panic. Phoebe had barely touched her, but had that been enough for her healing powers? Could she tell the truth of what Ember had done?

Eventually she unfastened her shawl and gave it to Ember. 'Most of the women in the castle would probably kiss your hem for good luck.'

'Then they'd probably catch something. This place is not sanitary.' Ember tied the shawl around her waist. 'Thanks, Phoebe. For getting me out of here.'

Phoebe shrugged. 'I meant what I said. I cannot get you ready for a wedding in here. Guards! Are you not ready? How long must we linger in this despicable place? My lady has been comprehensively cleared of any crimes by the king himself.'

Guards were found, and Phoebe bullied them into escorting them from the dungeons. They were taken to a portalling alcove, where Ember pretended to be impressed by the magic, and then – thank the Lords! – exited opposite her old chambers.

She was almost nostalgic for them now. Which was stupid, because she wouldn't need them much longer. It would be back to the Clockwork City, and her small bed under the eaves, and Pa forgetting she existed and the boys treating her like an unpaid servant.

But at least no one will be trying to kill me.

And with any luck, Yskaran royal brides wore as much jewellery as Yskaran royal brides-to-be, so she'd be returning home with a lot of portable wealth.

The first part of her plan had worked out just fine. The rest would, too. It had to. She just needed to be royal enough to get the king's crown, and then she could get away from Rhaell—

—from Bronadyr—

No! She had to get home. That was the point here. It wasn't about what she was running *from*, it was what she was running *to*.

The fact that she was leaving that lying bastard behind was just a bonus.

She and Phoebe were escorted to her chambers, where guards filled every corner.

'This is absurd,' Phoebe said. 'Are we to be allowed no privacy?'

'King's orders, miss,' said the one with the most stripes on his shoulder.

Ember went to the window, where bars were being crudely hammered in place. She scanned the skies, but they were empty.

Phoebe strode into the bedchamber. 'In here, too? No. This is unconscionable. This is to be your queen. How dare you enter her bedchamber! How dare you lay eyes upon her bed!'

Ember watched in astonishment as Phoebe strode to the dressing room and grabbed a soldier by his collar.

'How dare you,' she hissed, 'look upon her garments? Did you touch anything?' She eyed the open drawers. 'Did you?'

The man – taller than Phoebe by several inches, muscles straining at his tunic, armed with sword and crossbow – stammered, 'N-no, miss!'

Phoebe put her face right up in his and snarled, 'If I find a single fingerprint I shall defenestrate you.'

The man blinked.

'Throw you out of the window,' came a voice from behind Ember, and she jumped.

It wasn't Rhaell. But he had the same sort of laconic delivery. He was a little older, beard flecked with grey, and wore authority like an old, well-fitted suit of armour.

'Out of the bedchamber,' he ordered, and the guards obeyed. 'Balcony guards are forbidden to look inside, or you'll be fed to the hafmey.'

'But, Captain—'

'Remind me who's in charge here?' said the older man wearily.

'You, sir,' said the protesting soldier, and they all filed out, until only two remained in the outer chamber.

'It'll have to do. You're a flight risk,' he told Ember. Taking off his helmet, he saluted somewhat desultorily. 'Captain Brock, Your Grace.'

Ember sighed. 'You're the actual Captain of the Guard?'

'I am, ma'am. I'll give you as much privacy as possible, but I'm afraid orders are orders, and none of us can refuse the king.' He nodded to a couple of soldiers, who brought forth a heavy length of chain.

'Brock, no,' said Phoebe, as if he was a dog who'd just brought in something disgusting.

'I'm sorry,' he said. 'It's a long chain, you'll have plenty of movement around the chambers.' He directed one of the men into the bedchamber.

'You're going to literally chain me to the bed?' Ember said.

'It's the largest, heaviest thing,' explained the captain. He did look genuinely regretful. 'Your Grace, if you wouldn't mind taking off your boot...?'

'And how am I meant to dress her with a chain on one ankle?' Phoebe demanded.

'In skirts, I should imagine,' said Brock.

'And her current clothing? Am I to cut it off?'

'To be honest, yeah,' said Ember, who was still wearing the Rakaa clothes she'd put on at the hot springs – *where I was having sex with Rhaell* – which were now stained with blood. 'I ain't gonna be needing them.'

'And underthings?' Phoebe said.

There was a short silence. Brock winced.

'I don't expect I'm gonna be needing them, either,' Ember said, and allowed the captain to chain her ankle.

He did at least take off the manacles on her wrists before he left, apologising once more.

'Well, isn't this a charming new development,' said Ember. A chain on her ankle, guards in her living room, and if she peered out of the window, she'd probably see gargoyles spying on her.

'A little increased security around a wedding is normal,' said Phoebe, as she gathered up Ember's Rakaa boots. 'Especially as there was an intruder reported earlier.'

'An intruder? Where?'

'Of all the places,' said Phoebe, 'the butcher's stores.'

Ember stilled for just a second, then asked lightly, 'What were they after? Knives?'

'They didn't take anything. Just made a mess with some pig's blood,' said Phoebe, dropping the boots into a sack. Her gaze met Ember's for just a second. 'Strange thing is, the place was lousy with people, but nobody saw a thing.'

'Weird,' said Ember, not touching the stone under her shirt.

'Very,' said Phoebe.

'Yeah,' said Ember, and made her way, clinking, into the bedroom, where she stood and looked at the bed for a long moment.

She'll be chained to the bed until you put an heir in her. Only a couple of days ago the prospect of being stuck in bed with Rhaell for days would have thrilled her.

'It won't be as bad as all that,' Phoebe said, standing beside her. 'He's not a bad man.'

'He lied to me,' Ember said. She glanced at her maid. 'And so did you.'

Phoebe went still.

'You said you'd known him all your life,' said Ember, and watched Phoebe's hand come up to touch the faint scar on her cheek. 'You knew he was the prince, and you still let me go on believing he was—' Her voice broke a tiny bit. 'He was my friend.'

'He was. He is,' said Phoebe. 'That hasn't changed.'

'No? You don't think he hates me now, too?' Ember clinked over to the bed and sat down.

'He'll come around,' said Phoebe desperately. 'I'm sorry. I

wanted to tell you. But he wanted to get to know you. He wanted—Look, everyone here is terrified of him. You've heard the stories. They call him a monster.'

'He is,' said Ember, because when she closed her eyes, she could see him hacking off Ikrai's head.

And worse, she could see the love in his eyes when he looked at her. She could hear him murmuring endearments to her as she drifted off to sleep in his arms. She could feel the passion in his kisses, recall the thrill of his touch, drown in the scent and taste of him—

What kind of monster could lie to her with every look and every touch?

'He just wanted you to not be terrified of him,' said Phoebe. 'To get to know him. As himself.' She paused, and added quietly, 'To not hate him.'

'Well,' said Ember, 'he failed.'

CHAPTER 30

'Well, Nykisa,' said the old man. Rainbow knew he was the king now. Nobody else would have ever dared to defy Mama. 'What use have I for you now?'

'I can still take care of him,' said Mama, as she cradled Rainbow. Her face was bruised and swollen, and so was Rainbow's. The cut on her face hurt more than anything she'd ever known.

Well, maybe not anything. They'd taken Deer away, unconscious and bleeding more than Rainbow ever thought a person could. Those horrible, deep wounds on his back had gaped open as they carried him out.

They'd picked up his wings, his lovely wings, and his tail and horns, as if they were disgusting bits of gristle, and thrown them on the fire.

'He's a child,' said Mama. 'He needs—'

'He needs training as a future king, not mothering,' said the king. 'He has tutors in history and politics, and he will begin training with the master-at-arms tomorrow.'

He looked around the room, as if wondering if there was anything else he needed to take. Rainbow wanted to tell him Deer's toys were in the other room, but she didn't want them to be thrown on the fire, too. Maybe she could get his little wooden dragon back to him somehow.

His attention had already left Mama, but she brought it back.

'Tomorrow? But he needs to heal. He'll need days in the Sacred Waters, he can't—'

'Do not,' thundered the king, and then dropped his voice to a terrifying purr, 'tell me what to do.' His gaze fell on Rainbow. 'Come here.'

'No,' said Mama, not letting go of Rainbow.

'What did I just say?' sighed the king and unsheathed his sword.

'I'll go,' said Rainbow quickly. 'Please don't hurt my Mama.'

The King eyed her as she forced Mama's arms to give her up. 'So long as you behave yourself, child, I'll have no need to. What is your name?'

'Rain—' She caught the glint in his eye. His sword was still in his hand. 'Phoebe, Your Grace.'

'Of?'

Rainbow didn't really understand this. 'Of ... the ... attic?'

Mama cleared her throat. 'I am of Oaksthorpe. Her father was of Vaesturness.'

'Ah,' said the King. 'Yes. A soldier. Died at Gluyver's Point. I recall it now.'

'He laid down his life for Her Highness,' whispered Mama. She never spoke of Rainbow's father; or of Deer's parents.

'You married beneath yourself,' said the King. 'Still, useful enough, I suppose, to have a wet nurse who could stand to look at ... it. We'd have had the devil of a time trying to recruit one.'

He was talking about Deer. Mama said it had been her privilege to care for Deer after his own mother had died. She said she'd been Deer's mother's closest friend, that she'd loved her very much, and that it was the least she could do for her.

She'd never said Deer's mother was the king's daughter.

'Well, you can go,' the king said now, and Rainbow looked back at her mother in surprise.

'Go?' said Mama. 'Leave the attic?'

'Yes. No need to hide away up here now. The boy will be educated as a member of the court. You can go back to Oaksthorpe. I've no need for you now.'

'I,' began Rainbow's mother. She looked at Rainbow, clearly torn. 'But Deer— Bronadyr...'

'Has no need of you,' said the king. 'Come, child.'

Rainbow began to trot after him, then stopped at the king's next words.

'I'm sure there's a place for you in the kitchens.'

'Kitchens?' said Mama. 'But— You said we could leave.'

'I said you could leave. Phoebe here will be staying. Come.'

Rainbow froze, darting looks between Mama and the king.

'But I want to stay with Mama,' she said.

'I don't care what you want,' said the king. 'You've proven yourself a good little spy over the years. You're going to report to me now, instead.' He showed her a bracelet on his wrist. Little charms hung from it. 'I hear the boy calls you Rainbow. Perhaps that can be your code name. Come.'

'I'm staying,' Mama said.

'No,' said the king, impatient. 'You're leaving. The child stays. Go back to Oaksthorpe and live the life of a genteel widow. There will be money provided, since your husband left you none.'

'Why can't she stay?' said Rainbow, panicked. 'I don't want to be your spy!'

'She's going to go back home and tell everyone in Oaksthorpe all about Prince Bronadyr, isn't she?' said the king, looking right at Mama. 'That the heir to Yskara is a beast, that even as a child he took down several soldiers, that he's barely civilised. That by the time he's grown he will be a one-man army.'

Mama sniffed and wiped away a tear. She nodded.

'But he isn't,' said Rainbow.

'He will be when I've finished with him,' said the king grimly. 'And there will be no other rumours about his parentage, will there? There will be no stories of children hidden in attics, of wings being cut off, or the like, will there?'

'No,' said Mama, so quietly it was almost inaudible.

'Good. And in the meantime, you, Phoebe, will have a nice warm bed in the kitchens and plenty to eat and the prospect of promotion. Why, perhaps you could even work above stairs one day,' he said, still looking at Mama. 'If you are very good.'

Rainbow didn't understand all this, but Mama nodded, and so she did, too.

'Will I see Deer?' she said.

'Who?'

'He is Prince Bronadyr now, my love. That is what we must call him,' said Mama.

'But,' said Rainbow, 'that's the monster's name! That's what people in court say! There's a hidden monster!'

'Who says this?' said the King. 'You will report them to me.' He leaned down and said to her, 'You will report everything you hear to me.' His eyes were very blue. The same blue as Deer's. 'Do you understand?'

Mama said, 'May I say goodbye?'

He shrugged as if this was of little importance to him, and Rainbow ran to her mother.

She cried. Mama cried. They promised to write, although Rainbow wasn't sure either of them would be allowed.

Then Mama whispered to her, 'You must look after him for me, Rainbow. I promised his mother I would, and now you must.'

'I promise,' Rainbow whispered.

'He needs someone here who will love him. And you don't have to call him Bronadyr. That's the name the king gave him. He has another name. One his mother chose for him before he was born, from his father's people. It can be a secret. Just between you two.'

'What is it?'

'Hraeulfr. Rhaell, perhaps, for short.'

'As a secret?' Rainbow said, between her tears. 'A secret from the king?'

'Yes,' said Mama. 'From everyone.'

CHAPTER 31

When the knock came at the door, Ember actually expected it to be Rhaell.

'Pathetic,' she muttered to herself, as the guard spoke with a woman. Why would he come to see her now? To tell her how much he hated her? How miserable their lives would be?

'I should—' started the guard, but he was swept back by the woman entering Ember's sitting room.

'Don't be ridiculous,' she said. 'I am the king's cousin. The Promised One and I are to be related by marriage. You will leave us.'

'They're not allowed,' said Ember, not getting up from her chair. The remains of supper were spread out in front of her, but she'd lost her appetite after a few bites. Her brain was working overtime, making and discarding plans. 'I'm to be watched at all times.'

'Absurd,' said Lady Sarea as the guard locked the door behind her. 'You are the Promised One.'

'Yep,' said Ember, sighing. 'No getting away from that, is there? Trust me, I've tried.'

Sarea took a seat opposite Ember, further down the table, her pet dragon curled around her shoulders. Its beady eyes fixed on Ember, who wondered if it could talk, or if the lesser dragons were lesser in every way.

'Yes, I heard.' She glared at the guards in the room. 'I have also heard that you bleed, Your Grace. Many women do not. Tell me, do you have the pains, too? The few times I bled my stomach was in absolute revolt.'

The guards stiffened. 'I must confer with you,' said one to the other, and they both scrambled for the bedchamber.

Sarea raised an eyebrow.

'Neat,' conceded Ember.

'Easy. Men usually are. Now. Do you really bleed, or is it a trick?'

'Why would I tell you?' said Ember.

'True. After all, if you don't bear my esteemed cousin the prince an heir, I will inherit.'

'Only if you outlive him,' said Ember.

She met Sarea's amethyst gaze.

'May the Tree protect and shelter him,' said Sarea, making the symbol of the Tree with her hand.

'May it indeed,' said Ember.

'I admit he will be a better king than his grandfather,' sighed Sarea. 'Albeit that won't be particularly difficult. His cock hasn't rotted off from the pox for one thing.'

'Ew,' said Ember. Then, 'Really?'

Sarea shrugged. 'Six wives and only one child? After dear Queen Amatheis met such a dreadful and untimely end so shortly after having provided him with an heir, they say the King of Peace enjoyed his freedom a little too much. Five healthy young wives, each of them examined by the finest healers in Yskara, and not a single surviving child. But you, Ember Hart of the Iron World, you bleed regularly, do you not? You will provide Prince Bronadyr with a whole stable of infants.'

'You keep babies in stables?'

Sarea reached out and picked up a bit of cheese tart to feed her dragon. 'Zoo? Cave? Where do the Rakaa live?'

'In perfectly pleasant houses,' said Ember, suddenly so angry she couldn't believe she'd ever been frightened of this woman. 'Did you have a purpose for coming here, or was it just to insult my fiancé?'

Sarea smiled with actual tenderness at her dragon as it ate the tart, which made her next words come as a bit of a surprise.

'Why did you want to steal a yellow stone from my house? Don't look so coy, the thief was obviously you.'

'Obviously?' said Ember, too taken aback to think of anything else to say.

'Mmm. You were seen with the prince, of course, skulking around, fucking in doorways. Then he causes a nice distraction, my dear niece reports a thief, and who's missing?'

'I don't know what you're talking about.' Ember was more consumed with realising Rhaell had been the one carrying in the body of the mantis than she was wondering what Phoebe had done with the jewels she'd stolen from Sarea's room.

'No? You have an interesting collection of jewels there, Your Grace. Honouring the Ancestors, is it? One for Ruvaen the Rogue, one for Mnorir the Mystic? They complement Prince Bronadyr's quite marvellously. Searching for the Heart of the Tree, were you?'

Ember opened her mouth. She closed it again.

'I have been second in line to the throne my whole life,' said Sarea. 'You don't think I have prepared myself for it? I read every scroll in that library. When Nephinae died I truly thought my time had come. Nobody expected the child to survive. Dreadful, misshapen thing, he was. Those awful stubbly wings. And the face.' She shuddered. 'Sometimes I think Nephinae would be glad she never saw it.'

'Is literally everyone here blind?' said Ember. Why did they all think Rhaell was ugly?

Sarea cocked her head. 'You truly don't find him repulsive? He's so...' She waved her hands as if to indicate excessive size. 'Do you get him to take you from behind so you don't have to look at him?'

Ember fantasised about leaping over the table and shoving her thumbs into Sarea's eye sockets. 'No, I get him to take me from behind so I can come like a fucking freight train,' she said, a retort that probably would have worked better if Yskara had freight trains. 'Sad news for you, isn't it? From second in line, you'll go further down the list with every baby I pop out.'

'You don't have to,' said Sarea. She leaned forward. 'We both know the possibility of you surviving giving birth to his monstrous get is slim. Spare yourself. We can make a bargain, you and I.'

Ember raised her eyebrows. 'What could you have that I could possibly want?'

Sarea glanced around, then made a gesture in the air. Rhaell had done something similar when he wanted to stop anyone overhearing them.

'You could've done that sooner,' Ember pointed out.

'But it's more fun to embarrass them. Listen. You don't want to be queen. Don't lie, you've spent most of your time here trying to escape. You're collecting those stones to heal the Tree and use it to make a portal home, aren't you?'

Ember eyed her suspiciously. 'And if I was?'

'I can make it for you. I'm a skilled portal-maker,' Sarea said, amethyst eyes gleaming like Ruvaen's Stone. 'Once the Tree is healed I can send you home.'

I don't want to go home. Ember didn't even know if that was true anymore.

Sarea continued. 'You're missing some stones, aren't you? That's why you're marrying the prince. To get your hands on the Royal Stone. But I'm the King's cousin. My great-great grandfather was King Braedam, descended directly from Ysarriel herself. If only it had been Onas who died in that stupid accident and not Jaonos bloody Yllanala, I would be queen now. I can get it for you.'

Ember folded her arms. 'I still need the Wisdom Stone and Ephyrea's Stone.'

Sarea waved her hand as if these were minor concerns. 'Wynric's is with the bones of the Great Dragons. I assume that's why you were in the Shadowed Mountains? Once you've got the others, I'll fly you over the area on a vyanka, we'll find it in no time.'

She doesn't know about the Great Dragons.

'And what's in it for you?' Ember asked.

Sarea eyed her for a long moment before she said, 'I want the throne. With you gone, there's just my monstrous cousin and one old man standing between me and it. I'm prepared to wait for the king to die, but the prince?'

'Yes,' said Ember tightly, 'the prince?'

Sarea watched her like they were opponents in battle. 'When you were attacked by the Myr,' she said, 'you healed awfully quickly.'

'Must have been Phoebe's skill,' said Ember.

'Or Gaeleath's Stone. The old texts say each stone has special powers. What, I wonder, would the Stone of Death do?'

Ember held her gaze and didn't blink.

'You would be free of him. No more pretending to enjoy fucking a monster. No more fearing his babe will rip you to pieces. I saw Princess Nephinae,' Sarea hissed, eyes flashing. 'Torn apart from the inside as that abomination clawed his way out.'

Abomination. 'You want revenge on him?'

'I bear my cousin no malice,' said Sarea quietly. 'But he does not wish to be king, and the country doesn't want him either. I would be a good queen. I have trained for it.' She stood, her dragon flexing its wings on her shoulder like some kind of giant collar. Their combined shadow loomed over Ember. 'If we use Mnorir's Stone on him tonight, you won't have to marry him. We will retreive Wynric's Stone and then I shall give you Ysarriel's, and send you home.'

She wants to kill Rhaell.

Ember could have everything she wanted. She could go home, away from this insane place, back to Pa and the boys and her normal life in a normal world. She could leave Rhaell and his lying, his manipulation, his biting betrayal of her. She'd never have to look at his beautiful, hateful face again. Never touch him. Never lick the salt from his skin or hear his groan of pleasure in her ear or feel the thick heat of him inside her.

And all I'd have to do is kill him.

Ember stood, slowly, the chain at her ankle clinking. She reached inside her neckline for Mnorir's Stone, gleaming black upon its chain. She watched Sarea rear back, ever so slightly.

'If anything at all happens to my fiancé,' she said slowly and clearly, 'if he has an accident, if he's ill, if he breaks a fucking nail, I will tell the king and everyone in the castle what you have just said to me.'

Sarea's lovely face blanched.

'You will leave,' Ember said. 'You will never speak to me again. And you will remember that I carry death around my neck.'

'You'll regret this,' hissed Sarea, backing away.

'Probably,' said Ember. Without taking her eyes off the other woman, she called, 'Guards! Lady Sarea will be leaving now.'

Sarea shook her head as she moved away, sweeping her long skirts aside with a grace Ember would never manage if she practised for a thousand years.

'Does Prince Bronadyr know?' Lady Sarea said, as the guards came to unlock the door for her. One stood beside Ember, as if she might try and make a break for it.

'Know what?'

Sarea smiled, the expression almost pitying. 'That you're in love with him?'

The words pierced Ember like a dagger to the heart. She laid one hand on the back of the nearest chair, hoping like hell it didn't look like she was about to crumble to her knees and weep.

She didn't love him. She hated him. Hated him with a fire

that burned hot and strong, violent in its intensity. Hated him with everything she had. Hated him from the very bones of herself.

I don't love him. I don't, I don't. It was the biggest lie she'd ever told herself.

'Goodbye, Lady Sarea,' said Ember, her voice nearly steady. 'I'll see you tomorrow, when I become the highest-ranking woman in the land.'

Sarea just gave her a half smile, and left, and Ember crumpled into the chair she was gripping.

'Your Grace?' said the nearest guard, as the other locked the door.

'I'm fine,' Ember snarled at him, although that was a lie, too. She was going to get married tomorrow, to a man she loved and hated in equal measure. How the hell was she going to get through it?

If the dragon never came, if she never got the final stone, she'd be trapped here forever. In this suite of rooms, chained to the bed, while Rhaell either ignored her or mechanically fucked her until his grandfather gave up on getting an heir. She didn't know which was worse.

If only she hadn't gone after that stupid stone from Baron Varne's mansion. If only she'd left that stupid girl to be sacrificed – this could be Dandelia's problem now! She would probably love to be the queen, popping out babies for her handsome hunk of a husband. If only, if only!

If only it had been Onas who'd died in that stupid accident.

Then Rhaell wouldn't even exist. Sarea would have inherited the throne, and who would the Promised One be then? Would they even need a Promised One? Would the land be blighted if Onas had not come to the throne?

The magic had been failing for a few generations...

If only it had been Onas who'd died in that stupid accident.

Ember raised her head. 'Holy shit,' she said.

~

His suite of rooms in the castle was exquisitely decorated, of course, as befit the heir to the throne, but Rhaell had never really liked them much. All the lines were so perfectly clean and elegant, the furniture impersonally beautiful, the view immaculately bland. It was a suite that belonged to a perfect, elegant, refined and graceful prince. Someone impersonal and bland.

Not a man who towered over the brawniest stevedore and had to file down his horns every few months.

Ember liked my horns.

Rhaell poured another drink and tried to wash away the memories of her with it. Bad enough they had to go through with this charade tomorrow, but now every memory of her he had was tainted. Every time she'd smiled at him, caressed him, kissed him – it had all been a lie. A means to an end. And now they were stuck with each other.

A knock sounded at his door. 'Fuck off,' he called, lighting a sootweed.

'It's Lady Sarea.'

He poured more vodka. 'I said what I said.'

'I really think we should speak.'

Rhaell rubbed at the stubs of his horns. 'First time for everything,' he said, but he was intrigued enough to haul himself to his feet and pad over to the door. No guards here to open it for him. Apparently, nobody thought the Beast needed guarding.

Sarea stood there with her little dragon curled around her neck. It was cute, really, but somewhat pathetic after the Great Dragon he'd actually met.

'Well?'

His cousin looked him over, her lip curled. Rhaell hadn't bothered with a shirt or shoes; he just stood there in a pair of low-riding trousers that displayed an awful lot of his beastliness. The hair on his chest. The scars from his fight with Ikrai. The sheer offensive size of him.

He aimed his sootweed smoke away from her. She did not appear to appreciate the courtesy.

'Drink?' he said, waving his glass at her and turning away. He heard her hiss of indrawn breath as she clocked the ruin of his back. 'I've Vatnabian vodka or there's some weird fruit stuff from Paren. Do you drink weird fruit stuff?'

'No, thank you,' said Sarea, and he heard the quiet click of the door behind her, followed by the deadening of sound he knew was her casting a silence ward. She always had been good at wards.

'Fine.' Rhaell threw himself into a chair. 'What do you want to talk about so privately?'

Sarea's gaze roamed his body, as if trying to understand something.

'Revolting, aren't I?' he said cheerfully, saluting her with his glass.

'Your bride doesn't seem to think so.'

Rhaell snapped, 'Ha!' so forcefully he nearly spilled his vodka.

'Oh dear,' said Sarea, still standing neatly by the door. 'I thought you were quite intelligent.'

'Me? No. I'm a beast. Everyone knows that. Dumb as an aurochs.'

'Then being the king will be a trial for you,' said Sarea.

He sighed. 'What do you want, cousin?'

They'd never really spoken before. Most of the court didn't speak to Rhaell. They were either terrified of him or disgusted by him, often both. And since Rhaell found most of them to be insufferable bores, this suited him just fine. He'd spent a bit more time with Sarea than the rest, what with her being the next in line to the throne, but she'd usually managed to avoid anything more than a cutting remark. And everyone knew the Beast did little more than grunt.

'To offer you a wedding gift,' she said.

'How kind of you.' He braced himself for some kind of cruel joke.

'To set you free,' she said, and he sat up a bit straighter.

'What?'

Sarea smoothed her immaculate skirts. 'It's no secret I want the throne,' she said. 'But I can't have it if you're still alive. The old man, I can wait out, but not you. I could kill you, of course.'

'You could try,' said Rhaell, without any particular malice.

'Yes,' said Sarea, with a strange look on her face. 'Or I could offer you a way out. It seems to me, cousin, that you've never wanted to be king.'

'Want doesn't have a lot to do with it,' said Rhaell.

'No. But if it did? If you had a way to ... vanish? We'd both get what we want.'

Rhaell set down his glass and leaned forward in his chair. 'And what is it,' he asked, 'that you think I want?'

Sarea looked at him more directly than she'd ever done, and said, 'I think you want to escape all this. I think you don't want to be king, and you never did. I think you hate this court and everyone in it, especially the man who cut your wings off. I think the only person in the whole castle you've ever liked is that maid, Phoebe, which is why you got her a job with the Promised One, and now I think you like the Promised One so much you'd happily shank Phoebe for her.'

'Is that a threat?' said Rhaell. He wasn't armed, but he didn't need to be.

'No. I am just ... making an illustrative point. If I could find a way for you to leave here, forever, with your bride, would you take it?'

Of course I would. But he couldn't, because that would leave Sarea as the heir. And also because Ember hated him, he reminded himself. And he hated her, too.

And yet.

And *yet*.

Rhaell picked up his glass and threw back the contents. 'You might as well tell me your plan,' he said.

~

Picking the lock on her shackles was easy. Ember was, after all, the daughter of the best clockmaker in the Clockwork City, and the best thief, too. She'd been picking locks with hairpins since before she knew her own name.

The guards had been forbidden from entering her bedchamber, and so Phoebe slept on a pallet at the foot of her bed instead. But Ember wore Ruvaen's Stone around her neck, and by now she knew how to make herself even more silent and still than ever before.

She stepped past Phoebe's sleeping form, made herself a portal, and stepped through on the third opening into a room filled with treasure.

It made Kasteladdor's jewel tower look like a child's toy box.

Gems and jewels sparkled at her from every surface. Stands held tiaras and crowns, there were cases full of necklaces and bracelets, and whole rows of rings. Jewelled chains were draped on mannequins, and there were clothes made of real silver and gold thread, studded with gems. Several suits of armour stood in their entirety, exquisitely embossed, enamelled and jewel-encrusted.

One of them, which almost gave Ember a small heart attack, was the Beast's, complete with its fearsome horned helmet. She went up to it, traced the beautiful leaves gilded onto the horns, and for just the tiniest fraction of a moment allowed herself to remember what it had felt like to caress the stubs of Rhaell's horns. How his breath had hitched and he'd made an involuntary sound, and how if she pressed her body against his she could feel his cock throb.

She exhaled hard, and stepped back. She wasn't here for reminiscences.

She turned away, towards the undoubted centrepiece of the room. Ysarriel's Crown stood on a stand of its own, surrounded by werelights even in the middle of the night. The forks and branches of the golden circlet gleamed, the tiny jewelled leaves winking in the light, the green stone at the centre glowing as she neared it.

'If only it had been Onas who'd died in that stupid accident,' Ember said. The court still mourned the death of the king's young companion who had died on the way to their wardship in Vaesturness. Two boys left their home, and one arrived, into the company of strangers.

Two boys left, and one arrived.

When our native land be stolen, she shall restore it.

Ember had a handful of jewels in her pocket. Green stones weren't exactly hard to come by in the wedding regalia of the royal bride of Yskara. She wasn't the best jeweller in the business, but she could prise out one stone and wedge another in. The king was half-cut most of the time, he wouldn't notice.

If he even was the king.

Ember took a breath, let half of it out, and made a grab for the crown.

It wouldn't budge.

She felt around it to see if there was a wire or a catch holding it in place. She lifted up the dummy head it stood on. She ran her knife under it. It wouldn't move.

Ember grabbed her knife – one she'd stolen at dinner – and tried to prise the stone free, but of course it wouldn't move. Only royalty could take this stone, and she wasn't royal. But she tried again, and again, teeth gritted and eyes burning with tears. 'Lords fucking *dammit*.'

She'd been so sure. The boy who would be King Onas had died on the way to Vaesturness, probably killed by Jaonos Yllanala, and then Jaonos had taken his place on arrival at Vaesturness. It was simple. It was obvious. It was the sort of ruthless thing he'd do.

And if Onas wasn't really Onas, and therefore not the king, then the Royal Stone couldn't really belong to him. And she could steal it. Ember the thief, wearing the Stone of Ruvaen the Rogue, could steal *anything*. And that would be a thing so smart the dragon would come and offer her the final stone.

But Ysarriel's Stone wouldn't budge.

Ember sat down on the nearest cabinet and wiped her eyes with the back of her hand. King Onas was the rightful king of Yskara, and the only way for her to get that stone was to become a member of the royal family herself.

She hadn't been smart, and the dragon wouldn't come. She'd end up married to Rhaell, being hated by him for the rest of her life, and probably once he figured out she couldn't really give him an heir he'd stop even hate-fucking her and she'd just be locked in her rooms forever. Or the king would arrange for her to have some kind of accident just like his wives.

The air in this stupid gilded room with all its pointless jewels was stifling. Ember needed to be outside, breathing in the cold night, muscles burning as she climbed something. When was the last time she'd climbed anything?

She swiped back her tears, went to the nearest wall and made the sign of the Tree. 'I want to go somewhere I can climb,' she said.

The cut on his finger was small, but it smarted. Rhaell held it under the running stream of Sacred Water until the blood stopped and then dried it on a towel.

It was a good choice he'd made. He told himself that as he wandered back into the bedroom to pour himself another drink. Even if he had to go through with the ceremony tomorrow, he'd be free of Ember soon enough. Sarea would get what she wanted, and he ... he could do whatever he wanted.

He stopped in the middle of the room, glass to his lips, as he realised he had no idea what that even was.

He was the prince. He was the Beast. He had duties to carry out and a destiny to fulfil. He wasn't allowed to want things for himself. The last time he'd even thought about choosing his own future he'd been flying through those attics with Phoebe at his heels.

Maybe he'd go see Mama. She was still living in Oaksthorpe. Phoebe got letters from her frequently, which she passed on to him. She always asked, quite carefully, after him. Nobody would ever be allowed to know that the mother of a maid actually knew the heir to the throne. Mama had never been stupid.

What would she have told him to do now? Would she have condoned his bargain with Sarea?

He thought about the way she'd betrayed him to save her own daughter. Yes. She'd tell him to do what was necessary for the person he loved most.

And as much as Rhaell passionately hated Ember, he loved her even more.

He tilted the vodka to his lips, then paused. Through the glass, it almost looked as if something huge was flying past the window.

He lowered the glass.

'Fuck me.'

There was something huge flying past the window.

The green Great Dragon turned her head as she passed his window, and he could've sworn she winked at him.

The glass shattered on the floor. Rhaell skidded to the nearest wall and made the sign of the Tree. 'Take me to Ember!'

The roof of the bridge across the gorge was covered with tiles that seemed from the land to shimmer like gold. Up close, Ember could see they were just some kind of cheap metal, hammered into place. Fool's gold, her mother would have said.

They were cold under her backside as she sat in her nightgown and shawl, dressed not unlike she had been that first night in Yskara. When she'd tried to run and the hafmey had nearly eaten her and she'd tried to seduce Rhaell, then passed out in his arms.

When he'd had the opportunity to tell her who he was, and that all her fears were unfounded, and he'd kept his beautiful mouth shut.

She was slightly sheltered by a chimney stack, but the wind was still cold up here, hundreds of feet above the gorge. Below her, water thundered over the falls, from the Sacred River into the Sacred Sea, which stretched off into darkness. She couldn't see the mountains where she'd been kidnapped by Rakaa and Rhaell had fought to the death and they'd fucked each other into the sort of bliss she never knew existed. And all the while he'd been lying.

'It's times like this I really wish I smoked,' Ember said out loud, and a voice replied, 'That could be arranged.'

She startled, losing her balance and nearly falling. But Ember Hart, who'd been climbing like a ferret since before she could remember, never fell. Her fingers and toes dug in, found a hold on the cold tiles, and she looked up as a rush of cold air blew her hair back from her face.

'Holy shit!'

'Hello to you, too,' said the dragon.

'You came!'

The dragon settled herself on the roof of the bridge and looked Ember over. 'Why are you up here?'

'I wanted to think.'

'Oh? About what?'

'About— I thought you could look into the hearts and minds of mortals,' said Ember.

'Well, yes,' said the dragon, 'but it isn't very polite.' She tucked her wings on her back and said, 'You figured something out. About the king.'

Ember slumped, curling her arms around her knees. 'No, I didn't. I thought I had, but I was wrong.'

'Were you?'

Ember grunted out a sigh. 'Look, I'm not having a great day here. I've been locked in my rooms being fitted for a wedding dress to a man I hate and who I'm pretty sure hates me right back; someone just offered to kill him for me, and I tried to nick a crown that can't be nicked unless I go through with said wedding to said man who hates me, et cetera.'

'Well,' said the dragon. 'That's a lot.'

'You're telling me.' She stared moodily out at the dark ocean. The twin moons reflected off the distant waves.

'Especially since you're wrong about most of it.'

Ember's head swivelled round so fast it hurt. 'What? You mean the king isn't really the king? Then why couldn't I take his crown?'

The dragon shrugged. Ember would not have believed a four-legged animal could shrug.

'He might not be the rightful king, but he is still the king.'

Ember's lips moved as she tried to work that one out. 'Is it like me being the Promised One? I wasn't supposed to be here, but I am here, and so I'm ... it?'

'What makes you think you were not supposed to be here? You are the thief your prince needed.'

'Am I, though? I've hardly stolen anything.'

'You have five of the seven stones, and you know how to get the other two.'

'Four,' said Ember glumly, and Rhaell had two of those.

The dragon cleared her throat, which was a terrifying prospect. 'Here. Don't drop it,' she said, and her foreleg extended, claws up.

Nestled in them was a small yellow jewel. It glowed softly.

Ember's jaw dropped. 'You're giving me the stone? But why? I ain't smart. I wouldn't be in this mess if I was.'

The dragon chuckled softly. 'Oh, Ember Hart. You're nearly there. Take this stone, and perhaps it will help you to see the rest of it.' She hesitated as Ember reached out. 'You have considered being careful what you wish for?'

'Hah,' said Ember bleakly. 'I get the stones, I can go home. Never have to see Rhaell again.'

'Yes,' said the dragon gently. 'Exactly.'

Ember took the stone. It was warm in her hands, and the pads of the dragon's claw were rough, like those of a dog's. She tucked the stone into the pocket of the belt she wore over her nightgown.

'How can I thank you?' she said.

The dragon got carefully to her feet. The roof trembled as she moved. 'Be smart, Ember Hart,' she said. 'Be brave. Brave as a ferret.'

Ember felt her eyes grow wide. *You can do it, little ferret.* 'How—?'

But right then a section of the chimney beside her exploded and Rhaell grabbed her, shoving her behind him and drawing his sword. He was barefoot and shirtless, his scarred back gleaming in the moonlight.

'Good evening to you too,' said the dragon drily.

'Rhaell, what the fuck?' snapped Ember, stepping around him, which was a mildly risky business given the slope of the roof. 'She's my friend.'

'She's also capable of turning you into ashes,' said Rhaell, then as an afterthought, 'and half the castle, too.'

'I could probably burn the whole castle,' said the dragon thoughtfully, 'but I'd have to take a rest in the middle.'

That sent Rhaell into a fighting stance, his blue eyes almost glowing with rage.

'She's not going to hurt anyone,' Ember said urgently. 'What is wrong with you?'

'I protect what's mine,' Rhaell snarled.

'Right, of course, you'll be king one day,' said Ember sourly. 'Fine. Go ahead and antagonise the giant predator that breathes fire.' To the dragon, she apologised, 'Sorry about this one. It appears I can't get rid of him.'

Rhaell stiffened at that. The dragon let out a huff of laughter.

'So it seems,' she said. 'Well, our business here is concluded, Ember Hart. Perhaps we shall meet again some day.'

Ember began to say she'd like that, and then remembered she'd be going home. 'Can you travel between worlds?' she asked. 'Wait, stupid question, of course not, or we'd have noticed.'

'Would you?' said the dragon. She nodded to Rhaell, and said, 'Keep protecting what is yours, Prince Bronadyr.'

Her huge feet moved on the golden roof, and Rhaell tensed, but the dragon simply launched herself into the air, great wings drawing a powerful downdraft that had Ember involuntarily grabbing Rhaell to steady herself.

He grabbed her back, his free arm dragging her down against the roof as the dragon's tail swept over the roof, cold air sending her hair and nightdress flying. Ember found she was clutching him, and not because she was afraid but because she wanted to. Her body was a treacherous bitch, and it craved the warmth of his skin, the strength of his arms, the sheer solidity of him. She breathed in his bitter orange scent – and shoved him away, disgusted with herself.

She stood up and tugged down her nightdress. 'What are you even doing here? Your *Grace*.'

For a tiny fragment of a moment, she thought he looked hurt, and then he curled his lip at her as he got to his feet. 'Forgive me for defending my castle from a fucking dragon.'

The castle. Not her. 'Your castle, is it? Did something happen to the king? May the Tree protect and shelter him,' she added sarcastically.

'I have lived in and defended this castle my whole life,' Rhaell snapped. 'I care about it and the people in it. You understand that concept? Caring about other people?'

'Hey,' Ember said, jabbing her finger at him. 'I've worked my fingers to the bone for other people since the day I came screaming into this world. I cook, I clean, I go out and nick stuff to sell so I can pay the rent to the disgusting landlord who always leers at my tits and offers me a special deal if I'm very nice to him.'

'Oh, I'm sure that wouldn't be a hardship for you,' said Rhaell, looking down at her with more contempt than she'd ever seen on a human being before. 'You'll fuck anything to get what you want, after all. Even an obscene Rakaa cock.'

Ember's fist flew at him, hard, and if he'd been anyone else the punch would have smashed his nose like a ripe plum. But he was Prince Bronadyr, the Beast, and he was faster and stronger than anyone else. He caught her fist in his hand and snarled down at her, teeth bared like the animal they said he was.

Rage boiled over in Ember and exploded from her mouth. 'I'd rather go back there and be treated like an unpaid skivvy in a filthy city,' Ember growled, 'and fuck my repulsive landlord than ever see you naked again. You *disgust* me.'

The words were out before she could stop them.

The hand holding her fist turned to stone, and she saw the blow ripple over him, tightening every muscle until his face was a drawn mask of fury.

He jerked his hand from hers and turned away, and Ember saw his shoulders heaving as he fought himself under control.

Disgusting. Repulsive. Monstrous. Deformed. He'd lived with those words all his life. For some reason that escaped Ember, people here seemed to genuinely believe he was all those things.

You're not ... horrified by me?

'Fuck,' Ember muttered. The cold wind blew her nightgown against her legs as she stepped forward. 'Rhaell— I didn't mean—'

He flinched away from her reaching hand, and when he glanced back at her, his face was colder than the depths of the ocean.

'Why,' he said, 'would I give a fuck what you think?'

'I didn't mean physically,' she said, althought she didn't know why she was trying to clarify this. 'Literally the only thing I like about you is your body.'

He turned fully back to her then, a mocking smile on those beautiful lips. 'Sure it is, Sparks. Couldn't drop your knickers fast enough for me, could you? What happened, Ikrai turn you down?'

Well, that was what she got for offering an olive branch. 'Fuck you,' Ember snarled.

'How about the Myr?' persisted Rhaell. 'If you're into murderous beasts. The hafmey could probably get you off. I seem to remember you like being eaten.'

Ember's whole body jerked with the need to hit him, but he was faster, and she froze, forcing her fists down before he could grab them.

'You're disgusting,' she said.

'Sticks and stones, Sparks,' Rhaell said, spreading his hands. His laugh was the angriest sound she'd ever heard. 'Disgusting, revolting, grotesque, I've heard them all. I'm a monster. I'm an abomination. But what does that make you, who actually wanted to fuck me?'

'Don't flatter yourself,' she sneered. 'You were a means to an end.'

'An end? I seem to remember you finished every time,' taunted Rhaell. His lips curved. 'And there were a lot of times.'

'You think I don't know how to fake an orgasm?'

'Practised on your landlord?' he shot back.

'He'd never be stupid enough to believe me,' Ember said. 'You know, if I didn't loathe you so much I'd pity you. Practised your oral technique on girls who wouldn't fuck you?' She saw the shame flicker across his face and knew she'd scored a hit. She forced her lips into an insulting smile. 'You're pathetic.'

He loomed over her, so close she could see the fierceness in his eyes, the tightness of his jaw, the pain and fear under all his anger. *I did that.* Her smile hurt, flickering at the edges, her eyes burning.

He deserved it. He deserved to be in pain, miserable and shamed. She wanted to see him cower, whimpering like an animal, broken and bleeding and hurting like she hurt. She wanted to destroy him.

Her fists curled with helpless rage, smile crumbling under the threat of tears. How could he just stand there, breathing down at her, eyes glowing in the dark like he was some kind of primal god, so beautiful it hurt to look at him. How could he have decieved her and betrayed her, made her fall in love with him, made her vulnerable to him, and then crushed her heart in his stupid giant fists.

Rage spilled from her eyes in hot tears.

'I hate you,' she ground out.

His nostrils flared. His chest heaved. He bared his teeth at her like the monster he was.

He smelled like bitter oranges and rage and everything she'd ever wanted.

'Fuck you,' Ember sobbed, and grabbed him in a kiss so savage she was sure it drew blood.

Rhaell growled into her mouth and crushed her body against his, his tongue in her mouth, his fingers digging into her flesh. All the tension that had wound tight in Ember snapped and heat roared in its wake, taking over her wits and her senses.

She found herself backed against the chimney, hitched up off her feet as Rhaell kissed her like he was dying, and she wrapped her legs around him and mashed her hands into his hair. His hips surged into hers, the thickness of his erection grinding into her and drawing a desperate moan from her throat.

He still smelled like bitter oranges.

'Fuck me,' she gasped, and Rhaell's teeth sank into her lip as he tore at her nightgown. She wrestled with the front of his trousers, ripping them open and grasping his thick, hard length in her hand. The heat and the throb of him had her craving like an addict.

His first thrust forced a sound from her, a desperate wordless cry of fulfilment. His thick cock felt so right inside her. She'd never needed anything like she needed this.

Rhaell's eyes burned into her, the blue of a consuming fire. And Ember ignited.

He surged into her again and again, tongue plundering her mouth. His hands gripped her hips so hard she knew they'd leave bruises and she relished it. She bucked into his hold, fingers digging into his scalp. Her thumbs found the stumps of his horns and forced a groan from him.

'Fuck,' he gasped, almost helpless, and then he was biting down on her neck and hammering into her so fast she barely had the breath in her to cry out as her orgasm rushed in, hot and fast.

Rhaell made a gutteral sound, and then he was roaring against her skin, his hips pumping as she screamed her pleasure to the night sky.

He shuddered, breath coming harsh against her skin, fingers grasping and releasing handfuls of her flesh. His breath stuttered, chest heaving, a gasp escaping his lips that she realised in her daze was laughter.

He was laughing at her. He was still inside her and he was laughing at her. Ember pushed at his shoulders, then shoved, her pleasure dissolving in cold shreds around her.

'Fuck you,' she muttered, the tears threatening her again.

That made him laugh harder as he withdrew from her, leaving her chilled and empty, the sound harsh. 'You just did,' he muttered, and sobbed out another laugh. 'Leaves and branches, Ember, I'll never be fucking free of you, will I?'

He turned his face away and moved to fasten his trousers, but not before Ember caught the glint of tears on his cheek.

'You will tomorrow,' she said, steadying herself against the wall, tugging her nightdress down over her hips. 'Soon as we say the vows, I'm gone.'

His head snapped round. 'The dragon gave you her stone?'

Ember clutched at the pouch on her belt that held it. Its weight was reassuring in her hand.

'Just one more to go,' she said. 'I tried to get Ysarriel's Stone to leave sooner, but the king is still the king and I ain't royal yet.'

Rhaell stood tall and beautiful in the moonlight, his hair dishevelled, skin gleaming with sweat as his chest heaved from pounding her so hard. How was it possible for one man to make her feel so good and so awful? Why did she let him have this power over her?

'I am,' he said.

Hope surged in her, soured with sharp misery. 'And you can just walk in and get it?' she said.

'You said you tried,' Rhaell said, and Ember fished between her still-tender breasts and raised Ruvaen's Stone at him.

'Thief's Stone. Got me right in there. Could've taken anything I wanted, except for the thing I actually wanted. But I'm assuming there's actual security on that place?'

'More than one easily distracted guard, at any rate,' Rhaell said, not looking at her.

'What, you don't think you could go another round, just for the sake of getting rid of me?' Ember narrowed her eyes as his gaze whipped to hers. 'Don't pretend you wouldn't hate-fuck me into the middle of next week if it'd get me out of your life.'

The look on his face could have frozen fire. 'Hate-fucking?' he said. 'Is that what this is?'

'You said you'd fuck me with all my arms and legs broken,' Ember said.

He shoved a hand at his hair. 'I said I *could*, Sparks. Big difference.'

'Oh, the Beast has nuances?'

'The Beast,' gritted Rhaell, 'is a role I play. People expect a violent monster, they get one. But you've already decided that's what I am, so I won't waste my time explaining myself to you. The security,' he went on, as if their last exchange hadn't happened, 'around the jewel tower is strong. Multiple guards, and magic wards, too. I reinforced them myself. Absolutely nobody is getting in there until the king himself approaches tomorrow morning.'

The thought briefly occurred to Ember that if she slid a knife into the king's ribs, Rhaell would be the king. But she wasn't going to commit murder to get what she wanted.

Rhaell glared at her, his hands on his hips.

Probably. She probably wasn't going to commit murder.

'But the Thief's Stone got you in?' he said, head tilted as if he was thinking.

'Right in, past whatever security you've got.'

He whistled, his eyes going distant.

Ember waited. Whatever Rhaell's faults – and there were many – he wasn't stupid. He could come up with a half-decent plan sometimes. His exit strategies sucked, but that was where Ember had the advantage.

Don't get in if you can't get out. Ember looked at Rhaell, standing there on the roof with his hair blowing in the wind and his eyes narrowed in calculation, and knew she'd never get out. She could be worlds away and she'd still be consumed by him.

She'd been maimed and drowned and kidnapped for these stones; she'd nearly died and so had Rhaell, and poor Caeda had gone to half a grave. She'd lied and killed and lost her heart. And Lords help her, but she didn't even want the stones anymore.

But if she stayed here and married the man she loved, his hatred would kill her.

'I have an idea,' Rhaell said eventually, looking up at her, and the look in his eyes was a man at the end of a terrible journey. 'You're not going to like it.'

Ember blew out a breath and met his eyes for what felt like the last time. 'I'm all ears, Buttercup.'

CHAPTER 32

On the day Ember's arrival had been foretold, the city had been bedecked with flowers, streamers and bunting. Silver and green filled every street, canopied the river, and decorated every excited citizen. The castle had been unrecognisable under its festive trimmings, the Great Chamber groaning under the weight of flowers and people. Everyone wanted to say they'd been there. The air of excitement had been contagious.

The people lining the river to watch the prince sail to his wedding a month later were somewhat more subdued. The city was possibly even more decorated, but the cheers were a little less cheerful. Somehow, the people had worked out that their Promised One was little more than a sacrificial lamb, to be given to the Beast as a brood mare.

He had killed his mother. He would probably kill his wife. It was hard to cheer that.

The Beast was easy for them to recognise as he stood in the prow of the boat. Taller and broader than any other man in Yskara, he wore a green tunic that was so heavy with silver adornments it was practically armoured. Huge epaulettes crowned the shoulders, spiked into the shape of the Tree, and from them fell a cape of green and silver leaves. Braid and brocade covered everything. Even his boots were shiny with embellishment.

And there was a coronet. A smaller, simpler version of the King's crown, studded with gemstones and so sharp it had drawn blood when he touched it. His hand throbbed as it hung by his side.

Rhaell stepped off the dock onto the path leading to the Sacred Tree. It was lined with members of the court, and dignitaries from all over the continent. He saw only a blur of faces, more sick with nerves than he ever had been facing an opponent in the arena. He followed the guards leading him to the edge of the clearing, where he was to await Ember's arrival.

The king stood under the Tree, waiting, too. He had written the vows they were to recite, and for their blood vow he had retrieved the jewelled knife that had been embedded in Ember's chest when she fell from the sky. His eyes gleamed like he knew he'd won.

Rhaell did not look at Ysarriel's crown. He couldn't.

It's too late to change anything now.

His palm throbbed. He'd lied to Ember when he said it didn't mean anything. It meant everything.

Trumpets sounded before he could think about that, and he turned to see the crowd murmuring and peering around down the path. Ember's ladies came first, four birds of paradise strewing real jewels into the path as if they were rose petals.

Ember would love that, he thought, and then cursed himself. Because Ember was following them, and she wasn't stopping to pick up jewels. She couldn't, because her dress was a cage.

It was a cage made of silver, and fashioned into the shape of the Tree, but fastened around her waist was a cage, nonetheless. Gaps between roots and branches flashed her bare legs, her modesty barely concealed by the trunk of the Tree. There was nothing beneath the skirt. He supposed this was so the Beast could start rutting his bride as soon as the vows were said.

Above her waist, the solid silver Tree rose into branches that covered her breasts and shoulders, the leaves made of gemstones. It wrapped around her neck, leaves and branches a gentle chokehold. There was no back to it, and no sides, just the Tree, barely covering her breasts.

Her hair had been bulked out and teased into a long mane. Her face and arms were painted with silver, leaves and branches twining over her skin. Only one part of her remained unadorned: her left hand, ready to be sliced and joined to his.

Over the cage was a heavy skirt, split at the front to show the tree's trunk, and unsurprisingly green. It glittered like a beetle's wing. This was, Rhaell realised as she came closer, because it was made from beetles' wings, shaped into leaves and interspersed with real precious stones. The whole thing was as stiff as a bell, and clearly so heavy she could barely walk in it. Which was probably the point.

And worse, she was still chained up.

Rhaell felt the rage build in himself, even as he told himself he hated her. No woman should be brought to her wedding in chains.

Brock's eyes met his, and he could see his frustrated anger reflected there. It very nearly boiled over when Brock unfastened the cuff on his arm and fastened it to Rhaell's.

'We're to be bound together in the ceremony,' he growled in a low voice.

'But only by silk,' said Brock. 'King's orders. Sir.'

Ember's left hand was clenched into a fist.

He couldn't look at her as she was chained to him. Couldn't take in the splendour of her dress and her jewels. Couldn't bear to see the hatred and fear he knew would be in her eyes.

He took her hand, her left in his right, their arms extended past the ridiculous bulk of her skirts, and began to walk. Slowly, because she was wearing a fucking prison cell. Her hand was cold and still in his, fingers loose, like holding hands with a corpse.

Near to the king, stood Sarea, resplendent in Yskaran green. Rhaell did not look at her.

The king watched them approach with a triumphant smile. His gaze flickered over the chain, his smile widening a little, and Rhaell wondered if he could lunge at the old man and throttle him with it.

He was backed by a dozen guards.

Beside the king, stood a page bearing a cushion, on which nestled a coronet. Ember's coronet, a more delicate version of his own. She would be crowned as his princess after their vows were said.

Ember didn't speak at all. Didn't look anywhere but straight ahead. Barely moved but for her small steps inexorably forward, until they had no more ground left to cover, and stood under the golden branches of the Tree.

Under his shirt, the stones he wore gave a throb of recognition. He felt Ember's hand tighten momentarily, as if her stones had done the same thing. He wondered where she'd hidden them.

'May the Tree protect and shelter you,' the king said, his voice magnified by a charm, and the assembled worthies murmured the same. 'We come to witness the solemn and sincere joining of these two souls in a sacred union before the Tree.'

Rhaell waited for the king to ask if they came willingly. He did not.

'First these petitioners must be named under the sacred leaves and branches, so that the Tree may know their full sincerity. Your whole and full names,' he warned, spearing Ember with a look. To Rhaell, he waved a prompting hand.

'Bronadyr Onas Hraeulfr of Yskara,' said Rhaell, watching the King's eyes narrow at the name his mother had given him.

Beside him, Ember lifted her chin, and said clearly, 'Ember Hart.'

'Your full name,' the King repeated in a fierce mutter.

'That is my full name. We couldn't afford fancy extra ones,' Ember said, and Rhaell nearly smiled.

The stones he wore throbbed faster and faster, in time with

Ember's rapid breaths, and her fingers tightened involuntarily around Rhaell's.

He squeezed them back. 'Breathe,' he murmured. Just as he had at their betrothal. Ember dragged in a breath and let it out. Another. Another.

The stone at his wrist pulsed. He saw an answering light from her chest, shining through the silver branches. From the corner of his eye, the Tree seemed to glow...

And suddenly the pulse of Aywin's Stone began to slow, taking his heart with it, until it seemed to beat to a strong, steady rhythm. A rhythm with an echo.

It's her. I can feel her heart.

Somewhere under the sound of it, he heard the King's voice.

'Bronadyr Onas Hraeulfr of Yskara, do you swear to bind yourself in sacred marriage to this Ember Hart?'

Rhaell looked down at her, and even under the silver and the gems and the beetle wings and the make-up and the hairpieces she was still his Ember, and she made him smile.

'No,' he said.

CHAPTER 33

A shocked silence fell over the clearing. Ember felt power throbbing through her veins.

'No?' said the king. His face darkened. 'Boy—'

'I'm not a boy,' said Rhaell. 'I haven't been a boy since you cut off my wings.'

The assembled crowd drew in a shocked breath.

'And you,' he said, reaching under his doublet with the hand not holding Ember's, 'are no king.'

Onas drew in an outraged breath, but it died on his lips as he saw what Rhaell had fastened around his neck. The Stone of Ysarriel, glowing green.

'How?' whispered Sarea.

Onas's hand flew up to his crown, where Ember had set, with shaking fingers, one of Rhaell's decoys.

Ember knew she wasn't much of a jeweller. But she'd managed to fix Ysarriel's Stone into a pendant for Rhaell, just as she'd wedged Wynric's Stone into a previously priceless heirloom for herself.

'What is this ... this joke?' the king hissed.

'It isn't a joke,' Rhaell said. He squeezed Ember's hand, and she squeezed his right back. 'We hold six of the seven pieces of the Heart of Yskar.'

'Impossible,' breathed the King.

'How?' came Sarea's voice again, louder.

Ember glanced over at her and smiled. Only Rhaell was close enough to see the tremor in it. 'We did something ... smart,' she said.

The stones pulsed. The Tree seemed to blaze with a sudden light.

'Guards,' said the king, not taking his eyes off them.

Rhaell turned so that he was facing Ember. He spoke in a clear voice, so everyone in the clearing could hear it.

'I, Bronadyr Onas Hraeulfr of Yskara, will not be marrying Ember Hart this day,' he said.

'And nothing in this world or the next could make me marry you, either,' she said, and a small, shocked laugh escaped her as she spoke.

King Onas's hand smacked into her face so fast, and so hard, that for a second her ears rang and her vision blurred. Someone pushed her, and she stumbled.

It was Rhaell, shielding her with his body even as their hands were clasped together. In his left hand she saw, as she blinked her vision into clarity, was a sword.

'By its leaves and branches,' he snarled quietly, 'you will not touch my wife.'

There was a shining sound, such as many swords might make being unsheathed at the same time.

Wife.

The truth of it pulsed through her body, throbbing in time with Rhaell's heartbeat. She was his wife, and had been since they'd cut and bound their hands together last night, before the authority of the six Stones of the Ancestors.

Only someone wearing Ruvaen's Stone could enter the jewel

tower. And only Ember could wear that stone. And only a member of the royal family could take Ysarriel's Stone.

Rhaell's plan had been simple. Marry in secret that night and turn the wedding into a coup.

'Sarea wants the throne anyway,' he said. 'Let her have it.'

Ember had stared at him, standing there on the roof above the gorge as the wind whipped his hair. 'Do you really think she'll let you live if she takes the throne?' she said.

He'd shrugged. 'That's my problem, not yours. You'll be long gone,' he said, and the sick pain of that had nearly brought Ember to her knees.

But she'd knelt before him on the roof, knelt as Coldonians did before the statue of their chosen High Lord, and she'd told him the marriage vows that Coldonians made.

'I promise to be faithful and true to you, to honour you with my body and cherish you with my soul, for as long as we are in the world together.' And Rhaell had repeated the words back to her as he cut their hands and bound them together with the muddy scarf that he'd kept with him all this time.

She had felt the marriage bond snap into place as she clasped his hand and hadn't tried to stop the tears from flowing down her face. She'd been married to him for just a few hours. And now she was going to leave. Forever.

But not before she'd fulfilled her destiny.

Ember stepped out to stand beside her husband, the man they called a monster and a beast. The boy who'd been locked away and mutilated, ridiculed and shamed, who'd been forced into the role of executioner and killer. The man who kept a toy dragon and a muddy scarf in his pack and kissed her so sweetly she might die from it.

The newly made marriage scar on her palm throbbed as she squeezed Rhaell's hand. 'I am his wife,' she proclaimed to the court of Yskara. 'And proud to be so.'

The three stones she wore pulsed in time with the three Rhaell wore. And with a seventh stone.

She smiled.

'I don't know what stupid trick you think you're pulling here,' hissed the king. Louder, he said, 'You have said your vows?'

'We have.' Ember glanced at Sarea, who looked steaming.

'You have cut and bound your hands?'

They displayed their matching scars to the court. 'We have.'

'By whose authority did you wed?'

'By the authority of the Ancestors.' Rhaell gestured to their glowing stones. Behind them, the Tree lit up the clearing. The court murmured and nodded to each other.

King Onas gave a horrible smile. 'By its leaves and branches, it is done. You are bound by blood.'

For as long as we are in the world together. Rhaell looked down at Ember. His eyes shone with so much emotion she couldn't possibly identify it all.

'Take them to the tent,' said the king.

'The tent?' said Ember. This wasn't part of the plan.

'What tent?' said Rhaell, as guards began to shepherd them around the Tree. He held her as close as her stupid skirts would allow.

'Is this some part of the—' Ember began, halting as she saw the tent in question.

It was not, as she'd expected, a venue for feasting. It was not for a private part of the wedding ritual.

Or rather, it was, but not a part anyone had warned her about.

'Are you fucking kidding me?' Rhaell muttered, digging his heels in.

The tent was beautiful and luxurious, open at one side to reveal the opulent interior. Draped with green and silver hangings, carpeted and scattered with cushions and throws, there was only one piece of furniture within.

A bed.

'That had better not be for what I think it's for,' Ember said.

'I don't think it's for a nap,' said Rhaell, staring in horror.

'The newlyweds will consummate their union,' cried the king, his voice still magically magnified. 'Here in the hearing of all, under the branches of the Tree! May the Tree bless and protect your union!' he shouted, and a hundred voices shouted it back.

'No,' said Ember.

'Are you deranged?' said Rhaell.

The king's eyes shone with an unholy light. 'By the Tree,' he snarled, 'you will do your duty, boy!'

'We are not having sex in full view of the court,' said Rhaell flatly. Beneath his sleeve, Aywin's Stone was glowing so red it showed through the fabric.

'We're not animals,' laughed the king. 'We'll close the tent flaps.'

'You're insane,' said Ember. People had begun to follow them now, watching with some consternation.

'Guards,' said the king, and men came forward. 'Chain her to the bed.'

'You cannot be serious,' said Ember, as the men tried to push her forward. 'Get the fuck off me!'

She'd been pushed and pulled like this before. Some cove in an alley who tried his luck and assumed she'd be helpless. She'd smashed his head against the wall and run for it. But these were large, armed men, and there were a lot of them.

Rhaell struck out with his sword. Ember wished to the Lords she wasn't wearing a bloody cage of a dress, and shoved at them as hard as she could. Hands dug into her arms. Beside her, Rhaell roared, and she saw three guards go down, but he was hampered by his hand being bound to hers and he was trying to fight men who pressed in too close, and Ember felt panic overwhelm her dragon heart and shrink it back down to a rabbit's, and—

A roar sounded in her ears. The stone at her breast pulsed.

Not Ruvaen's Stone. Wynric's.

Do something smart.

The guards would do what the king said. But if he wasn't the king anymore...

'Change of plan,' Ember gasped. She clutched Ruvaen's Stone in one hand and reached out to Rhaell with the other as he whirled to slash at a guard, grabbed the green stone that swung from his neck and yanked it free. *I can take it now, I'm royal.*

Because right now, King Onas was still the king, and she was bound in blood to his grandson. But in about thirty seconds—

'Sarea!' she yelled. 'Catch!'

The pendant sailed through the air, and Sarea lifted her heavy skirts in one hand and stepped forward to catch it, looking mildly bewildered as to where it had come from.

Ember kept her hand on Ruvaen's Stone and strode forward, past guards who suddenly didn't notice her, and grabbed Ysarriel's Crown from the King's head. Then she calmly walked to Sarea, unveiled herself, and said, 'Would you have a dagger, Your Grace?'

'What the hell is going on?' hissed Sarea, handing over a small jewelled knife as Rhaell continued to fairly easily fight off the guards coming at him. Ember had the feeling they weren't trying very hard. He was their commander, after all.

Ember prised the green decoy stone from the crown and let it fall unheeded into the grass.

'Oh, we're staging a coup,' she said. 'We'll need to borrow this crown in a minute, but first I need to make a modification. If you'd hold it steady for me?'

Sarea's fingers closed around the crown, and Ember saw her knuckles whiten.

She glanced up as she replaced Ysarriel's Stone and saw the thoughts chasing across Sarea's face at lightning speed.

'This wasn't the plan,' she said.

'What plan?'

'Mine and Bronadyr's plan!' hissed Sarea.

Ember's fingers fumbled on the glowing green stone. Rhaell

had plotted with Sarea? Before or after he'd made the plan with Ember?

Had he ... made a back-up plan?

Of course he had. He didn't trust her, after all.

'And what was your plan?' she said, grasping the Royal Stone in her fist, her marriage scar throbbing against it.

'Steal the crown, kill the king, declare myself in his place, send you home,' said Sarea.

'I see.' Ember's knife worked on a stubborn claw of the crown's setting. 'And was this going to happen after we said our vows?'

'I was going to step in when the king asked if anyone knew of a reason why you could not be wed,' Sarea said.

'Nice. Dramatic,' said Ember numbly.

But whatever else Sarea and Rhaell had plotted without her, Ember never got to hear, because the king shoved her to the ground, the crown rolling from her hands.

'Guards!' yelled King Onas. He drew his sword, but it was a ceremonial rapier, and he clearly hadn't used one for years. 'Take this woman—'

'Fuck's sake,' Ember muttered, and kicked out with her ankle.

Nobody else had remembered she was still chained to Rhaell, including, it seemed, Onas. She used the chain to trip him and rolled back out of his way, grabbing the crown as she did and tossing it up to Sarea, who placed it neatly on her head.

And as she did, the whole clearing filled with green light.

Ysarriel's Stone glowed brighter than it ever had before, even in the presence of all the other Heart stones, and beneath it Sarea emanated light.

Just as Ember had when she'd first touched the Tree.

Queen Sarea gleamed like polished ivory, her hair a river of rubies, her eyes shining amethysts. Beside her, Lord Addor fell to his knees, and then so did the nearest courtiers, and even some of the guards.

'Guards, stop her,' cried Onas, from the ground.

'Do not obey a false king!' roared Rhaell, and his voice echoed around the whole clearing. He whirled in a devastating circle, knocking down every soldier surrounding him, Aywin's Stone flaring bright red.

Then he swung gracefully to his knees, holding out his sword to Sarea, then deliberately laying it down.

'I pledge fealty to Queen Sarea, First of her name, True Descendent of Ysarriel the First Queen,' he said, voice magically magnified.

'I pledge fealty to Queen Sarea, First of her name, True Descendent of Ysarriel the First Queen,' said Lord Addor, gazing up at his wife with both awe and terror.

After that the murmur rose up from courtiers, guards and servants. Under it, Ember could hear Onas shouting that he was the true king, but no one could hear it under the sound that grew to a roar.

And when it died down, Ember and Sarea were the only ones still standing.

'And will you pledge fealty to me?' purred Sarea.

'Usurper!' yelled Onas. 'Usurper! Guards!'

Sarea's dragon flew down to land on his chest. It blew a tiny flame into his face, scorching his eyebrows.

'Rhaell,' said Ember, not taking her gaze off Sarea.

'Yes?'

'What was that word in the prophecy? That you said could be translated differently? The land is blighted, or...?'

'*Skoli*,' he said. '*When our native land be stolen.*'

'Stolen,' Ember repeated thoughtfully.

'This is treason,' snarled Onas.

'*When our native land be stolen, she shall restore it*,' said Ember. '*And power shall be restored to the rightful.*'

'I am the rightful king! King Onas, third of his name! The blood of the royal line flows through me!'

'Does it?' said Ember.

'Does it?' echoed Sarea, one brow raised enquiringly at Ember.

She'd planned a coup, but she didn't know the truth.

Sarea had probably intended to kill Onas.

'Tell me,' Ember said, 'about your childhood.'

'What?' The king's eyes rolled at her as if she'd gone mad.

'What?' said Rhaell.

'You were a hostage in … where was it?'

'Vaesturness, but what does this have to do with—'

'And you made friends there you still have today,' Ember said. Wynric's Stone warmed her skin.

'What does this have to do with—'

'Answer her,' said Rhaell, looming over his grandfather. Ember wondered briefly why he ever bothered with the Beast's fearsome helmet, when he could be quite terrifying enough on his own. But his presence by her side warmed her.

He lied to you, betrayed you, and trusted you so little he made a back-up plan. Don't feel warm about him.

'Yes, I made friends, several of them are here at court, and believe me, their armies will overpower any coup you think you can—'

'And you still mark the death of one of them,' Ember said.

'Jaonos Yllanala,' said Rhaell, slowly. 'We commend him to the Tree every year.' His expression invited Ember to explain where the hell she was going with this.

'I imagine you were close,' she said. 'Grew up together, did you? Must have been a shock to leave behind everything you knew and live among strangers.'

The king seethed silently at her. The dragon batted him on the nose with its tiny claws.

'How did he die?' Ember said.

'This is madness,' said the king.

'In a storm at sea,' said Rhaell, as if reciting a well-told tale. 'On the way to Vaesturness.'

She saw the realisation come over him.

'On the way to Vaesturness,' Ember repeated, and as Rhaell made a sign at her, her voice grew in power until it filled the clearing. 'Two boys left, and one arrived. To live among strangers, people they'd never met before. How terrible that poor Jaonos died in that storm. It must have been by the providence of the Tree that the rightful heir to the throne survived, eh?'

The silence was sticky.

'Lies,' said the king in a thready whisper.

'Of course, nobody could prove anything,' said Ember. 'Nobody would know that the boy who left and the man who returned were not the same person. People change so much as they grow. Why, you might be a small child with wings and a man with none,' she added, and saw Rhaell's knuckles go white.

'This is treason,' the king shouted. 'Treason! Guards! Cut her down!'

'Belay that order,' said Brock.

'You!' screamed the king.

Brock gave Ember a look that said she'd better have some goddamn proof of this.

'Can anyone here deny that Queen Sarea is clearly the true descendant of Ysarriel, the First Queen?' said Ember.

Sarea stood tall and beautiful, glowing with unearthly power. The crown on her head seemed to turn her into a mythical beast of horns and antlers, an ancient goddess wreathed in power.

Lords, I hope this won't backfire on the whole kingdom.

'If only there were someone we could ask,' Ember said. She felt giddy with power. 'Someone who remembers the founding of Yskara.'

Beside her, Rhaell picked up her thread. 'All the Ancestors are dead and gone. Apart from one.'

They all turned to face the Tree. It was glowing now, the trunk almost pink. The stones at Ember's breast heated so intensely she was amazed her silver dress didn't melt.

Ember looked at Rhaell, who nodded and jerked his head at

Brock. The Captain of the Guard came and dragged the erstwhile King Onas to his feet, shackling his wrists behind him. He held out something to Rhaell.

A key. Rhaell unlocked the chain at his wrist and knelt to unlock Ember's ankle.

He looked up at her from the ground as he freed her. But it was just a chain. Just a physical thing. The scar on her palm would remind her she was bound to him for as long as they were in the world together.

Her stomach hollowed as she glanced at the Tree.

'I'll have your head for this,' the king sneered. 'I'll have your skin.'

Brock didn't even appear to hear him.

'You ready?' said Ember. She held out a hand to help him up, and he kept hold of it as he stood.

The twin scars on their hands throbbed. Ember looked up at him, this man she loved and had sworn to hate.

'Ember,' he said, his voice dropping. He made the sign to remove the magnification of her voice. 'I don't know what's going to happen when we do this.'

'Neither do I,' she said. She glanced back at the struggling king. 'I think we just pulled off a coup.'

'I think we did. But listen.' He took her other hand, and looked down at her with those blue, blue eyes. 'Ember, if this works, if the Tree is healed and magic is restored, we can open a portal and send you home.'

Ember went so cold the stones felt like coals against her skin. It was what she wanted. It was best for both of them. She couldn't stay with him.

'And I ... I wanted to ... I need to—'

Ember shook her head rapidly. Tears burned her eyes. 'Don't say it.'

Sincerity blazed from him. 'Ember, I'm sorry.'

She startled. 'What?'

'For not telling you who I was. For letting you believe I was someone else. I'm sorry. You deserved better.'

She stared up at him. *Did you think he was going to tell you he loved you?*

'I—' she began, and ran out of words. 'I'm sorry, too,' she said. 'I didn't mean what I said, about just trying to marry you to get out of marrying ... er, you. I never meant that. I was just angry. And desperate.'

'To get home.' He nodded, face bleak.

I am home. I'm with you. 'I faked it,' she blurted. 'I can't give you heirs.'

An incredulous laugh escaped Rhaell, and he muttered, 'Yeah, I did think you were supposed to bleed for slightly more than a few hours.'

Ember felt her face burn.

'You know,' said Rhaell, his thumb stroking her hand. 'You could have not said those vows.'

Ember groaned. 'Okay, first off I didn't know that was an option, and second of all, so could you.'

Rhaell gave her a bit of a smile. 'I know.'

Her heart leapt. Did that mean—?

'I hate to interrupt,' said Sarea. 'But would you mind? You haven't sworn fealty to me, and if you hang around much longer it'll make me look bad.'

She took off the crown, and the glow faded from her skin. 'I'll be wanting this back,' she said, handing it to Ember.

She looked down at it, and felt the thrum of power at having all six stones so close together. The Tree seemed to pull at them, Ephyrea's Stone desperate to be reunited with the rest.

Ember looked up at Rhaell, and his blue eyes burned down at her.

'Fortune favours the brave,' he muttered, and then he swept her into his arms and kissed her.

And Ember kissed him back. Her free arm wound around his

neck, holding him to her. Her hand pressed into the ridges and troughs of the scars on his back. *I've got you.*

She kissed him back, because it was so good, the best she'd ever had, and it had been hours since she had. *Hours.* After all that time wanting him and not having him, all those weeks of longing, she'd had him for such a brief time. The night by the Sacred Sea, the days and nights in the Rakaa village. That first, endless night, when she couldn't get her fill of him. When everything felt perfect, felt right, as if she'd been made purely for those moments of desperate bliss.

She kissed him back, because after this she never would again. Because she had to leave, return to where she belonged, go back to her real life. Because she didn't belong here.

Because Rhaell hadn't asked her to stay.

Because he'd said he was sorry, and not that he loved her.

Tears spilled from her eyes, and she didn't stop kissing him. When she stopped it would be over. They'd heal the Tree and he'd send her home. And she'd never feel the heat of his skin or the softness of his lips, she'd never see the blue of his eyes blaze with passion, or light with laughter, or warm with love. Because he didn't love her.

But she would be bound to him for as long as they were in the world together.

She wished he'd never apologised, and she could go on hating him. Hating didn't hurt.

It was Rhaell who pulled back, and she went with him, until he gently cupped her jaw and stopped her.

'Ember,' he murmured, his eyes soft and dark. She couldn't bear to look at him.

'Let's get on with it,' she said, and marched towards the Tree, towing him after her.

CHAPTER 34

Don't go. Don't go.

Rhaell felt the words in every beat of his heart. But it was the only thing Ember wanted. The only thing she'd ever wanted. Since the moment she fell out of the sky and into his arms, all Ember Hart had wanted was to go home.

She said herself she was desperate. He'd nearly taken that away from her, the chance to go home where she belonged. Back to her family. Back to her world, where people weren't bound into marriage by blood oaths, where Myr didn't try to feed her to fish and Rakaa didn't kidnap her. Back to safety. Leaving his world entirely.

And just like Ruvaen leaving Ephyrea, she would take a piece of his heart with her.

He let her tow him towards the Tree, the crown glowing on her head. He hadn't been lying: it did suit her. They could take it back. She could rule beside him, as his queen, wise and brave and joyous—

But she was going home. It was what she wanted.

All too soon they stood before the Tree, its bark glowing, pink light forcing its way out between the cracks. Ephyrea calling to

Ruvaen. He understood her desperation. He'd been bound to Ember less than an hour and already the thought of being parted from her tore at his heart.

She might not have meant her vows, but he had. And even if she thought nothing of their binding, he did. He had sworn to honour and cherish her, to take her as his wife for as long as they were in the world together. And even if they weren't in the world together, he belonged to her, body and soul.

It could never be undone, not by death, not by the Tree.

'Oh, bollocks.'

He looked down to see her fiddling with the clasp at the back of her neck, and nearly laughed at the mundanity of it when his heart was breaking.

'I can't get the bastard thing undone,' she muttered.

'Let me,' said someone, and he somehow wasn't surprised to see Phoebe there. She unfastened some hidden clasp at the back of Ember's neck, and the silver tree loosened enough for her to pull the stones clear of it. The heavy beetle wing train fell from her shoulders.

Ember took a deep breath, and Rhaell watched her breasts move beneath the silver branches. *Of all the things to memorise, you pathetic rat.*

Phoebe gathered up the silver and the fabric, and hesitated. 'Your Grace—'

'Ember.'

'Ember. I'm...' Phoebe, never lost for words, stood mouthing like a fish. Finally, she said, 'It's been a privilege to serve you.'

'It's been a privilege to have you as a friend,' said Ember.

Phoebe nodded jerkily and stepped back.

Ember glanced up at Rhaell and handed him the crown. She took two pendants from around her neck, and Rhaell unfastened the one the Rakaa blacksmith had made him. He tore his sleeve when it wouldn't roll up, and removed the vambrace. She handed him the crown.

Ember held Ruvaen's Stone in her hand, then gave a sharp tug, and this time, it finally came free.

She looked up at him again, briefly, then back at the Tree, and together they pressed all six stones against the bark.

Pink light blazed from the Tree, so bright it blinded him. The stones in his hands heated until he couldn't touch them anymore, but that didn't matter because the Tree held them, the bark absorbing them into itself.

Ember's fingers curled around his. *Hold onto me. Don't let me go.*

The light and the heat grew, until Rhaell stepped back, pulling Ember against his body to shield her from the inferno. She wrapped her arm around his waist and stumbled back, turning her face from what had been the Tree.

It was barely even visible anymore. Even the outline of it had disappeared into the blinding light, which grew and grew until it filled Rhaell's vision, filled the clearing, filled the sky.

And then suddenly, it wasn't there and never had been.

A woman stood there, the blazing pink light from her chest slowly fading to a glow. She wore a long, draped robe, her hair unbound nearly to the floor. Her face was so lovely it hurt to look upon.

Rhaell took a deep breath, of air that felt brand new and filled his lungs with...

With magic.

They'd done it. Magic had been restored. He could feel it, thrumming through the earth below them, through the trees and the water. The air felt elastic, as if he could simply spring into it, swim up into it as if it were water.

Ember stirred in his arms, and all the magic in the world couldn't hold together Rhaell's shattering heart.

They had restored the magic, and now he had to send Ember home.

Tell her. Tell her how you feel. Beg her not to go.

He clutched at her, desperate to hold on for just a minute

longer. When she looked up at him, the light fell golden on her face.

Ember glowed, so lovely it hurt to look upon her.

'My child,' came a voice, lilting and musical, and they both turned to the woman who stood where the Tree had been. 'How I've longed to see you.'

~

Every person Ember had met in Yskara had seemed to be inhumanly beautiful. Every one of them tall and ethereal, willowy and slender, with faces like those of angels. Sapphire eyes and cornsilk tresses around every bloody corner.

The woman standing where the Tree had been would make every one of them look like a misshapen goblin.

'Ephyrea?' Ember said, because who else could it be?

The angelic woman smiled. Her heart glowed within her chest; the heart they had restored.

'My child,' she breathed, gliding forward. 'How you have grown.'

Ember looked around. By the treeline, she saw Brock still holding Onas's chains. He knelt on the ground, weeping. A few feet away, Phoebe stood clutching her bundle of Ember's clothing. Nearby huddled her four ladies, their exquisite gowns torn and dirty from cowering on the ground. Well, at least they were still alive.

'You have freed me. But where is your father? Where is Ruvaen?' demanded Ephyrea.

Beside her, she heard Rhaell swear.

'You and Ruvaen had a child?' No wonder Ysarriel had been angry.

Ephyrea tilted her lovely head, the motion birdlike. 'He took a piece of my heart with him. I knew he would keep you safe.'

Was she talking to Rhaell? But his mother had been the

princess, and his father Rakaa... weren't they? There was no one else in the Ancestor's eyeline. Only herself, and that wasn't possible.

'Do you not know me?' said Ephyrea, standing before them. 'Did your father not tell you?'

In Bleakburn, there were temples and shrines to the High Lords and Ladies. Ember had found herself leaving tokens under the hooded statue of Lord Ruven more than once, offering a quick prayer to the High Lord of Thieves, but she'd scoffed at the penitents begging Lady Feara for some luck in love. Her statues were always depicted as beautiful young maidens, buxom and bountiful, often modelled after some fashionable young pin-up of the day. She smiled out of the stone, her saucy wink seeming to promise someone would be getting lucky and it might be her.

This cool, pale creature with her eyes full of distant green stars was nothing like the statues.

Her hand reached out, and Ember froze. Beside her, Rhaell tensed, his hand tightening on hers.

'Um,' said Ember. 'My father is a clockmaker.'

A tiny wrinkle appeared between Ephyrea's perfect brows. 'A...?' she looked around the glade, as if only just seeing the people there. The deposed king, in his ornate finery, Brock in his armour with his green and silver surcoat, the ladies in their complicated dresses and overstyled hair.

Ephyrea herself wore a column of draped silk, her hair falling in a loose sheet almost to her bare feet. Her gaze travelled upwards, to the mighty castle of Yskara, standing high on the cliffs, towering over even the Sacred Forest.

'The trees do not sing the same song, and it is very quiet,' she said. 'The moons are shy and the stars will not chatter to them. How long has it been?'

Rhaell cleared his throat. 'Many, many generations,' he said. 'Lady Ephyrea, forgive me – Lord Ruvaen has not been seen for thousands of years.'

'Thousands?' said Ephyrea. 'But you are grown, it has been no more than a hundred or two...'

'Er, how long do you live for?' muttered Ember to Rhaell, who gave her an incredulous look.

Just then, Ephyrea's hand touched Ember's cheek, the fingers cold and glowing faintly. Ember felt the power of the stones thrum through her with a new heartbeat – Ephyrea's heartbeat. Which wasn't surprising since the stones comprised her heart.

'Oh,' she said, her lovely eyes widening. They were a deep green, the colour of a meadow in springtime. 'You are ... diluted.'

'Excuse me?' said Ember.

'My blood is in your veins, and my darling's too, but so many others...' Ephyrea's fingers trailed over Ember's face to her neck, and she wanted to squirm away.

'Possibly all the generations in between?' said Ember, and mentally shook herself. 'Look, I can't be your descendant. I'm from another world.'

'Yes,' said Ephyrea dreamily, 'Ruvaen always was skilled at slipping between worlds. He raised you there?'

'Maybe he raised *a* child there,' Ember said carefully. 'But not me. My father is a clockmaker, and my mother is ... was ... a—'

She felt it then, something inside her answering to Ephyrea. A sort of tug, something reaching out to the ethereal being gazing at her with childlike interest.

'She was a thief,' she whispered, and Ephyrea clapped her hands in delight. Ember exhaled – partly relief that the strange woman wasn't touching her anymore, and partly in shock at what she'd just revealed.

'Yes! He could steal the songs from the birds, my love. And he passed it to you? His piece of my heart?' She put her hand to her chest, which was still glowing. 'I can feel you here.'

'Not ... exactly.' Ember sighed. 'I ... sort of ... stole it.'

Ephyrea clapped her hands again. 'You *are* his!'

'No, I'm...' Ember gave up. 'Sure, fine. He was my million-times great grandfather. You're my million-times great grandmother. And you've restored all the magic to the land.' She looked around, suddenly realising what should have been obvious from the start.

The Tree had gone.

Where it had stood was a piece of scorched earth, not even any roots or branches remaining. The melted, twisted remains of the pendants and vambraces lay on the burnt ground, but the crown was gone.

Ember had a feeling that if she looked for Sarea now, she would not find her.

'What happened to the Tree?'

'Tree?' Ephyrea glanced over as if she hadn't the faintest idea what they were talking about.

'The Tree. The Sacred Tree,' said Rhaell. His eyes were wide. 'That gave us all our magic.'

'That's going to send me home,' Ember cut in sharply. The Tree was the portal between worlds. That was what all Rhaell's scrolls had said. She needed the Tree.

Ephyrea blinked at them, then laughed a tinkling, bell-like laugh that should have sounded delightful and somehow just sounded kind of creepy.

'Child,' she said. 'You are home.'

Ember stumbled, and Rhaell caught her.

Home. *I'm not. I can't be.* Home was the Clockwork City, where the three rivers met. Home was smoke and smog and filthy streets. Home was a cold hearth and a lecherous landlord. Home was Pa and the boys.

Wasn't it?

'But the magic is restored,' said Rhaell, squeezing Ember's hand.

'The magic did not come from the Tree. The magic made the Tree.'

Ephyrea looked around, at the forest glade, the river rushing by, the castle on its clifftop. 'Before the castle, before Ysarriel, before the stupid Tree ... this was mine.'

She waved her hand in an arc, and flowers grew.

'You were here before the Tree?'

'Yes. I made it to explore. To see what and who else was out there. To find someone to love. And I found someone. Brave and kind and wise.'

'Ruvaen?'

Ephyrea looked surprised. 'Ysarriel. Oh ... our love was sweet, and pure as the mountain springs. To love a friend, is it not the sweetest love in the world?' She sighed. 'I have never had a greater love. I do not think I ever loved Ruvaen as much as I loved Ysarriel.'

'But ... what happened?'

'What happened?' Ephyrea's golden face darkened. 'My sweetest friend Ysarriel happened.'

Her hair, which had flowed behind her in a sable river, now rose as if a wind blew it. Her emerald eyes flashed with lightning.

'My Tree,' she said, 'my beautiful Tree, that connected all the worlds known and unknown. Ysarriel tapped its power, and it made her mighty. It made all of us mighty. We raised castles and flew with dragons. We dreamed and dreamed, and our dreams became real. And the Tree fuelled all, its power running through us like a river with no end and no beginning. But the Tree's power was not limitless.'

'It has been failing recently,' Rhaell said.

'It was failing since long before your birth,' said Ephyrea. 'It began drawing its power from the earth, but that wasn't enough. Then, from the other worlds it connected. I well remember visiting and finding its leaves and branches petrified. The people,' she added in disgust, 'were using it for fuel.'

Fuel. Ember thought about the sarel mines, the sarel furnaces, the sarel stones. All named after Sarel, High Lady of beginnings, births, and miracles. Ysarriel.

It was us. We killed the Tree.

'But she wouldn't stop. Would never give up her power. Ysarriel claimed the land as if it was her right, and she bled it dry. None of them would stop. Only Ruvaen, handsome Ruvaen, would listen to me.' She gazed at Rhaell. 'He looked a little like you. Well, not *like* you, but handsome.' She giggled.

'See, I told you you were handsome,' Ember hissed, digging her elbow into his ribs.

'He was a rogue of lightning speed and mischief,' Ephyrea said dreamily. 'No woman could withstand his charms. I didn't even try. I took him into my bed, and I begged him to listen. But even my darling could not stop his wife. She took and she took, and when we begged her to stop, she accused us of treason.' Her brow wrinkled. 'She said we had been having an affair.'

'And you ... hadn't?'

'Well, of course we had, but we thought she didn't know,' Ephyrea said dismissively. 'Her rage and jealousy knew no bounds. She beat and tortured me. She used my Tree – my Tree! – as my prison. Only my darling Ruvaen took a piece of my heart with him and hid it away. To become you,' she added, touching Ember's cheek with her cold, cold fingers. 'My scion. My heir.'

'Yes, about that,' said Ember, but Ephyrea wasn't listening.

'And now it is gone,' she said, gazing at the small circle of scorched earth that was the only marker of the Tree's presence. 'It can imprison me no longer. And I shall retake what is mine.'

'You mean the castle?'

Ephyrea blinked up at it. 'That? No.' She waved her hand, and a distant rumble came to Ember's ears.

'Leaves and branches,' muttered Rhaell, his eyes wide.

Ember twisted in his arms, and as she did she heard people screaming. The ground shook.

The castle was crumbling.

'It took a day to raise, and less to fall,' sang Ephyrea.

'What are you doing?' gasped Rhaell. 'There are people in there.'

Ephyrea shrugged.

'No – please,' said Ember. 'Stop. There are people in there. Your people. My people,' she tried. 'They don't deserve this.'

'But I don't like the castle,' said Ephyrea crossly.

'Then get the people out and then bring it down. After it's evacuated,' urged Ember.

Ephyrea gave a great childish sigh. 'Fine.' She waved her hand, and the rumbling ceased. Ember could still see bits falling off, but no more cracks appeared.

'Thank you,' she said, trying to find a smile to appease the crazy woman. What the hell were they going to do?

'No!' The howl came from the former King Onas, who Ember had completely forgotten even existed. 'My castle! My kingdom! What are you *doing*?'

'Your kingdom?' Ephyrea looked beautifully confused again. 'Who are you?'

'I am King Onas!' He was still being held by Brock, who was beginning to look fed up.

'Well...' said Ember.

'King Onas ... of...?'

Ephyrea moved faster than a snake. Her hand was suddenly at the king's throat, and he froze, eyes wide. 'You are...' She stepped back, surprised. 'You are king of nothing.'

Ember exchanged a look with Rhaell, who quietly let go of her hand and reached for his sword.

Her hand throbbed, the cut on her palm making itself known. Her fingers felt empty and cold without Rhaell's around them.

'What treason is this? Ephyrea said, as if she'd been offered a sweet and decided to decline it.

'I am – it is lies – I am—'

Ephyrea made an elegant motion with her fingers, and lightning crackled between them. 'I have sworn,' she said conversationally, 'to kill the usurpers who stole my land.'

'Your land?' said Rhaell. He had one hand on his sword.

Onas slumped on his knees, Brock standing over him in a somewhat cursory manner.

'He is not Ysarriel's kin,' said Ephyrea, peering down at Onas. 'He is twice a false king.'

'So, you don't need to kill him,' said Rhaell.

She shrugged, the lightning fizzing in her palm. 'He is still a usurper,' she said, and her hands raised.

'Stop! Wait, please!' Striding across the glade, Rhaell pleaded, 'Show him mercy. A great leader should show mercy.'

'Why? He stole my land.'

'He mutilated you,' Ember pointed out, hoisting up her skirts to follow him.

'He's my grandfather,' Rhaell said. His sword was in his hand now. 'My blood. Show him mercy. I beg you.'

Ephyrea went still. Her head turned, very slowly, her eyes taking their time to find him.

Fuck. Of all the things to say...

'He's not really his blood,' Ember babbled, rushing forward. 'He's actually half Rakaa, did you know that? And they've no quarrel with—'

'Fine, I will kill you both,' Ephyrea said over her, and turned her palms towards Rhaell. The lightning flew, striking him in the chest.

Ember didn't even have time to scream. She hurled herself at Rhaell, faster than she even knew she could move, and wrapped herself bodily around him as they both hit the ground. He landed with a grunt, and Ember felt the lightning hit her back.

If Ephyrea had some notion that Ember was her kin, it didn't stop her blasting more lightning at her. Ember was pinned by the heat of it as power flowed through her, filling her with blinding light like the machines she saw at fairgrounds back home. *Electricity*. She was filling with electricity.

Her muscles contracted, breath robbed from her body. Beneath her, Rhaell gasped, and a charred smell filled her nose. *She hurt him. She hurt him and I will kill her for it.*

Electricity crackled through her veins and along her skin. Ember rose, lightning pulsing with her heart, and turned to face Ephyrea.

The bright, unnatural light lit her face with shock, which only deepened as Ember reached out and grabbed her hands.

'Get,' she snarled, 'your nasty little sparks *off my husband*.'

She shoved, and Ephyrea flew backwards, the lightning abruptly ceasing. Ember stood, heaving with power, light crackling around her. It sparked and fizzed, and she gulped in a breath, suddenly aware that the few remaining people in the clearing were staring at her with horror. She felt as if all the power and magic in the world had filled her up, and her body could barely contain it.

'Ember?' gasped a weak voice behind her, and the lightning abruptly fizzled out.

'*Rhaell.*' She was on her knees beside him in an instant, reaching for the charred fabric of his tunic and gagging at the smell of burnt flesh. 'Oh Lords – Phoebe, help—'

Phoebe was there beside her, drawing in a sharp breath. 'Oh,' she said, her voice dissolving into horror. 'I don't know if—'

'Do something!' Ember snapped, and behind her she heard a nasty laugh. Ephyrea, coming back for another round. 'We have to get him out of here.'

'Where? How?' Phoebe's hands were on Rhaell's chest, her face twisted in fear.

'Did you ... steal my power?' said Ephyrea.

'Save yourself,' Rhaell breathed, his face grey.

'Fuck's sake, idiot, not without you,' Ember snapped.

'You absorbed it,' Phoebe whispered to Ember. 'You didn't steal it ... you ... maybe you can use it to heal him—'

More lightning landed next to Ember, searing Rhaell's arm. 'Fuck off!' she snarled, blasting a hand behind her. She heard a scream.

'You do lightning now?' coughed Rhaell. It was a horrible wet sound.

'Yes, and I'm going to—' Fuck, what was she going to do? How could she get him away from here, from Ephyrea's terrible power?

Wait, she'd opened portals before, and that was before the return of the magic. She made the sign of the Tree – *but the Tree doesn't exist anymore, what's the damn symbol for the land itself?* – and drew a desperate square in the ground. Light seared up where her finger dragged. She grabbed and pulled at the turf, and oh, thank the Lords, a square of light and sound flowed up.

'What is...?' murmured Ephyrea, coming closer.

Hooves on cobblestones. Factory whistles. The bells of Lord Ruven's temple. *The Clockwork City*.

Ember grabbed Rhaell and was half an inch from pulling him through the portal when Phoebe yelped, 'No! Never the first one!'

Fuck, fuck. Ember shoved it shut, then yanked it open again. The Rakaa village, horned heads turning and smiling at her. The house with the cabin bed where she and Rhaell had made love all night—

Lightning hit her back.

She shoved that portal closed and yanked it open again and this time, leapt in without even looking where it took them.

Lightning seared through the gap, and Ember just saw Phoebe grab the hatch and pull it closed as she tumbled through after them.

There were rocks and running water, but Ember didn't notice any more than that. She tore at Rhaell's clothing, exposing the horrible wound on his chest that smoked and charred. His head lolled, his fingers loose against the ground.

'The water,' she gasped, and Phoebe said, 'I don't think—' and Ember snarled at her, so Phoebe grabbed Rhaell's other arm, and they dragged him to the river, Ember crawling in on her knees to hold him in her arms with his chest under the surface. His breath rasped, that awful wound pink and black and raw.

'Heal him,' Ember begged of her friend. 'You have to. Please.'

'Ember, I— This isn't sacred water, the Tree is gone. I don't know how,' said Phoebe. Her hand clutched Rhaell's, her eyes streaming tears.

'Try harder,' shrieked Ember, clutching Rhaell's body to herself and willing him to heal. Her body was still full of lightning, and she poured it into him with the full force of her desperation and love. She couldn't lose him.

'I've got you, I've got you,' she sobbed, as if it was a magic chant that could bring him back to her. He'd saved her so many times, from the Myr, from Ikrai, from the Sacred Sea, and now it was her turn to save him.

The water ran cold over his body, shifting him in her lap.

Ember felt as if all the lightning in the world had filled her, and now she forced it into Rhaell, drawing more power from the earth, driving her will into him, drowning his pain with her love. Her eyes squeezed shut, her arms around him, barely aware of the wind of the water or anything but him.

'You have to survive,' she gasped, tears running unheeded down her face. 'I love you.'

His body rolled in her arms as the current pushed at it, her heavy skirts dragging in the water.

'I love you more than life, more than breath, more than home. I will make any bargain to save you. I need you. I love—' Her voice broke into a fierce sob. 'I love you.'

'That's a lot to live up to,' Rhaell murmured, and her eyes flew open.

He looked up at her, eyes bluer than the sky.

'I mean it,' she whispered.

'By its leaves and branches,' whispered someone nearby. Maybe Phoebe. Ember didn't care.

'You love me?' said Rhaell, struggling to sit up, and Ember gasped. 'You weren't just saying that because you thought I might die?'

'No,' Ember said, staring at him. His chest was healed. 'I don't think you're going to die.' His arm was healed. 'I think you...'

She leaned back to look up at him. All of him. At the horns that grew from his skull, at the wings that rose over his back, at the tail that lashed her legs under the water. She couldn't widen her eyes enough.

'Lord Ruven and all his little angels,' she breathed.

'What did you *do*?' That was Phoebe, somewhere behind Ember.

'I healed him,' Ember whispered. She'd healed all of him. Healed the wings King Onas had hacked away and the tail he'd severed and the horns Rhaell had filed down even though it hurt, so as to look less frightening for her.

He didn't look frightening now. He looked *magnificent*.

'Yeah? I feel kind of— Whoa,' Rhaell yelped, stumbling in the water, and Ember reached to steady him. 'Like I can't stand, I'm unbalanced, I—' He frowned at Ember. 'What are you looking at?'

His wings were stunning, rising above his shoulders in a display of black, blue, purple and green, gleaming like a sarel-oil slick. The strong bones that ran out from his shoulder blades were so thick with feathers they looked almost furred. Points like claws crowned the joints. His upper body was completely bare, clothes shredded and lost in the river, and over his shoulders and upper arms trailed wild symbols, dark as his wings, burning through his skin.

And his horns... They rose from his dark hair, gleaming the same oil-slick black as his wings, curving inwards and then out again into wicked points. They made him look fierce, glorious, a warrior.

'It's what you were meant to be,' Phoebe wept. 'Deer – you're my Deer.'

He frowned up at her from the river, managing to gain his feet with his legs braced wide against the gentle current. 'You haven't called me Deer in a long time.'

'You haven't been Deer in a long time.'

'Deer?' said Ember.

'I'll explain later,' said Rhaell, reaching over his shoulder, his expression almost fearful. 'Ember, do I have fucking wings?'

'You do,' she said. 'And they are *gorgeous*.'

He did not look like he believed her, so Ember scrambled to her feet and grabbed him in a bruising kiss.

He was here, he was alive, and he felt complete in her arms, so much so that Ember wondered how she'd never noticed the absence of his wings. Her hands greedily felt at the skin covering the ridges of bone growing from his shoulder blades, the cartilage and muscle beneath, the feathers sprouting from his skin. She was right, the tiny feathers did feel like fur, soft and damp under her fingers.

Rhaell made a sound against her mouth. 'Does that hurt?' she murmured.

'No.' His eyes were half closed. 'It feels good.'

Ember grinned as a second thought occurred. She raised her hands to his head, burrowed her fingers through his thick hair, and grasped the roots of his horns.

'Fuck,' he groaned sharply against her mouth. 'Ember.'

'You like that?'

'Like isn't a strong enough word,' he gasped. 'Ember ... you don't— I'm a monster now.'

Ember sucked on his lower lip, as plump and delicious as ever. 'A gorgeous, beautiful monster,' she said, rocking her hips against him, wishing she wasn't wearing her stupid wedding skirts so she could feel his body reacting to hers. She wondered if a Rakaa cock was different to a human one. *Won't it be fun to find out?*

'You said you loved me,' he said, eyes desperately searching hers. 'Can you love me like this?'

She laughed against his mouth. 'Rhaell, I loved you as a guard, I loved you as a liar and I love you even more as a Rakaa. I love the bones of you.'

He pressed his forehead to hers, breathing deeply, his horns touching the top of her head. 'Good,' he said, voice breaking a little, 'because I love you so much, I think I might die from it.'

'Please don't,' she said, her laughter almost a sob. 'I need you to live for me.'

'You're the air in my lungs,' he promised, and his desperate mouth found hers again.

She kissed him deeply, her beautiful monster, twined herself around him and lost herself in the sensation of his new body. He was alive, he was whole, he was hers. She had no idea what the future was going to hold, if she could ever get home, if she even wanted to. She didn't know where home even was. She didn't know if Yskara would fall to Ephyrea or if they could reclaim it, but she knew Rhaell would be by her side and right now nothing else mattered. Nothing at all.

She'd probably have torn their clothes off and fucked him right there in the river if Phoebe hadn't coughed loudly and said, 'Apologies for interrupting this adorable scene, but I think we have company.'

Ember tore her mouth from Rhaell's but didn't let go of him as she looked around, a little bleary-eyed with passion.

They were in a rocky river valley, lined with scrubby trees and scree, behind which mighty peaks soared. The river flowed shallow and rapid over rocks and shallow drops, wide and fresh from the peaks behind them.

Lining both sides of the riverbanks were a dozen or more large Rakaa, faces and bodies painted with streaks of paint, spears and bows and mighty axes in their huge hands.

Ember smiled hopefully, scanning their faces for anyone familiar.

She was met with a dozen fierce scowls.

'Hi,' she tried, Rhaell's arms tight around her. 'Um, any of you know the Jolvista, of the Moonlit Highlands?'

There was a bristling sound as dozens of weapons were brandished.

'We are Taveen of the Savage Heights,' growled one, a very large Rakaa who had his horns carved with intricate symbols. 'We spit upon the Jolvista.'

'Oh good,' said Ember weakly, suddenly jarringly aware they were largely unarmed and that she was wearing half a mile of sodden beetle wings and silver. 'Us too.'

'Are they going to hurt us?' muttered Phoebe.

'I really hope not,' sighed Rhaell. 'I'm not sure I can stand up straight yet.' He flexed his wings, grimacing.

'Friends,' said Ember, letting go of him to raise her hands peaceably, 'I'm sure if we sit down and talk about it, everything will be just fine. I—'

She broke off as a piercing cry broke the sky, and all three of them looked swiftly upward. A pair of dragons wheeled above, the sunlight glinting off their scales and feathers. Purple and red and blue flashed in the light.

Rhaell shaded his eyes and turned to watch them wheel and chase each other. 'I don't think that's our dragon,' he said.

'No. I don't think so. But maybe they know her,' said Ember, and turned swiftly at a sudden sound coming from the Rakaa, as if they were all moving at the same time.

They were all kneeling.

'Um, okay,' said Ember.

'He has returned,' whispered one Rakaa.

'The rumours were true,' breathed another.

'What?' said Rhaell, looking around at the kneeling warriors, each with a fist over their hearts. Their leader raised his head, carved horns catching the light. He gestured with one large hand to the markings on Rhaell's back and shoulders.

'Hraeulfr, son of Koenulf,' he said. 'Lost Prince of Damholm. You have come home.'

EPILOGUE

Above them, the castle shuddered.

'Hold true,' Sarea commanded. Sweat dripped down her brow, which was not the regal look she was going for, but right now needs must. There was no point being the queen if there was nothing to be queen of.

She felt the magical scaffolding climb the West Wing, supporting and strengthening what Ephyrea had tried to destroy. Across the bridge, the East Wing was half crumbled, only the ancient Keep still standing. But there was nothing she could do about that now.

Ephyrea had made her court there, and anyone unfortunate enough to have survived the collapse now served her.

There! The final part of the grid rolled into place, and Sarea stood frozen, muscles locked, until she was sure it would hold.

She let out a breath. 'We have it,' she said, letting go of Lord Addor's hand on one side of her and Lady Feynrith's on the other. 'Well done, everyone. Get some rest.' She turned towards the exit of the cave. 'What is the situation with food?'

'The kitchens are partially destroyed, Your Grace,' said a guard. 'But the food for the wedding feast was protected by a ward.'

'Good. Send some guards with the porters and bring some up. Have someone collect bedding, we'll stay down here tonight.'

'I thought the castle was safe now?' said Lady Feynrith, and Sarea tried not to curl her lip at her old enemy.

'Safe from collapsing on our heads. I don't trust that bitch Ephyrea not to make incursions in the night.' She reached the entrance to the cave, and let the cool salt breeze cool her skin. The setting sun turned the waters of the Sacred Sea to molten gold and glittering jet.

Most of the castle inhabitants didn't know about these caves, but Sarea was not an ordinary castle inhabitant. She had known since she was a small child that she was only one unfortunate accident away from becoming the heir to the throne, and had prepared for it accordingly.

She had not expected to be defending her castle against a goddess on the day of her accession, but Sarea was nothing if not versatile.

Below them on the rocks, teams of guards, maids and even the odd nobleman were helping to bring Sacred Water to the wounded, of which there was a terrible number. Beyond them waited the hafmey, eyes glowing with avarice over the spilled blood.

'Any trouble from them?' she asked.

'Not since you cast the protection charm, Your Grace,' replied Lady Eyvinby. 'Ameer is keeping an eye on them. He says Sehari is beset by similar creatures.'

'How interesting,' said Sarea, who had absolutely no interest in Sehari but felt she ought to cultivate its ambassador. She'd need all the allies she could get right now. 'Do make sure the Ambassador has everything he needs.'

The dragon on her shoulder flicked its tail against her neck, and she turned in the direction it indicated. A page hovered, hands and knees filthy with mud and soot. In his hands was something small and shiny.

'Ah. If you will excuse me,' she said, and swept away, down the rocks to a small chasm above the sea. She held out her hand, and the boy handed over the trinket he held.

Yes, this was it – battered, slightly tawdry, and not very impressive if you looked close. Rather like its previous owner. 'Well done,' she said. 'Go and get something to eat.'

She gathered her tattered skirts, and leapt the distance across the churning water, landing on the slippery rocks and narrowly avoiding a fall. People were watching. The queen could not be seen to stumble.

She straightened her crown and turned her back on her people. Then she held up the bracelet the boy had brought her, and sorted through the charms on it. A Sehari fig, an Addoran snake – that was interesting, she'd come back to it later – and here. A little crystal rainbow.

She held it up to the light of the dying sun, and said, 'My spy. Attend.'

The crystal rainbow in her hand heated and glowed, and for a moment nothing happened. Then someone muttered, 'Fuck.'

Sarea waited. Onas had spies; of course he did. He had them all over the land, in every enemy court and especially every allied one. But his most important spy had always been right here in the castle, keeping tabs on his monstrous heir. Sarea had never known their name or identity, just that Onas would sometimes boast that the 'rainbows whisper secrets to me'. He'd fondle his charm bracelet, subtle as a frog.

Eventually a figure flickered into view, translucent against the rocks, ducking down as if afraid of being seen.

'Your— Your Grace!'

'Not who you were expecting?' Sarea said.

'No ... I mean, yes, of course, Your Grace. The rightful queen of Yskara.' The spy gave a furtive bow. 'Is ... what happened to ... is he...?'

'Onas? Still alive, I believe, although in what state is anybody's guess. Ephyrea has him.' Sarea allowed herself a shudder. The woman was insane, and cruel with it: Onas was probably being killed very slowly and painfully. 'She has taken the Keep; I control the West Wing for now. We are a nation at war,' she said grimly.

'I see,' said the spy.

'And his grandson?'

The spy hesitated. 'He is not the prince anymore, Your Grace. He conceded the throne.'

'All the more reason to keep an eye on him. Report.'

The spy looked around and lowered her voice. 'He is safe. He is healed.'

Sarea had not seen Ephyrea's attempt to murder Bronadyr, but enough people had told her about it. 'And the girl? The destruction of the Tree prevented her from leaving?'

'Yes, Your Grace.'

That was a blow, she had to admit. She'd been counting on banishing the Promised One, who didn't look like a threat but definitely was one. But perhaps she could turn it to her advantage.

'Did she really manifest Ephyrea's power?'

The spy hesitated. 'I... It's unclear if she manifested or absorbed it, Your Grace. But it was enough to heal the prin— To heal Rhaell.'

Rhaell. She had forgotten that was one of his names. Now he had a wife who could perform powerful magic – a wife who was the scion of both Ruvaen and Ephyrea.

Sarea regarded her own hand as it held the charm bracelet. Smooth skin, neatly-kept nails, tasteful jewellery. Her own hand. But now the hand of a queen who channelled the power of her Ancestor. The strength of Ysarriel the First Queen flowed through Sarea, and in a tiny corner of her mind she could admit this terrified her.

'The girl has power,' she said. 'And he has none. If we are to retake Yskara, we will need her.'

'Your Grace,' said the spy frankly, 'I don't think you're going to get her.'

Sarea narrowed her eyes. 'Then it will become your job to persuade her,' she said. There must be other scions. Not every Ancestor had bred children, but did that matter? Ember Hart seemed to be the descendant of a piece of Ruvaen's heart, or something absurd like that.

The spy straightened. 'Your Grace,' she said. 'With all due respect, I don't work for you. My loyalty is to Rhaell and Ember.' She lifted the rainbow pendant from beneath her collar. 'I wish you all the luck, but I won't be—'

'You think I'll be any more lenient towards your mother?' Sarea whipped out, and saw the blow hit. 'She has a pleasant life in Oaksthorpe, as it stands. It would be a shame if that had to change.'

The spy closed her eyes. Her mouth almost – almost – crumpled. But she was a servant, and a servant of the Crown at that, and she controlled her expression.

Sarea gentled her voice. 'All I require is your reports. What the Promised One and the prince are doing now. Whose alliances they seek. What powers they manifest.'

'I ... I will not betray their trust anymore—'

Sarea stamped her foot impatiently. She was tired and cold and filthy, she faced sleeping in a cave with peasants and she had to defend her brand new kingdom against a psychopath with immense powers – and the coming days were only going to get worse.

'I can send your mother a case of wine or I can send an assassin,' she snapped. 'Which is it to be?'

The spy slumped. 'Rhaell has been restored to his half-Rakaa heritage,' she whispered. 'He has wings and a tail. The Rakaa have claimed him as their prince.'

Sarea barked out a laugh. 'The Beast has truly become a savage? Marvellous.' A thought occurred to her. 'Do you think the Rakaa will ally with us against Ephyrea?'

'I doubt it,' said the spy tiredly. A sound came from behind her, and she turned towards it. 'Rhaell isn't exactly pleased about any of this.'

'And the Promised One?' Sarea supposed she'd better get used to the girl's real name. 'Ember?'

'She ... she might.'

'How have her powers—'

But this time someone on the spy's end called her name. 'Phoebe? Are you coming?'

Sarea smiled at the panic on the girl's face. 'Don't worry. I think I shall keep on using your code name, Rainbow.' As her spy's image flickered and faded, Queen Sarea said, 'I think we shall be of great use to each other.'

Acknowledgments

Thanks must go to:

The magnificent, supportive and gloriously ridiculous Naughty Kitchen for everything; but specifically the wine, Mat Baynton's Bottom, lockpicking, and 'trebuchets are very on brand for you Kate.'

Jan Jones, for everything.

And everyone else who kept me going while I was being told fantasy romance will never sell, it's just not popular, omg Kate can't you just write something cute about cupcakes...

Charlotte, for putting up with me going 'Surprise! I sort of wrote a romantasy without telling you,' and then letting me draw my own maps and things.

Taylor Swift, who's got me through some shit.

My cats, who after a couple of utterly horrendous years are still there for me, even when the Pride has lost its king. Because even Ysarriel herself would even pledge fealty to His Most Spikalicious King Spike of Spikington, the true King of All Things. You are beautiful idiots and I love you.

ONE MORE CHAPTER

The author and One More Chapter would like to thank everyone who contributed to the publication of this story…

Analytics
James Brackin
Abigail Fryer

Audio
Fionnuala Barrett
Ciara Briggs

Contracts
Laura Amos
Laura Evans

Design
Lucy Bennett
Fiona Greenway
Liane Payne
Dean Russell

Digital Sales
Laura Daley
Lydia Grainge
Hannah Lismore

eCommerce
Laura Carpenter
Madeline ODonovan
Charlotte Stevens
Christina Storey
Jo Surman
Rachel Ward

Editorial
Kara Daniel
Charlotte Ledger
Lydia Mason
Laura McCallen
Ajebowale Roberts
Jennie Rothwell
Caroline Scott-Bowden
Emily Thomas
Helen Williams

Harper360
Jennifer Dee
Emily Gerbner
Ariana Juarez
Jean Marie Kelly
emma sullivan
Sophia Wilhelm

International Sales
Peter Borcsok
Ruth Burrow
Colleen Simpson
Ben Wright

Inventory
Sarah Callaghan
Kirsty Norman

Marketing & Publicity
Chloe Cummings
Grace Edwards
Emma Petfield

Operations
Melissa Okusanya
Hannah Stamp

Production
Denis Manson
Simon Moore
Francesca Tuzzeo

Rights
Helena Font Brillas
Ashton Mucha
Zoe Shine
Aisling Smyth
Lucy Vanderbilt

Trade Marketing
Ben Hurd
Eleanor Slater

The HarperCollins Distribution Team

The HarperCollins Finance & Royalties Team

The HarperCollins Legal Team

The HarperCollins Technology Team

UK Sales
Isabel Coburn
Jay Cochrane
Sabina Lewis
Holly Martin
Harriet Williams
Leah Woods

And every other essential link in the chain from delivery drivers to booksellers to librarians and beyond!

ONE MORE CHAPTER
YOUR NUMBER ONE STOP FOR PAGETURNING BOOKS

One More Chapter is an award-winning global division of HarperCollins.

Subscribe to our newsletter to get our latest eBook deals and stay up to date with all our new releases!

signup.harpercollins.co.uk/join/signup-omc

Meet the team at
www.onemorechapter.com

Follow us!

 @OneMoreChapter_
 @onemorechapterhc
@onemorechapterhc
 @onemorechapterhc

Do you write unputdownable fiction?
We love to hear from new voices.
Find out how to submit your novel at
www.onemorechapter.com/submissions